The Cusser Club

Randall Northcutt

The Cusser Club

ISBN: 979-8-35093-306-2 (print)
ISBN: 979-8-35093-307-9 (eBook)

For Kathy

1

Friday, May 23, 1969
Dix Knob, Texas

I'M AN EXPERT AT ASS WHOOPING. THE RECEIVING END, NOT the giving end. On the last day of school before Memorial Day weekend, 1969, I strolled out of Dix Knob Junior High fantasizing about summer break and the upcoming Treasure O' the Knob Festival. This brief indulgence in reverie proved my undoing.

As I stepped into the sunlight, my arch enemy, Galton Grails, grabbed me in a headlock, spun me to the ground, and buried my face in gravel. Quality entertainment is a rarity in rural East Texas, and the certain prospect of a gruesome mauling instantly attracted a cheering crowd. Grails outweighed me by forty pounds, and I was no match for his incessant rage. My rapier wit backfired earlier in the year when I saddled him with the nickname "Butt Crust" after an amusing wardrobe debacle during the school musical production of *Oklahoma*. My classmates quickly picked up the moniker and when the girls passed notes in class, they simply referred to him as "BC," or "Crusty."

Throughout the year, I'd been Galton's punching bag, and the final Friday of the spring term was especially brutal. A fist to the nose lit up my brain with a burst of stars. With a vicious punch to the kidneys, I pissed myself. This was especially gratifying to Galton, and he howled in demonic glee. My adversary was a deranged doppelgänger of Johnny Cash. Black jeans, black pointed cowboy boots, and a black shirt with tacky pearl snap buttons. A grotesque Neanderthal unibrow, greasy hair, and rotten green teeth topped off this swank fashion ensemble.

He fancied himself as a real life Groovy Muffscout, swaggering around the hallways flirting with the girls. Grails would make gross comments, and they would giggle and bat their eyes in a lewd little game, just to see who could get the biggest reaction from the troll, without actually having to touch him—a sophomoric ongoing contest to draw out the maximum grossness from Galton. The bravest contestants would gag and make *Yurk* and *Glurx* noises behind his back. Of course, none of them ever followed through with their flirtatious frivolity. Truth be told, Galton Grails couldn't get laid in a monkey whorehouse with a boxcar of bananas.

The brute rolled me over, kicked me in the gut, grabbed my throat in an excruciating choke hold and yelled, "Teddy Nutscalder thinks he's the last weenie in the sauerkraut! A pretty boy. A ladies' man. The fact is, he's just a puny, smart aleck ass kisser. Teacher's pet and prod-gity."

A voice from the back of the crowd yelled, "It's pronounced p-r-o-d-i-g-y, you inbred half-wit."

"Who said that? Just stick around and I'll stomp your ass next. Just like Nutscalder here, who thinks he's a genius. He ain't so bright. He's just a scrawny, dick headed ... puny ... little ... dick head."

A hushed murmur fell over the assemblage as onlookers pondered the sheer magnitude of Galton's towering intellect.

Another gut punch squeezed the last drop of pee out of my bladder, and as I lay dazed and gasping, he raised his boot above my groin for the coup de grâce.

"Crushed nuts for Nutscalder!" Slimy spittle sprayed the rabble of spellbound spectators.

As he prepared to trounce my testicles, Coach Mason rushed in and broke up the fight. He pulled Galton off of me and gave him a couple of swift open-handed jack slaps to the head. A massive Texas A&M championship ring turned palm-down ricocheted off the thick Cro-Magnon skull with each wallop. The resulting *clack-clack* drew a slew of "woos" from the happy horde of bystanders. The Ring Dinger Maneuver was standard practice among coaches and a remarkably effective corporal punishment technique. Sporting an Aggie crew cut and ice-blue eyes, the muscular athletic director acted with unwavering decisiveness in every situation.

Our ninth grade English teacher, Nora Hawkins, came running out of the building with her paisley skirt billowing in the breeze. She had a figure like Marilyn Monroe with an hourglass waist and tits like a couple of 1957 Cadillac bumper bullets. Miss Hawkins knelt by my side, produced a handkerchief, and wiped my nose. Sacrificing pride, I faked serious injury, to get a little sympathy and a close-up view of her glorious cleavage.

Coach Mason shifted the ever-present wad of Red Man chewing tobacco from one cheek to the other and spat a thick stream of gelatinous goo across the top of Galton's boots. He then raised his hand to the bully's face, pinching his thumb and forefinger together.

"I'm this close to finishing the paperwork to ship you off to the Gatesville Reformatory. You've got all these kids running scared, but you won't be so tough in there."

Miss Hawkins looked up from dabbing my nose and chimed in, "Every teacher in the school has signed off on it. The forms are complete, and all you have to do is lick a stamp."

Coach slapped him on the side of the head once more.

"Grails, I bet those fellas at Gatesville would elect you prom queen. A little mascara, some lipstick, and you could be a fairy princess, or the belle of the ball." Mason made a not-so-subtle thrusting gesture with his pelvis.

"Now get the hell out of here. I'm sick of looking at your ugly mug. Drag a toothbrush through your mouth every once in a while! Your breath would knock a buzzard off a gut wagon."

Onlookers erupted in laughter. Galton flipped them the bird.

Against Miss Hawkins' protests, the coach hoisted me off the ground.

"He's a tough little turd knocker, Nora. Don't worry, he'll be fine." Mason flexed his enormous biceps as he lifted me out of the dirt. Miss Hawkins smiled and rolled her eyes as he made a half-hearted effort to dust me off and straighten my collar.

"Nutscalder, you're a walking, talking shit magnet. That snarky mouth of yours is really gonna get you crippled or killed someday. I swear to God you must have a death wish. Between your daddy and Grails, I'm surprised you ain't a bloody pulp every day. You need to keep your head down and your trap shut." He bent down close to my ear and whispered, "Son, it's okay to be smart, but it's not okay to be a smartass." That stung, but I was grateful when he turned to the remaining bystanders and shooed them off.

"What the hell kind of name is Nutscalder, anyway?"

"It's an Americanized truncation of the Germanic surname Nusskas…" Before I could complete my sentence, the coach abruptly thumped me on the forehead, right between the eyes.

"See there! You don't get it. That was a rhetorical question, Nutscalder. *Nobody* gives a shit." He grimaced at the sight of the urine spot on my pants, and let out a deep sigh of exasperation. "Beat it, kiddo. School's over for the summer, and the campus is officially closed. Keep a plug in that sarcastic diarrhea of the mouth. It's going to be your downfall."

Miss Hawkins smiled and told me to keep the handkerchief. Bosom skyward, she locked arms with the coach and they strolled off like a couple of star-struck lovers.

A menacing squall line formed on the south horizon, and an invisible wave of low rolling thunder rumbled through the river basin. Spring had been fairly calm, but the summer heat was ramping up and so was unpredictability. Gulf Coast weather is a fickle bitch. Sunshine and gentle breeze one minute, and a hurricane force ball blaster the next.

Attempting to salvage a modicum of dignity, I pinched the bridge of my nose to quell the bleeding and untucked my shirttail, covering most of the embarrassing stain. Brushing off red dirt, grass burrs, and Grail grease, I hurried east along the adjacent railroad track to the solitude of my after-school hideout.

The Grotto was an abandoned concrete bunker built into the high end of the levee embankment of the Missouri-Pacific railroad bridge, traversing the Sabine River. Constructed in the 1930s, it formerly served as a Corps of Engineers' alcove for flood gauge equipment. The wooden facade had long since rotted away and the opening was now concealed by a thick curtain of kudzu and trumpet vine. Iron ore in the soil seeped through the microscopic pores of the cement and stained it a rusty red. It was my private hideout, shared from time to time with my only two friends and an old stray dog named Humper. Cool in the summer and warm in the winter, it served as a cozy refuge from bullies, an abusive father, and the ghost of a dead sister.

This high vantage point provided a clear view of everything on the Riverfront Levee Road and straight across the water into The Grove, a small community on the Louisiana side of the river where all the old Black folks lived.

Rick's Casablanca Bar and Grill was a stone's throw below my concrete cave. The sprawling open air Caribbean style drinkery was built high on stilt pilings, painted stark white, with a bright tin roof and wrap-around porch. It was the town's watering hole and melting pot. If your money was green, Rick Blaine didn't care about your civic standing or the color of your skin. From this concealed position, I could observe everything happening at the popular saloon. The music was great, and the antics of tipsy locals provided endless entertainment.

At just after four o'clock, the bar was already overflowing with out-of-towners. Metal detectorists from all over the south were pouring in for the holiday festivities, testing their skills at finding the legendary "Treasure O' the Knob," a stolen cache of rare gold coins that went missing after a running shootout between two bandits and a passel of fuzz during a devastating storm 11 years earlier. The jamboree infused money into our declining hamlet and was always a lively spectacle to kick off the summer.

Next door to Rick's place was the dilapidated Knights of the Mystic Chalice Fraternity Building, a 19th century, two-story, gray brick edifice surrounded by more barbed wire and chain link than a maximum-security prison. The city elders condemned the structure when flood waters undermined the foundation during Hurricane Audrey in 1957. Walls fractured, windows broke, floors buckled, and the building leaned askew. After a lengthy legal battle, the dwindling K.O.M.C. membership went bankrupt, leaving the grand old building to rot.

Lichen-covered gargoyles crouched under rotting eaves and a murder of crows kept constant vigil atop the sagging roofline. It was a spooky, cursed place, where kudzu and English ivy fought a silent war for dominance over the crumbling walls.

The secretive lodge hall occupied the second floor of the building, away from street noise and curious eavesdroppers. The bottom floor had once been an upscale pub named after General George Armstrong Custer, who helped restore justice in Texas during the lawless days following the Civil War. Profits from the bar subsidized the shady exploits and occult rituals of the secret society. Before the fence went up, vandals defaced the *Custer Club Taproom* sign to read instead as *Cusser Club*, and the locals simply adopted the name for the property.

Across the mighty Sabine, on the Louisiana side, sat a cluster of colorful wood plank shotgun houses neatly nestled among a thick stand of pecan, pear, and peach trees. I retrieved my Captain Kidd spyglass hidden in the underbrush and peered across the river at the yellow homestead nearest the water. Aunt Tilde Kellum was rocking on her porch with a pair of ancient opera glasses, staring back at me. She smiled and waved, and I waved back.

Tilde was the town fortuneteller and tarot advisor. The aged sage was rumored to be a descendant of the famous New Orleans Voodoo Queen, Marie LeVau. The beloved Obeah woman gave good counsel to the lovelorn and grieving. Folks would come all the way from Houston and Shreveport to get straight advice from old Tilde. She was no one's auntie and everyone's auntie. Dix Knob had lots of churches, with lots of preachers, but Tilde Kellum was the undisputed spiritual leader of our quaint little border community.

Aunt Tilde had a pet pangolin named Rufus. A Nigerian businessman gifted the rare beast to her after she removed a malicious curse, that caused him to stutter. The animal was intended for ritual sacrifice, but Tilde didn't dabble in the dark arts. She was dedicated to a more saintly calling. Consequently, Rufus lived a life of leisure.

I took my Radio Flyer wagon across the railroad trestle a couple of times a month and gathered up rotting logs to dump in the pen with Rufus. The scaled prehistoric creature would eagerly tear apart the wood pulp with powerful claws and devour a smorgasbord of beetle larvae, termites, and grubs. My efforts pleased Aunt Tilde immensely. She knew my family history and used her influence to help me out when things got tough at home.

A tiny cascade of dust and pebbles tumbling over the opening of the Grotto interrupted my train of thought. It was a sure sign someone was approaching from the railroad tracks above.

My oldest friend, Mickey O'Dell, peeked around the corner and smiled. He was ginger-haired and stocky, with arms the size of syrup buckets. A pint-sized Hercules, Mickey was the only guy in school Galton Grails avoided. Mic was everyone's pal, but for some reason, he considered me his best friend. Stumbling behind him was Tommy Crum, a tall, lanky boy with unruly blond hair, a fabulous Doc Savage tan, and very thick glasses. We had all been together since kindergarten. Mickey reached in a paper sack, tossed me an apple fritter, and spoke first.

"We ran into Sara Tyler at the bakery and she told us that Greasy Galton stomped your ass again. She was really worried you might have gotten hurt. I think that big tittied girl is in love with you. She thinks you're soooo handsome." Batting his eyelashes and shrilling his voice for a feminine effect, he added, "Yeah, buddy! The biggest boobs in junior high. That frizzy blonde might be the prescription to make a real man out of you. You should plow that valley, Teddy boy."

A conversation with Mickey was like smoking a hand-rolled cigarette made out of rough-cut tobacco. You got the full, robust flavor of his thought process, along with all the burrs, stems, seeds, and miscellaneous bug parts.

I said, "Good god, Mickey, your mammary obsession is truly disturbing. You really shouldn't judge girls solely by their bust size." It was the only retort I could come up with, and I meant the statement as an insult, but Mickey took it as a compliment.

"Size isn't the only consideration. Jiggle and bounce plays an important role as well. But back to the subject at hand. Sara's got the hots for you, Teddy. Everybody knows it, by the way she practically swoons every time you speak to her. If you gave her some sugar, I bet she would let you play blap between those Titanic Tah-Tahs. Sara's got true nine-point nine knockers, scientifically calculated on the O'Dell Mammary Scale."

Sara Tyler is what rednecks call a "sugar dumpling." Kind of cute, but dumb as a box of rocks. She's that paradoxical girl you find in every East Texas town. Shapely, with hair that constantly combats any attempt at coiffure. An awkward understudy of the social graces, who is slow to recognize irony or insult. I have to admit, what God denied in brains, he more than made up for in curvaceousness. Sara had killer curves. All the other girls poked fun at her, but in reality, they were just jealous. The entire male population dismissed any minor intellectual deficiencies outright, favoring her overwhelming geometric attributes.

Tommy belonged to a very religious family and was a tad uncomfortable talking about girls, so he changed the subject abruptly. Holding up his book satchel and taking a deep bow, he said, "Teddy, I've got something that will cheer you up. I was helping the school librarian close up for the summer, and I made an unauthorized withdrawal for you."

He handed me a thick leather volume: *Melchior and Dipdottle's, The Methods of Great Actors,* an encyclopedic compendium of the stars of stage and screen. Loaded with the secrets of movie stars and Broadway greats, it was our favorite book. Tommy's uncharacteristic venture into lawlessness genuinely impressed me, and using my best Sean Connery impression, I croaked, "Do you think they'll miss it?"

Tommy shook his head. "Are you kidding? Look at this check-out card. Our names are the only ones on it. Nobody will miss this moldy old book."

Mickey snatched the card off the inside cover, took a lighter out of his pocket, set the paper on fire, and threw it at me. "Problem solved, Teddy boy!"

I cursed when the flame singed my eyebrows. Both boys roared.

Melchior and Dipdottle's masterpiece of theatrical instruction was the passport out of our piss ant village. *The Dix Knob Tattler* published a gushing review of our performance in *Oklahoma,* and with such critical acclaim, we pledged to pursue the acting craft. Mickey dreamed of following in the footsteps of Audie Murphy and John Wayne. Tommy leaned toward Shakespearean theater. I was more interested in writing and directing. We knew it was a stupid pipe dream, but what else was there to occupy three poor boys in an East Texas cesspool that God forgot? Devoid of an audience or venue, we simply tried to outwit each other with whimsical gestures and outlandish vocabulary. It was our private game, played daily, ad nauseam.

I coveted the book, and it pleased Tommy that I was pleased. He said, "Hey Teddy, you promised us another installment of *Mutant Teens on Mars*. I'm dying to hear how the Gorgax battle plays out.

Do the slimy reptilian invaders get cremated by Lars Lazer and Dirk Deadly?"

"I'm just about finished with the final chapter. I'll have it figured out in a day or two. I've got a real neat twist in the works for the ending. You'll both like it."

Mic kicked the dirt, twisted my arm behind my back, and clamped my forehead in a paralyzing Fritz Von Erich iron claw.

"You said that last week, you slacker! Have you got writer's block? Am I gonna have to beat the story out of you?" I struggled to no avail. Tommy poked Mic in the ribs in a half-hearted attempt to come to my rescue.

"C'mon, masser Mic. Let the po' white boy go."

Mic loosened his grip a bit. "Say the infamous words, Teddy Boy, and I'll let you go!"

"Science fiction is *not* literature." I screamed in cowardly capitulation.

O'Dell made me repeat the insulting phrase every time I made some excuse to procrastinate on my writing. He gave me a vigorous Indian rub on the scalp before letting me go.

Tommy said, "That old Underwood typewriter is still in the window of Pressman's Pawn Shop. He marked it down to twelve bucks. I went in a couple of days ago and tried it out. The 'Z' and 'L' are broken, but all the other keys work okay. I told him we were saving up for it, to launch your writing career. He said he would throw in a new ribbon if we would get it out of his way. I figure you can pencil in the missing letters. Maybe change Lars Lazer to Lars Laser. You wouldn't have to make so many corrections. You're a great storyteller, so don't pay any attention to Mickey. He's just razzing you about

Squeaky Sullivan and that fight y'all had in English class last semester."

Miss Hawkins had come up with the bright idea of "Fabulous Fiction Friday" in an effort to make English class more interesting—as if such a thing were even remotely possible. She encouraged students to read their stories aloud for extra credit. Samantha "Squeaky" Sullivan and I were the only ones who participated regularly. She was a sarcastic writer wannabe with a self-righteous attitude and big buck teeth. I presented an ongoing serial narrative about a group of super kids developed in a government eugenics lab, who got stranded on Mars after the project went sour. There, the exiled heroes battled a plethora of ferocious aliens and flesh-eating monsters. Squeaky Sullivan plagiarized *Nancy Drew* mysteries and everyone knew it. I got applause, and she got yawns. On one occasion, I got a standing ovation after Lars crushed the cranium of an evil Lizard Overlord and rescued a beautiful Alien Princess—scantily clad, of course. In a fit of resentful rage, Sullivan hollered, "Science fiction ain't litter-uh-chewer," and the guys taunted me with the put-down whenever the mood struck.

Music reverberated up the hill into the Grotto, as patrons packed the gin joint below. The river basin and trestle dyke created a strange acoustic phenomenon when Rick Blaine fired up his big Wurlitzer jukebox. The O'Kaysions were singing "I'm a Girl Watcher," and the triple echo was comical.

Tommy switched the subject to treasure. "Do you think they'll find anything this weekend? That old man from Livingston found an 1861 five-dollar gold piece last year, right behind the First Baptist Church. An expert from Austin said it was worth at least $500."

Mic wiped custard off of his chin and tossed the paper sack in the fire pit. "Stinky Rucker found a Spanish doubloon just half a mile up the road from here. Hell, he didn't even have a metal detector. It was just laying on top of the riverbank after a thunderstorm. The money he got from selling that piece paid his rent at Miss Norvell's boarding house for nearly a year."

Tommy said, "That gorgeous blonde TV reporter was on Channel 3 last week speculating about the identity of the robbers. She hired a private investigator to track down the remaining witnesses. After all these years, nobody has a clue who pulled off the great heist."

I was an outspoken scoffer. "The story has too many holes in it. The thieves passed through here and lost a little loot on their way west, but I don't believe the rest of the treasure is anywhere in the Knob. I think some of the local shopkeepers are planting a few coins around town to keep interest going. All these metal detector nuts pour into town every Memorial Day weekend hoping to strike it rich. The local proprietors make a killing on the poor schmucks."

Mickey stood up, pulled the kudzu back from the opening, and peered down the hill. "No doubt about that. Look at Casablanca. Standing room only, and it's not even five o'clock. Every hotel and flophouse is booked solid and charging double. The sheriff even ran all the whores out of the Grand Dee Motel up on North Jackson Street to make room for real, overnight paying customers. There's twice as many people as last year. Rick's already got them studying his diagrams."

Mr. Blaine hung a map of the town with multicolored tacks denoting the date and place where hunters had located a gold piece over the past decade. Red string connected the pins, and a group of enthusiasts gathered around the parchment, taking notes, while electronic dealers displayed the newest metal detector models on the wraparound porch. One seller had a plastic five-gallon bucket of sand filled with metals at varying depths, demonstrating the power of a new double loop coil design.

After an hour of observation, speculation, and small talk, Mickey announced he needed to get home. He was the man of the house, and his mother always required help with three younger siblings. We made plans to meet back at Casablanca on Saturday morning. Rick would slide us a few bucks to hose vomit off the porch and sweep up litter that accumulated after a raucous Friday night.

Mic said goodbye, but Tommy stayed behind. He was the only kid in town more pitiful than me. His mother had miscarried several times before her pregnancy with him, and some quack in Baton Rouge gave her a butt load of hormones and steroids to help her come to term. The pharmaceutical cocktail left Tommy with a lovely bronze complexion, early onset cataracts, and a penis the size of a Czechoslovakian summer sausage. None of us would shower with him after gym class. It was just too humiliating.

Tommy's parents ran the Palisades Movie Theater. They were an unhappy couple. Burtis and Edna Crum had fallen out of love a long time ago, but tolerated each other for Tommy's sake. They rarely appeared in public together. Burtis spent most nights on an old army cot in the theater office and Edna became a religious nut. She stayed up watching fiery evangelists on late night TV, and would have sporadic visions of Jesus and Satan. Whenever the Spirit seized her, she would rip her clothes, gnash her teeth, and speak in unknown tongues. I'd witnessed her gyrations a time or two during sleepovers. A little frightening, and a lot funny. Fortunately, she didn't foist any of the pious crap on Tommy. I suppose she figured his disability was enough penance for a lifetime.

More dark clouds rolled in, and the mood turned somber. Tommy reached in his satchel and handed me an article from *Time* magazine explaining Kelner's Phacoemulsification, a new surgical procedure by a famous ophthalmologist in New York. Developed in 1968, the revolutionary ultrasonic method was the most promising treatment for cataracts. Preliminary trials were encouraging, but the procedure was horribly expensive. Tommy's vision was deteriorating at an alarming rate, and his desperation was palpable. The thick glasses magnified his eyes, and when the light was just right, you could see the milky film behind his pupils.

He said, "Last year I could see across the river into The Grove. Now I can't even distinguish the other end of the trestle. I bet this Yankee doctor could help. My mom would move heaven and earth for me, but it would take a miracle to raise the cash for this new treatment."

He realized his lapse of etiquette. "I'm sorry, Teddy. I didn't mean to prattle on about my mother."

I slapped him on the back and cut him off with a forced laugh. "Think nothing of it, Tommy."

My mother left when I was eight years old. When my twin sister died, there was no reason for her to hang around. Her little princess was gone, and she lost all interest in family life.

Tommy hung his head and sighed. He was despondent, and I didn't know what to say, so I put my arm around his shoulder and gave him a hug. We knew each other's thoughts and just sat in silence for a while. Each with our own cross to bear. Sporadic raindrops slapped against the kudzu leaves and lightning discharged behind another onslaught of clouds invading from the Gulf. The grumble of thunder was constant, and gloom was as thick as blackstrap molasses.

Another cascade of pebbles interrupted our morbid contemplations. A breathless Mickey O'Dell returned. Running at breakneck speed, he stumbled down the path, falling on his hands and knees at the entrance of the Grotto. He rocked back on his haunches, red-faced and gasping.

"Guys ... jeezus ... guys ... that pretty Turnbow girl ... she's on the trestle ... and I think she's going to jump!"

2

MISSY TURNBOW STOOD DEAD CENTER OF THE RAILROAD bridge, on the edge of a steel girder, staring down at the churning waters of the mighty Sabine. She didn't go to public school. I'd caught glimpses of her around town, but we didn't really know her. She was high society, and we were the sediment at the bottom of the social barrel.

Mist settled on her long black hair, and it glistened like tiny violet gems in the cloud-muffled light. She was wearing one of those Catholic schoolgirl uniforms—a pleated tartan skirt with white knee socks and saddle shoes. There was nothing for her to hold on to.

Fragmented thoughts repeated like a broken record in my head. *Do something, dummy. Do something.* A neuron finally fired in the back of my brain, and I spoke without thinking.

"You know, it'd be a damn shame if the prettiest girl in town got swallowed up by this dirty creek. Why don't you take a step back? Let's chew the rag for a while."

She made a motion with her head like she was going to look at me, but abruptly turned back. "Just go away and leave me alone!"

I crept forward, holding my hands out, trying to maintain a non-threatening posture. The mist turned back into a drizzle.

"The truth is, I just got my ass whipped by the school bully, and I've had a pretty crappy day, too. But even in a mountain of despair, there is always a stone of hope. I can't remember who said it, but I recite that line just about every day. Why don't you come back to our private hideout and we'll talk things over?"

Tommy and Mic meekly backed me up.

"Yeah, we can't just leave you—"

"Never forgive ourselves—"

"Please go away," she said, but this time with a little less conviction.

I inched closer, trying not to alarm her. "We're not going to do that. Now, here's the deal; the Missouri-Pacific 6:15 is going to come roaring down these tracks any minute, and we're all going to be in a hell of a bind if we don't get off this rusty old bridge."

Her shoulders slumped, and I thought she might reconsider the situation until she lifted her arms as if preparing for a swan dive.

I leapt forward and grabbed her waistband, giving it an awkward tug. She stumbled back a step, teetering on the edge of the girder.

Lightning flashed overhead and a gust of wind caused us to sway. I firmed my grip and pulled hard, falling backward on my butt across the steel rails. A split second later, she landed in my lap.

We sprawled across the tracks just long enough for me to catch a whiff of her perfume. The girl was back on her feet in an instant, glaring down at me.

Flashing a toothy grin, I said, "My name is Theodore Roosevelt Nutscalder. My friends call me Teddy. These two goons are Mickey O'Dell and Tommy Crum."

She didn't flinch. I had never seen her up close. Sea-green eyes, a honey complexion, and manicured nails accentuated a flawless form. I was instantly smitten. This girl was the complete package. A goddess among troglodytes.

She took a step toward the other boys and they parted like the Red Sea.

"Get out of my way and leave me alone. You can't help me with my problems."

Enchanted and a bit perturbed, I wasn't about to let her off so easily.

"Now hold on a minute. I just busted my scrawny ass, and the creosote on these crossties ruined my best pair of jeans. I deserve an explanation, for the effort, at least."

She continued walking away at a faster pace. We trotted behind, wondering what was going on inside that pretty head.

She suddenly spun around to face us. "Don't follow me. You'll just make matters worse. I'm caught in a tree, the forest is on fire, and I can't get down."

Mickey and Tommy looked at me in confusion.

I said, "It's a writer's metaphor, you morons."

A moment of silence followed as the girl gathered her thoughts.

"If anyone sees me with you guys and it gets back to my..." Her voice trailed off, and it was obvious she wasn't ready to trust us. She looked straight up and silently mouthed something as if appealing to a higher power. Then she gazed straight at me with a profound despair in her eyes.

"You're really sweet for offering to help, but you just can't. No one can. It's a no-win situation all the way around. Other people are involved and ... it's complicated. Just leave me alone and forget you ever saw me."

For a moment, I thought she would break down, but she just squared her shoulders, turned, and ran away, the granite stones crunching with each graceful stride.

Mic and Tommy shrugged and looked at one another as I peered across the river. Tilde was still rocking on her porch, with those old opera glasses. She had seen it all.

* * *

The Missouri-Pacific 6:15 rumbled through the Delta carrying lignite coal from strip mines in Harrison County at the north end of the Sabine River valley. A few pieces would fall off at the sharp dog leg curve leading up to the trestle, and we gathered it to fuel a fire pit in the Grotto. We dumped our haul while discussing the unusual events of the day. Ideas and theories were ricocheting like pinballs in an arcade.

Tommy voiced the overriding question. "How could a rich high society babe be so desperate at her age? It doesn't make any sense. Do y'all think she committed a crime or got in trouble at school?"

Mickey snapped his fingers. "I'll bet she's having boyfriend trouble. Maybe she's pregnant! Since she's a Catholic, maybe we should tell the priest over at Immaculate Conception. They have to keep secrets, don't they?"

I squashed the idea immediately. "It's all speculation, guys. She's in some kind of predicament, and even a well-intentioned move could make her situation worse. She asked us not to tell anyone, so we won't. Understood?" Both shrugged and nodded.

Mickey lamented the fact that his mother was going to be furious at him for being late and appealed for us to intervene on his behalf. Tommy and I agreed we would concoct some alternate version for Vera O'Dell to get him out of hot water should it become necessary. We set the Casablanca cleanup for 9 a.m. the next morning.

We parted ways and, as I headed home, the trestle scenario replayed in my mind. Every guy fantasizes about the knight in shining armor routine at some point in his life. Boldly riding to the rescue of a beautiful damsel in distress. Every smart guy also knows it's absurd, but that doesn't keep heroic thoughts from seeping through the barrier of logic and reason.

The weather settled, so I lingered by the Sandstone Quarry for a while. Like everything in Dix Knob, it was dilapidated and outdated. The wheat-colored blocks fell out of style, and when the quarry closed, the town began a downward spiral. Interstate 10 bypassed the town and Eisenhower's dream became our nightmare. Snubbed by progress and frozen in time, our crappy little village was circling the drain like a stubborn turd in the toilet. High school graduates staged a mass exodus at the beginning of each summer to find jobs along the industrial coast. Most never returned. "Only the dead and dying" was the town's unspoken motto. The Treasure O' the Knob Festival was one last pitiful gasp for revival.

Rhinelander Dix founded the town in the late 1800s when he discovered the huge outcropping of compacted quartz and feldspar. Formed by Huronian glaciers a billion years ago, the huge knob-like formation was ideal for mining with the technology available in the late 1800s. The quarry carried the town through tough times and a depression, but the decline started after the Second World War and ate away like an insidious disease.

Rusted draglines, cranes, and rock saws littered the floor of the quarry. Sweet-gum saplings and Johnsongrass found a foothold among a million cracks and crevices. Dirt bike trails scarred the stone remnants and terraced rock face. Galton Grails went down there daily, zig zagging around on his old smoke-belching motorcycle.

A stagnant seep pond filled the lowest point. Green slime covered the surface, and the alkaline water was devoid of aquatic life and too toxic for swimming. Anglers threw carp and alligator gar in the pond, but even the robust bottom feeders would bloat and go belly up within a few hours.

On the opposite side of the quarry, local potheads gathered for their weekend ritual of drug-fueled debauchery. Campfires and munchies. Lots of sex and music. Very little harm. The idea of "Free Love" was gaining traction throughout America, and the local hippies did their part to promote the movement.

Clydell and Cletus Barge, the cannabis kings of Kushner County, were holding high court. Clydell and Cletus were popular purveyors of homegrown hempage.

All dopers met up on "The Rim." It was the perfect place to do business and smoke weed. You could *literally* see the cops coming for a mile, and when they arrived, the stoners would just fling their stash into the seep pool below. No evidence. No crime. Truth be told, nobody really cared anyway. Townsfolk considered Clydell and Cletus more of an infestation than a menace.

The carillon bells at the Methodist Church chimed 10:00, so I figured it was safe to go home.

I spent most nights next to the town dump on the lower end of Kickapoo Street, in a ramshackle two-bedroom frame structure, also occupied by my father. He was a mean drunk. My mother left seven years earlier after the death of my twin sister, so he took solace in a whiskey bottle.

Of course, this sad state of affairs was all my fault. My sister Tessa got sick and died instead of me. Yoked with this stigma, I avoided "home" whenever possible.

I approached the house quietly, carefully choosing my steps to avoid any noise. There was no movement inside. The front door and windows were wide open and an oscillating metal fan clattered on the coffee table. The screen door squeaked a bit, so I spit on the hinge to silence the racket. I needn't have bothered. Nathaniel Nutscalder was passed out on the couch. Still dressed in overalls smeared with asphalt oil and cutback tar, he cuddled a fifth of *Old Rebel,* while the Houston weatherman gave dire warnings on a grainy Zenith in the corner. I swiped a cigarette off his rusty TV tray, lit up, and blew smoke in his face to see if he would stir. He didn't. The dung heap was out for the night. I could sleep solid.

There was a chicken leg and bologna slice in the fridge. Better fare than most nights. The milk curdled, so I threw it out. Saltines and ketchup made dessert. The water heater was working, so I took a hot bath and used the leftover water to rinse my clothes. All the piss and most of the creosote came out. My luck was turning.

Nightmares terrified me in the past. I used to wake up in a cold sweat, but time had castrated the most of the demons, and my subconscious mind concocted all sorts of delightful scenarios to cope with anger and justify my existence. Visions of my sister were a strange comfort in a morbid, metaphysical way. Tessa's ghost had grown up with me. She wasn't the second grader who lay in the coffin on that frosty February morning seven years earlier. She was a teenager like me, and her caustic wit and passive-aggressive attitude had grown more complex with age.

It had been a hell of a day. I was dead when my head hit the pillow.

* * *

Daddy, Momma, and Tessa walked through the department store, awed by the Christmas decorations and an extravagant collection of expensive toys.

"Nathan, let's get Tessa this beautiful dollhouse."

"Yes, honey, and that little pink bicycle too!"

Tessa giggled. Her mottled blue skin, bloodshot eyes, and purple lips contrasted nicely with a strawberry print dress and white leather go-go boots.

"Momma, I want another Barbie. Momma, I want some candy. Momma, I want a push-up bra with some fishnet pantyhose, and spiked heel stilettos."

"Yes, darling, anything you desire. Nathan, perhaps we should ask Teddy if he wants Santa to bring him a gift."

"Teddy boy, you don't need anything from Santa this year, do you?

"Just one thing."

"What would that be?"

"A ten-inch Bowie knife to cut all of your fucking throats."

3

KUSHNER COUNTY SANITATION DEPARTMENT OPENED THE automatic mechanized landfill gates at 7 a.m. sharp, Monday through Saturday. The rumbling, rusted, ill-greased cogs served as an alarm clock for the few residents remaining at the end of Kickapoo Street. Humidity was high and my clothes were still a bit damp, but I put them on anyway. The old man was still comatose on the couch. The cupboard was bare. No breakfast today.

I had an hour before the rendezvous at Casablanca, so I decided to take a stroll by the Turnbow house for a look-see. The Bell Telephone directory provided an address. Storm clouds cleared out overnight and the first Saturday of summer break promised to be a scorcher.

Number Eight, Fairhaven Street, was on the north end of town. I settled into a casual jog and it only took 20 minutes to get there. Work trucks lined the street. Caterers, plumbers, landscapers and painters were busy ensuring the Upper Crust remained the Upper Crust.

The Turnbow residence was the most spectacular. A massive two-story Greek Revival mansion with four white columns and an elaborate widow's walk crowning the roof. There were no cars in the driveway, so I took a chance and walked around to the back yard.

I concocted a lame excuse of looking for a lost pet if anyone inquired. So many laborers were moving around the neighborhood that no one took immediate notice of me. I allowed myself to relax a bit. The back yard looked like a movie set. There was a broad covered patio decorated with custom furniture, along with topiary shrubs and St. Augustine grass, all trimmed to perfection. Flowering plants filled a large glass greenhouse. Conflicting emotions ricocheted through my head. I wanted to see Missy again, but I simultaneously feared rejection. This foray into her domain might seem creepy to a girl in her social strata.

The enormous greenhouse was at least 40 feet long and had two large metal drawers labeled "Mulch Butler" built into the back wall. These slid on rollers connecting the outer yard and the inner greenhouse. An elderly gentleman was loading fertilizer and potting soil into one, and removing dry stems and wilted cuttings from the other. He frowned when I came into sight.

I said, "Sorry mister, I didn't mean to intrude. Just looking for my lost kitten. A calico. Have you seen her?" He shook his head and pointed to his ears. Deaf as a hammer. The jig was up. This was my cue to exit. Turning to leave, I glanced up at a second-story window.

A ghastly, pale-faced woman stared down at me. My heart fluttered with panic. I waved, but she scowled and jerked the curtains shut.

I was in a wide-open sprint by the time I reached the street. My cross-country training came in handy, and I was back at the town square in record time.

Midtown was already hopping. Treasure hunters crowded the sidewalks and parks, gliding their metal detectors over right-of-ways and vacant lots. Some were negotiating with locals for temporary access to lawns and private property. Many of the homeowners posted signs reading 50%-50% or 60%-40%, letting the electronic adventurers know what split they expected if anything turned up.

The Treasure O' the Knob Festival was certainly a boon for our struggling township. The whole idea was ridiculous to me, but there was no doubt the event was getting bigger every year. I marveled at the pitiful schmucks trying to strike it rich off a legend shrouded in mystery.

In the summer of 1957, Hurricane Audrey surprised forecasters as it rapidly gained strength and barreled into the Gulf Coast. The crabs knew it was coming. Thousands of the crustaceans clogged roads and sidewalks in a mass migration to higher ground. Amused newspaper photographers snapped pictures for morning editions that would never be published. Stinky Rucker, the village idiot, ran door to door, telling everybody the storm was going to be a killer. He had barely survived the Labor Day hurricane that decimated the Florida Keys in 1935. Folks say he went crazy cremating corpses in huge open fire pits following that storm.

The story goes that during the evening of June 26th, a couple of desperados robbed a wealthy coin dealer in New Orleans. Some reports say it was two men. Others insist it was a man and woman. A vigilant neighbor raised the alarm, and the perps fled in a stolen 1949 Ford Coupe just as the cops closed in. A chase ensued across western Louisiana and the Sabine River into East Texas.

The sliding mesh three-speed transmission was not one of Ford Motor Company's stellar engineering achievements. Also known as a crashbox, the Coupe's drivetrain faltered just over the Texas border and left the robbers afoot. With a heavily armed posse in hot pursuit, the pair fled to Dix Knob and apparently got separated just as Hurricane Audrey slammed ashore.

Twenty miles south of town, the Sabine Estuary swelled and reversed the water flow back up the river in a devastating flood surge. With sustained winds over one hundred miles per hour, the gargantuan storm was one of the worst in U.S. history. No one was prepared. 500 people died and dozens went missing. Both robbers vanished.

The official version states one sustained a wound but may have gotten away. One twenty-dollar gold piece, found a week later, had an obvious bullet nick and folks assumed the bag of booty deflected a shot. Some of the loot dribbled out at various points along the burglar's chaotic path, and that's what the detectorists had discovered so far.

After a running shootout, the other unfortunate outlaw fell into the turbulent river, and was never seen again. Lots of conspiracy theories emerged.

Searchers discovered coins on the riverbank and several other places along the route of pursuit, but it was only a tiny fraction of the total haul. The rest remained a mystery.

With rapid advancements in metal detecting technology, the search took on new life and interest was growing each year. Kushner County sheriff, Otho Wheat, thought the gold was at the bottom of the Sabine, washed out by the storm surge along with the bandit's body.

Panic, confusion, and desperate rescue efforts delayed the manhunt in the days following the aftermath of Awful Audrey.

At any rate, the celebration injected cash into our lagging economy. Everybody benefited to some degree, so doubters like me and the sheriff kept mum, to avoid dissuading the influx of tourists.

Mickey and Tommy had already started the cleanup by the time I reached the bar. Mickey hoisted a bag of trash on his shoulder and motioned me over.

"Mr. Blaine told me he'd give us five dollars apiece if we did a good job. There's a TV crew from Channel 3 Houston coming to interview him and the sheriff about the robbery and festival. They're going to film it right here at the bar. He said he'd even pay a little extra if we would straighten up the chairs and wipe down the tables."

This was good news. I hadn't seen a five-dollar bill in a long time. Our stray canine friend, Humper, was even getting in on the act. The short-haired pit bull-boxer mix scoured the parking lot for chicken bones and chip crumbs, doing his part to make the place presentable. The old cur had been around as long as I could remember. Humper was the unofficial town mascot, and everyone in the Knob threw morsels when he passed. Aunt Tilde said he carried a melancholy soul, and with her blessing, no one dared to harm the mutt.

We hustled hard, and the parking lot and surrounding area up to the Cusser Club fence was spick-and-span in less than an hour.

Tommy had some new clip-on sun shades for his glasses. It made a remarkable improvement in his appearance. He looked like a bush pilot, and I told him so. He puffed out his chest and grinned like a Cheshire cat.

He replied, "These were a gift from Dr. DeSilva, that Cuban surgeon at the hospital. He told my mom these would block some of the ultra-violet rays and slow down the progression of my cataracts." He was almost giddy.

We went inside and started wiping down tables and baseboards, making sure the chairs were nice and orderly.

The local handyman, Arthur Rumkin, was busy repairing a broken window in the ladies' restroom, damaged the previous evening when two hookers tried to skip out on their tab at last call. He was a jack-of-all trades, erstwhile ballroom dancer, Korean War vet, and a conspiracy theorist with more tattoos than teeth.

Rumkin was a yakker. A shit stirrer. An embellisher of tales. He knew all the juicy gossip and wasn't shy about slinging it. To say he was slightly schizoid would be an understatement. I was curious about the Turnbow clan, so I tried to lather him up with some clever acting skills.

"Mr. Rumkin, you keep a finger on the pulse of the community and I was wondering if you could give me the inside scoop on some highbrows from the North Side?"

"Which ones would that be? The Englands? The Kuykendalls? The Hildebrands?"

"I was curious about the Turnbows."

"Jeezus, Teddy, how much time do you have? The sad tale of the terribly tragic Turnbows would fill a library."

"Maybe you could just give me the *Reader's Digest* condensed version."

"This wouldn't have anything to do with a little raven-haired beauty, would it?"

I feigned embarrassment and even managed a slight blush. I hung my head and brushed the floor with my foot. Melchior and Dipdottle would have been proud. My motivation was transparent, so I thought I'd ham it up.

"Aw, man, you won't rat me out, will you?"

Rumkin slapped me on the shoulder and laughed. "I hate to tell you this, but they'll never let it happen."

"Who's they?"

"Are you brain-dead, boy? Her family, of course. They are not gonna let *you* ... get anywhere near ... little miss sweet stuff."

The dialogue was turning into a lecture, so I changed strategy.

"It's not like that at all. Sure, I like Missy. Who wouldn't? But I'm no fool. I just want to plan for a future friendship. I thought some background information might keep me from putting my foot in my mouth. Conversation fodder, if you know what I mean."

"Gotcha, little man. Gotcha. Well, let's see now. Grandaddy Turnbow made all his money in the oil business. He was one of the first wildcatters during the Kilgore oil boom back in the '20s. His son, Missy's father, moved down to the Knob in the late '40s and made his fortune in petroleum transport. He died in Hurricane Audrey back in '57. Folks say he was trying to help rescue some stranded motorists and got swept away himself. He turned up, washed ashore, in Deweyville, bloated in his boxers. The truth is, he was out catting around with a car full of whores, got drunk, and drove off a bridge, but you didn't hear that from me."

Rumkin cursed loudly and stuck a filthy thumb in his mouth.

"Damn it! That's the second time I've cut my hand on this window. Now, where was I?"

"Whores on a bridge."

"Oh yeah. That's right. Anyway, his wife got all bummed out about it. Mrs. Turnbow got hooked on drugs and started seeing a psychiatrist. She sent the daughter off to a private boarding school. Damn shame, sending her off alone. Then that Nollen Embers guy came on the scene and started sniffing around. He got his hooks in the widow. Her name is Maris. Anyhow, that greasy son-of-a bitch got her to marry him. Everybody in town says she was all doped up and didn't know what she was doing, but I think she was just scared and lonely. Nollen was after her money, for damn sure. Her lawyer, Hyrum Bell, stepped in at the last minute and had her sign some papers protecting most of the fortune. He mysteriously vanished shortly afterward. Embers got a piece of the pie, but not all of it. Folks say he deals in stolen cars and runs a bunch of chop shops scattered all the way down the coast to Biloxi. I don't know. Maybe, maybe not. That guy has been indicted for all kinds of crimes, but never convicted. Witnesses mysteriously disappear. He's a slippery eel for sure. He's running for mayor and making all kinds of wild promises about bringing in new business to the area. Pie in the sky stuff. Hell, nobody wants the job, but nobody wants him to have it either. That's about it, in a nutshell."

It was a big nut. There was a lot to digest. I thanked him and told him not to worry about the broken glass and sawdust on the floor. I'd clean it up after he finished. Mic and Tommy carried out the last of the trash as I stood on the brass foot rail and polished the mahogany bar.

Built in 1959 after the Cusser Club flooded, Rick's Casablanca Bar was a tribute to the 1942 Warner Brothers blockbuster movie starring Humphrey Bogart. The main movie character's name was Rick Blaine. Our Mr. Blaine's given name was Rayford, but everyone called him Rick for obvious reasons, and he considered it an honor. Blaine looked a lot like Bogart—tall, dark, and handsome, with a stern gaze and a slightly receding hairline. He even adopted a Bogart-esque manner of speech to go along with his persona. The resemblance was uncanny. Casablanca was decorated with posters from the movie. A beautiful, dewy-eyed Ingrid Bergman silently pleaded for compassion while the stern gaze of Conrad Veidt and Claude Rains kept a watchful eye on the patrons. Someone even donated a ceramic reproduction of the iconic Maltese Falcon. It was a prop from a different Bogart film, but no one cared. The massive ebony bird stood silent watch, perched on a shelf above the Wurlitzer jukebox.

Rick was the undisputed expert on the gold heist, shootout, and disappearance of the loot. He kept a scrapbook with all the past newspaper clippings and magazine articles regarding the mystery.

He emerged from his office dressed in a cream-colored silk jacket and black slacks.

"Fellas, Casablanca hasn't looked this good in years. Y'all did a fine job. Here's a fiver for each of you, and a jar of nickels I took out of the Wurlitzer. Grab a soda and some snacks. If you're quiet, I'll let you sit behind the bar and watch the interview."

We cheerfully obeyed and divided up the nickels as we guzzled Grapette. A minute later, the sheriff's car pulled in with a TV van trailing close behind. Boards creaked under the strain as Sheriff Otho Wheat ascended the steps from the parking lot. He was a mountain on two feet. A quintessential Texas lawman who never called for backup, he kept his thumb on the scales of justice to make certain it didn't tip too far in either direction. He was widely respected, with a keen sense of fairness. Occasionally, he would let minor offenses like consensual prostitution and private gambling go with a stern look. As long as no one was getting hurt and no one got cocky, he was inclined to let some of the small stuff slide.

The Sheriff shifted uncomfortably in an undersized chair while the film crew set up equipment, tested microphones, and adjusted lighting. Rick discussed camera angles with a shapely reporter, sporting an impossibly short miniskirt and platinum blonde hair.

Mickey stuck his nose up to mine with a shit-eating grin on his face. "Do you think she bleached her bush, too?"

Grapette erupted from my nose as I tried to control my laughter. Rick turned and arched an eyebrow.

He said, "Okay, fellas. Hit the road. You can watch the interview on TV after the ten o'clock news."

Tommy went home and Mickey invited me to lunch at Casa O'Dell.

4

THE O'DELL'S HOME WAS A BIG, SPRAWLING, CLAPBOARD MAZE with multiple add-ons, constructed over the years to accommodate an expanding family. A hodgepodge of different colored shingles smattered the roof, and the low-hanging branches of an ancient cottonwood tree shaded the entire structure like a mother hen coddling her chicks.

Mickey's father was in prison for manslaughter. Pete O'Dell previously worked in the local slaughterhouse, gutting hogs. A big jolly oaf, he was the constant butt of practical jokes by his fellow butchers. After being startled by a prank bullhorn, Pete reflexively struck a co-worker, knocking him into an industrial sausage grinder. An arm was severed at the shoulder and the stupid bastard bled to death before help arrived.

The new district attorney, eager to prove himself, prosecuted poor Pete to the full extent of the law. An inept public defender fumbled the ball, and Pete was doing a dime in the state prison at Huntsville.

Mrs. O'Dell did domestic work on the North Side, cleaning, cooking, and ironing 10 hours a day. She was a saint. Mickey felt bad about his behavior at Casablanca and, in return, promised me a hardy meal. His three younger sisters met us at the door. When he reached into his pocket and pulled out a handful of nickels, they squealed and hugged him. Ranging in age from 5 to 10 years, none of them resembled Mickey, thank God. The youngest had a curly Orphan Annie hairdo and an adorable lisp because of a slightly bifurcated tongue.

My stomach growled as I entered the kitchen. Chicken and dumplings, green bean casserole, cornbread, and peach cobbler covered a large rough plank dining table draped in a cloth of stitched flour sacks. After a second helping, I told Mickey I would help him with the chores.

A hinge had come loose on his older sister's bedroom door, so we put our heads together to see if we could fix it.

Mic's 17-year-old sister, Brandy, was a voluptuous creature with big brown eyes and chestnut hair. Everything was in the right place. And when I say everything, I mean *everything*. Heads turned wherever she went. When she walked down the street, her ass jiggled like two coons wrestling in a tow sack. She oozed sensuality and was a popular dancer at Muddy Mike's Gentlemen's Club, a river bottom titty bar across the Louisiana state line in Beauregard Parish.

Cajuns, outlaws, roughnecks, and rednecks plopped down large dollar for a little glimpse of Heaven. Brandy O'Dell and a Coushatta girl named Danni Redhawk were the stars of the swamp show. The sassy babes performed an Annie Oakley and Pocahontas routine that included a blow-up kiddie pool, leather whips, and strawberry syrup. Despite obvious historical anachronisms, the sultry extravaganza was immensely popular.

Since Big Pete's unfortunate incarceration, Brandy was the undisputed breadwinner of the family. She started ragging on Mickey the moment we got to her door.

"If you made any money at Rick's today, you need to give it to Momma. The light bill is due and the Kuykendalls are leaving for Colorado next week, so she's only going to bring home half pay. I can't carry the whole family on my back."

Mickey snorted. "I've got a few bucks. I'll throw it in the pot."

Brandy didn't let up. "Even the young'uns go around town gathering up discarded Coke bottles for a nickel apiece. It ain't much, but they're trying. You need to find some yards to mow or something."

"Dammit, Brandy, I would, if daddy's old beat up mower worked! Why don't you just rub that big ass of yours on a few more rednecks…"

A heavy glass ashtray sailed past my face and glanced off the side of Mic's head. He dropped the screwdriver and stormed off.

Rubbing his noggin, he shouted, "I've got to find some bigger screws. The holes in the door frame are all stripped out. You gotta quit swinging on the door when you practice that vulgar pole dance routine!"

Nonplussed, Brandy sat down on her vanity stool, touching up her makeup and spraying her hair. I couldn't resist a glimpse, and she caught me immediately in the mirror's reflection. Her instincts about men were razor sharp, and her mouth curled up in a wicked smile.

"So, what's on your mind, you little pervert?"

She caught me red-handed, so I retreated to a "poor-pitiful-me" posture.

"I made five bucks today. I'll put it in the pot if you will save me some leftovers tonight. My dad usually drinks whiskey for dinner and isn't real diligent about keeping the pantry stocked."

Immediately, her demeanor changed. She rose from the chair, walked over, and reached up with her forefinger under the pretext of straightening my hair.

"You've got a cute little cowlick right here."

She toyed with the curl for a second, stood on tippy toes, and glanced over my shoulder to see if anyone was nearby. The vixen playfully put her thumbs through my belt loops, pulled me close, and gave me a vigorous shake at the hips. I was glad my shirttail was out. A tingle ran up my spine as I watched her saunter back to the vanity stool.

"Keep your money. You can come over and eat with us anytime. We're not starving or anything, but Momma works a lot of long hours. Everyone in town knows my occupation, so I just want Mickey to step up. He needs to contribute something. Daddy's not coming home any time soon. Nobody in Austin is listening to the appeals. I make fairly good money, but things have been slacking off at the club. The good Baptists in Beauregard Parish are protesting and taking down license plate numbers in the parking lot. There's nothing Muddy Mike can do to stop it. The clientele is dwindling. Most of the oilfield workers don't give a shit, and they even throw rotten tomatoes at the little old church ladies, but it just makes matters worse. The Beauregard Parish sheriff is actually pretty nice. He tries to act as a peacekeeper, but he's fighting a losing battle. He's got constituents and elections to consider just like Otho Wheat."

She stood and took one last look at her impeccable makeup before turning back to me. I had unconsciously taken another step into her room. She grabbed my collar as I retreated.

"You're a handsome little guttersnipe. I suspect you're going to be a heartbreaker someday." Brandy bit her bottom lip seductively. Her breath was spicy and hot. "When you get a little older, come over to Mike's. We'll find a dark corner and I'll give you a nice lap dance." Brandy knew exactly which buttons to push. It didn't matter if a man was 9 or 90.

I got a little woozy as the blood rushed to my nether regions. She stuck out her tongue and licked the air an inch from my chin. I couldn't breathe for a few seconds.

Mickey returned with a coffee can full of old bolts and screws, and we managed to repair the hinge despite my trembling hands.

Missy Turnbow and Brandy O'Dell were opposite sides of the same coin. Missy was the kind of girl that inspired works of art, poetry, and thoughts of manly virtue. Brandy inspired men to drink hard liquor, lie to their wives, and write bad checks.

After repairing the door, Mic and I took turns popping the clutch on an old 1951 Dodge flatbed pickup. Pete O'Dell bought it for a hundred dollars to haul hay during the summers, but he landed in prison before he got it street worthy, so we just drove it up and down the back roads for fun, until the sheriff's deputies would send us home. We did a few other chores, and I used a handy trick to get a rust stain out of the kitchen sink with a sliced lemon and a dab of bleach. Vera O'Dell was so impressed she invited me to stay for supper and a sleepover. She offered to call my father for permission, but I said he was working late and wouldn't miss me. He didn't give a rat's ass, and I suspect she knew the truth.

As I touched up paint on the porch rails, Coushatta Danni pulled in to pick up Brandy in her beat-up 1959 Pontiac Star Chief. The car was a rusted-out land yacht with a different hubcap on each wheel. It could easily accommodate eight or nine people. The paint was originally a beautiful Copper Canyon Poly, but our morbid coastal climate had oxidized it down to a dull Pig Shit Sienna. The girls huddled in the front seat for a few seconds, and Danni leaned out the window and pulled down her tube top, gracing us with a quick boob flash. Tires spun, gravel flew, and two slightly sullied sirens were off to the swamp show.

5

THE INTERVIEW WITH RICK AND OTHO AIRED ON CHANNEL 3 after the ten o'clock news. Sheriff Wheat addressed the glaring discrepancies in official documentation. Law enforcement didn't do an investigation of the crime until much later, because of the confusion caused by Hurricane Audrey. Memories faded and priorities shifted. He skillfully dissected critics who postulated a cover up or incompetence.

Rick discussed conflicting eyewitness accounts. A neighbor had seen two men exit the victim's home. A service station attendant in Moss Bluff reported seeing a man and a woman. The shapely reporter advanced the possibility of three or more criminals. Sheriff Wheat thought this theory was unlikely.

He said, "The more perps involved in a crime, the more likely someone will slip up and get caught. The rarest date pieces, which are well documented, never turned up at any coin shows or auction houses. It is logical to assume they were lost. Criminals are greedy. If there were other culprits, some evidence would have surfaced over the previous 11 years."

That's the last thing I remember as I fell asleep on the couch.

* * *

"Daddy, I think Tessa is sick."

"Momma and I are trying to sleep. Leave us alone."

"She was coughing, but now she stopped, and her lips are blue."

"Dammit Teddy, get out of here or I'll blister your ass with a belt."

"I'm sorry, Daddy."

* * *

At 6:40 a.m. Sunday morning, we awoke to a calamity at the end of Pearl Street. Mickey's 5-year-old sister ran into the living room with wide eyes and a broad grin.

"Teddy, Mickey, they founded some tweasure!"

Barefoot and half dressed, Mickey and I ran to the end of Pearl Street to where it intersects with the Riverfront Levee Road. Tommy was already there. Two dozen locals gathered, and the police were roping off the area and pushing back rubberneckers.

Mic said, "What's going on, Tommy? What did they find? Why are the cops here?"

"Mom heard a scream and saw a woman crying and waving her arms, so she called the police. Apparently, the lady found two ten-dollar Gold Eagles right next to the river, in the same hole with some bones."

The crowd pressed in as a sleek black Buick Riviera pulled up. The cops pushed the gawkers aside to make a path for the car. Dr. DeSilva climbed out wearing a starched white clinic jacket. Otho Wheat took him by the arm and led him to the retainer wall at the edge of the water. We squeezed through the crowd for a better look.

A middle-aged woman in denim shorts sat on the muddy ground, wiping her eyes next to a high-tech metal detector. A young deputy I didn't recognize was pouring some coffee out of a thermos bottle and gently interrogating her. Dr. DeSilva bent over a shallow hole, pulled a fountain pen out of his pocket, prodded the ground, and emerged with a bone. Otho crouched down to his eye level.

DeSilva announced, "A human mandible … jawbone."

Otho stood upright and repositioned his white Stetson hat.

"Doctor, are you absolutely certain it's human? Could it be an animal bone?"

The physician used his handkerchief to polish a tooth.

"Have you ever seen a wild animal with a gold crown?"

The lawman threw his shoulders back and bellowed. "Deputies. We've got a crime scene. Finish roping it off. Elbows and assholes. Everybody else back up a hundred feet … now!"

The woman sobbed uncontrollably as the crowd dispersed. Dr. DeSilva pulled a syringe out of his black bag and gave her a shot in the arm. Deputies hustled her into his car. We climbed a nearby chinaberry tree to continue our observations. The morning was already sweltering and the thick green canopy provided a welcome refuge.

Brushing his hands together with a satisfied smirk, Mickey said, "That's the bones of the robber, for sure. That thief got shot, and the backwash from the flood buried him deep in the mud. Case closed."

Tommy bounced on the limb, nearly knocking both of us off our perch.

"No way, dumbass. The flood waters couldn't have buried the thief at this location. Do you see the retainer wall? They didn't even construct it until about five years ago. This entire area was dug up and the county work crew trucked in tons of dirt. Dozens of laborers were digging around on this site. If a whole human body was in the ground, someone would have noticed during all that excavation. Those coins and that jawbone were accidentally hauled in here with the fill dirt, from somewhere else."

The argument continued as deputies set up a white canvas tent over the site, drove stakes in the ground, and made a neat little grid with kite string. I jumped out of the tree when Tommy and Mic's "discussion" deteriorated into threats of eye gouging and high-pressure enemas.

I said, "Fellas, there's nothing else to see now, so I'm going to head over to Kickapoo Street and put in an appearance. Let's meet up at the Grotto at five o'clock, then we'll head over to Rhinelander Park for the festival."

I retrieved my Keds from the O'Dell place and headed home. Brandy's door was shut, but the aroma of strawberries filled the hallway, so I knew she was safe in her bed. On one hand, I felt sorry for her; on the other hand, I admired her spunk. She was independent and strong. Stronger than most guys I knew.

6

NATHANIEL NUTSCALDER WAS A 39-YEAR-OLD ALCOHOLIC with no prospects. Educated as a civil engineer, he landed a cushy job with a tri-state bridge contractor straight out of LSU. He married his college sweetheart, Cassie Vinman, and a set of twins were born three weeks before their first anniversary. Everything was right with the world. Nate brought home the bacon, and Cassie spent her days doting on her daughter, Tessa.

The fairy tale unraveled in the seventh year. Tessa developed a chronic cough, fainting spells, and seizures. Specialists were consulted for over a year, but no one provided answers.

I awoke in the early morning hours of Sunday, February 11, 1962, to my sister gasping for air. I covered my head with a pillow and ignored her. An hour later, the first rays of dawn filtered through the window, highlighting her wide-eyed corpse staring at me from her twin bed. The skin was mottled and purple. Her lips were blue, and the whites of her motionless eyes were as red as the Satin Valentine Heart taped to her headboard. I jumped up and gave her a vigorous shake, but she didn't move. I told my father, but he scolded me and threatened to whip me with a belt.

* * *

The house on Kickapoo Street appeared quiet, and a squeaky sprinkler spewed water over the sidewalk and a weed-infested lawn. With wet shoe soles, I stepped through the door and immediately slipped on the greasy linoleum, crashing into my father's TV tray. Two Camel cigarettes escaped the pack and rolled onto the floor. Before I could get back on my feet, Nathaniel erupted from the bathroom and kicked me in the ribs, knocking the breath out of me.

"Dammit, cigarettes cost money you worthless turd. Quit being a pussy and get up. You ain't hurt. I got chores for you."

As I crouched on all fours, gasping for breath, Nathaniel gouged my shoulder with a pair of rusty garden pruners, and screamed, "You're going to trim every blade of grass in that yard to an exact height of three inches. I'll be out there in half an hour to measure it. If it ain't exact, I'm really gonna beat your sorry ass. Now get to work."

I vomited bile and limped out the door. The morning sunlight intermingled with droplets from the sprinkler, forming a pastel rainbow against rotting garbage matted against the dump-ground fence. I imagined this as a vision from God, so I took the pruners and cut the hose into four pieces. I hurled the tool at Nathaniel's pickup, where it lodged firmly in the grill. Another wave of vertigo and nausea racked my body, so I stumbled across the street to a vacant lot to hide in a rusted-out Studebaker abandoned there.

The driver's seat had been removed, and the headliner hung down like a shredded curtain. When I crouched on the floorboard, with the dash at eye level, I could view the front of the house without being seen. It was an excellent position to lurk undetected when I wanted to determine my father's mood and inebriation level. The windows were opaque with grime, so concealment was a cinch. The back seat served as a makeshift bed on those nights when the bastard was in a rage.

After half an hour, Nathaniel walked out of the house, and sank up to his ankles in mud from the still running hydrant. Retribution would be brutal, but I couldn't help enjoying a sublime sense of satisfaction at his spastic rage. A string of violent curses ensued as he tried to shake the sticky muck off of his boots. He didn't notice the pruners protruding from the Chevy's grill.

The bastard screamed and shook his fist at the heavens. "Theodore Nutscalder, you're gonna regret the day you were born!"

That day was long past.

I scrunched down as he shaded his eyes with his hand, searching the neighborhood. Still fuming, he retrieved keys from a peg behind the front door, fired up the old pickup, and raced down Kickapoo toward town.

I rubbed my sore ribs and waited a few more minutes. Gathering courage, I ventured back into the house. To say our relationship was deteriorating was an understatement. His anger at me, and the world in general, was growing exponentially. He was off the rails and I put nothing past him, including murder. In his bedroom nightstand was a snub nose 38 wrapped in a greasy rag. I unloaded the revolver, took the spare cartridge box, replaced the gun, and hid all the bullets behind the water heater.

Another wave of nausea washed over me, accompanied by a sudden urge to pee. I stumbled to the bathroom and splashed water on my face. The urine was red. Not the first time. It would pass. I cleaned up with a damp towel and rinsed my hair in the sink.

Suddenly a board creaked on the front porch. I froze and strained to listen, simultaneously planning an escape route out the back. A gentle knock rattled the screen door.

"Is anyone home?" It was a female.

As low voices murmured, I crept into the living room and peeked through the window. All I could see was a delicate feminine arm holding a brown paper sack. Smoothing out my hair and straightening my collar, I opened the door.

Miss Hawkins smiled while Coach Mason scraped mud off of his shoe on the edge of the step.

"Hello Teddy, is your dad home?" Nora cooed.

"Nah, he's gone to town. Should be back in a few minutes. Would you like to come in and wait?"

Miss Hawkins shifted the sack and took a step forward. Mason grabbed her arm.

The coach said, "Look here, Nutscalder, we don't have time to visit. We have to get over to Rhinelander Park and help set up for the festival. Aunt Tilde Kellum sent a word across the water. Said you might need some help. Nora picked up some grub, and I went by the Church of Christ Share Shop and grabbed some duds. Preacher Perkins twisted my arm and wouldn't let me go until I loaded up this box. Come on, Nora, we've got to go."

Miss Hawkins shot him an angry look. Mason winced and cleared his throat.

"Er … uh … well … listen Teddy, I'm in number 210 over at the Harvest Row Apartments. If you ever get in a bind, come on by. We'll talk." He leaned down to her ear and rubbed his nose in her hair.

"Are you happy now? We did what we came to do. Now, let's go."

"Will we see you at the festival tonight?" Miss Hawkins asked as she pushed Mason away and handed me the grocery bag. The coach squeezed past her and placed the box over the threshold without stepping inside.

I replied, "I plan to be there if my old man doesn't go too far off the rails. He's been on a bender for a couple of weeks now. Thanks. I appreciate all the great stuff."

She put a hand to her throat, spun on her heels, and ran down the walk. Coach Mason scowled, backed off of the porch, and examined the house with a critical eye. It wasn't hard to imagine what he was thinking as he stared at the cracked windows, peeling paint, missing shingles, and rotting eaves.

He narrowed his eyes and pointed at me. "Take care, Teddy. I expect you to go out for the high school track team next year. I need an anchor for the 4x400 relay, and I think you're the man." He hesitated for a moment before joining Miss Hawkins at the curb. She gave a brief wave as he opened the passenger side door of his Mustang Fastback. Tires screeched, glasspacks barked and they were gone.

As I set the grocery bag on the kitchen counter, the phone rang, and I nearly jumped out of my skin. My father's boss, the county road commissioner, was on the line.

"Tell Nathaniel he has an opportunity for some overtime. News is spreading about that woman finding those coins alongside the jawbone, and downtown parking is going to be a cluster-fuck this evening. Otho Wheat asked me to help with the gridlock. Nate can earn a few extra bucks if he can stay sober. I need him to be at the gazebo in Rhinelander Park at 6 p.m. sharp, but if I smell whiskey on his breath, the deal is off and I'll give the OT to Sudsy Monkhouse."

"Thanks for calling, Commissioner. I will leave him a note, but I wouldn't bet a plug nickel on the liquor situation."

"Yeah, you're probably right. Maybe I'll just call Sudsy. The muttonhead has the IQ of a tadpole, but at least he don't drink. Hey, next year you'll be old enough to work the summer months shoveling asphalt on the pothole crew. I'm paying $1.60 an hour for temporary help. It ain't as much fun as washing windows in a whorehouse, but it's honest work, and the paychecks don't bounce."

"I'll keep that in mind," I said, as I replaced the receiver.

Aunt Tilde always came through when times got tough. I have no idea where she got her information, but she always knew when I was scraping the bottom of the barrel. Miss Hawkins loaded the grocery sack with milk, bread, eggs, and sliced ham. A box of Wheaties. Pork 'n beans, saltines, and an enormous block of cheddar. After a triple decker sandwich, I gobbled down a bowl of Wheaties and scrawled a note about the commissioner's offer, leaving it on Nathan's TV tray.

Preacher Perkins stuffed the box with cast-off clothes. It was so full; the bottom was busting out. His Sunday sermons were full of hellfire and brimstone, but the rest of the week was enlightened kindness. He was always looking out for the downtrodden. I rarely went to church and felt a little guilty, so I paused for a moment and uttered a word of thanks to The Carpenter from Galilee. Right on top was a slightly faded pair of bell-bottom jeans, and a nice long sleeve button down silver shirt with a subtle diamond pattern woven in the fabric. Store tags were still on it. There was a black ink stain on the cuff, but it didn't matter because I'd roll the sleeves up, anyway. A pair of brown corduroy pants were way too long in the inseam. Tommy would like those. Deeper down was a variety of shirts, underwear, and a wide split leather belt with a heavy brass buckle embossed with a lion's head. At the bottom of the box lay a pair a black leather penny loafers. The soles were lightly worn, but the uppers were unblemished. The shoes were half a size too large, but I didn't care. I would keep the ratty Keds on my feet and take the premium leathers to the festival in the grocery sack, switch out a block from the park, hide the tennis shoes in a hedge, then switch back again at the end of the night.

Donning the new clothes, I admired the reflection in the mirror. The outfit looked tailor made. The guy staring back at me grinned like a jackass eating briars. A spark of confidence flickered inside. I sponged off, brushed my teeth, located my father's razor in the medicine cabinet, and shaved some peach fuzz off my upper lip and chin using castor oil as a lubricant. I had once overheard Danni and Brandy discussing its suitability for certain delicate areas.

I hid the remaining clothes in the attic and as I stepped off the pull-down ladder, the front door opened. Tucking the new shoes under my arm, I bolted out the back door. Scaling the hog wire fence, I heard the old man scream.

"Get your ass back in here, you delinquent shit. I'm not done with you."

I turned and flipped him off with both hands.

"Maybe not, you vicious old bastard, but I'm done with you."

7

THE COMMISSIONER WAS RIGHT. DOWNTOWN WAS PACKED with visitors and cars were bumper to bumper as far as the eye could see. Every shop on the square was open, and Rhinelander Park had transformed into a genuine carnival, complete with game booths, grub stands, and holiday lights strung between the trees. Miss Hawkins and Coach Mason were putting the finishing touches on a portable dance floor. He squinted at a carpenter's level and didn't look happy.

The woman who found the jawbone was sitting on a park bench surrounded by admirers. With a solemn face and animated gestures, she repeated her harrowing story. The two ten-dollar Gold Eagles were mounted on a piece of velvet-covered cardboard in her lap. A reporter from *Treasure Hunter's Digest* snapped pictures and scribbled in a little spiral notebook.

Aunt Tilde sat on a park bench, puffing on a cheroot as passersby nodded and smiled. A pimple-faced boy from the Corn Dog Concession rushed by and offered her a lemonade. She reached for her purse, but he waved her off. Everyone courted Tilde's favor, even though she never asked for it.

I approached her, held out my arms, and spun around like a runway model. She chortled, eyeing me from head to toe.

"Them's some fine threads, Teddy. You look downright handsome. Sporty."

"Miss Hawkins and Coach Mason came by with this, and a lot more. I know you sent word across the water. You're my guardian angel, Aunt Tilde. You always know when I'm down on my luck."

She winked and motioned me to come closer.

"Teddy, it's all about doing the right thing. The philosophers call it altruism. I've had some visions about you. There is a young lady in this town who needs you. Maybe not today. Maybe not tomorrow, but believe it or not, you're the only one who can help her. Not the law, not the clergy. Only you."

I must have looked befuddled. She touched her hand to her heart and said, "Just keep your ear to the ground and your mind open to the possibilities. When the time comes, you'll know it."

Allie Kiem, the proprietor of the funnel cake stand, snuck up behind her, then stealthily reached around and laid a hot pastry on the bench next to her. She whispered something in Tilde's ear. The old soothsayer laughed and said, "I told you it would all work out. Children are gonna come when God's ready to send 'em to you!" Allie gave her a kiss on the cheek and hugged her neck.

Tilde turned back to me. "You'll know when the time comes. It may be a little thing. It may be a big thing. It will definitely take some courage, but you'll be ready. Now go on and enjoy the party. Oh, one more thing. There's a little dinosaur in my back yard that's getting mighty hungry."

"Me and the boys will come by tomorrow and deliver Rufus a feast fit for a king."

She slapped her thigh and laughed. "Grubs and termites will be just fine."

Tyler's Bakery was on the northwest corner of the town square. I stuck my head in the door and inhaled the sweet, yeasty air. The smell was glorious. Sara was working behind the counter with her mom. She smiled and waved while each strand of her hair grappled with a helpless hairnet. I gave her a thumbs up and she puckered for a long-distance air kiss. God definitely has a sense of humor. Sara was unabashedly mamma-rific. Mrs. Tyler was as flat as Vera O'Dell's ironing board. Being flush with cash, I indulged in a two-bit fried apple pie. Sara picked the largest one out of the glass case and when I gave her the five-dollar bill, she handed me back five one-dollar bills.

"Sara, you gave me too much change."

For the benefit of the other customers she said, "Oh, my goodness, sir. I'm so sorry. Let me fix that."

She winked at me, took the money back, and gave me six one-dollar bills in return, plus a Kennedy half dollar.

"Save me a dance."

I leaned in to give her a peck on the cheek, but Missy flashed across my mind and I pulled back. It was a chickenshit retreat, and

I felt like a jerk. Her shoulders slumped for a moment, but then she perked up and said, "You look really nice. Are you meeting someone?"

"Just those two crazy rogues that are dumb enough to hang out with me."

Sara's mouth morphed into a huge grin. "Yeah, I suspected as much. They're outside the window right now, making goofy faces at me."

I turned just as Tommy and Mickey pranced through the door, making kissy gestures and batting their eyes.

"Where were you? I thought we were supposed to meet up at the Grotto?" Mickey said with an edge of irritation in his voice.

"I'm sorry guys, I got sidetracked." I pulled up my shirt, revealing the bruised ribs. Tommy bent down for a closer look. "Jesus, Mary, and Joseph, what in the hell happened?"

"What do you think happened? I knocked over my father's TV tray and this was the punishment."

Mickey silently mouthed a curse and turned his face away in disgust. "I gotta give it to you, Theodore; you can take an ass whoopin' better than anyone I know. You rebound pretty fast. And look at you, all gussied up, eating some of Sara's sweet pie. You are definitely ... what's the word I'm looking for...?"

"Resilient," Tommy responded.

"Yeah, resilient, with a big ass chunk of dumb luck. Just like I always say, Teddy gets whupped, but he don't stay whupped. Guys, it's getting pretty crowded in this joint. Let's find another place to perch."

Waving goodbye to Sara, we crossed the street and climbed on the pedestal of Rhinelander Dix's statue at the center of the park.

The monument was actually Confederate General P. T. Beauregard. There was a slight resemblance and a clever shyster passed it off on the town elders the year after our founder died of silicosis in 1904. My ninth-grade history teacher said she saw one exactly like it in New Orleans. They probably stole this one from the same foundry.

A band was tuning up and testing the microphones in the gazebo. Jaycees and the Masons were running carnival game booths, along with several other clubs. I saw Nathaniel guiding traffic with a flashlight and an orange flag. Shaking with delirium tremens, he looked like a zombie. The miserable prick had fallen far. Once a respected engineer on his way up the corporate ladder, he now assaulted his liver with cheap booze while filling potholes on the lonely back roads of East Texas.

An eruption of laughter from the crowd interrupted my solemn thoughts. Straining to look over the throng, the source of jocularity was immediately clear. Our old friend Humper was living up to his name.

Prim and proper Millicent McLeod brought her champion Afghan hound, Damsa, to the festivities and tied her to a park bench while she ventured to a snack stand. Humper promptly mounted Damsa, enthusiastically giving her "The Business," as a rhythmic chant rose from the crowd: "Humper, Humper, Humper. Hump her."

Miss McLeod fainted, and a gaggle of old biddies rushed to her side, fanning her face with napkins and paper plates. Undaunted, the canines continued their brazen display of vigorous copulation. The laughter had an uplifting effect, and I pushed the bitter sentiments of my father to the back of my mind while enjoying the raunchy display of pooch pounding. Except for Millicent, everyone was having a good time, especially Damsa.

In perfect step with the carnal fervor, three high school girls had coaxed Tommy off the pedestal and were playfully prodding and tickling him. A leggy brunette said, "I heard a rumor about you. Everyone in town says you are very well endowed." The other two girls snickered, picked up the baton, and ran with it.

"Wonder weasel...

Firehose...

Trouser snake...

Pocket python."

Tommy blushed and turned to me and Mickey, his eyes pleading for help behind his coke-bottle glasses.

Mickey guffawed while I capitulated, "Sorry, Tommy, I can't help you out with this situation. You're on your own." Another one of my signature chickenshit retreats, but this one was funny.

Mickey shoved me aside, cleared his throat, stuck out his chest, and made a grand sweeping motion with his arms. Speaking in a remarkably convincing Irish brogue, he said, "Lovely lassies ... I must inform you ... the rumors you've heard are all true! When he walks into the shower after gym class, we all hang our heads in shame. None of us measure up."

The girls were relentless with their titillating torture. Poor Tommy was the color of a Lincoln Rose. Proud of his performance, Mickey turned to me and said, "Tell us, Mr. Nutscalder, what is your opinion of Tommy's mannish, macho puberty?"

"Both of us put together wouldn't measure up to Tommy's tremendous toolage."

The girls were in a frenzy of laughter. They continued poking Tommy, and he was gyrating like a praying mantis on a hot plate.

Mickey turned back to me and murmured, "In these circumstances, I always ask myself, what would Melchior and Dipdottle do?"

"Mickey, you've revved 'em up. Now you need to ease back the throttle before poor Tommy throws a rod."

"Haha. Throws a rod. That's real funny. Very apropos."

Mickey jumped down from the pedestal and spread his arms out in reverent appeal.

"Ladies, I beg a moment of solemn utterance. Tommy is not yet a man of the world. He requires experienced ladies, like yourselves, to provide feminine, yet robust guidance in matters of courtship and love."

The five bawdy revelers melted into the crowd with Mickey gesticulating in a most elegant manner. The sight brought a smile to my face and joy to my beleaguered heart.

Mickey and Tommy were my sole tether to sanity. Relaxing, I leaned back against the statue and gazed out over the crowd, soaking in the general splendor and merriment.

A band fired up, and the dance floor came alive. Brandy and Danni, wearing matching tube tops and hip huggers, passed out flyers for Muddy Mike's until some of the local wives complained and a deputy made them stop. Unfazed, the sultry vixens joined the rest of the revelers in dancing, games, and gastronomic debauchery. I had plenty of doubts about the Treasure O' the Knob, but the festival itself was an undeniable success.

Just as the sun dropped behind the horizon, a gold Cadillac Brougham pulled to the edge of the curb and Missy Turnbow climbed out of the back seat. The rest of the world dissolved into a cloud of vapor as my mind focused on a vision of pure beauty. Her hair was pulled back in a thick braid, revealing every inch of her flawless complexion. The lady I had seen in the second-story window struggled out of the car behind her, visibly unstable on her feet. My heart quickened. Would she recognize me? The Caddy slowly pulled away and my old man directed it to a parking space reserved for VIPs.

The pale woman leaned heavily on a cane as Missy guided her to a park bench. A swarthy man in a gray pinstripe suit and slicked-back hair joined them. He shook hands with passersby and handed out cards. Missy kissed the woman on the forehead and stood behind, stroking her shoulders. It had to be her mother. I suspected the man was her stepfather, Nollen Embers, and slid down off the pedestal, determined to get a closer look.

Arthur Rumkin was running the ring toss booth, so I made my way over to the game hut and laid three nickels on the counter. Stuffed animals of all shapes and sizes crammed the stand. Two smaller kids were trying their luck. Arthur smiled broadly, showing a hodgepodge of bridgework attached to his five remaining natural teeth—artificial choppers, worn only on special occasions.

"Hello, Teddy. You're looking mighty sharp this evening. Are you ready to try your luck?"

Absentmindedly, I took the rings and handed them off to the kid next to me. "I just need some information, Mr. Rumkin. Is that Missy Turnbow's mother and stepfather on the bench where Humper and Damsa were … uh … copulating?"

Arthur stood on his tiptoes and nodded.

"Indeed, Master Nutscalder. That's Nollen and Maris, alright. He must be dragging his family out for a PR stunt. Already campaigning for mayor. Did you see that god-awful billboard he put up next to Kutz's Cleaners? His picture looks like a gangster out of a 1940s B-movie. Greaser sumbitch."

"No, sir, I haven't seen the billboard. All of this mayor stuff seems a little strange to me. It's just the end of May, and elections aren't until November."

"Not this one, Teddy. Old Vic Grisham resigned as mayor. His wife has cancer. Terminal case, I heard. The town is just about bankrupt and nobody on the city council wants to step up to be mayor pro-tem. They're calling a special election for mid-July. There's some weird bylaw on the books from a long time ago. The problem is, no one has the guts to run against him. I think folks are afraid of that slimeball. He's got a reputation for hiring goons to do dirty deeds. Everybody that opposes him seems to develop a run of bad luck." Arthur paused for a moment and jutted his chin toward the trio under discussion.

"Don't turn around. It looks like they're moving this way. Here, Teddy, toss a few rings. Hurry, they're coming closer!"

He handed me six more rings, and I started throwing them at the soda bottles mounted on the waist-level table. Rumkin was staring past me and wasn't paying any attention to my feeble efforts. He muttered, "If you can reel in that little mermaid, I'll dance at your wedding." Suddenly he threw back his shoulders and yelled, "Ladies and gentlemen, we have a grand-prize winner!"

He grabbed a large white unicorn, shoved it in my arms, and spun me around. I was face to face with Missy Turnbow. Taken aback, I smiled and held the stuffed animal forward. Missy glared at me like I was offering her a dead cat. Her mother frowned and poked me in the thigh with her cane.

"That's the boy I saw trespassing in my yard!" she said with a forcefulness disproportionate to her feeble appearance.

I opened my mouth to speak, but Missy frowned and interrupted me. "No, Mother. That was the Chilton boy you saw in the yard. He was helping his father trim the hedges. I don't know this young man."

Nollen Embers appeared out of nowhere and grabbed Missy's arm.

"Meroticia, your mother is exhausted. Help her to the car. I'll be along in a minute."

She jerked away from his grip and took Maris' hand. Missy turned for a second and our eyes met, but the moment was over before I could read her expression.

Embers cocked his head and scrutinized me with a disgusted look on his face, as though I were a dog turd stuck to his shoe. Arthur Rumkin read the awkward situation and intervened with another obnoxious carnival bark.

"Ladies and gentlemen, mayoral candidate Nollen Embers will try his hand at the ring toss. Gather 'round and let's see if he can out-perform this young whippersnapper!"

The startled man looked at the encroaching crowd and reluctantly took the proffered rings. I didn't stay to watch.

Dejected by Missy's rebuff, I started toward Kickapoo Street and passed Tyler's Bakery just as Sara was turning the door sign from open to closed. She jumped when I tapped the window with the unicorn's snout. Upon recognizing me, she unlocked the door and pulled off the hairnet. Unruly locks tumbled over her shoulders in a delightful, frizzy explosion. Without a word, I gave her a kiss on the cheek, handed her the stuffed animal, and backed away. She hugged the furry beast as she locked the door and lowered the shade.

The festival was rocking, but I wasn't in the mood for mirth. Perhaps I could beat Nathaniel home, retrieve my new duds, and sleep across the street in the Studebaker or at the Grotto.

Noisy footsteps echoed in the dark, accompanied by a familiar voice singing a bawdy stanza of "*The Whores of Sailortown.*" Mic and Tommy emerged from an alley, sweaty and disheveled. Tommy had his glasses off, fiddling with the frames.

"Looks like somebody got lucky," I said as Mickey strolled up with his shirt unbuttoned, chest out, and arms flexed like the body-builder, Charles Atlas. Lipstick smudges glistened on ruddy cheeks.

He wiggled both index fingers in front of my face. "Thomas ain't a man yet, but the boy has been molested in a most delightful, lecherous, groping fashion. I tried to defend our lanky friend, but alas, I succumbed to the delicious torture myself, as you can clearly see!"

I looked at Tommy for his commentary. "Teddy, those girls were really aggressive. I think they were drunk. Look at this; they bent the frame of my glasses."

"That's all you've got to say? They bent your glasses? Not a word about three high school hotties harassing your hooter?"

The rose complexion reappeared. Mickey grabbed him in his signature Von Erich headlock and tousled his hair. "The boy is an idiot. You should have been there, Teddy. Those girls had Tommy twirling like a dervish. He didn't even cop a feel." He gave Tommy a vigorous Dutch rub on the noggin, and said, "C'mon, boys, let's all go back to the party and scope out some more chicks."

My enthusiasm for the celebration had waned, but I had nothing better to do. Home held no great attraction. The guys sympathized when I told them about the encounter with Missy and Mic put it in the proper perspective.

"You know, Theodore, guys like us ain't welcome anywhere on the social ladder. You try to climb up a rung and the guy above you just kicks you in the teeth. The obstacles are too much. Her family will despise you. Missy is a sho'nuff beauty, but you can't keep up with the money or fashion situation, and what are you going to wear when she invites you to a dinner party?" He flipped the collar of my new shirt. "Secondhand duds just won't cut it. Forgive the severity of my comparison, but everyone in that ritzy cartel will ridicule you. Heartbreak and humiliation, my good man, heartbreak and humiliation. You are better off letting that little bird fly. Our kind don't fit into no romance novel. In real life, the good guys never win."

Deep down, I knew he was right.

Folks were still pouring into Rhinelander Park. The festival was packed. Mr. Rumkin had turned the ring toss booth over to someone else and he was gliding across the dance floor with a long line of single ladies, each waiting their turn. What Arthur lacked in looks, he more than made up for in grace.

Mickey was in his element. Girls giggled as he smiled and complimented their appearance. He jiggle-flexed the muscles of his chest in the most amusing manner. He was the strongest guy I knew, but he rarely fought, and could disarm the Devil with his smile. I envied his congenial nature.

The band was hammering out a pretty decent version of Creedence Clearwater Revival's "Proud Mary," when a man in muddy overalls strolled up to the gazebo and held up a 2500-year-old gold Greek stater. Everyone was awestruck. The music stopped and the fellow boldly stepped up to the microphone.

He said, "I'm Bert Levy. My brother Miles and I just found this rare beauty about 50 yards from where the young lady found those two Gold Eagles this morning." The crowd clapped loudly and converged on the gazebo for a closer look.

Bert stepped down and rubbed the treasure with a dirty handkerchief. Nollen Embers tried to speak, but the curious crowd drowned him out. All eyes were on the lucky detectorist. The piece was magnificent. I'd never seen anything like it. It was thick and irregular ovoid, featuring a high relief impression of Alexander the Great in profile wearing an elaborate battle helmet. This wasn't some clever decoy planted by a local shopkeeper. This coin was the real deal.

Tommy laughed and poked my sore ribs with his elbow. "Teddy, you can't be a scoffer any more. That coin shoots down all your theories about this treasure festival being a big flimflam. Nobody would plant a rarity like that in the dirt."

Mickey said, "Lots of folks have been making fun of these detector dipsticks, but no one is laughing now. That piece is probably worth six months' wages for the average guy around here. Imagine what we could do with the money from just one coin like that!"

The locals were clamoring for a closer look, and the excitement was electric. Mr. Blaine was speaking with Bert Levy. Both men smiled and shook hands. Rick motioned us over.

"Boys, I just made a deal with this gentleman to display the rarity at Casablanca. This will make the news all over Texas and Louisiana. By tomorrow, the Knob is going to be crawling with yokels and clodhoppers, and I plan to cash in on them. We'll be serving lunch and nickel beer until the tap runs dry. I'll pay each of you guys two bucks an hour to bus tables and wash dishes. If you hustle, I'll throw in a little tip share to boot.

We responded simultaneously, "Yes, sir!"

The barman smiled. "10 o'clock sharp. Look presentable. I run a classy joint."

The band fired back up, and the revelers were more animated than ever. Dancers spilled off the crowded stage onto the lawn.

A cluster of porta potties lined the southwest end of the park and I got a sudden urge to pee. My bruised kidneys were working overtime, so I told the guys I'd meet up with them later at the Dix statue. Summer was just beginning, but the heat and humidity encroaching from the Gulf of Mexico was already at a stifling level. The smell around the turd traps was revolting.

I stepped into the nearest privy and unzipped. Little Willie was reluctant, and he hesitated a long while before allowing the blood-tinged urine stream to flow. It was like pissing shards of glass. As I shivered and shook off, a commotion outside grabbed my attention. I opened the door to an infuriating scene. Sara Tyler was in a tug-o-war with Galton Grails and two of his toadies. Galton clutched the stuffed unicorn by the horn while the other two boys popped her bra strap and goosed her tushy. Not wanting to relinquish hold of the animal, she was pretty much defenseless.

Suddenly, something snapped inside me. Brandy and Danni always joked about men and their "Big Bag of Buttons." Some could be pushed. Others were forbidden. Some girls like Brandy O'Dell know where all the buttons were. When to push them, when not.

Some girls, like Missy Turnbow, just pushed buttons randomly because of inherent grace and beauty. Girls like Sara Tyler unintentionally pushed buttons by pure sweet innocence, and a noble desire to protect the fairer sex.

Rage welled up and my Big Red Button got pushed. Smacked, bashed, hammered. Sara pleading for mercy, with tears rolling down freckled cheeks. Clear snot running out of her perfect little nose. Cringing with every lustful prod.

I transformed into a man possessed. My legs started churning, and I bolted headlong into Galton, bashing the top of my head into his chin. A satisfying crack resounded as rotten teeth clacked together with the force of the blow. Spitting blood, he stumbled back, flabbergasted.

"Pardon me, Galton! Your grungy filth blended in so nicely with the overwhelming smell of shit, I didn't see you standing there."

Okay, okay, it wasn't the best Shakespearean, "Mealy mouthed, flap-eared knave, I have done thy mother" insult, but it worked.

Spluttering incoherent expletives, he stumbled around like a drunkard and let go of the unicorn. His toadies glared, and Sara beamed.

"You're a dead man, Nutscalder!" Grails screamed as he launched a right hook that smacked me in the temple. The bully was still a bit off balance as he swung, and I accidentally stepped on his foot, forcing him to fall headlong against the door of the nearest port-o-piss. The privy rocked and sloshed as the unfortunate occupant bounced against the plastic walls.

A bloodcurdling scream pierced the air and Coushatta Danni erupted from the plastic privy, pulling up her panties. I took a step back and let the scene unfold in all of its magnificent glory.

Red-polished fingernails cut three perfect parallel lacerations across Galton's cheek. Platform pumps connected to the left patella, hyper-extending the bully's knee. The reprobate folded like a cheap suit. Danni kicked and pummeled Grails as a mixture of English and Koasati curses streamed forth in a luxurious cascade of poetic profanity.

Indian warriors are often memorialized in literature and song. They are brave men, celebrated for honor, and their fearless fighting skill. None are a match for the rage of a Native American woman interrupted *en urinae.*

Dalton struggled back to his feet, limping on his wounded knee. His toadies faded into the darkness. Sara wiped her eyes. I laughed aloud. He turned, facing me, bloody teeth gritted, fists clenched. I put up my dukes and braced for a brutal assault, simultaneously imagining how my mangled body would look laid out in a coffin. A moment later, I felt a firm grip on my shoulder. I spun around to face Sheriff Otho Wheat.

The Sheriff barked, "What's all the ruckus? What the hell is going on here?"

I straightened up and said, "Greasy Galton was harassing Sara. If you will excuse my crude turn of phrase, he and his stooges were groping at her goodies."

Danni instantaneously transformed into a demure, defenseless damsel in distress. In a sweet southern belle accent, she said, "Yes, and the mean sumbitch tried to force the door on the latrine while I was trying to relieve myself. My lady parts were momentarily exposed to public view. It was a horrific intrusion. I am so embarrassed." She fanned her face with her hand and even whipped up a few tears. "I believe I'm getting the vapors. I feel a bit faint." It was an Oscar-worthy performance. Melchior and Dipdottle would have been positively orgasmic.

Sara sniffed pitifully, clutched her unicorn, and nodded in affirmation. Otho's countenance darkened. Galton turned to walk away.

"Fucking lying Injun whore," he muttered under his breath.

Apparently, that was the last straw. The Sheriff rushed forward and grabbed Grails by the hair. "Get your sorry ass in the patrol car, Butt Crust. You're going down to the station."

The rascal cut his eyes toward me. The sheer fury and hatred made the hair on the back of my neck stand up. I'm sure he would have killed me right then and there if he had the chance. The sheriff passed the bully off to a deputy standing by a Plymouth patrol car. He cuffed Grails and made sure his head whacked the doorjamb a couple of times on the way into the back seat.

Otho gagged as he wiped the grease from Galton's hair on his pant leg. He yelled at the deputy as he drove off. "Check that boy for lice before you book him. I don't want an infestation spreading through my jailhouse."

The deputy waved casually and beeped the horn in affirmation.

Otho growled, "All you troublemakers disperse. No more ruckus."

Danni gave me a wink and a hip bump. "That's the last we'll see of Crusty for a few days."

Sara hugged the unicorn and mouthed, "Thank you," with trembling lips. She really was pretty-ish. I couldn't help but feel a surge of genuine admiration for the girl.

I said, "What are you going to do with that gaudy animal? I wouldn't blame you if you stuffed it down the hole of one of these plastic crap shacks."

A playful, pouty expression spread over her face. "Teddy Nutscalder, you can be a real asshole sometimes." She nuzzled the pony's neck and stepped closer until she was toe to toe with me. "For your information, I have a little hammock in the corner of my bedroom for all of my animals." She kissed the beast on the snout. "He's going to stand watch over me while I sleep ... and bathe ... and get dressed."

I experienced a pang of envy for the stuffed stud. Blood rushed to my face. Sara giggled and kissed me right on the mouth before backing away.

"I can read you like a book, Teddy Nutscalder. I'm patient. Everybody thinks I'm an airhead, but they're wrong. You don't know what you're missing." Her ample bosom heaved in immaculate synchronicity to her closing statement.

8

(Memorial Day)

I COLLECTED MY OLD TENNIS SHOES FROM THE HEDGES AND Mickey, Tommy, and I retired to Casa O'Dell for the rest of the evening. Brandy and Danni brought home a bag of leftover corn dogs, paid for with a wee sneaky peek, no doubt. Everyone feasted on battered tube steak, slathered with mustard and ketchup.

My belly full of lard, and anxieties at bay, sleep came easily. The sheriff would sequester Galton from society for a day or two, and Nathaniel Nutscalder was undoubtedly drinking his overtime. We had excellent prospects for earning some dough at Casablanca on Memorial Day. I dreamed of the old Underwood typewriter in the window of Pressman's Pawn Shop. I could finally bring Lars Lazer and Dirk Deadly to life in a grandiose style. Even if I had to pencil in the "Zs" and "L's."

An unexpected thunderstorm with marble-sized hail rolled through the delta overnight. The electricity flickered, and a tornado touched down near Bridge City, busting up a few barns, but nobody got hurt. By daylight, the skies cleared.

Vera O'Dell cooked up bacon, eggs, biscuits, and cream gravy for breakfast, and I ate like a hog. Brandy woke up just as we were finishing and walked through the kitchen wearing nothing but a wife-beater undershirt and bikini bottoms. Vera scolded her, but she ignored the reproach. The boondock angel gulped a cup of coffee and ran her fingers through my hair as she walked by.

"You need a haircut, shaggy boy," she said as she playfully tugged at the little curls along the nape of my neck. It was true. My hair was always unruly, and it insisted on curling up in an annoying feminine manner, if it grew past the top of the collar. We walked out to the porch and when the cool breeze hit Brandy's skin, a delightful reaction occurred underneath the thin cotton frock. Using a pink rubber band, she took her time gathering up her hair in a ponytail, making sure Tommy and I got a nice, long, luscious, lingering look.

She said, "Take a seat, boys, and I'll lower your ears." Within 20 minutes, she had barbered us both.

"Theodore, I believe we look quite presentable," Tommy said as he looked at his reflection in the window and repositioned his clip-on shades over slightly bent spectacle frames.

"Yes, Mr. Crum, Miss Brandy is a talented wizard with the shears."

The erstwhile barber was standing behind Tommy, and playfully goosed him between the legs. She said, "I heard some tales about Tommy's adventure with those high school skanks, and I've come up with a new nickname for him—Attila the Hung." Tommy blushed. Mic snickered. The day showed promise.

After sprucing up, we headed to Casablanca, hoping to get on the clock a little early. Conversation turned to the recent treasure finds.

"Maybe we should look into getting one of those metal detectors," Mickey said as we walked down Pearl Street and turned on to Riverfront Levee Road. "Think about it. If we just found one or two coins, it could pay for Tommy's trip to see that specialist in New York, and maybe get a *good* lawyer to look into Daddy's case. Teddy, we could slap some paint on the Kickapoo Street chalet. Fix it up some. Maybe get your old man off your case for a while."

Mickey was a genuine paladin, and always thinking of others. I hated to shoot him down, but reality intervened. "We're talking about sixty to seventy dollars for the cheapest model. We would have to do a lot of odd jobs to come up with that kind of cabbage, and there's no guarantee we would find anything. I hate being a pessimist, but..."

Mickey slapped me on the head and said, "Quit being a wet blanket all the time. Of course they're expensive, but our four-eyed friend may have an answer for that problem. Tell Theodore about that repo man over on Bolton Street."

Tommy shook his head. "C'mon, Mickey, I was just mouthing off. It's way too dangerous to get into his warehouse. That repo guy carries a gun and has a big old mean guard dog."

Mickey interrupted. "There is this repo guy that works for Nollen Embers. He has a warehouse on Bolton Street. The building is packed with cars, motorbikes, and all kinds of cool, repossessed stuff. Arthur Rumkin was telling Tommy's dad about a high-tech Fisher M-Scope detector he saw in the building while he was working on a leaky toilet. If we snatched it…"

I couldn't believe my ears. "So, we're resorting to crime now? Mickey, what is wrong with you, man? That's the craziest idea ever."

O'Dell was unfazed. "Aw hell, I'm just talking about a little B&E. Is it really a crime to steal from a thief? A repo guy that uses loopholes in the law to cheat people? It's one thing to run a pawn shop like Mr. Pressman, where people voluntarily bring stuff in for a cash loan. It's another thing altogether when the repo man grabs your stuff on the sly, in the middle of the night."

I said, "That's a pretty twisted train of logic, and it sounds like the guy is a tough hombre. You really need to think this through. The idea sounds pretty risky."

"I got a plan," Mickey said. "I'll do it with or without you guys."

A quarter mile from Casablanca, stenciled pasteboard signs lined the road.

Rarest Coin of the Hoard on Display … Nickel Beer with every Entrée … All day Happy Hour on Cocktails.

It was only 9:45, but the parking lot was full. Schlitz and Busch kegs lined the porch. Several of the detectorists were using machetes to hack through the tangle of weeds and briars intertwined in the fence of the old Cusser Club property. So far, the only things turning up were bottle caps and pull tabs. Humper was barking and growling at the destructive interlopers.

One guy stumbled upon a skunk den and got a face full of spray. The stench spread over the area and all the other treasure hunters scattered. The unfortunate victim puked up his guts, ran to the river, and dove in, coming up for air every few seconds and then re-submerging, like a self-baptizing religious nut. A merciful southern breeze coming off the Sabine Estuary slowly diluted the nauseating sulfur smell.

A perturbed Rick Blaine emerged from his office buttoning a silk jacket and warned the searchers about water moccasins and rattlers. "And that mean old dog will bite you." It was a little white lie, thrown in for good measure.

All of us locals knew that wasn't true. Humper had been around 11 or 12 years and had never even snapped at anyone or nipped at a heel. I doubt he had enough viable teeth left to bite, even if he wanted to. One tourist turned to Mickey and said. "Will that old mongrel really bite you?"

With a wide-eyed and crazed expression, he replied, "Hell yeah, that sumbitch will tear your damn leg off if you get him riled up. He don't like that high-pitched squeal of those metal detectors. Drives him nuts."

Tommy and I laughed. Humper was a thousand times more likely to lick your face or hump your leg.

Sara Tyler pulled up in a bright red 1962 Ford pickup with her mom in the passenger seat. Mrs. Tyler didn't drive and Mr. Tyler was chronically ill, so all the cops just looked the other way and let her make deliveries, although she didn't have a license. Sara spied me coming down the steps and glanced in the rearview mirror, attempting to straighten her hair. A look of hopeless exasperation clouded her face as her ill-tempered locks refused to cooperate. It was obvious she had been up since the wee hours of the morning helping with Rick's big order.

Mickey elbowed me in the ribs. "I'll give Mrs. Tyler a hand with those pastries, and you can help Sara with her luscious goodies."

Tommy even joined in on the teasing. "Yes, Teddy, give her a hand. Or two."

I sauntered over, trying not to smile too broadly at the sight of her. She wore a red apron over tight jeans and a lavender-colored blouse, all smudged with flour, cinnamon, and icing. Sara spoke without looking up.

"God, I am so embarrassed. I never thought I'd see *you* here. I've been up since 3 a.m. and must look horrible!"

I couldn't stifle a chortle. "I know you've been working all night. You look fine, and you smell delicious." She bit her lower lip as she unlatched the tailgate. I grabbed a big box of sticky buns and followed her. Her perfect bubble butt jiggled delightfully as she ascended the steps. The view was spectacular.

Rick caught me looking, donned a devilish grin, shook his head, and pointed me to the kitchen. Thumping me on the ear as I passed, he said, "Boy, you better stay out of trouble while you're on these premises." He tried, but failed, to inject a tone of seriousness into the comment.

The other guys were following Patti Wheat's directions, arranging the delicacies, so I fell in line. Patti was blonde, tall, slender, and graceful, a perfect contrast to Otho's gruff exterior. Rick promised a share of the Memorial Day proceeds to the public library fund, and Patti was there to ensure everything went smoothly. The cooks and servers deferred to her judgment, and Rick was perfectly content to step aside and let her run the show. Her feminine touch would bolster profits and everyone knew it.

Rick emerged from the storeroom with bar towels and white aprons. We slipped them on and went to work. Sara blew me a kiss as she was leaving, and the guys razzed me with noisy smacks while Rick admonished me for letting her go without a real kiss. "When you get to be my age, you'll never pass up an opportunity to get some sugar from a pretty little darling who is so obviously willing."

Patti patted me on the back and said, "Don't listen to them, Teddy. I think it was sweet. You're much more of a gentleman than they are." Her comment, although well intended, just made my embarrassment worse.

Patrons poured in, and Miguel, the master chef, fired up the grill. The smell of burgers, fries, catfish, and boudin filled the air. Customers consumed nickel beer as fast as the draft master could pour. Standing room only. Sheriff Otho Wheat showed up and raised a half-hearted fuss about beer service before noon. Patti ran him off.

Bert Levy sat at the bar showing off the gold tetradrachm. The magnificent specimen sparkled on a white leather jeweler's tray. We got busy bussing tables and by 1:00, Rick started serving tequila shots and Harvey Wallbangers. By 1:15, Bert was shit-faced. Casablanca was rockin'-and-rollin', more like a New Year's Eve party than a Memorial Day picnic. Mic, Tommy, and I worked like convicts on a chain gang, earning our two bucks an hour.

A black Lincoln limo pulled up in the parking lot as I was sweeping off the wraparound porch. The chauffeur hopped out and opened the rear door for a tall, distinguished gentleman with thin gray hair and black-framed glasses. As he emerged, a hush fell over the bar, and all you could hear was the whirling of the ceiling fans. I glanced back as Rick straightened his collar, snapped his fingers, and motioned for the crowd to rise. Everyone stood in silent unison.

The driver walked up to me, touched the brim of his cap, and said. "Young man, would you tell Mr. Blaine that Governor Preston Smith would like a word with him?"

I nodded, but didn't move. Rick was already sauntering down the steps with a broad smile and his hand extended. "Governor, what brings you to my humble establishment?"

The statesman shook his hand and said, "Good to see you, Rick. I was in Port Arthur giving the keynote address at a petroleum conference when I heard news of treasure turning up in the Knob." He pointed to the chauffeur. "My man Franklin has been following the story on the radio and filled me in on the facts. Fascinating. Came to have a look. Mayor Grisham said the latest find was on display right here at Casablanca."

Rick bowed, pointed up the stairs, and the governor ascended while acknowledging the patrons and staff alike. He shook hands or made eye contact with everyone in the place. Preston Smith carried Kushner County with 91% of the vote in the crowded Democratic primary election against Don Yarbrough, Dolph Briscoe, and Waggoner Carr. He was one of thirteen children born to Central Texas tenant farmers, and Dix Knob folks preferred him over the rich, hoity-toity candidates. During those days, whoever won the Democratic nomination won the state. In the general election, his Republican opponent, Paul Eggers, never stood a chance.

The governor sat down at the bar and studied the coin while Patti Wheat coaxed coffee down Bert Levy's throat to sober him up a bit. Preston reached into his coat pocket, pulled out a checkbook, and started writing. Without speaking, he presented the promissory to the detectorist. Levy's eyes widened, both men shook hands, and Franklin escorted Alexander the Great to a lockbox in the limo.

The Governor graciously declined libation and vittles, and Mr. Blaine nudged him off to the corner by the Wurlitzer. The popular politician's facial expression took on a serious countenance during the muted exchange. After several minutes, Rick looked up, scanned the room, found me, and silently mouthed, "Where is Mickey O'Dell?" I pointed to the kitchen. He and Tommy were taking advantage of the brief interruption of service to catch up on dish washing.

Rick made a quick nod toward the door. Message received. I ran and got Mickey, who was slinging suds over dirty plates and greasy spoons. "Hey, man. I think Mr. Blaine wants to introduce you to the governor."

Patti Wheat pushed past me, grabbed a damp bar towel, wiped the sweat off Mickey's face, and straightened his hair. "Stand up tall, shake his hand, look him straight in the eye, and say, It's an honor to meet you, sir."

Mickey nodded in agreement, and timidly walked through the swinging doors into the dining area, unconsciously wiping his hands on the apron.

A reporter from *The Dix Knob Tattler* was preparing for a photograph of the two men. Mickey hesitated, but Rick motioned for him to join them. The photo op was perfect. The camera shutter snapped, a bulb flashed, and a historic moment was memorialized.

The governor made another pass around the bar before leaving, laughing and joking with constituents. The patrons indulged in countless high-spirited toasts after the encounter, and the rest of the afternoon was a hectic blur. Six p.m. rolled around and we had racked up eight hours of pay. Rick called us over to the bar as Patti Wheat collected the library fund share from the day's proceeds. He gave us each a twenty-dollar bill, and Patti gave us three dollars more apiece.

Rick said, "Don't pay 'em too much, Patti. They'll get spoiled and expect it every time they show up for the job."

Tommy and I hadn't spoken to Mickey about his introduction to the governor, and his voice cracked when he addressed our benefactor.

"Mr. Blaine, all of us guys are grateful for the opportunity to work. We all need the money. I'm especially grateful for you stepping up to the plate for my dad. Do you think Governor Smith can help my family?"

Patti Wheat turned her back and wiped her eyes with a bar towel. Rick took a deep breath and puffed out his cheeks as he exhaled. "I don't know, Mickey. Even the governor has limitations. There are channels to navigate. Court filings, parole board hearings, and stuff like that. Strings have to be pulled. Favors called in. Palms greased. It all takes time. But he's a good man. He'll help if he can."

For the first time in my life, I saw Mickey O'Dell break down and sob. He covered his face with the apron. Patti ran to the kitchen, Tommy sniffed, and I fought back tears of my own.

Rick grabbed Mickey by the nape of the neck and gave him a gentle shake. "Okay, boys, you are officially off the clock. I'll expect to see you next Saturday morning for our ritual parking lot sweep and vomit scrub." It was just the bromide we needed to break the tension. Mickey wiped his eyes one last time, before we shed our aprons and headed out.

A merciful evening breeze cooled our sweaty duds, as we paused to pet Humper. The jolly hound was scarfing up scraps thrown off the porch by tipsy patrons. We sat on the bottom step while Mickey gave us a rundown on the three-way conversation with Rick and the governor. Most of it I surmised from the recent exchange.

"Mr. Smith seemed eager to help. He knows all the judges in the appeal courts. He's got friends on the parole boards. Lordy, I hope he comes through."

Tommy patted Mic on the back. "My folks campaigned for Governor Smith in the last election. They ran ads at the theater before every movie. Mom's a yellow dog Democrat and knows a lot of his cronies. She'll make sure he's frequently reminded of the unjust situation with your dad." Mickey was fidgeting and wringing his hands, hungry for encouragement.

I said, "Listen to me, Mickey. The ball is rolling. Rick made an appeal. The most popular governor in Texas history acknowledged you, so keep your chin up. Justice will prevail in the end."

Mic stood and stretched. "Thanks, guys. I needed that. Let's stop by the house and tell Brandy and Momma the good ... what the hell is that crazy dog doing?"

Tommy and I looked around, confused by the outburst. Nothing seemed out of order. Mic pointed toward the old Cusser

Club building and whispered, "Look in the bushes, just behind the fence, below the K.O.M.C sign."

Tommy adjusted his glasses and squinted. "Holy Toledo, it's Humper. How the heck did he get inside the compound? That place is a fortress."

The old cur was sniffing around the entryway door to the first-floor pub, and suddenly vanished.

"Did you see where he got inside?" I asked.

Tommy responded. "He was on the porch with us for a while and just a minute ago he was sniffing around that big clump of wisteria."

I sprinted toward the fence line nearest the street, but Mickey caught up with me and grabbed my sleeve.

"Hold on a minute, Teddy. Let's make sure nobody's looking. We don't need none of those drunk Boudreauxs snooping around. Let's saunter over real leisure like, and have a look at that wisteria bush growing on the fence."

The huge plant was blooming late and covered with honey bees. Intertwined in the chain link, the thick vines and spindle-shaped flower clusters formed a giant natural umbrella that extended four feet on either side. Mickey got on all fours and crawled underneath. "Keep a lookout for any snoopers. If anyone comes by, just pretend you're taking a piss."

Tommy unzipped. "If anyone gets too close, I'll just wiggle my hose and scare 'em off."

"That'll damn sure do the trick," Mickey replied as he ducked under the lowest vines.

He emerged a minute later with mud on his hands. "Yep, there's a hole in the fence. The heavy vines pushed up the chain link, leaving a nice gap. I can tell where old Humper has done some digging too. The opening is almost big enough for a skinny guy like Tommy Boy, and with a little work, you and I could squeeze through, Theodore."

Tommy and I took turns looking. Mickey's assessment was spot on. Some wire cutters and a little elbow grease with a pry bar would do the trick. We agreed to meet back at 6 a.m. on Tuesday with grubby duds and tools. Most Memorial Day revelers would be gone, and we could work unobserved. Tommy headed out to the Palisades Theater for evening projector duty. It would be a quick shift. *Night of the Living Dead* was the feature film and George Romero's cult classic was making one last curtain call before being relegated to late night TV reruns.

Mickey rearranged the vines to conceal our discovery, and we headed to Casa O'Dell.

9

MONDAY NIGHT WAS AN EMOTIONAL ROLLERCOASTER AT the O'Dell household. Vera paced the floor and wept as Mickey and I related the events of the day. Even Brandy shed tears and hugged her brother. He was the hero of the day, and I was proud of him. We turned in at midnight and sleep came easily after busting our humps all day at the riverfront bar.

Tessa pestered my fatigue-muddled mind all night until a merciful noise on the front porch awakened me at 5 a.m. I shook Mickey awake, and we crept to the window. It was the newspaper delivery boy.

"Sorry, guys. I was trying not to disturb anyone. I thought you might like a couple of extra copies of *The Tattler* today, no extra charge. It's got a big front-page story I think you'll enjoy." Mickey thanked him and retrieved the periodicals emblazoned on the front page with the headline:

Gov. Preston Smith visits Dix Knob. Buys Greek Treasure Coin.

Below was a half-page picture of Mickey shaking the politician's hand while Rick Blaine smiled approvingly.

In the kitchen, Vera spread the paper out on the dining room table, patting and smoothing the page as though it were a rare piece of silk. The youngest sister retrieved her reading glasses without being told.

Mickey stood behind Vera and wrapped both arms around her neck. "Now Momma, don't get your hopes up too much. It ain't gonna be quick, and it ain't gonna be easy. Mr. Blaine said so."

She leaned her head against his muscular shoulder. "At least now I have some hope. Maybe my prayers are finally being answered." Mickey laid his twenty-dollar bill on the table next to *The Tattler*. "Here's a few extra bucks for the light bill." I reached into my pocket, but Mickey waved me off. "We can't hang around for breakfast, Momma. Teddy and I have some stuff to finish up at Casablanca, so we're gonna get an early start. Maybe I can add a couple more bucks to the pot later on today."

I was pondering Mic's deception when Brandy appeared from the hallway, dressed in full-length pajamas, much more modest attire than the day before. She said, "Are you guys gonna be back for lunch? If so, I'll make sure a hot meal is on the table." This uncharacteristic flirt with domesticity surprised everyone in the room. It was my turn to contribute. "Thanks, Miss Brandy, but we'll get lunch on the run. I'll buy a bag of hot links at Obermeyer's and have 'em delivered. Y'all have done a lot for me and I really appreciate the hospitality. I'm going to earn my keep."

Brandy stood on her tiptoes and planted a kiss right on my lips. My nostrils filled with the intoxicating aroma of cigarette smoke and strawberry syrup.

My clothes were dingy after two days of wear, so Mickey lent me some blue sweatpants and a white Mexican wedding shirt. It was too wide in the shoulders and a little too short at the tail, but the ensemble was comfortable. I donned my tennis shoes and Vera threw my soiled attire in the washing machine along with the rest of the family clothes. I felt right at home.

Mic suggested a visit to Tyler's Bakery for breakfast, as he emerged from the tool shed, pulling a drawstring atop a large, waxed, canvas bag.

"What the heck is that?" I asked.

"It's an offal bag. O-F-F-A-L." He spelled out the word as if I was stupid. I let it go.

"Daddy would swipe 'em from the slaughterhouse. These are for pig guts. Lips and assholes. You know, all the leftover swine parts they use for bologna, hot dogs, and potted meat. I threw some of Daddy's tools in here. A crowbar and some wire cutters. That should get the opening in the fence wide enough for us to get through."

The bakery was busy, but Sara nudged her mother aside to wait on Mic and me. We ordered ham croissants and cinnamon rolls. Sara rang us up on the register and as I reached in my pocket, a deep voice behind me said. "Little lady, I'll cover breakfast for these young men. Throw in some Yahoos and a couple of kolaches." Mic and I simultaneously spun on our heels and came face to face with Nollen Embers. A newspaper was tucked under his arm, his eyes were bloodshot, and a gauze bandage covered his right hand. He handed Sara several bills and told her to keep the change. Turning back to us, he asked, "Gentlemen, may I have a moment of your time? It's very important." He motioned to the door, and we followed him across the street to a park bench near the statue. He plopped down, obviously exhausted.

Embers eyed the offal bag with curiosity bordering on suspicion. Mickey held it up so the outline of the crowbar was clearly visible and said, "We appreciate the generosity, Mr. Embers, but Theodore and I are on a tight schedule today. We're heading down Kickapoo Street to fix some warped boards on the Nutscalder's back porch."

Mic reached over and lifted my shirt, exposing the bruised ribs. "Teddy tripped and fell a couple of days ago and damn near punctured a lung. We gotta get those steps fixed before this clumsy stooge kills himself. So tell us, what's on your mind?"

Satisfied with the explanation and visibly more at ease, Embers reached in his pocket, fished out a cigarette, and lit up. "Have either of you fellows seen Meroticia, er, uh, Missy? There was a … misunderstanding … and she took off late last evening and hasn't returned home. Her mother and I are worried sick."

We shook our heads. He nodded to me and continued, "She is a very troubled young lady. Insanity runs in the family. Her mother is a paranoid schizophrenic, and I apologize for how she acted toward you at the festival." He pointed across the lawn to the spot where Arthur Rumkin was running the ring toss booth. "Maris sees villains in every shadow and thinks everyone is out to get her. It's very distressing. Poor Meroticia picks up on the delusions, and it keeps her in a constant state of confusion. She gets upset and rebellious at the least little thing. Now she's run off and hiding from us."

Mickey said. "Missy doesn't exactly circulate in our social circle. We see her around town from time to time, but we don't know her. Doesn't she attend a private school outside of the Knob?"

Nollen winced. "That was her mother's idea. I think it made matters worse. I should have put my foot down and kept Meroticia at home, but I didn't want to step between a mother and daughter..."

The man seemed sincere, but there was still something shifty about him. I said, "Mr. Embers, don't beat yourself up too bad. God knows we've all had good intentions come back to bite us in the ass. Missy seems like a nice girl, and we're eager to help. Mic and I are real civic-minded in that regard. I've got to tell you straight up, there's an air of mystery about the Turnbow clan. We'll keep any additional information you care to share in strict confidentiality." I didn't want to be offensive or make the man angry. I just wanted to bait him out a little. He unfolded the newspaper and looked at the front page and then at Mic.

Mic put on a smug little smile and said, "Not my best side."

The man straightened his back and took a deep breath.

"It's a fine photo, and I appreciate your honesty. I know there are lots of rumors floating around about me. Nothing's true. In my line of work, I constantly come into contact with unsavory characters. I occasionally hire recovering addicts to give them a second chance. Keep 'em straight and clean. Give them a purpose. A leg up. I run a wrecker service and trucking business. There are a lot of crooks in that line of work, so folks always assume the worst. I get it. I really do, but…"

The man suddenly stood up, reached into his pocket, and pulled out a handful of change and a couple of wadded bills. "God almighty, listen to me. I'm prattling on like an old woman. I didn't mean to unload all this personal garbage on you guys. I'm just worried to death about my sweet Meroticia. Please keep an eye out for her. I'm desperate to find her." He deposited the money in Mickey's outstretched hand and gave us each a business card. Embers put his hands together under his chin in a gesture of friendly supplication. "Gentlemen, get to a payphone and call me if you see her. There will be a nice reward for anyone who helps me find my step daughter. I never forget a favor. I'm good to my friends." He looked back and forth at each of us for acknowledgement. I nodded, and Mickey gave him a curt salute.

With a deep sigh, he turned and shuffled toward his Caddy parked across the street. Mickey elbowed me and said, "By the way, Mr. Embers, if you need any help putting out your campaign signs, we're for hire." Nollen didn't turn around but held up his hand and flashed the okay sign.

I glanced back toward Tyler's Bakery as we turned to go. The sun was climbing over the horizon and there was a glare on the window so I couldn't see inside. I waved anyway, just in case Sara was watching.

The walk to the Cusser Club property was contentious. Mickey was playing the Devil's advocate and thoroughly demolished my defense of Missy Turnbow.

"Look Teddy, I'm not saying Nollen Embers is a straight up guy, but you must admit his explanation would explain a lot of what happened last Friday on that old railroad bridge. Missy was acting pretty strung out. I think she was seriously considering self-harm. When I climbed up out of the Grotto and saw her standing there, rocking back and forth, it was almost like she was in a trance or something. Nobody in their right mind would stand on the edge of that old trestle, even on a dare."

I said, "We don't know the whole story. She was certainly acting strange, but there may have been a good reason. I have a feeling we're missing some pieces of this puzzle."

He shoved the offal sack into my hands. "Hold this sack while I rearrange my package. These damn pants are too small for my boys. I'll never catch up to Tommy, but I ain't going to stifle any opportunity for expansion." Mic rearranged his unmentionables, re-tucked his shirttail, snatched the sack out of my hand, and continued.

"I know you are defending her because she's pretty, and I get it, but she blew you off in a damn rude manner at the festival. I was otherwise engaged, but you told me about it yourself, and Arthur Rumkin is spewing his first-hand account all over town. When you take everything we know about her and boil it down, we're only left with three explanations. One—she is as crazy as a peach orchard boar. Two—she's a spoiled rich girl just rebelling against her parents. Or three—she's just a conniving little bitch."

Mickey had a point, and I was out of arguments.

As we turned onto Riverfront Levee Road, Tommy was waiting for us under the shade of a mimosa tree at the edge of the K.O.M.C. property, dressed in faded overalls and a shabby, straw, cowboy hat.

Mickey chortled as he quickened his pace. "I think Señor Crum is *incognito*."

As we approached Tommy, he pulled the hat farther down over his brow.

"I thought we agreed to wear a disguise."

Mickey bent forward with a deep belly laugh. "You're some kind of scrawny bumpkin, and Teddy is a Mexican groom looking for a bride. That's rich."

Tommy was perturbed at our stocky companion. "Oh yeah? Well, at least we tried. You're dressed the same as every other day."

Mickey put his fists together in front of his belt, striking a bodybuilder pose. "I can't disguise my macho virility. This perfect physique defies any attempt at camouflage or subterfuge." Tommy and I both shook our heads and looked at each other. It was our turn to laugh.

Tommy was showing us the flashlights he requisitioned from the theater when a patrol car turned on Riverfront Levee Road and pulled up alongside us. Tommy tossed the torches into a clump of Johnsongrass. The deputy who arrested Grails rolled down the window and asked about our business.

Tommy said, "We are just heading down to Casablanca to clean up the parking lot, like we always do after weekends and holidays." He smiled, crossed his eyes, and tipped his hat like a true hayseed.

The deputy snorted and looked at Mic. "What's in the bag?" My heart skipped a beat and Mickey swallowed hard.

Tommy came to the rescue again. "That there is a crowbar we found over on Pearl Street. It might have fallen off a city work truck."

The junior lawman found the explanation highly amusing. "Them damn city boys are a bunch of nitwits. They ain't got a thimble full of brains between 'em all."

He reached into the glove compartment and pulled out a grainy mimeograph copy of Missy Turnbow's picture. "This little rich babe has apparently flown the coop, and her parents are frantic. Have you guys seen her?"

Mickey pulled Nollen Embers' business card out of his pocket. "Deputy, we got the complete story from her stepfather twenty minutes ago over at Rhinelander Park. He even bought us breakfast at Tyler's. We're keeping our eyes peeled, but we ain't seen hide nor hair of her."

He put the car in gear. "Okay, fellas, stay on the lookout. She's a real cutie. Be hard to miss. Even in this crappy picture, she looks..." The deputy took a long look at the image and arched his eyebrows. "Just call us if you see the girl. The Sheriff doesn't like being left out of the loop. He'll have questions. Personally, I don't give a rat's ass. All those snobs on the North Side can jump in this shit-stain river for all I care." He turned the car around in the Casablanca parking lot and gunned the engine, leaving skid marks on the pavement before careening back toward midtown.

We breathed a sigh of relief, and Mic congratulated Tommy on a fine performance as he relayed the story about Missy's disappearance and our meeting with Embers. Tommy retrieved the flashlights and we made our way to the Cusser Club fence. One last glance around the area assured us that no one was observing our movements. Except for a slow-moving beer truck lumbering toward

Casablanca, traffic was light and Aunt Tilde had not yet nestled into her rocker.

Scooching under the vegetation, Mickey took the tools and got to work. Five minutes later, he had doubled the size of the opening in the fence, providing just enough room to slide through on our backs. The property inside the compound laid untended for years, and tall stalks of ragweed, thistle, and toadflax provided excellent cover.

We silently crawled on all fours toward the faded green entrance of the first-floor pub. All the windows were boarded up and a rusted chain secured the brass pull handle to a crudely installed eye bolt screwed into the door frame. The bottom half of the door was rotted out and splintered from stress and strain of foundation shift and constant exposure to the elements. The lower hinge had pulled away from the frame and Humper was gaining access to the building through the narrow gap that appeared.

Tommy suddenly gave out a loud yelp. "Ouch! Guys, don't make any sudden moves. Look up." I turned my head toward the Cusser Club sign. Affixed to the sagging awning was a hornet's nest the size of a beach ball. Agitated by our movements, the insects were swarming. One of the vicious beasties popped Tommy on the shoulder. Fortunately, his thick T-shirt and overall strap deflected the poisonous stinger, so the wound was minor. We slid sideways in a crab crawl away from the hive. Within a few seconds, the menacing activity subsided.

Mickey tapped the middle hinge with the crowbar and it disintegrated like a stale crumb cake, allowing us to force the gap wide enough to squeeze through.

A three-inch layer of fine sand covered the pub floor. Watermarks stained the walls halfway up to the ceiling, evidence of the flood eleven years earlier. It obliterated a profile mural of General George Armstrong Custer up to his chin—a fitting end to the pub's notorious namesake. Someone had spray-painted "Custer had it coming" on the back-bar mirror—a sentiment shared by many. Small animal bones were scattered around the place, and we didn't know if the skeletal remains were drowned critters or roadkill dragged in by Humper. The old cur's resting place was evident behind the bar. He was nowhere to be seen, but a wallowed-out area of dirt and a chewed-up tennis ball marked his lair.

As I was looking under the bar for anything salvageable, a rat scurried across my foot and I lurched back into a wooden panel below the back-bar mirror. A loud, audible click sounded, and the panel popped open to reveal a hidden compartment. Two more rodents scampered by, and I screamed like a six-year-old girl. My companions guffawed at my alarm, but helped me up.

Mic shined a light into the compartment. "It's a shaft that goes up toward the second floor, but this old building is so catty-wampus that the boards are busted and splintered, blocking the opening about eight feet up."

Tommy tugged on a dangling chain and said, "This is an old-fashioned dumbwaiter. My dad said this building was a speak-easy during the prohibition years, and a hideout for bootleggers. They probably used this little elevator to haul illegal liquor back and forth between floors."

I began pushing on other panels and found another compartment littered with colorful seltzer bottles. "Man, this place is full of surprises. I wonder how many more covert nooks and crannies there are in this place?"

Sunlight filtered through cracks in the weathered boards covering the windows. Mickey stood on tiptoes and peered out through a gap. "I can see the parking lot and most of the front porch of Casablanca. No one is in sight. I think we made it undetected. This bottom floor is a wreck. There's nothing of any value here, so let's have a look upstairs."

In the back corner of the bar was a steep, narrow stairwell leading up to the second floor. We fired the flashlights and headed up single file with Mic in the lead and me pulling up the rear. A few feet from the top, a step gave way and Mickey cried out in pain.

"What happened?" Tommy asked.

"I fell through a rotten board, and I skinned my shin. It hurts like hell, but I'll live."

From that point on, we tested each step before putting full weight on it.

As we reached a landing at the top of the staircase, a gust of wind triggered a low, mournful moan from the decrepit structure. An intimidating, heavy oak door blocked our way. Gruesome mythical creatures were carved into the dark-grained wood. Imps, demons, serpents, and orks glared at us in silent warning. The door facing was chiseled and gashed along the edges, but still firmly intact, evidence of an attempted break-in before the fence went up.

Mic took his crowbar and started hacking away at the knob and keyhole, slamming his muscular shoulder against the obstruction every few seconds until it finally splintered. Tommy and I joined the assault, and after 10 minutes of relentless battering, the door finally gave in. The spine-tingling screech of heavy hinges announced our breach of the mysterious lair.

A shattered skylight provided a modicum of light, illuminating the eerie inner sanctum of the Knights of the Mystic Chalice. A dozen crows squawked and fluttered out through the damaged roof. Floorboards, warped from the foundation failure, made each step a challenge.

As we gazed around the room in amazement, Tommy said, "Man, Hurricane Audrey really did a number on this old building. We're probably the first people to set foot in this place in a decade or more." The walls were covered with elaborate wood paneling, carved with the cryptic symbols of the mysterious fraternity. A large portrait hung high on the back wall, surrounded by an opulent gold foil frame. The bearded, sober subject was arrayed with a resplendent chain collar and a multitude of medals. His gaze seemed to follow us around the room.

Mic and Tommy lifted me up so I could read the inscription on the brass plate below the painting.

I said, "Gentlemen, this is the most honorable Faustus Muffberger, Grand Master and founder of the Ancient and Illustrious Order of the Knights of the Mystic Chalice, A.D. 1844." The dry-rotted canvas crumbled at the slightest touch. His gaze seemed self-righteous and haughty, so I reached up and thumped Faustus' left eye and nose, leaving a hole in the portrait. "How dare you gaze at us with such contempt! Curse your carcass as it rots in the grave; meat for the maggot and conqueror worm. Behold the new kings of the Mystic Chalice!"

I expected applause from my companions, but they were embarrassingly uninspired.

Mic said, "What the hell was that all about? Are you trying to jinx us or something?"

"Alright already, so it wasn't my greatest improvisation. Let's keep looking. Maybe there is something we can pilfer from this place."

Four thrones sat atop a raised dais in each corner of the room. Dozens of ornately carved chairs lined the walls at a slightly lower level. A magnificent ebony wood altar rose from the center of the lodge floor. Faint sunlight filtered through particles of dust, illuminating a skull resting in the center. On the west wall of the room, a spiral staircase ascended to a platform near the ceiling beside a glass porthole-shaped window. Ubiquitous cobwebs hung from every surface.

Mickey nudged the skull with his crowbar. Trembling with trepidation, he picked up the head. "It's heavy. Carved out of soapstone. Amazing detail. Do you think it's worth anything?" He waved the morbid object in front of Tommy's face. "Give us a kiss and pledge allegiance to the Mystic Chalice!"

Tommy recoiled and let out an uncharacteristic curse. "Put that damn thing down, Mic. You and Teddy are going to bring us bad luck. Let's get out of here. This place is giving me the heebie-jeebies."

Mickey chuckled and replaced the calvarium in the exact center of the altar, where he found it. "C'mon, Tommy Boy, grow some balls. Let's have some fun. Nobody knows we're here, and what are they going to do if they catch us? All the members are dead or wasting away in an old folks' home. Knobbers don't give a hoot about this old building. Let's look around and see if there is anything valuable we can salvage. Maybe we can make a few bucks."

We began thumping and pounding on the ornate paneling. Spiders scurried and cockroaches sprinted, unaccustomed to mortal intrusion. Within a few minutes, Tommy found the upper opening of the dumbwaiter, hawked up a big loogie, and spat it against an obstruction. "Something must be wedged in the chute. Just a bunch of shattered boards and rusty nails. Nothing else to see here."

I located a concealed closet filled with ceremonial robes of crimson and black. Dusty, musty, and slightly moth-eaten, the garments were tattered but still wearable. Trimmed in silver braid, the garments were tailored of a heavy velvet, emblazoned with embroidered skeletons and mythical serpents.

Fascinated by the finery, I said, "Brethren, let us don these royal vestments and ascend to the thrones of the exalted knighthood!" Climbing to the top of the spiral staircase, I sat on the bench and peered out of the porthole. The glass was covered with a dingy film, but I wiped it with a sleeve until I could see across the river into The Grove. My friends positioned themselves on the gaudy, baroque seats in the south and east corners.

Using his flashlight, Tommy examined the heavy wooden lectern in front of his station. He fingered an indentation, and the top slid aside, revealing a metal plate embossed with writing. He studied the inscription for a moment, stretched his arms out to the side, threw back his shoulders, and proclaimed, "I am the Subterranean Horluth. I rule over the nocturnal creatures that slither below the fetid loam, feasting on the flesh of the quick and the dead. Heed my command all ye vile monstrosities that coil and cling and creep, unseen, through caverns measureless to man, down to a sunless sea."

Hooting and hollering in approval, Mic followed suit, locating the hidden switch where he stood. Studying the ritualistic words, he declared, "I am the Imperial Cyclops. My all-seeing eye pierces the veil of darkness and death. I summon all the wretched souls who sipped of every sinful sweet and unremembered fell asleep. Awaken and obey my command, thou forsaken spirits, and wreak havoc on those who would violate their vows and bring dishonor to our noble order!"

After fiddling with a frame next to the porthole, a shutter popped open, exposing the duties of my high station. Struggling to stifle a laugh, I stated, "I am the Serpentine Wyvern. Forever vigilant, I guard the portals of this sovereign citadel with scimitar and mace. Imposters and interlopers, I eviscerate and maul, casting their entrails upon the steps of this sacred temple as a warning to others!"

We congratulated ourselves with a hearty round of applause. Crows peered through the hole in the roof and cackled their objections, but we paid them no heed. The Imperial Cyclops pronounced us the new custodians of the Cusser Club and illustrious heirs to the chalice knighthood. Our spontaneous performance was flawless, and I envisioned Melchior and Dipdottle's sublime approval.

As we converged at the altar, Tommy said, "Who came up with all this stuff? Faustus Muffberger must have been a pretty creative dude. It's a shame this old club died on the vine. I guess the younger generation just lost interest."

Mic replied, "It was a different era. Back in the 1800s, when they built this place, there was no TV or radio. This was a swanky, private club, where guys could meet, have a few drinks, and trade stories, without their women nagging 'em to death. What do you think, Teddy boy?"

"I think I need to stop by Obermeyer's and order hot links for tonight. I also promised Aunt Tilde we would drag the wagon over the river and collect some grub for Rufus."

The guys nodded, just as Tommy's flashlight flickered and died. Enthralled by the thought of deciphering more of the mystic works, we agreed to come back with fresh batteries for a more thorough exploration. As we were leaving, Mic paused by a massive, seven-foot tall fluted column with a tarnished brass sextant mounted on top. He rubbed it with his hand and shined his fading flashlight beam up close. He exclaimed, "Hey guys, do you know what they carved this column out of?" Tommy and I leaned in and inspected the rich burgundy wood with subtle black specks and swirls of orange. I shrugged. "It's beautiful, Mickey, but what is it?"

He licked his finger and rubbed away more of the grime, growing visibly more excited by the second. "They carved this column out of pure Amboyna burl. It's a really rare and valuable wood. My uncle Murl has a cabinet shop and does a lot of custom stuff for rich folks in Houston and Lake Charles. Desks, chairs, and bookcases. He uses this type of wood for ornamental veneers and decorative inlay."

Tommy leaned closer and used his sleeve to polish a section. "Okay, so it's pretty wood. So what?"

Mic grabbed us both by the collar. "Last summer, while I was helping him move a turning lathe, a guy came in with some salvage stuff and my uncle paid him forty bucks for a piece of Amboyna burl the size of a loaf of bread."

Tommy's jaw dropped as I did a quick calculation in my head. At 12 inches in diameter, the object was at least thirty times that size.

Tommy said, "Jeez, if that's true, then this chunk of timber is worth several hundred bucks."

Mickey grinned and rubbed his hands together greedily. "I'll trade in this crowbar for daddy's old hand saw. We'll cut it to pieces and take this big, beautiful bastard out of here one chunk at a time."

Exhilarated by the thought of easy money, we descended the staircase to find Humper lounging in the sandy wallow, wagging his tail. He didn't seem the least bit surprised to find us there. He followed us, playfully licking our faces as we crawled back to the fence. Aunt Tilde was busy sweeping her porch, and no one else was near, so we made a clean exit.

Tommy said, "Hey, since we're already kinda dirty, let's crawl under the porch at Casablanca and see if there is any loose change that fell between the boards over the holiday weekend. Nickel Beer and tequila shots. Lots of stumbling drunks. We might get lucky."

Mic reached into his pocket and pulled out the change Nollen Embers had given him.

"Teddy has to save his money for the hotlinks, but if we find another quarter and we could feast on some of Sara Tyler's giant, custard-filled cream puffs." He looked at me, licked his lips, and wiggled his eyebrows. "Now, wouldn't that be nice? All warm and sweet and squishy. Just like Sara. What do you say, Theodore?"

"That's a real knee slapper, Mic. Real classy. Chortle, Chortle. Ha-ha."

A vision of Sara's voluptuous body covered in sticky custard flashed across my mind. I should have been ashamed.... I wasn't ... but I should have been.

Seven nickels, three dimes, and a quarter later, we crawled out from under the pilings and brushed off. The accumulation of dust from the Cusser Club, cobwebs from the fraternity hall, and mud from the dank underbelly of the bar took a toll on our appearance. It wasn't even noon, and we already looked like a bunch of migrant cabbage pickers.

Tommy flared his nostrils and sniffed the air. "Do you guys smell something?"

The strong smell of roasted coffee and diesel oil filled my nostrils. The odor of burning lignite.

Mic glanced up toward the trestle. "Look up the hill. There's smoke coming from the Grotto!"

10

THERE WAS NO MISTAKE. SOMEONE HAD INVADED OUR hideout. Gathering courage, we quietly made our way up to the railroad track and circled around to enter from above. Mic insisted that military strategy dictated an assault from high ground, so he led the way with the crowbar in hand.

I whispered, "I'll pull back the kudzu and you wallop whoever comes out." He nodded in agreement.

My heart pummeled my bruised rib cage as I pulled back the vegetation. Mickey rushed in with a menacing snarl. "Don't move, you sorry bastard or I'll...!"

A bloodcurdling feminine scream followed, and Mic jumped back, knocking me into Tommy, forcing all of us backward on our butts like a row of dominoes.

Mic shot back up on his feet and said, "Oh my god, I am so sorry. We didn't know who was here. Are you okay?"

Missy Turnbow huddled against the back wall, trembling uncontrollably. Mic stood motionless. I eased around him, and she recoiled at my approach. I held up my hands. "Nobody is going to hurt you. We saw smoke coming from our hideout and we thought some old hobo had trespassed." My companions backed me up.

"Yeah, we thought you were a tramp…

Wino…

…Bum."

Missy's left cheek was red and swollen. Coals sputtered and crackled in the firepit. She apparently tried to start a fire with the lignite and some damp straw. Her pink blouse and jeans were sooty and wrinkled. We stood quietly by for a minute until she settled down and finally spoke.

"I didn't know where else to go, and remembered you said there was a hideout near the trestle. I didn't have any trouble finding it. This gravel trail leads right to it."

I squatted down to her eye level and smiled. "Yeah, it's really not much of a secret. Lots of people know about it, but we are the only ones who come here. It's just a poor boy's hidey-hole."

Mic and Tommy stomped out the smoking embers and pulled the vines aside to let the place air out.

Missy struggled for words. "I'm in a serious predicament, and I needed time to think. I'm sorry about the fire, and all the mess. I'd better go. I can't drag you guys into this. That would just make matters worse."

Tommy spoke up. "Wait a minute. It's obvious you're in some kind of trouble. We ain't got much in the way of money or material things, but we're pretty resourceful. I've known Mic and Teddy all my life. Despite an obvious lack of refinement, they're upstanding, honorable guys, and I can assure you we can all keep a secret if that's what you're worried about."

Missy covered her face with her hands and quietly sobbed.

There are pivotal moments in life when your perception of the world changes forever. After my twin sister died and my mother left me with an alcoholic father, all hope of an idyllic childhood vanished. When Tommy was told that blindness was inevitable, his depression morphed into an oppressive enemy, kept at bay by a thin thread of hope in the slow grind of medical progress. Mickey O'Dell was forced to sit idly by and watch his sister debase herself in front of lecherous men in order to pay the family's bills. Every day in Dix Knob brought us one step closer to being devoured by the Gaping Maw of Despair. The whispers, the pity, and even well-intentioned charity yokes a guy with an indelible stain that extinguishes his pride and sense of self-worth. But when a person comes along suffering an abasement even worse than yours, there is a moment where rage drowns your own shame and ignites a fire of fortitude to rescue another human.

This was that moment.

Missy stood, wiped her eyes, and slowly unbuttoned her blouse. I simultaneously beheld the most beautiful and most revolting thing imaginable. It was as if a giant vacuum sucked every other thought and emotion out of my soul.

She pulled her camisole down to that crucial point and squeezed her eyes shut in shame. Her shoulders and breasts were covered with scratches, bruises, and bite marks. Not from a playful puppy or petulant child. Not from a boyfriend overcome by a brief moment of passion. Gnawings. Vile, deliberate abuse. My head swam as I attempted to wrap my head around the depravity. Tommy turned away. Mickey slumped against the concrete wall and slid to the ground in disbelief.

"Your stepfather." The words were out of my mouth before I could stop. Missy nodded and buttoned up. A long period of silence passed before anyone spoke.

Mickey hung his head and stared at the ground. "We saw Nollen Embers this morning at Tyler's Bakery. That son of a bitch bought us breakfast and offered a reward if we found you and brought you back. I can't believe that smug bastard. When I see him, I'm going to beat him to death with this crowbar."

Humiliation consumed Missy, and she turned away, folding her arms across her wounded chest.

I said, "Let us help."

Tommy was pacing back and forth, wringing his hands. The wheels were turning. He whispered, "We can't help if we don't know the problem. Tell us what's going on."

"I wouldn't know where to start."

"Just start, and we'll sort it all out."

She sat down, wrapped her arms tightly around her legs, and rested her chin on her knees. Tommy and I assumed the same position. Mickey remained slumped against the wall, muttering curses.

I said, "Just let it out. It will do you good."

Missy stared blankly ahead. Her shame was heartbreaking. When she finally spoke, the narrative poured forth like a cleansing torrent.

"When my mother married him, he would do these creepy little things. Sneak into my bedroom. Make an excuse to get something out of the medicine cabinet while I bathed. Mom sent me off to boarding school. I don't know if she suspected anything or if she was just overwhelmed with grief at my father's death and wanted me away from her own depression. When I got older and came home for holidays, he would get more and more aggressive. He started drugging Mom. When I finally tried to stand up to him, he warned me to keep quiet or he would have her committed to a mental hospital. He threatened to have her subjected to electric shock treatment, or a lobotomy. Turn her into a vegetable."

I interjected. "I really don't think they do that kind of treatment anymore."

Missy shook her head. "You don't understand. It doesn't matter. He's got influence, and knows a lot of dirt on people in high places. He's determined to have his way. Even if they didn't operate on her, he could still have her committed. With all of her problems, it wouldn't take much. Bribe a doctor. Find a crooked judge to sign off on it. I've thought about telling the sheriff, but it would just be my word against his. I try to avoid him, but it doesn't work. He gets off by scaring me. It's a control thing, and he's relentless. Last night, Mom was in a stupor so I tried to hide in the greenhouse, but he cornered me. He was high on dope. While he was forcing himself ... I bit his hand. He drew back to hit me and knocked over the Ficus tree. I guess there was a wasp nest in it. They stung us both." She touched her swollen cheek. "The little brutes actually saved me. He's allergic to them. He ran into the house and I ran away."

Tommy said what we were all thinking. "So, has he actually … done the deed?"

"Not yet, thank God. He was on the verge last night. He likes to dominate. Nollen uses his mouth and gropes with his hands while staring me down. He enjoys seeing the terror in my eyes and gets excited when … I struggle."

Mickey jumped up, stumbled outside, and fell on all fours, retching. "I'd kill that sumbitch if I could get hold of him. I have four sisters and I can't imagine anything like that happening to one of them. Hell, I would stand up in court and tell the judge and jury I did it. Make my old Daddy look like a saint."

He rolled over on his back, fists clenched. Tommy ran to Mic's side and motioned me over. "Guys, we've got to go to the police. This thing is too serious for us to handle. Otho will know what to do."

Missy lunged forward and grabbed Tommy's arm. "Don't you understand? Nollen gets away with everything. He's got lawyers. He's got money. I have nothing. If the sheriff arrests him, he will be out on bail in an hour. He always slithers out of trouble. He brags about it all the time. It's a thrill. It's a game to him, and he always wins." She slumped to the ground next to Mic.

My mind was in vapor lock. Tommy laced his fingers behind his head and rolled his eyes back and forth like he always did when he was deep in analytical mode. He said, "Maybe we could hide her in the Cusser Club building until things cool off."

Mic stood up and pulled Missy back to her feet, "Hey, that's a great idea, Tommy boy! Nobody would look for her there. We could take turns guarding her until we figured out something better. I'll bet Brandy and Danni could help us out. They're savvy. They'd know what to do."

I was still grasping at straws. "Let's examine our options. If we try to hide Missy, it will just trigger more alarm. If the whole town starts looking, this thing will spin out of control. The fewer people involved, the better. We have to take charge and manage the situation." I turned to Missy. "In this little town, word spreads real fast. Every minute that goes by, more folks are going to get involved in the search. Just for the sake of argument, what would happen if you went home today?"

She rubbed her eyes and thought for a moment. "I suppose I have to go back. I can't leave my mother alone. I have this nagging fear in the back of my mind. He's going to do something to my mother and blame it on me. I've got to go home. Nollen usually leaves town on Wednesdays, and drives to New Orleans and Biloxi to check on his businesses. Sometimes he stays gone overnight. I'm afraid to show up alone. Would you guys come with me? Maybe that will put him off..." Her voice cracked, and she started rocking back and forth. I motioned for the others not to interfere. We kept quiet and just let her cry for a while. I figured a thorough emotional washout would do her good, and it gave me more time to think.

The guys looked at me for guidance, and I said, "We need to get her away from here. If anyone sees us all together, there will be a lot of uncomfortable questions. I may have a better idea." They looked at one another and nodded. I formulated a plan and verbalized it for her benefit.

"Mickey and I saw Embers this morning. He knows we are on the lookout for you. He also knows you won't tell anyone your reason for running off because of his threats against your mother. What if we showed up with you in tow, and told him we found you sleeping in an old abandoned car across the street from my house on Kickapoo Street?"

Mickey perked up. "Yeah. I told that sumbitch we were going to your place to fix the porch. It dovetails perfectly with the plan. It just might work. Missy could tell him she went out for a walk, and got surrounded by those stray junkyard dogs, locked herself in the car, and waited till morning. It's kinda far-fetched, but it's not unbelievable."

Missy said, "He might believe it. He'll want to believe it, because he doesn't want any more trouble. It would invite more scrutiny and hurt his political aspirations. But there's one big problem. How do we get all the way across town without being seen?"

Tommy took off his straw hat and put it on the girl's head. "Do you think you could stuff your hair up under it?" Missy twisted her hair up in a big knot on top of her head and then covered it with the hat. She pulled it down tight over her ears and brow. "If I keep my head down, maybe no one will see my face."

Mic inspected her efforts. "That might work. We can smudge your cheeks with a little soot. But there is one conspicuous problem. How do you cover up that delightful little..." He made an hourglass motion at the level of her derriere. Tommy gasped and Mic realized he had made a colossal blunder. "Oh god, Missy, I'm so sorry. That was a sick comment to..."

She put her hand over his mouth. "Shhh. Stop worrying. In a weird sort of way, it's actually kind of nice to have some attention from guys my age. It makes me feel … less dirty." We were all buoyed by the droll misstep of our muscular friend.

I took off my Mexican wedding shirt, and Missy recoiled at the sight of my bruised ribs, but said nothing. "Here, put this on over your blouse. I apologize for the sweat and dirt, but maybe it will cover up your figure." She smiled for the first time since we met her. It was fleeting, but it was lovely.

Tommy said, "Do you think you could walk like a guy?" He waddled around like Daffy Duck, and she giggled. The tension was easing.

Mickey swatted at him. "Hell, that will attract more attention than if she just walks normally."

Missy said, "I think I can change my stride. This shirt covers me up pretty well. You guys are the best. I mean it. No one has ever stepped up to help me. I'm really grateful."

Tommy slipped off the T-shirt under his overalls. "Teddy, put this on. We can't have you walking through town bare-chested. Those neon ribs are sure to attract attention."

I pulled the T-shirt over my head while Mic helped Missy with some final adjustments to her disguise. "If you walk behind us, maybe we can get you to Kickapoo Street unnoticed."

As we prepared to leave, Tommy examined the offal sack, testing the draw strings. "I've got an idea spinning around in my head. You guys go on without me. I need to get back to the Palisades, anyway. The projectors have to be loaded for tonight's feature. Give me a ring later on and let me know how it works out."

As Mic and I walked Missy down the railroad track toward town, we discussed her fictional route to the South Side and gave her some trivial details to add some color to her backstory in case anyone got inquisitive. I would show her my hiding place in the trusty Studebaker. For the plan to work, she had to be completely at ease with the strategy.

* * *

There were still a few tourists in the Knob, and Division Street was busy for a Tuesday, but it worked to our advantage. Congested traffic distracted the drivers, and no one seemed to take much notice of us.

I ducked in Obermeyer's Meat Market and placed an order for the hot links, and paid an extra dollar for delivery to Casa O'Dell. My friends hid in the alley behind the dumpster while I checked out, and when I returned, Mic was filling Missy in on my family history. He went into morbid detail about how my twin sister died in her bed, and how my mother had abandoned me to an abusive father. Mic told her about his own father's conviction, and the family burden that resulted from his unjust incarceration. He admitted being duped by Nollen Embers' bogus version of events, but told her I stood fast and didn't believe a word of it. She smiled at me, listened attentively, but said very little. This was Mic's way of letting her know we had empathy for her plight. It was good therapy for him and her.

As we passed Rhinelander Park, a county dump truck ground to a halt beside us. My old man was driving, and he was furious. "Where the hell have you been? That stunt you pulled with the garden shears punctured the radiator and cost me thirty bucks to fix."

I replied, "Well, just pardon me for a moment while I check my *give-a-shit-o-meter!*"

He huffed and opened the door to get out, but I slammed my weight against it, smashing his leg. He let out a scream and cursed so loudly that everyone in the park turned to look. Missy cowered behind the vehicle. I grabbed the offal bag from Mic, jerked out the crowbar, and said, "You stay in that truck, you hateful son-of-a bitch, or I swear to God, I'll bash your fuckin' head in."

Mickey tried to diffuse the situation. "He's been staying with me, Mr. Nutscalder. We've been doing some odd jobs around town trying to earn some spending money."

I pushed him aside and pulled the remaining bills out of my pocket. "I've been man-whoring up at the retirement center. Those old ladies love a young buck."

Mic shoved me aside and reasserted himself. "Don't believe a word Teddy says, Mr. Nutscalder. He ain't giving those old gals a pickle tickle or nothing like that. He's just dancing for 'em. They love to see his little heinie shake." He turned his back, put his hands behind his head, stuck out his butt, and shook it from side to side. Brandy's artistic influence was clear. My father's face morphed into a crimson rage. He wasn't believing a word of it, and the fact we were blatantly lying just stoked his fury all the more.

He started to reply when another truck caught up with us and honked the horn. The brawny cigar smoking driver stuck his head out the window and yelled. "C'mon, Nate, get a move on! We're already late to the job site. You're going to get us both fired."

"This ain't over. Not by a long shot," my father muttered. I gave him the double middle finger salute as he drove off.

Mickey patted me on the back. "I think that went rather well, Theodore. No one was maimed or killed. What do you think, Miss Turnbow?"

The girl pulled the shirt collar up over her face. "Oh my God! I can't believe you guys. That was so courageous. I can't imagine speaking to an adult like that."

I thumped the brim of her hat and bent down, looking directly into her gorgeous green eyes. "It's more akin to desperation than courage."

The incident gave our new friend a lift in spirits. I think she believed we might actually be able to help her. She opened up and became downright chatty. Missy told us about the cruelty she endured at boarding school. How the other girls continuously teased her about her mother's mental condition and the suspicious death of her father. Even the nuns chastised her about her budding womanhood and provocative appearance to the point she intentionally rumpled her hair and tried to dress sloppily.

Always the purveyor of perfect perspective, Mic summed it up nicely as he said, "You can't win in this world. You're either too ugly or too beautiful. Too rich or too poor. Too smart or too stupid. If you're not dead center of the pack, you're an outcast."

She kept her face turned as cars passed and when we finally reached the end of Kickapoo Street, I escorted her to the abandoned Studebaker. She climbed in to absorb the grungy ambiance, fingering the torn headliner and even laid down on the floorboard, internalizing each detail.

Nathaniel wouldn't be off work until late afternoon, so I suggested we go inside the house to put the finishing touches on the plan. Stepping through the rusty screen door, her jaw dropped as she scanned the squalid living room and dilapidated furnishings.

I said, "Not exactly on par with Fairhaven Street." Embarrassed, she shrugged, not knowing how to reply. I regretted putting her on the spot, so I changed the subject. "Are you hungry?"

"Famished."

I escorted her to the kitchen and threw together a Dagwood sandwich with the grub Miss Hawkins brought by. Missy gobbled it down in a most un-ladylike fashion. Mickey raised an eyebrow and said, "I never thought I'd meet a girl who could wolf down a hoagie faster than my sister, Brandy. Don't inhale it. We're not in that big of a hurry" She laughed so hard she almost choked. I patted her on the back and asked, "Do you want to clean up a little?" She nodded and handed me the Mexican wedding shirt and straw hat. I showed her to the bathroom. The swelling in her cheek was subsiding. She used my comb to untangle her hair, and I made a mental note to save any raven strands that remained.

"I'm really nervous. What do we do now?" she asked.

Mickey said, "I figure we should call the sheriff's office and let them take you home. They expect it. We saw a deputy this morning, and he showed us your picture."

Missy grimaced. "I didn't know the cops were already involved. I bet my mother called them before Nollen could stop her. That's going to really complicate things."

Mic shook his head. "Maybe, maybe not. If they show up with you, it will certainly put your stepfather on guard. It may give you a reprieve from his advances. At least for a day or two. I think Tommy has a plan in mind. He's the mastermind of our little group. He grabs onto a problem like a dog with a bone and won't let it go. If there is a solution, he *will* figure it out."

She was unconvinced, but reluctantly agreed. "Make the call."

I reached for the phone, but Mickey snatched it away from me. "I'll do the honors. The dispatcher is a friend of Momma's. She'll recognize me and it may avert some awkward questions." He looked up the number and dialed.

"Hello, this is Mickey O'Dell. I found Missy Turnbow. No, no, no. She's fine. We're at the Nutscalder residence at the end of Kickapoo Street. Theodore and I spoke to a deputy this morning and he told us to call right away if we found her. Just following orders. Yeah, she got mad at her folks and took a skedaddle last night and got lost. We're visiting with her now. She's really sorry about all the fuss." He winked at Missy as he listened to the dispatcher's instructions. "Nathaniel Nutscalder's place; right next to the landfill gate. Okay, we'll be waiting on the porch." He hung up the receiver. "They are sending a car over. Everybody take a deep breath and stick to the story. No matter what. That's the only way this is going to work."

Missy and I both breathed a sigh if relief. Mic wrote down the phone number to Casa O'Dell and gave it to her. "Hold on to this number. I have four sisters, so there's someone home to answer almost anytime, day or night. If you get in a pinch, just let us know. We'll come running."

We were only outside for a minute before the sheriff arrived. He parked his car at the curb and stared at us for a long moment before stepping out. Missy took a deep breath and walked right up to him.

"Sheriff, I'm so embarrassed about all of this trouble. I've been fighting with my parents about school and I did a stupid thing. I stormed out last night, got lost, and ended up sleeping in that old car across the street after being chased by a pack of dogs." She pointed at the Studebaker and, as if on cue, three of the strays appeared at the landfill gate, snarling and barking. Missy moved in close to the sheriff's side. A nice touch.

Mickey stomped on a warped porch board. "I came over this morning to help Teddy repair this porch. Suddenly we looked up and there she was!"

The dogs were getting noisier by the second. Otho pulled a 45 automatic out of his holster and fired one shot. The biggest dog dropped, and the others ran.

The sheriff picked up the spent shell casing and said, "Young lady, you take the front seat. You two hooligans in the back."

The sheriff was mostly silent all the way to Fairhaven. Missy explained how she didn't fit in well at the Catholic school and wanted to come back to the Knob for senior high. She prattled on, and I worried about her overplaying the part. Missy glanced back at me and I frowned and drew my hand across my throat. She got the message.

When we pulled up, Maris and Nollen were waiting by the curb. Missy went straight to her mother, who hugged her and then scolded her for the misadventure. Nollen was pacing back and forth with his hands stuffed deep in his pockets, nervous as a crippled goose in a pond full of alligators. We kept to our seats while he and Otho had a terse exchange. The ladies moved into the house, as Embers nodded at the sheriff's remarks.

When Sheriff Wheat returned to the car, he lit a cigarette, stared straight forward, and said, "I wasn't born yesterday, so make no mistake; I ain't buying any of this shit-brick story." He glanced back in the rearview mirror before continuing. "Y'all got anything to say to me?"

A lump formed in my throat. We had to give him something.

Mic said, "Teddy talked to Missy more than me. He can fill you in on the details."

I leaned forward and said, " The school situation is bad, but Mic and I believe the story goes a lot deeper than that. Missy thinks there may be drugs involved. Nothing she can prove. Embers might be taking advantage of her mother's habit and illness. We suspect he's going after Missy. You know, in a nasty, perverted way. Is there anything you can do?"

"Do you have any witnesses? Any proof?"

"No, sir."

"I can keep my ear to the ground, but that's all. There's nothing I can do *officially* unless Maris makes a complaint and is willing to press charges. The courts are reluctant to act on family related sexual misconduct. It's too hard to prove. Unless we have a credible adult witness, they'll just write it off to teen hysteria. It's a shitty situation, but that's just the way it is."

Otho gripped the steering wheel and let out a long sigh. "You guys want me to drop y'all off somewhere?"

Mic replied, "If you could drop us off at my house, we would be much obliged. We're having hot links for supper. You're welcome to join us."

The lawman snuffed out the cigarette in his ashtray and patted his belly. "Thanks for the offer, but I would die of heartburn if Patti didn't kill me first."

As we rode through town, everyone waved. Otho acknowledged with a nod and muttered each person's name under his breath. It was 5:00 on the nose as we pulled into the gravel driveway of Casa O'Dell. Danni was picking up Brandy for their nightly foray to Beauregard Parish and the swamp show at Muddy Mike's.

Brandy sauntered up to the patrol car and puckered her lips at the sheriff. He rolled down the window, and she leaned in, almost touching him, but not quite. "What did these little turds do this time, Sheriff Wheat? Pee on the sidewalk? Steal some candy? Look up Sara Tyler's skirt?" She winked at me. Her irreverence was legendary. Women hated it. Men loved it. She knew it.

It was Otho's turn to perform. "Aw girl, you've got it all wrong about these fellas. You and I are in stellar company. They're the heroes of the hour. Found the little Turnbow princess and got her safely home to the loving arms of her family."

Brandy blew an enormous bubble with her gum. When the orb burst, she licked it off her lips provocatively. "No shit! I may have to amend my opinion about these rogues."

Danni hollered from her car, "Come on, Brandy, we're gonna be late … again!"

"Gotta go. Those roughnecks get real irritable if they don't get their full quota of titties." She leaned over and gave Otho a quick peck on the cheek. In the blink of an eye, they were gone.

Otho shook his head and said, "If I were a real straight-shooting lawman, I would arrest both of those girls and send them off to juvenile detention. They're both underage."

My smart aleck mouth blurted, "Then you would have to help the sheriff of Beauregard Parish quell the riots."

A low, throaty chuckle erupted into a full-fledged guffaw. "Indeed, I would, Master Nutscalder! Indeed, I would."

Since the back doors of a patrol car won't open from the inside, Otho had to exit the vehicle to let us out. I must have flinched while climbing out. He grabbed my collar and pulled up my shirt, exposing the colorful contusions along my thorax.

Mic said, "Sheriff, that there is Nathaniel Nutscalder's handiwork. Theodore has been pissing blood, too."

Otho bent down to study the lesions. "Hmm ... why don't we take a little trip over to Dr. DeSilva's office for a professional opinion?"

"I'm alright. The bleeding from my kidney stopped this morning. The worst is over. It's healing up on its own."

Otho put his hand on my forehead. "Are you coughing up any blood?" He looked at Mickey for the straight answer. He just shrugged. "Promise me you will call my office if you run a fever, or get short of breath." I nodded and Mic crossed his heart.

"I'll have a little 'Come to Jesus' meeting with your daddy."

"Please don't bother, Sheriff. It won't do any good. He blames me for all his woes. I'm used to it. Don't waste your breath."

A sly smile emerged as the lawman pulled down my shirt and straightened his Stetson hat.

"I have a God-given talent for persuasion. My little pep talks are very inspirational and always enthusiastically received."

11

Supper at Casa O'Dell was glorious. Hot links, corn fritters, and homemade vanilla ice cream. The younger girls and I took turns on the hand crank ice cream maker, while Mic related our modified rescue story to Vera.

She hugged each one of us. "Meeting with the governor and now this! Pete will be so proud of you, boys. I can't wait to tell him on visiting day." The poor woman was starving for anything uplifting to relay to her incarcerated husband. "I'll sleep better tonight, knowing that God is finally answering my prayers." Vera got on the phone and spent the rest of the evening relating details of our heroic endeavors to everyone she knew.

Mickey was all lathered up about the prospect of salvaging the Amboyna wood for some quick cash. "Let's cut off a two-foot section. Something we can easily handle. A little teaser for my Uncle Murl.

Maybe we can make enough money to buy a bus ticket to Huntsville for Momma. I need a new pair of jeans and you need some new tennis shoes. Those puppies stink to high heaven."

I inspected the ratty Keds. They had served me well, but alas, Mic was right. They were falling apart at the seams and smelled like catfish Charlie fermenting in a yak herder's bed sack. I wondered if Missy had noticed. My mind turned to a promise I made three days earlier.

"When we finish, I have to visit Aunt Tilde and Rufus. I promised her I'd cross the water on Monday. I'm late."

"I'll go with you. We better fatten up old Rufus. If you break a promise to Tilde, she might put a curse on you. Turn you into a frog or a dog. That's what the colored boys on the Louisiana side tell me."

"I think those guys are pulling your leg, Mickey. Aunt Tilde would never put a curse on us, or anybody else for that matter. She says, 'Good or evil; whatever you put forth in the world will eventually come back to roost on your head.' I'm not sure about all the visions and magic stuff, but I believe that."

We settled in for the night and watched *The Curse of the Werewolf* on the tiny black and white Philco Autovision TV. It was a remarkably un-terrifying movie. Me, Mic, and his three younger sisters all fell asleep on the living room floor. I woke up early and took a hot soaking bath while the rest of the family snoozed. I had to cover myself with a washcloth when the middle sister wandered in and peed without so much as a how-do-you-do. Modesty is a rare commodity in a home with six occupants and one bathroom.

Vera washed my new duds the day before and ironed them to perfection. I was glad to shed the sweatpants and Mexican wedding shirt. I wiped off the Keds and doused them with aftershave from the medicine cabinet, but it didn't help much.

Mickey put a pen and paper by the telephone and extracted a promise from each of his sisters to make detailed notes if Missy Turnbow called. We were both surprised at Brandy's sincere interest in the subject. She and Sheriff Otho Wheat had the same instincts for BS. She was suspicious of our sanitized version of the previous day's events.

We called Tommy and told him everything went exactly as planned. He pledged to meet us later at the Grotto for our jaunt over the trestle to The Grove. He never missed an opportunity to visit with Tilde and marvel at all the trinkets, amulets, and charms.

Mic grabbed a handsaw out of the tool shed and we headed to the Cusser Club. When we reached the fence, Aunt Tilde was on her porch, opera glasses in hand. We waved, and she waved back. We wanted to enter unobserved, so we loitered on the edge of the Casablanca parking lot and considered our options.

Mic said, "We will just have to hang out in the Grotto until she leaves the porch. I hope it ain't too long. Uncle Murl closes the cabinet shop early on Wednesdays, to eat fried chicken and play dominoes at the Methodist Church."

The words were barely out of his mouth when a brand-new Buick Electra 225 convertible pulled up in front of the yellow cottage. Three well-dressed ladies bailed out, eager for Tilde's clairvoyant revelations.

We took advantage of the distraction and were under the wisteria in an instant. The hornet's nest was bustling with activity, so we gave the irritable creatures a wide berth.

Upon entering the ground floor, we found Humper curled up at the bottom of the dumbwaiter shaft. He whimpered and feebly wagged his tail. He looked sick. We knelt down and gave him a scratch behind the ears. Mickey said, "Poor Humper is getting old. Look at his eyes. There are clouds behind his pupils, just like Tommy's."

It was true. I felt a pang of guilt for not noticing it before. Mickey thumped a flea off my arm and said, "When we score some moolah, maybe we can get him one of those newfangled flea collars and an old blanket to sleep on. We could buy a bag of bologna ends and chicken necks from Mr. Obermeyer."

I leaned over and nudged my friend. "That's a lot of maybes. You're a good guy, Mickey O'Dell. Always thinking of others. Even an old cur like Humper. We can't do any of the things we've talked about this morning until we put some muscle behind that saw blade." Without another word, my companion gave the aging mongrel another affectionate head maul before hurrying up the stairs.

The Amboyna column appeared even bigger than the day before. Mic pushed against it, but it didn't budge. Further inspection revealed the massive pedestal was bolted to the floor.

"C'mon, Nutscalder, we are going to have to get this thing horizontal before we can carve it up. Flex those scrawny muscles and help me topple this big, beautiful sumbitch." We applied our shoulders to the object as he counted down. "One, two, three, push." The floor splintered. After six repetitions, the pillar fell to the floor in a deafening crash. A plume of dust filled the entire chamber, and the brass sextant broke off and bounced across the unlevel floor. A wall panel behind us popped open, revealing a cache of rusted ceremonial swords.

While the dust settled, I took a moment to examine the blades. The leather wrapped handles crumbled at the touch. "Pretty awful shape, but we might polish these up and rework the handles with some leather scraps."

Still coughing from the dust, Mic fingered the tip. "That might work. They should bring a couple of bucks at the Saturday flea market. Let's come back to these later. A bigger prize awaits." He shook the handsaw, making a warbling sound.

The saw was dull, and progress was painfully slow. We took turns working the cut. My arms were quivering with exhaustion a half hour later when the top twenty inches finally separated and fell away. Mickey hammered on his chest and made a Tarzan yodel like Johnny Weissmuller. The falsetto ululation triggered a symphony of cackles from the crows on the roof, as he hoisted the log on his shoulder. "Payday awaits, Cheeta."

I responded with a monkey hoot, like jungle man's simian sidekick.

As I glanced toward the altar, a spark of inspiration struck. "Let's take that skull to Aunt Tilde. It would make an interesting addition to her collection of charms and talismans."

Mic tossed the log down the stairs and it tumbled end over end before coming to rest against the wall below the mural of General Custer. We shoved it through the gap in the door and rolled it to the edge of the property. The Buick raced out of The Grove just as we crawled under the fence. As we dusted off and hid the skull under a pile of brush, Tilde Kellum emerged from her front door, stuffing a wad of cash into her bra. She crossed herself in the Catholic manner and lit a twisted cheroot cigar before plopping down in her rocking chair. I had seen her perform the same ritual a hundred times.

Mickey said, "After we unload this bauble, we will get Daddy's wheelbarrow to take across the river. It's bigger than that rinky-dink wagon of yours, and will save us some time, too." I agreed, and we took turns lugging the wood chunk a half-mile uphill to Murl's cabinet shop. Mickey snickered as I struggled with the weight, but I wasn't about to let him outdo me.

The elder O'Dell was locking the front door of his shop as we arrived.

"Uncle Murl, I have something you might find interesting," Mic said as he hoisted the heavy block up to the man's face. Murl's nostrils flared as he sniffed the sweet herbaceous scent of freshly cut end.

"A-m-b-o-y-n-a!" dragging out the syllables in a swell of admiration. "Where did you find this beauty?"

I said, "Rolled off a garbage truck right in front of my house. Darndest thing. I was going to throw it on the burn pile, but Mickey said it was a valuable piece of rare African wood."

"Southeast Asian," the artist replied as he rubbed the fluted surface. "I fell in love with this wood while I was in Burma during World War II. Buddhist monks decorated their temples with it." He unlocked the door and said, "Come inside, gentlemen. My domino game can wait."

Murl O'Dell's shop was filled with cigar humidors, jewelry boxes, liquor cabinets, and wine racks. Each piece was inlaid with exotic woods of all colors, flawlessly sanded and lacquered to an impeccable sheen. He poured linseed oil in the palm of his hand and slathered the surface of our prize, rubbing vigorously. The subtle details of the grain emerged, and he licked his lips like a lonely hermit admiring a sexy girl. The man was a decisive man of few words. "Twenty now. Twenty Friday."

Mic poked out his bottom lip in a churlish pout. "Well, I was hoping for a little more, but it's a deal if we can borrow that big garden cart of yours for a couple of hours."

Murl never looked up from the object of his caress. "You can have the damn cart."

"Done," Mickey said as he plucked two Hamiltons out of the man's hand.

"If you boys find any more, I'm always buying."

* * *

The heavy-duty garden cart would carry five times as much as the Radio Flyer, and twice as much as Pete's wheelbarrow. We threw in a pickaxe and four-pronged potato hoe, useful implements for gathering the rotten pulp for Rufus. Mickey figured the time saved might allow us to get back to Dix Knob and go shopping for jeans and shoes before day's end.

The MP 12:20 was already rolling across the Sabine, so we had to wait before we could cross over to retrieve the skull. I always delayed a few minutes after a locomotive passed before heading over the metal truss trestle. The vibration from the train caused the corroded paint to flake off and turn into a fine caustic powder that lingered in the humid air. It was laced with lead, mercury, and other toxins, and Arthur Rumkin claimed the poison dust would make your dick shrivel up. His medical expertise was questionable, but I wasn't about to risk it.

When the caboose passed, a chilling scene confronted us. Galton Grails had Tommy Crum in a headlock, while three of his minions took turns peering through his thick glasses. Galton's black shirt accentuated the inflamed, pus oozing lacerations on his left cheek. His head was shaved bald.

Grails said, "I caught Mr. Magoo walking along my railroad track. He refused to pay the toll, so I'll just take all his money." He rifled through Tommy's pockets and held up a crumpled wad of bills.

Mickey yelled, "Rocks, and the high ground, Teddy Boy!" We mounted the tracks, grabbing the sun-scorched slag rocks before our adversaries caught on to the strategy.

"Toadies first," I replied. My first throw was too high, and the boy just ducked.

"Guts and nuts, Nutscalder. Guts and nuts!" Mic screamed as his first volley found its mark, striking the nearest flunky in the groin.

Galton pushed Tommy to the ground and stomped hard on his back. "You guys take O'Dell! I've got a score to settle with Nutscalder."

I grasped a stone in each fist and braced myself as Grails charged. The other three ruffians converged on Mic as he hoisted the pickaxe out of the cart.

I stepped aside and tried to trip Grails as he swung at me. The strategy I used at Rhinelander Park didn't work. His fist struck my left collarbone, and my arm exploded with an electric bolt of pain. I saw him favor the left knee for a millisecond and realized that Danni's well-placed kick must still be sore.

Crouching low, I lunged and hit him at the waist. Clutching his left thigh, I tried to force the knee backward, but the bastard was too strong for me. He threw three hard kidney punches, and I collapsed in a heap. Going down, I gave one last shove against his kneecap and heard an audible pop. Galton screamed in agony and faltered just long enough for me to escape his grip and crab crawl out of reach.

I glanced up just in time to see Tommy jump on him from behind, wrapping his arms around the stumbling bully's neck. Grails bucked and twisted, but Tommy held onto him like a champion rodeo cowboy. Still on all fours, I scurried forward and clasped my arms around the thug's ankles. It was a pathetic effort, but effective. He toppled face down in the rocky slag with Tommy riding his back all the way to the ground. We both held fast, knowing we had a tiger by the tail. We couldn't run. We couldn't let go.

As Galton screamed threats of castration, a shadow emerged over my shoulder. I braced for a blow, figuring the other three attackers had dispatched Mickey and were now turning on us.

A light tap on my shoulder. The sun was in my eyes, and all I could see was the naked end of the pickaxe handle.

"Gentlemen, you may cease your exertions," Mic said as he stepped on Galton's neck. "Matters are well in hand." Our liberator was sporting a black eye and a bloody lip, but seemed completely oblivious to the wounds. The metal head of the pickaxe was missing. I pictured it buried in a toadie's head. Mic took the heavy wooden stave and whacked Grails twice on the crown of his head. The implement made a satisfying, hollow *tock-tock* sound with each cranial percussion.

Grails howled, "For fuck's sake, O'Dell, that's too much. I'd never do that to you."

Mickey's eyes widened in comical amusement.

"You expect me to believe that? You sumbitches ganged up on Tommy, beat him up, and stole his money and his glasses. By the way, where are those glasses? If there is one scratch on those lenses, I'm going to shove this stick all the way up your ass until it comes out of your mouth." *Tock-tock* as the ax handle kissed the bully's naked scalp again.

Galton winced and yelled, "Virgil, find them damn glasses before this fucker puts another knot on my head!"

I looked around and saw a timid face peek out from behind the railroad signal shack twenty yards away. The toadie yelled, "I ain't getting nowhere near O'Dell. He whooped all three of us with that ax handle. I'll bring the glasses halfway if one of them other boys will meet me. Otherwise, you can kiss my ass, Galton."

Mic bent over to the bully's ear and shifted his foot to the middle of his back. "Galton, it sounds like your buddy Virgil needs a little encouragement." *Tock, Tock. Tock.* Three more head knots.

"Virgil, get your sorry ass over here .... *now!*"

Tommy was sitting on a crosstie, squinting, desperately attempting to see where the voice was coming from. I volunteered to meet the boy halfway, and as I approached, Virgil was cleaning the lenses with a sweaty shirttail.

He said, "I didn't bend these glasses. I swear to God they was already bent."

"Yeah, I know. Some girls bent them while they were tickling him a couple of nights ago at the festival."

Virgil shrugged his shoulders, held out the glasses at arm's length, and took two steps back before speaking. "Galton is really pissed at you, Nutscalder. He blames you for getting arrested. He's on a strict curfew now, and can't be out after seven o'clock at night. Can't get caught drinking or smoking, and a big list of other stuff. They found lice on him at the jail and shaved his head and balls with a dry razor. He's got a flaming raw crotch burn, real bad. He's out to get you. Fair warning. Don't tell him I told you. Tell Mickey O'Dell he won't get no more trouble from me—ever."

"Where are your other two buddies?" I asked.

"They done took off. I'm taking off too. Galton's gonna be in a foul mood for a while. We'll be steering clear of him for a few days. Y'all hold him down until I can get out of sight."

With that, the boy turned and ran down the tracks. I handed Tommy his glasses and turned back to the developing hostage situation. Mic was tapping the steel rail right next to Galton's ear. *Tock, Tock, Tock.* Several greasy blue buboes glowed on the bully's noggin.

Grails whimpered, "Jesus, sweet Jesus, don't hit me no more."

Mickey raised his voice to the sky and shouted. "We have a convert! A repentant sinner who is calling on the name of the Lord for salvation. Hallelujah! I'm filled with the Holy Spirit." Mic cupped his ear and gazed toward heaven. "What's that, Lord? Should we baptize the evil asshole before he resumes his wicked ways? Thus saith the Lord." *Tock, Tock.* "Can I get a witness up here?"

O'Dell reduced his opponent to a miserable mass of quivering flesh. He twisted his captive's arm behind his back and lifted him off the ground. "To the river, Butt Crust. It's time to atone for a lifetime of sin and remorse. Brother Tommy, would you grace us with a hymn for the occasion?"

Tommy waved his arms above his head and shuffled his feet on the crunchy railroad slag, dancing like a fanatic at a tent revival.

"Amen, Preacher Mic, please join me in that fine old Hosanna we all turn to in times of tempest and trouble!"

I was sinking deep in sin,
Far from the peaceful shore,
Very deeply stained within,
Sinking to rise no more;
Then the Master of the sea
Heard my despairing cry,
From the waters lifted me–
Now safe am I!

Love lifted me,
Love lifted me,
When nothing else could help,
Love lifted meeeeeee…!

Mic joined in the soulful refrain. Nutscalders aren't churchgoers, so I didn't know any hymns. Apparently, Grails didn't either. It was the only thing we had in common.

As we reached the river's edge, Galton fell to the ground on his knees, covering his knotty head with his hands, begging for mercy. "I'm afraid of the water, Mickey. I can't swim. I'll shit myself."

I put in my two cents' worth. "Don't torture the boy, Mic. Let me just piss on him."

Sporting wild eyes and a comical air of righteous umbrage, Tommy said, "Theodore! I'm no theologian, but I'm absolutely certain that God would not approve. To be truly repentant, the sinner *must* be submerged."

Mic offered Grails a way out. "I'll tell you what I'll do, Galton. If you can sing a single stanza of any church hymn, I won't dunk you in the river. Any hymn at all … 'How Great Thou Art?' … 'Rock of Ages?' … 'Amazing Grace?'"

Slobber was dripping out of the boy's mouth as his feeble mind searched for a tune. "Give me a second. Hold on, I'm thinking … Jingle bells, jingle bells, Santa Claus is coming to town…"

"No deal, dickhead! We're gonna go full Baptist!" Mickey yelled as he kicked Galton in the nuts and shoved him into the river. The miscreant did a noisy belly flop, sunk beneath the surface, bobbed twice, and finally came up sputtering. "I ain't gonna cause … *cough* … no more trouble for nobody … *cough, cough* … I'll do good, I promise."

Mickey raised the ax handle, "Hallelujah, praise the Lord. Let us all rejoice for a sinner who has seen the light of repentance and salvation!"

Grails sloshed ashore and hobbled off with one hand rubbing his knobby scalp, and the other holding up shit-laden breeches. None of us even considered pursuit. Mic had won the day.

A round of enthusiastic applause echoed from across the river. Old folks from The Grove had gathered on the riverbank to watch the spectacle. Melchior and Dipdottle would have been delighted. Mic took a bow and Tommy and I stepped forward for a curtain call. Tilde clapped and motioned for us to cross the water.

12

ON OUR WAY BACK TO THE CUSSER CLUB FENCE TO RETRIEVE the ceremonial skull, Mic filled us in on his part in the scuffle. "They were pummeling me pretty good when I grabbed the pickaxe. As I swung at Virgil, the damn iron blade broke free and flew off into the bushes. I panicked for a second, but immediately realized the handle alone was easier to maneuver and a much more formidable weapon. I whacked the biggest toadie right in the knackers, and he went down in a heap. Virgil grabbed the end, but I shoved it into his gut and knocked the wind out of him. The other skid mark saw the writing on the wall and ran off like a scared rabbit."

As we walked by Casablanca, Arthur Rumkin was painting a new set of foldaway shutters and whistled when he caught sight of Mic's bloody face.

"Jiminy Christmas. That's a real shiner! What the heck have you boys been up to?"

We filled him in on the fight and the scandalmonger was greatly amused by Mic's artistic scalp work and the spontaneous rite of baptism.

Rumkin exclaimed, "Classic! The whole Grails clan is a bunch of inbred reprobates and scoundrels. It's about time the delinquent boy got a comeuppance. Hey, I heard you guys saved the little Turnbow darling. Come on in and tell me all about it while I get some ice for Mickey's eye. The townsfolk say y'all found her in an abandoned car, cornered by a bunch of stray dogs, hysterical and screaming."

I said, "That's not exactly what happened, Mr. Rumkin. She was in the car and got frightened by the dogs, but she wasn't hysterical or anything like that. We called the sheriff's office just like we were told, and they took her home. That's all there was to it. The sweet girl has had some problems lately. Her mom is sick. What other rumors have you heard?"

Rumkin chipped some ice cubes out of the freezer behind the bar, wrapped them in a cup towel, and handed the poultice to Mic. "You guys are due for a reward from Nollen Embers. He was trolling all over town, telling folks he would pay a hefty reward to get his sweet Meroticia back home, safe and sound. Do you guys realize that the poor girl's name has e-r-o-t-i-c right in the middle? I don't think that's a coincidence. No wonder she prefers to go by Missy."

Rumkin was in full throttle yakkination and there was no off switch, so I figured we would indulge his verbal diatribe for a while to catch up on the rumor mill, if nothing else.

He continued. "Embers has been talking to a shrink up in Houston about getting Maris on a program at some special clinic." He used his fingers to make air quotation marks around the term "special clinic" as he drew out the syllables *ad infinitum*, as only a true East Texas redneck can. "Spay-shee-yull - cull-in-nick."

He laughed at his cleverness before continuing. "That sumbitch wants to get his hands on her money. If he gets elected mayor, there will be no stopping him. Marlon Kutz, who owns the cleaners off the square, was thinking about running against him, but dropped that idea after getting some late-night phone calls threatening to burn his store down. If Embers runs unopposed, he wins by default. I'm telling you boys, that greaser ain't no good. There are all kinds of rumors. Two of his competitors have vanished. Presumed dead. The DA over in Terrebonne Parish tried to get an indictment on murder last year, but dropped the charges after a key witness mysteriously disappeared. The fuzz can't get any evidence on him. He always gets away scot-free."

I was eager to help Missy, so I concocted a tidbit of slander, hoping it might filter through to Embers and distract him from his despicable advances for a while.

In a low whisper, I said, "I overheard some guys talking outside the Palisades yesterday. Apparently, some of Nollen's own business partners are about to stage a takeover. They mentioned a turf war with the Cajun mafia. I thought that was a myth. Have you heard anything like that, Mr. Rumkin?"

Arthur's eyes lit up in conspiratorial delight. I could visualize the schizophrenic gerbils swarming in his head.

"I will check into that, Master Nutscalder. Nollen is teetering on the brink of disaster. Everyone thinks his wife is crazy, but he might be the biggest loony of 'em all. You boys grab a soda on my tab. I'll leave six bits on the bar for Rick. Excuse me while I make a few phone calls." He bolted to the payphone down the hall next to the restrooms. We grabbed an RC apiece and rushed to retrieve the skull while Rumkin was busy adding grist to the rumor mill.

* * *

After stuffing the calvarium in a paper sack, we headed across the trestle. A few stray thunderheads sprinkled, making the crossties slicker than snot on a doorknob. Simultaneously cursing and praying, we slipped, skidded, and stumbled along the treacherous bridge, going single file straight between the rails. When we reached the other end, the fragrant smell of peach and plum blossoms, mixed with gardenia and honeysuckle, greeted our nostrils. It was morbidly humid and the light precipitation turned the atmosphere into a sauna. The Louisiana side of the Sabine was a step back in time. The tiny frame shotgun houses, brightly painted with narrow porches, were a remnant of the late 1800s southern working-class domicile.

Tilde Kellum's bright yellow home had a blue front door, emblazoned with a voodoo veve symbol of an open hand with a dove perched on the fingertips. No one but Tilde knew what the symbols represented, but the benevolent-appearing artwork was reassuring to all who visited.

The kind mystic was glad to see us. Rufus seemed to know a meal was coming. He paced back and forth in his pen, sniffing the air with his narrow, agile snout. The animal could have easily burrowed out of the enclosure, but seemed to have no interest in doing so. Everyone assumed Tilde cast a spell on the creature to make him stay put. I suspect he was content to be sheltered and well fed. The Louisiana Forestry and Fisheries employees frequently donated live meal grubs, propagated for zoos and aviaries. I provided some wild variety to his diet.

The three of us made quick work of the wood gathering. Citizens of The Grove piled up the limbs and logs from the previous fall pruning in a large mound behind an old community smokehouse. The decaying pile was ripe with termite larvae and beetle eggs. Within half an hour, we had delivered a cart full of mealy pulp to the enclosure and the primordial creature grunted heartily as he consumed the squirming delicacies. Aunt Tilde cackled and smiled as she watched the bark fly during Rufus' enthusiastic feeding frenzy.

We made a group presentation of the skull. Mic and Tommy appointed me as spokesperson.

"Aunt Tilde, we brought a gift to add to your collection of magical knick-knacks."

She switched the bag back and forth between her hands as if weighing it. Finally looking inside, perplexity turned to wonderment.

"Lordy, lordy, lordy, what a pleasant surprise. You boys brought old Tilde the skull from the Cusser Club Lodge!"

"How did you know?" Mic asked.

"Where else would you have got it? I've been watching the comings and goings across this muddy river for over 60 years. If those rich old white men knew I had possession of their ceremonial skull, they would spin in their graves!"

Tommy looked uneasy. "Do you want us to take it back?" he asked.

Tilde shook her head vigorously. "Heaven forbid! I'm gonna keep this wonderful gift. I'd never give up a fine prize like this! I was just stating a fact. Those old knights were scoundrels and libertines back in the day. They got away with a lot of illegal stuff during Prohibition. Rumrunners would come up the river from Cuba and Jamaica by way of the Gulf. They used all this secret society stuff to keep ordinary folks away. They called themselves the Knights of the Mystic Chalice. There wasn't anything mystical about their chalice. It was always full of booze. All the town's elite were members in the '20s and '30s, but by the time Awful Audrey hit, they were in decline. Barely anybody went upstairs by the mid-'50s. The taproom did real well, but the lodge members died off one by one until there were only a dozen left. They fought for a while to get the building fixed up after the big storm, but the expense was just too much. Some squatters moved in and out for a while until they put up that fence. When Rick Blaine built Casablanca, it was the death knell of that grand old building. There's nobody left to make a fuss about the skull. So tell me all about it. How did you boys find a way inside?"

We recounted the timeline about the discovery of Humper's secret passage, the Amboyna, and the robes. She nodded approvingly. "I'm impressed. No one has ventured into that building for years. Only crows, rats, and spiders. I'm going to put this skull in a place of honor on the tarot table. My clients will love that. I've had some visions lately. You fellows come on inside the house. I've got gifts aplenty for my allies against villainy."

I thought the last comment was peculiar, but the other boys didn't appear to take notice at all.

Shotgun houses are a very efficient design, with no wasted space. The front door opens into a living room; another door on the back wall opens directly into the kitchen, and a bedroom after that. The living room was twelve by twelve and served as her consulting suite. A round table was surrounded by four chairs and covered with a red silk cloth and a crystal ball at the center, just as one would expect. Tilde decorated the walls floor to ceiling with bleached animal skulls, feather collages, chalk drawings, dried flowers, rosary beads, and the prayer cards of saints and mystics. Photographs of satisfied clients were scattered throughout. There was a bronze-framed picture of a young, mixed-race couple hanging in a place of honor. Candles illuminated their faces and medals of Saint Anthony of Padua, the patron saint of lost persons, surrounded the photograph. The girl was a beautiful blonde and the handsome black man was muscled up like a linebacker. There seemed to be something haunting about them, but nothing I could put my finger on.

Tilde went into the bedroom and emerged with an armful of items and spread them out on the table. To Mickey she gave a fine dark brown leather vest with decorative tooling.

"I fashioned this vest out of genuine rhinoceros hide, blessed by Miriam Duvalier, a powerful voodoo priestess."

Mic put it on. "This looks kinda like the one John Wayne wore in the movie *True Grit*. Just my style. It's perfect, Aunt Tilde."

Next, she took a small Aladdin-style oil lamp out of a black lacquered box and handed it to Tommy. "I filled this lamp with the oil of an albino whale from the South China Sea. Every night before bedtime, you light this lamp and stare at the flame for five minutes uninterrupted. No more. No less. It will help soothe your troubled eyes and slow the progress of your disease." Tommy hugged her neck and whispered something in her ear.

She turned to me and held out a clenched fist. "This is for you to give to the girl that destiny implores you to help. When the time comes, you'll know it. Until then, keep it next to your heart." She opened her palm, revealing a silver chain necklace, with a heart-shaped green malachite stone pendant, wrapped in a web of fine copper wire.

"I hope I can live up to the challenge," I said as I slipped the necklace over my head. The stone was cool and soothing.

Tilde suddenly plopped down in the chair and let out a deep groan. Her eyes rolled back in her head as a violent convulsion gripped her body. We all gasped in horror. Within ten seconds the frightful seizure reached a crescendo and passed just as suddenly as it started. She glanced at each of us. "A storm of reckoning is coming. You boys are at the center of it. Be brave. *Alea iacta est*. The die is cast." With that, she rose and retired to the bedroom. "This old woman needs to rest. There are some trials ahead for me as well. I'll continue to petition the spirits for protection."

We took that as our cue to skedaddle. O'Dell pushed Tommy and me aside as he beat it out the door. Mic feared neither man nor beast, but supernatural affairs terrified him.

Jumping off the porch, Mic said, "That's some spooky shit. I love Aunt Tilde, but she scares the hell out of me sometimes."

As we headed back to the trestle, a frantic car horn honking from the Dix Knob side of the river interrupted our conversation.

There was someone in the Casablanca parking lot. Mic ran back to Tilde's porch and grabbed her opera glasses. "It's Brandy and Danni. Something is wrong."

13

BRANDY WAS WAITING FOR US AT THE END OF THE TRESTLE while Danni nursed the Star Chief at idle, afraid to kill the engine because of a bad battery.

She said, "Missy phoned the house and sounded pretty desperate. I could tell there was fear in her voice. Y'all want to let me know what's going on?"

Mic let the cat out of the bag. "Her stepfather must have made another nasty pass at her. I thought surely he would lay off..." His voice trailed off as he realized his mistake. It was too late for me to step in and stop him from revealing the real reason Missy ran away. As far as everyone else was concerned, the conflict was over the boarding school situation.

Brandy gritted her teeth and stamped her foot. "Dammit, I owe Danni five dollars. She said that dirty old pervert was diddling Missy.

I said nooooo waaaay, my brother and his sweet friend, Teddy Nutscalder, would never lie to me about something so important. But I guess I was wrong about you two." She punched Mic in the chest and twisted my right nipple. It hurt like hell, and I yelped like a scolded puppy.

Tommy threw up his hands and backed up before throwing me and Mic under the bus. "Honest to goodness, Brandy, I had no idea these two louses lied to you!"

Brandy continued, "Missy said the situation with her mom was coming to a head. She acted like y'all would know what she was talking about. Let's get back to the car before Danni runs out of gas. You guys need to get over to Fairhaven Street as quickly as possible and find out what's going on."

The old car was shaking and sputtering as we reached the parking lot. Danni popped open the trunk so Tommy and Mic could deposit their gifts. The rhino vest and whale-oil lamp found cushy company among a mishmash of leather whips, wigs, and lacy bras.

On the way over to the North Side of the Knob, Brandy filled us in on her brief conversation with Missy. The call was hurried. Embers was apparently skulking nearby and she couldn't risk getting caught on the phone. Brandy and Danni threatened to bail out if we didn't come clean with the entire story, so we told them everything. Bite marks and all. The incestuous abuse infuriated them, and they vowed to help. Missy told Brandy she would leave the back gate next to the alley unlocked. We should wrap a ribbon or handkerchief to the latch post, so she could see the signal from her second-story window and know we were waiting. She would try to sneak out at dusk and meet us behind the greenhouse.

I nudged Mic. "Let's use the money from your uncle Murl to buy a few gallons of gas and a new battery for this tuna boat. We're in over our heads. Maybe these clever girls can give us some ideas."

He nodded and tapped Danni on the shoulder. "Pull into the Gulf station and we'll change out that shot-to-shit battery and top off the tank. Theodore has a feeling we're gonna need some experienced feminine insight to deal with that perv-nasty bastard."

Mic pumped gas while the service station attendant switched the power cell. Brandy used her legendary charm to convince the guy to extend credit for the cost of the battery. As Mic climbed back in the car, Danni turned around, leaned over, and laid a big, sloppy kiss right on his lips.

He blushed and sputtered, "Say, Danni, I've got a little money left, and I'll wash your car and change the oil after we get done with this little chore." Danni laughed. Brandy snorted in derision. Tommy and I were inspired.

As we turned onto Division Street near midtown, traffic came to a standstill. Townspeople converged on Rhinelander Park, as shopkeepers and customers alike poured out of stores and restaurants. Distracted by the crowd, the driver of a VW Beetle ran up the rear end of a Mercury sedan, blocking the northbound lane. Sara Tyler's mother walked by the car, as Tommy rolled the window down. "Mrs. Tyler, what's all the ruckus about?"

"Some Aggie engineer has been going around town with an electronic contraption that looks like a hoop skirt, searching for the treasure. We all thought he was nuts. Apparently, he's found something." With that, she turned and hurried off. Traffic slowed to a crawl, so Danni pulled the behemoth into the nearest parking space.

Brandy handed me a red bandana. "Teddy, tie this on the metal spike on top of the gate latch post, and that will let Missy know you're there. This traffic isn't going anywhere until the cops come and sort out that wreck. Y'all can walk faster than we can drive. When they clear this up, Danni will drive on over to Fairhaven Street and park in the Kuykendall's driveway, next door to the Turnbow mansion."

Mic protested. "That will be awfully conspicuous. Forgive me, Danni, but if anyone sees this ghetto cruiser in that ritzy neighborhood..."

Brandy swatted at her brother. "We will hold back for half an hour to let you guys get in position and meet with the girl. If anyone asks, I'll just tell them I'm dropping a note in the mail slot regarding Momma's work schedule for the next week."

Brandy's voice trailed off and Danni shouted, "What the hell is that?" It took me a few seconds to figure out what was going on. Tommy had his head stuck out the side window, looking toward the park. He shouted, "It must be the Aggie engineer. That's the craziest contraption I've ever seen!" All four doors of the vehicle opened simultaneously, as we bailed out into an unusual sight.

A tall, slender fellow was outfitted with four wire hoops suspended by leather straps that formed a skirt from waist to ankle. Colored wires interlaced the hoops at various intervals and converged into a metal box strapped to his chest. Headphones completed the outfit. He spun, pivoted, moved forward and back, and side to side, guided by some mysterious signal emitted by the device. Dozens of curious onlookers followed him, fascinated by his odd gyrations. The hoops jiggled with each movement and reminded me of some antebellum undergarments I'd seen Vivian Leigh wear in *Gone with the Wind*.

He placed a stake in the ground, pulled a scrap of paper out of his pocket, studied it for a few seconds, and then headed off in the opposite direction.

Sara Tyler waved at us from the door of the bakery. Brandy and Danni reminded us of the rendezvous point and followed the Aggie treasure hunter, teasing him with the alluring feminine charms for which they were famous.

Tommy pulled some change out of his pocket and said. "I'm getting a hunger pang. Let's grab a jelly roll from the bakery before we head over to Fairhaven Street." My stomach growled loudly, in agreement with my bespectacled friend.

Mic thumped my stomach and said, "Borborygmi."

"Bor-bo what?" I replied.

"Borborygmi. The plural of borborygmus. The growling sound your stomach makes when you're hungry. Everyone thinks you guys are the intelligentsia of our little cadre, and I'm just the eye candy, but I know a thing or two."

Tommy shook his head and laughed. "Congratulations, Mickey, you win the vocabulary contest for the week. Teddy is the eye candy, at least as far as Sara is concerned." He pointed at the girl, who was urgently motioning us over.

Mickey reached over and tousled my hair. "We mustn't dawdle. Lady Boobaliscious beckons." Sara's frizzy strawberry blonde hair was pulled into a high fountain, and she was smattered with flour, sugar, cinnamon, and jams. She looked and smelled like a sexy pastry.

Mic made a yum-yum sound and Tommy said, "As the British would say; she's a bit of crumpet!"

Oblivious to our platitudes, Sara escorted us into the empty shop and loaded us up with sweets as she described the Aggie's strange movements through town.

"Daddy saw him from the window upstairs and thought he had escaped from the Rusk State Mental Hospital. Someone even called the sheriff. Otho said he wasn't breaking any laws and let him go. The Aggie found a couple of coins but wouldn't show them to anybody. A reporter from *The Tattler* said his homemade metal detector has a vay-lee-ants discriminator, whatever that is."

Tommy said, "Detectorists can adjust valence discriminators to ignore certain metals like iron ore, aluminum foil, or tin cans. Less time digging up worthless junk. This guy must be an electronics whiz kid. He might be closing in on the big haul."

Dusk was fast approaching, and Sara invited us to stay while she closed up the shop. Mic offered to pay for our pastries, but she refused.

"All this stuff is going to the homeless shelter after we close, anyway. You guys deserve a treat. I heard y'all got even with Galton Grails. Arthur Rumkin has been repeating the story, and now it's all over town." She looked at me, but I shook my head and pointed to Mic.

"O'Dell did all the work. He took an ax handle and single-handedly whooped Virgil and the other two boys before rescuing me and Tommy from Grails. Preacher Mic baptized Galton in the mighty Sabine. He's the hero. It was hilarious! You should have been there."

Mic basked in the moment's glory. "An O'Dell never runs from a fight. Truth be told, Tommy and Teddy had the scoundrel on the ground. I just tapped out a few punk knots on his ugly head."

I was getting antsy about the time, and was worried Missy might think we'd abandoned her. "Sara, thanks for the great treats. I wish you would let us pay. We would love to stay and help you close the shop, but we have another obligation and it's getting late."

Sara nodded and sighed. "Something to do with that pretty Turnbow girl, I'll bet. She's got the whole town talking. Y'all be careful. A lot of folks think she's just as crazy as her mother."

The statement caught me completely off guard. Thankfully, Mic spoke up. "I think Arthur Rumkin and some of the other gabby gussies have been spinning tales about her. Missy has some issues with her parents and the private school situation. That's all. This rumor mongering is going to hurt the girl, and she doesn't deserve it. It is a private matter and we want to help her keep it that way. Everybody picks on Missy because she comes from a rich family and her mother is craz… has some mental issues." His explanation seemed to satisfy Sara, at least on the surface.

She nodded thoughtfully and said. "I hope you guys can help her out. I know what it's like to be the butt of cruel jokes and rumors. It's no fun."

I bent down, hugged her neck, and kissed her cheek. "You're an angel, Sara Tyler." The other guys followed suit.

A gentle snap sounded as the door locked behind us. After a few steps, I looked back. Why did I always look back? Guilt, no doubt. Sara pressed her cheek against the window, and there was a heart-wrenching sadness in her eyes. A rock formed in the pit of my stomach. A stone of self-loathing. I needed a path to redemption, and a block down the street, inspiration struck.

"Guys, hold on for a minute. There's something I need to do."

I ran back to the bakery and knocked on the door. Mrs. Tyler had returned and was wiping down the countertop. She motioned for me to go away.

"Where's Sara? I have something for her."

Sara appeared out of the back with an armload of dirty linens and cracked open the door, but she didn't say a word. I took the malachite necklace off and slipped it over her head. "I believe this green jewel is the perfect contrast to that wild strawberry hair."

Sara's mouth dropped open as her mother yelled, "Leave her alone! Sara deserves a better guy than you, Theodore Nutscalder."

I backed out to the street, winked at Sara, and yelled back, "That's for damn sure!"

* * *

We reached the alley behind the Turnbow mansion, just as the sun nudged the western horizon. I couldn't reach the top of the latch post, so Mic and I hoisted Tommy up and he wrapped the bandana around the brass *fleur de lis* finial. The gate was unlocked, but we didn't dare enter the yard.

The three of us were peeking through the cedar slats when a gigantic burst of sputtering flatulence diverted our attention. We all turned to see an elderly stooped gentleman with an equally arthritic dachshund on a leash.

"What are you boys doing? Waiting on leftovers from the dinner table?" he asked.

Tommy replied, "Yes sir, just waiting on a handout. Mr. and Mrs. Embers are really generous to the less fortunate." He blinked several times and looked directly at the man.

"Nearly blind, eh, young man?" he said as he released another noisy ass blast.

Mic winked at me and jumped into the malodorous fray. "Yes sir, that's us. The Three Louskateers. Blind, crippled, and crazy." Pointing to me as he drew out the word craaaay-zeee. I donned a goofy grin and raised my leg and let out a single pitiful poot.

The old codger chuckled as he jostled the leash. "What do you think, Brutus? Cake and ice cream for these boys?" The weenie dog wagged his tail and snorted.

The gate opened, and Missy stepped through, bent down, and scratched Brutus between the ears. "Hello, Mr. England. I see you've discovered my little secret. You won't tell Nollen about this, will you? He would skin me alive if he knew I was raiding the pantry for these delinquent ne'er-do-wells."

Mr. England raised his hand to his mouth and made a zipper gesture across his lips. "The secret is safe with me, Missy. You boys drop by anytime." He pointed to the gate on the opposite side of the alley. "It's never locked, and I've always got a load of candy and snacks. My son-in-law is manager at the Piggly Wiggly. I can't figure out if the man really likes me or if he's trying to kill me. Maybe that's why Brutus and I are so gassy. Ain't that right, boy?" The dog responded by evacuating a remarkable turd torpedo, right in the middle of the alley in one smooth, fluid movement.

We said our goodbyes to the elderly interlopers and followed Missy to a hidden spot at the rear of the greenhouse.

She said, "Thanks for coming. Mickey, your sister, was so nice on the phone. She said she would help, and I am very grateful."

Mic's eyes opened wide. "My sister? Brandy? Nice? You must have her confused with someone else."

The night was sultry, but Missy folded her arms tight across her chest and shivered. "Well, she was really nice to me, and I need all the help I can get. Nollen got drunk last night and had that creepy look in his eyes. He makes my skin crawl. I hid in Mr. England's garden shed for a couple of hours while he cooled off. Some quack doctor came by yesterday and they're making plans to move my mother to some kind of private psychiatric clinic. I'll be completely alone in this house with him, and I'm deathly afraid. I called my aunt in Dallas to ask if I could stay with her, but she's almost as bad off as my mother and can't travel. Nollen would never allow me to get on a bus or train. He's got me over a barrel."

My mind was in full gear, but I was coming up with zilch. Tommy was fiddling with the mulch butler, sliding the drawer in and out of the glass greenhouse wall just like the elderly, deaf gardener I had seen on my first visit to the property. It would squeak every time he moved the device, and Mic lost his patience. "Stop monkeying around, man! You're gonna attract attention. Are you trying to get us caught?"

Tommy ignored him. He was inspecting the metal frame and dimensions of both drawers, and laid down on the ground to examine the casters and roller tracks underneath. He suddenly jumped up and snapped his fingers.

"It might work."

Mic, Missy, and I replied in unison, "What are you talking about?"

Tommy rubbed his hands together like a mad scientist in a horror movie. "My wickedly ingenious plan."

Maris called out of the second-story window. "Meroticia, where are you? I need help with my medicine. I can't get the bottle open."

Missy pulled her hair with both hands. "Arghhh! I'm going to lose my mind. I feel like the walls are closing in on me."

Tommy said, "Don't worry. You have the three of us, along with Mic's sister and Coushatta Danni. Keep your chin up. We'll come up with something to get Nollen off your … case."

14

WE PROMISED TO RETURN IN THE MORNING UNDER THE guise of looking for odd-jobs and collecting the reward Embers had promised. It was a flimsy strategy, but all we could come up with in a pinch. Missy was terrified, and I felt bad about leaving her.

When we got to the Kuykendall's house, my gut coiled up in a knot. Otho Wheat had his patrol car blocking the drive, with red lights flashing. He was standing with his hands on his hips, and Brandy was sitting on the trunk with her arms crossed, sporting a stern scowl.

She said, "We're not up to anything illegal. I was just leaving a note about Momma's work schedule for next week."

Mic jogged forward and put on a broad smile. "And we just stopped by to see Mr. England. He always has a bucket of snacks.

His son-in-law is a bigwig at the Wiggly. Anyhow, he was out walking old Brutus, so we didn't bother him."

Tommy and I had no choice but to go along with the misdirection. The sheriff pulled up his pants legs to the top of his black leather boots. "Uh huh? You know what this means, don't you?"

Brandy shook her head and donned a look of righteous indignation. "Yeah. You think it's all bullshit, and it really hurts my feelings. Just tell me one thing, Mr. Wheat. When have I ever lied to you? You've known from the very beginning that Danni and I dance at Muddy Mike's. You just told me these two goofballs helped find the little Turnbow darling. Just because we're white trash from the South Side, and daddy's in jail, you always assume we are up to no good."

Otho shook his pants legs back down to the ankle. "You girls are underage and I should turn you over to the juvenile authorities, for your own protection, but I never said anything about white trash!"

Danni leapt into the fray. "I tell you what, Mr. Lawman. If you tell us where we can find work that hauls down forty to fifty bucks a night, we'll stop jiggling our tits."

Brandy got in the passenger seat of the Pontiac and stuck her head out the window, her voice dripping with venom. "Do the math, Sheriff. At minimum wage, I would have to work a week checking groceries or car hopping at the drive-in to make one night's worth of wages at Mike's. I've got an overworked mother, a horny teenage brother, and three little sisters. If it isn't too inconvenient, Danni and I need to get to Beauregard Parish."

The sheriff realized he was embroiled in a losing battle. "Okay. Get your business done and get out of here. You ladies drop Mickey off at Casa O'Dell. Tommy and Teddy will ride with me."

Mic and I exchanged an alarmed look. I suspected this was one of those divide-and-conquer interrogation strategies. Fortunately, it was nothing so sinister. The sheriff had a little pow-wow with my father and felt like we should attempt a truce. He also told us that Dr. DeSilva arranged for an ophthalmologist from Longview to come down and examine patients once a month at Kushner County General. Tommy was at the top of the list, and his deputies were doing some gentle arm twisting to collect money for the visit in case the Crums came up short. I was curious to hear about Tommy's genius plan, but it would have to wait. Otho dropped me off at Kickapoo Street.

The sheriff said, "If your daddy is drunk or starts ragging on you, come get me. I'll wait a few minutes by the landfill gate and smoke a cig. Tommy and I haven't talked in a while. He and I need to catch up on world events."

As I walked up to the house, all the windows were open, and every light was on. I entered silently and crept to the kitchen door. Nathaniel was standing at the stove in boxer shorts and a wife beater undershirt, stirring a pot of beef chili. Hot dog wieners and buns were laid out on the counter.

"This is just about ready if you want some," he said without looking up. "I didn't touch any of the groceries you left in the fridge."

Wary of a ploy, I took a neutral approach. "No problem. I've been dining at Casa O'Dell for the last few days, while helping Mickey with some repairs and painting. Vera is a miracle worker in the kitchen, and always seems to have enough for everyone, with a bite or two left over."

As he turned to set the chili pot on a rusty trivet, I could see the black and blue skin just under his right shoulder blade extending down to his waist. Apparently, Otho's pep talk included a rigorous exorcism of worldly meanness.

I said nothing about the bruises and turned my attention to the water bill lying on the dinette. It was $7.49 and was already a week past due. In the spirit of detente, I pulled the remaining money out of my pocket and said, "Rick Blaine gave us a few extra bucks to help with the Memorial Day crunch at Casablanca. I can cover the water bill this month."

He looked over his shoulder at me for the first time since I walked through the door.

"I just got paid, and even scored a little overtime at the festival. By the way, thanks for taking the commissioner's call and leaving the note. If you pay the water bill, I'll budget out the rest of May and June, and stock up the pantry. We should be fine."

I found it encouraging that he used the term "we." It was the most civilized exchange we had had in years. I heard the patrol car crank and drive off. Otho had done me a huge favor I could never repay.

Nathaniel and I kept at arm's length the rest of the evening. He asked about the rescue, and I recounted the sanitized version of Missy's escapade. The misdirection worked, and he had not recognized her during our heated encounter on Division Street. After a few swigs from the bottle, he tried a feeble jibe about me being sweet on her, but I didn't take the bait.

I retrieved my clothes box from the attic and reacquainted myself with the remaining duds. The silver shirt I had worn all week was a little dingy, so I switched out with a not totally unattractive army green short sleeve shirt. A triple-layer yoke and oversized double pockets actually made my chest and shoulders look wider.

No hot water, but I didn't mind the cool bath after a hot day. There was a partial bottle of cheap shampoo that smelled like bay rum. It was a nice diversion from scrubbing my head with whatever scrap of bar soap Nate could pilfer from the county commissioner's restroom.

By the time I got out of the tub, my father was asleep on the couch cuddling a half empty fifth of Old Forester. The events of the week left me bone tired. A light easterly breeze filtered through the open window of my bedroom, and I was asleep in an instant.

* * *

Tessa was sitting on the edge of the quarry tossing dandelions into the seep pool below. Bottle flies swarmed around bald spots on her head. She gazed at me with grotesque, bloodshot eyes and reached up with two fingers to pull down her lower eyelids. Pointing at me with the other hand, she said, "Just remember, the eyes are always on you, sissy boy." Maggots fell out of her mouth as she giggled and went back to tossing flowers.

* * *

A loud pounding on the front door jolted me out of a deep slumber. It was still dark. Nathaniel cursed as he rolled off the couch and knocked over the TV tray. The clock on the stove read 3:40 a.m. Did it keep the correct time? I couldn't remember. My father limped toward the door and grabbed the knob, but didn't open it. "Who the hell is it?"

"It's Burtis Crum. Nate, I'm sorry to bother you at this ungodly hour, but this is a real emergency."

He opened the door, and Tommy pushed past my father and burst into the room with tears in his eyes and panic in his voice.

"Mickey's been shot."

15

THE DRIVE TO THE HOSPITAL WAS A BLUR. I MUST HAVE BEEN in a state of shock because I don't even remember getting dressed. Nathaniel pressed Burtis for details, but the man knew very little. "The shot woke us up, and I walked out to the front porch just as a patrol car came roaring down the street with the siren wailing. A neighbor came over and said there was trouble at the O'Dell residence and the boy was wounded."

Tommy was in the back seat with me, mumbling a plea to God for divine intervention. I was numb. Mr. Crum shaved corners and ignored the red lights. As we approached Kushner County General, it appeared as though every law enforcement vehicle in Texas had surrounded the hospital with lights flashing. The car lurched and scraped bottom as Burtis pulled up on the sidewalk next to the emergency room and killed the engine. Tommy and I bailed out and raced to the ER entrance. The automatic sliding glass doors clamored and rattled on filthy metal tracks and the stark white fluorescent glare in the waiting area accentuated blood stains on Vera O'Dell's tattered housecoat.

Brandy, dressed in a sheer strapless blouse and leather mini-skirt, was attempting to relay the events to Sheriff Otho Wheat between sobs. Black rivulets of smeared mascara stained her puffy cheeks.

A deputy stopped us. "Guys, we don't know anything yet. Mickey is in surgery. Dr. DeSilva is doing all he can to stop the hemorrhaging, but it looked real bad. Stay out of the way and don't interfere."

A nurse emerged with a clean gown for Mrs. O'Dell, and the sheriff stuffed her bloody garment into an evidence bag. He motioned toward the three youngest O'Dell sisters, still in pajamas, huddled in the corner under a dingy brown blanket.

As we made our way over, the youngest sister jumped up and hugged Tommy as he knelt down.

"One of them drunk rednecks followed Brandy and Danni home. He was mad and screamed they had taken all his money and didn't give him nuthin'. Mickey tried to run him off, but he pulled a pistol and started waving it at Brandy. Mic stepped in front of her and *bam*! It him in the stomach right here." She pointed to the left side of her belly.

Sheriff Wheat was barking orders to his deputies. "I want this son-of-a-bitch caught, understand? No stone unturned. Got it?" His men nodded and hauled ass.

Otho gathered up Vera and Brandy and gently guided them over to the corner where we were sitting. "Y'all hang tight right here. I sent Danni Redhawk with Constable Bennett over to Beauregard Parish to see if they can get an ID on the shooter. I've got to get on the radio and spread the word to the Highway Patrol. They might get lucky and snag him at a traffic stop." He handed Brandy a handkerchief. I know you're upset, but this is very important. You said the shooter was driving a late model Cutlass Supreme?"

She nodded. "Dark blue or maybe black, jacked up in the back, with fancy chrome wheels. I didn't get a license plate number."

She swayed and her legs gave out. I caught her on the way down to the floor. She collapsed against me and we both slid down the wall in a heap.

I wrapped my arms tight around her shoulders, as she nestled her head under my chin. "It's all my fault. I'll never forgive myself. Danni and I double teamed that guy at the club and looted his pockets. He got pissed, and we just laughed and tormented him. The bouncer threw him out. It was cruel and I shouldn't have done it. If Mic dies, I don't know what we'll do."

I kissed the top of her head. "Don't write him off just yet. Mic is the toughest guy I know. He's got the spark of God in him. Dr. DeSilva is a top-notch surgeon. He was a respected expert in Cuba before Castro took over, and Dix Knob is lucky to have him. All the nurses say he's a crackerjack in the OR."

At that moment, a nurse barged into the room and shouted, "Who's got O-positive blood type? The O'Dell boy has already had four units and needs more."

Nathaniel raised his hand. "I do, but I've been drinking. Teddy's got O-positive."

Burtis Crum rolled up his sleeve and motioned for Tommy to follow. "We've both got O-negative." The nurse looked doubtful, but Burtis said, "I am a veteran Army medic, and our type is the universal donor."

An attendant stepped up behind her. "Every second counts. Y'all come with me."

The radiologist, Dr. Linquist, was helping the nurses set up chairs and trays in the hallway outside the operating room door. "You guys are going to have to bear with me. I haven't drawn a unit of blood since my residency 22 years ago."

Linquist placed a rubber tourniquet on my arm and made one perfunctory swipe with an alcohol swab. Like a coward, I looked away and the needle stick burned like hell, but I managed not to flinch or cry out. My stomach churned. A black fog obscured the lights and the voices surrounding me descended into a deep well. I passed out like a putz.

* * *

I woke up in the hallway, lying on a gurney that smelled like mothballs and urine. No one was around. When I struggled to sit up, everything started spinning, and my stomach rebelled with a surge of nausea. After three attempts, I finally got my feet on the floor. Knees quivered like rubber bands and the first ten steps were wobbly. I slid along the handrails and when I reached the nearest room, the voices of Dr. DeSilva and Sheriff Wheat were audible through a crack in the door.

The surgeon said, "The bullet shattered his spleen, and I had to remove it. Probably a 38 Special at close range. Mickey lost a lot of blood. Fortunately, he was wearing a thick leather vest which caused the hollow point to splay out a bit before penetrating his abdomen; otherwise he would have hemorrhaged to death right on the spot where he fell."

Otho harrumphed and lit a Lucky Strike and offered it to the doctor, who was removing his surgical gloves and blood-spattered smock. DeSilva accepted the cigarette and took a long, deep draw while the sheriff lit one for himself.

"I guess you did surgery on a lot of gunshot wounds during the Cuban Revolution, when Castro was advancing on Havana."

I squeezed through the door as the physician replied, "Yes, far too many in those awful days, just before Christmas in '58. I still have nightmares. The main reason I came to this little town was to recover from the stress and trauma of those terrible times. I never thought I'd see it here, especially in someone as young as the O'Dell boy."

Both men spun around as the door squeaked behind me. Dr. DeSilva rushed to my side and grabbed my right arm. "You're bleeding, Teddy. When you passed out, the needle must have torn the vein as you fell. Let me bandage that arm." I looked down and saw blood seeping from a hole at the crease of my elbow. I hadn't noticed any pain until that moment. Otho guided me to a chair beside Mic's bed while the physician wrapped gauze over the wound.

The sheriff said, "Your friend ain't out of the woods yet. It's gonna be touch and go for a while."

Mic lay naked on the bed with bags of IV flowing into both arms. His skin was fish belly pale, and he moaned with each ragged breath.

Dr. DeSilva gave me a shot in the shoulder. "Penicillin to prevent an infection. You must leave. I'll sedate Mickey for several days to keep him from moving and rupturing the sutures. I'll keep Mrs. O'Dell posted. If you have any pull with the Big Man upstairs, I suggest you pray."

Otho hustled me back to the waiting area. The room was packed. Rick Blaine and Arthur Rumkin comforted the O'Dell clan. Sara Tyler and her mother served coffee and donuts to the hospital staff. The sheriff handed me off to Mr. Crum and said, "Get the boys home, Burtis. I think Teddy's still in shock. We are not making much headway searching for the shooter, so I've got to light a fire under some asses. We can't let that sorry bastard get away!"

Burtis handed me his keys and said. "Tommy's outside by the car. You go crawl in the back seat and hold that arm up over your head until the bleeding stops. I'll be along in a minute after I speak to Rick and Arthur."

Tommy was pacing back and forth on the sidewalk. "Did you see Mickey? Is he okay? The nurse said they'll transfer him to Hermann Hospital in Houston if they can get him stable."

"He looks bad. Real bad. Pale as a ghost. Drip bags attached to both arms. That's all I know."

Tommy nodded and pointed across the street. "He's been here since dawn."

Galton Grails was straddling his motorcycle in the liquor store parking lot. He glared at me with a slimy green grin and made a cutting motion across his throat. I flipped him the bird and yelled, "Go to hell, you shit-stain!"

He laughed, kick started the machine, and peeled off. Burtis pushed me into the car. "Come on, fellas. Let's not jinx ourselves. There are rough days ahead, and distractions are a liability."

* * *

Mr. Crum took us to the Pitt Grill for breakfast. Tommy and I couldn't eat.

We picked at hash browns and flapjacks while Burtis sipped coffee and said, "I'm going to level with you boys. This is a dangerous situation, and we must stay vigilant. Rick Blaine and Arthur Rumkin are going to set up a watch schedule at the O'Dell's house. A group of men are going to take shifts guarding the place. I would appreciate y'all running the Palisades for a day or two, while I do my part. Edna agreed to run the ticket booth and concession. Tommy will operate the projectors. Teddy, would you give us a hand cleaning up between features?"

I nodded. "I need to stay busy. Otherwise, I'll go crazy. Where is my father?"

"The county crews are searching the back roads for any sign of the Cutlass. Nate suggested the plan, and the commissioner agreed. The whole town is on edge."

I felt good about the fact Nathaniel was contributing. I held out very little hope of a meaningful reconciliation, but I allowed myself to indulge in a spark of optimism.

It was 10 a.m. when Mr. Crum dropped us off at the theater. Edna was sweeping the concession area and stocking the candy case.

She said, "The Turnbow girl came by. She inquired about Mickey O'Dell and I told her what little I knew. She was real fidgety. Seemed upset and nervous. I told her you guys would run the Palisades today. She said she would come back for the matinee at 2:30 and hurried off. That girl is a strange bird and I don't approve of you guys hanging out with her. The Turnbow clan has a sordid history; shady business dealings, wild parties, prostitutes."

Tommy got perturbed and scolded his mother. "Gee Mom, that's a real proper Christian attitude. Many people would look at our family and say that *we* are a strange bunch. They wouldn't be entirely wrong, would they? Missy is a nice girl, so don't judge her because of her family history. Her mom is sick. It's true that her real father died under questionable circumstances when she was still a toddler, but she's not responsible for that. She can't be held accountable for her step-father either. That's for damn sure."

Mrs. Crum winced at her son's rebuke and said, "I can be judgmental sometimes, but it's just because I'm trying to protect you from getting tangled up in a web of intrigue. I've known a lot of pretty, rich girls in my lifetime. Most of them are self-centered and conceited. They'll use you up and toss you aside." Tommy protested, but Edna raised her voice to drown him out. "You boys go back to the house, get a shower, and rest up for a while. Burt needs to be at the O'Dell's place by noon, so I'll finish up here."

* * *

Just as we arrived at the Crum residence, Burtis bolted out the door carrying an M1 Garand rifle with a sleek scope and an impressive flash suppressor.

I was flabbergasted. "Gosh, Tommy, your dad seems so meek and mild. What's the story with that gun?"

"Dad was a medic in North Africa during World War II, and saw a lot of action in Morocco." He pulled a White Owl cigar box from a cabinet next to the TV. It was packed with campaign ribbons and medals, including a Purple Heart, a Combat Medical Badge, and a marksman award. "Dad never talks about it. At least not to us. He gets together with Nurse Jurnigan at Rhinelander Park on Saturday mornings and they share war stories over donuts and coffee. She was a triage nurse at a field hospital in France during the war."

We showered and stretched out on the living room floor. Tommy snored as I dozed fitfully. At 2:00, we headed back to the theater to get ready for the matinee. A movie called *The Love Bug* featuring an anthropomorphic Volkswagen named Herbie was breaking box office records. I cleaned toilets and helped Tommy thread the projectors. When the movie started, I took a seat in the back row within earshot of the concession stand, just in case Edna got busy. The crowd was light.

Twenty minutes into the movie, Missy Turnbow walked in. She didn't see me immediately and stood in the aisle a few feet away, scanning the auditorium. She dressed like a socialite. Tight black slacks and a white satin blouse. I cleared my throat and stood. She rushed over and threw her arms around my neck and said. "I heard about Mickey. How is he doing?"

I recounted the early morning trip and the brief visit with the sheriff and Dr. DeSilva, but omitted my embarrassing blackout. "They are going to transfer him to Houston as soon as he's stable."

She nodded and rubbed her eyes. "Is there anywhere we can talk? I'm pretty sure Nollen knows the shooter."

I was stunned, and it took a moment to process the revelation. "Let's go to the projection booth. Tommy will want to hear about this bombshell."

She took my hand as we climbed the narrow staircase. It was stiflingly hot. As we entered the tiny room, Tommy was changing a bulb on one of the Simplex projector units, and was sweating through his shirt. He said, "Sorry about the heat, Missy. The AC is on the fritz and Dad isn't here to fix it. What's up?"

I replied. "She's got some info on the attacker. Nollen knows the guy."

Tommy pointed to a stool. Missy sat down and took a deep breath.

"When the doorbell rang at four o'clock this morning, I knew something was wrong. I crawled out to the landing at the top of the stairs and overheard two of Nollen's goons telling him a car thief did the deed. I didn't catch a name, but he's one of the chop shop flunkies. Embers went into a rage and ordered them to find the weasel before the cops did. He's coming unhinged. There's a rumor that some of his competitors are planning a takeover. Nollen is preoccupied with the hunt for the shooter and this turf war looming on the horizon. That's the only reason I could sneak out of the house and meet y'all here."

Tommy's eyes widened, and I knew what he was thinking. Arthur Rumkin fed my fallacy into the rumor mill, Embers' heard about it, and his paranoia was reaching critical mass.

Angry shouts from the moviegoers interrupted our conversation. Tommy jumped. "Dammit, I missed the end of the reel. Give me a second." His fingers moved nimbly as he made the switch. The Simplex flickered, and the patrons cheered as Buddy Hackett maneuvered Herbie onto the racetrack. Missy wiped sweat off her brow. Tommy looked at his watch and said, "We'll get a two-hour break at the end of this matinee. It's sweltering in this stuffy booth. I'll meet you downstairs in a few minutes. Perhaps we could use the payphone in the lobby to leave an anonymous tip with the sheriff's office."

I stopped by the lobby and told Edna about the AC. She filled three soda cups, and Missy waited at the bottom of the stairs while I ran one up to Tommy in the booth. As we strolled down the aisle to find a seat closer to the screen, I caught myself having impure thoughts just watching her sip from the straw.

It was twenty degrees cooler in the auditorium. We sat down and Missy laid her head on my shoulder. I felt guilty for enjoying the moment. Mic was unconscious in the hospital, the O'Dells were grieving, and here I was, falling in love. The 1968 version of *Romeo and Juliet* premiered the previous summer, and I cursed Shakespeare as Olivia Hussey committed suicide in the last scene. I cut her picture out of magazines and taped them to the headboard of my bed. The irony was tragic. Missy's resemblance to the actress was extraordinary. Dark hair, green eyes, flawless complexion. I never made the connection until that moment.

We lingered while the other patrons left and the credits scrolled across the screen. As I stroked her hair, an arm clutched my throat and a fetid breath assaulted my nostrils. Galton Grails snuck in behind us and caught me off guard. Locked in a hopeless choke hold,

I struggled to breathe. The bully pulled me across the back of the seat. I was flopping around like a rabbit in a snare. Missy jumped up out of her seat.

"You're hurting him! Let him go. He can't breathe."

Grails' grip tightened as he savored her alarm. "Piss your breeches, Nutscalder, and maybe I'll let you go. Piss your breeches like you did last week when I whooped your ass in the schoolyard. Mickey O'Dell ain't here to rescue you. If he lives, I'll kick his ass and make him watch while I bend Brandy over the back of a couch."

Missy pulled at his arm. "Let him go. You're strangling him." Galton twisted my body, wedging my legs between the seat backs. I was losing control of my cursed bladder, I couldn't swallow, and slobber was drooling out of my mouth. He pulled my hair and twisted my head to give her a full view of my agony. Missy straightened and pulled at the bottom of her blouse, seductively emphasizing her breasts.

"I'll show you my tits if you let him go."

Galton tightened his grip and ripped the bandage off my arm, opening the wound.

"If you give me a kiss *and* show me your tits, I'll let him go."

Missy leaned over the back of the seat and puckered her lips, pausing just inches from his face. "Oh Galton, I must tell you the truth; I would rather marinate in a barrel of cat piss and dog vomit than kiss you!" An instant later, she slapped him across the face and dumped the entire contents of her ice-cold soda in his lap. The bully screamed and loosened his grip just long enough for me to pull free.

Gasping for air, I motioned for Missy to run. Galton lurched across the seats, swinging his fist at my head. I dodged and grabbed his sleeve, pulling him off balance, buying me an extra second to get a head start. Missy was already racing up the stairs to the projection booth. I made it to the third step before Grails caught up with me. He seized my left leg and pulled me to the bottom. I spun over on my back and kicked him in the chest with the right. He grunted but didn't let go. An instant later, a metal film reel flew down the stairwell from the door above and smacked him in the face, leaving two bloody parallel indentations across the bridge of his nose. I kicked him in the throat. He released his grip, and I bolted toward the projection booth. I lunged into the room and Tommy slammed the heavy metal door just as Galton reached the top of the stairs.

I said, "That was a great throw, buddy."

Tommy shook his head. "Don't thank me. Thank Missy. She's the real, reel marksman!"

She said, "I won second place in the discus on track and field day at school."

Galton pounded on the metal door so hard that tufts of asbestos fell from the coated rafters above. "It's gonna be a long, hot summer, Nutscalder. O'Dell can't protect you anymore. Tell that little rich bitch I'm saving something long and hard for her. Tommy four eyes is gonna pay too!" The profane grumbling subsided as footsteps faded down the stairs.

Tommy placed his ear to the door before unlocking it. "He's gone. Let's get out of this oven and lay out some plans for our next move."

When we reached the lobby, Edna was standing at the entrance staring down the street. "What's going on? Why was that boy all wet? Do I need to call the police?"

Tommy replied, "Crusty is a bit of a drama queen. Don't worry, he'll settle down. Which way did he go?"

Edna pointed south. We headed north.

16

On the way to Fairhaven Street, we discussed calling the sheriff's office to leave an anonymous tip on Nollen Embers' knowledge of the shooter's identity. Tommy thought it was a good idea. Missy and I weren't so sure.

She said, "The more I think about it, the more he will just deny it. Worst of all, he'll certainly know it was me that squealed. Deep down, I know telling Sheriff Wheat is the right thing to do, but Nollen will concoct some airtight alibi, and I'm terrified of the consequences."

I replied, "Let's just take a step back from the situation and let it play out. Rick Blaine and Arthur Rumkin organized a watch party at Casa O'Dell, so they're covered. Everyone in town is on high alert and Nollen is distracted by the search. All of this hubbub will certainly work in our favor for now."

Three blocks from the Turnbow's residence, the conversation became moot. A string of squad cars paraded down Division Street followed by a wrecker hauling the mud-covered remains of a jacked-up, midnight blue Oldsmobile Cutlass with fancy chrome wheels. Pulling up the rear of this solemn procession was a county dump truck with Sudsy Monkhouse driving and my old man in the passenger seat. They pulled over to the curb, and Monkhouse stuck his arm out of the window and motioned us over.

Missy whispered, "What do we tell your father if he asks what we're doing ... together?"

"For once, I'm going to tell him the truth, or at least a version of it. Just smile and say Tommy and I offered to walk you home from the movie."

Sudsy pulled to the curb, killed the engine, and leaned out the window. He was a comical character, with big ears and a mouth full of oversized dentures, displayed in a perpetually lopsided smile. When Monkhouse was a teenager, he would dumpster dive behind the local bars and swig the foamy dregs out of discarded beer bottles, hence the nickname. He was on the wagon and sober for ten years now.

He said, "You boys are moving up in the world. Strolling around town with a pretty little filly from the North Side."

I put on the same embarrassment act I'd used on Rumkin at Casablanca. "Aw, Mr. Monkhouse, Tommy and I were just walking Meroticia home after the matinee. I'm helping Edna at the Palisades until Burtis finishes his shift guarding the O'Dell place. It looks like you found the getaway car. Did they catch the shooter?"

Sudsy rubbed his chin and glanced at my father. "I'll let Nate tell you about it," he said, waving us over to the passenger side.

My father grimaced as if he was unsure of what to say. "You guys need to get the young lady home. Sudsy and I found the deserted car on Morgan Bayou Road. Someone shot out the front tires and there's a lot of blood all over the inside, but no sign of the driver. This situation may not be over yet. Teddy, are you coming home tonight?"

Tommy answered him. "Teddy's staying with us, Mr. Nutscalder. He's helping me and Mom at the theater. I'm teaching him how to thread the projectors."

Nathaniel nodded. "Good. Good. It's getting late. You guys be safe. Maybe tomorrow will be a better day. Teddy, come on home when you get a chance. I've got a surprise for you."

Sudsy fired up the engine, ground the gears, and drove off. Tommy looked at his watch. "I've gotta be back to the Palisades in an hour, but I want to get one more look at the mulch butler in the back of the greenhouse first."

Missy laughed. "What is this fascination with my greenhouse?"

Tommy wiped his sweat-smudged glasses with a tissue. "I'm formulating a plan. A few more calculations and I'll let y'all in on it."

* * *

Missy scolded me for calling her Meroticia. She hated the name. I apologized profusely, and a coquettish smile declared her forgiveness. She guided us through a shortcut, behind the Piggly Wiggly along the water tower access trail, where we were less likely to be seen by the neighbors. Nollen's car was gone, so we had a window of opportunity to hear Tommy explain his grand idea. Listening to him was like watching a TV detective solve a complex case in reverse order.

"Okay, Missy. You said Nollen is allergic to wasps, right?"

She furrowed her brow and nodded. "Yeah, but how's that going to keep him from shipping my mother off to the asylum? How is that going to keep him away from ... me?"

"Two words. Dolichovespula maculata."

Missy looked at me and I shrugged, not having the faintest clue what he meant.

Tommy chuckled. "The bald-faced hornet. There is a nest on the awning of the Cusser Club property. It's about the size of a beach ball, and would fit nicely into one of these drawers. We simply wrap one of Pete O'Dell's waxed canvas offal bags around it in the cool, early morning hours before dawn, while the insects are docile, detach the stalk, and transport it here. We figure out a way to lure Nollen into the greenhouse, bar the door, and shove the nest inside. Walla! Let nature take its course."

Missy shoved me aside and grabbed the handle of the metal drawer. She moved it in and out of the glass enclosure as if she were seeing the device for the first time. She became animated. Almost giddy. "Dad-gummit! That could actually work! Sometimes he comes out here to smoke a joint. There's a small gap between the flagstones at the bottom of the entry door. A brick will wedge it shut. Exterminators did it last summer when Mom had the place fumigated for aphids and nematodes." She stepped back and her expression changed. "It's a complicated scheme. I would have to lure him in and get myself out. I'm not sure if I could do it. Let's see if I fit. Help me in." Tommy and I held her arms steady while she climbed into the nearest drawer and squatted down. As we pushed, the mulch butler squeaked loudly with the unaccustomed weight, but we were able to get her through to the inside. While pulling back, the casters slipped off the track and she was caught halfway in and halfway out. She looked up at us and said, "I guess I'm too fat to fit into this contraption." It was a ridiculous notion. The mere thought of Missy being anything but perfect was absurd.

Tommy hoisted the metal box up a couple of inches and re-centered the rollers on the tracks underneath as I lifted Missy out.

Tommy said, "There are some variables to consider. We've got some logistics to figure out. I have to make sure the offal bag doesn't smother the critters to death."

Missy said, "Nollen is an unpredictable control freak, so once y'all are in position, I'm going to have to figure out a way to lure him in at just the right time."

Tommy pulled a pocket watch out of his jeans and held it close to his eyes. "It's time for me to get back to the theater. You guys strategize for a while. Let's fine tune the plan and sleep on it." Missy gave Tommy a hug, before he turned and jogged down the alley toward midtown.

I said, "I have doubts about Tommy's plan, but it's a darn sight better than anything I've come up with."

Missy jostled the handles of the mulch butler and said, "Are you hungry?"

"Famished."

"I'll raid the fridge after I check on my mom. Stay by the back gate. You will be out of sight from anywhere in the house. I'll be back in a few minutes."

It was cooling down as the sun settled on the western horizon. I stretched out and gazed up at the emerging stars. The well-groomed St. Augustine lawn was softer than my bed at home. I tried to concentrate on Tommy's plan, but stupid romantic thoughts kept getting in the way.

In a few minutes, Missy returned with an enormous platter of food. "We're in luck. Nollen is still gone and Mom's watching *Lawrence Welk*. I shoved the food under the broiler for a minute to take the chill off. I hope it's warm enough."

We sat cross-legged with the plate between us and talked between bites. There was prime rib, potatoes au gratin, broccoli and cheese quiche, and crème brûlée for dessert. We shared a bottle of San Pellegrino sparkling water. I had never eaten so well and told her so. I couldn't tell if her expression was approval or pity. There were no napkins, so I wiped my mouth on my sleeve. She giggled and did the same.

She cocked her head to the side and studied me for a long moment. "I'm trying to figure you out, Theodore Roosevelt Nutscalder. You always look like you've got a question on the tip of your tongue that you can't quite spit out."

"Would you really have jumped off the trestle?" I asked, immediately regretting putting her on the spot.

Missy looked down at the ground and fiddled with the bottle cap for a moment before answering. "I don't know. Things have been getting worse with my mother's mental disease, and my disgusting stepfather. I'm exhausted by his terror tactics. I don't have any friends. I just wondered what it would be like to stand on the brink. Knowing that one thought, one step, one split second, was all that stood between life and death. Am I making any sense? Do you have any idea what I'm talking about?"

"Yeah, I've had some dark thoughts of my own. I think we all flirt with destructive feelings from time to time. My current toxic mindset is revenge. I'm fed up with the bullying. Just like today, at the theater with Galton. I'll take him down a notch if I ever get an opportunity."

Missy smiled as she piled scraps on the platter. "I want to apologize for the way I acted at the festival. I couldn't acknowledge you without raising suspicion. My mother has a lot of emotional issues, but there is nothing wrong with her eyesight. She recognized you right away. I knew I had to deflect her attention." Missy seemed embarrassed and changed the subject. "Your dad seemed a lot nicer today. Almost cordial. Are y'all getting along?"

"For the time being. Sheriff Otho Wheat had a pow-wow with him. He calls it a 'Come to Jesus' meeting. I think he roughed up Nathaniel. Gave him an incentive to be nice. At least for a while. Until he goes off on the next whiskey bender."

Missy laid on her back and laced her fingers behind her head. "Your dad's alcoholism and my mother's drug addiction. No wonder we're so fuc... fouled up. Sweet Jesus, let's talk about a different subject. Something upbeat, nice, funny. What inspired you to give Galton Grails the nickname Butt Crust? That's got to be a hoot."

"It all started when we were performing the musical *Oklahoma* for all the parents and elementary school kids. It was our first live performance. Sort of like a dress rehearsal in front of a forgiving audience. We had sawdust and shredded paper spread out over the stage for the last act so some of us guys could run out and slide across the floor on our knees before jumping up on a bench for the final chorus. Galton tripped, and tumbled over on his back during the maneuver, and a bunch of the junk lodged in his baggy costume pants. When he bent over during the finale, his crotch seam split and it all came bursting out, like he had crapped a bucket load of crusty shit. It was a real showstopper, and the audience went wild. Grails was humiliated and refused to take a bow at curtain call. When Miss Hawkins finally dragged him back out on stage, I yelled, 'Three cheers for Butt Crust!' Everyone stood and gave him a hearty 'Hip! Hip! Hooray!' The rest is history, and I've made an enemy for life."

Missy went breathless with laughter. It was magical. I was determined to keep the mood light, so when she finally regained her composure, I said, "On that first day we met, you used the writer's metaphor about being caught in a tree, with the forest on fire, unable to get down. Where did you learn that? Do you write?"

"If you promise you won't laugh, I'll tell you."

I crossed my heart.

She wrinkled her nose self-consciously. "I won a short story contest with a tale about a girl who turned into a garden slug after ruining the reputation of an innocent classmate. Catholic school stuff. The judges said it was positively Kafka-esque. I got a stupid little medal for it. St. Hildegard Von Bingen, one of the many patron saints of writers. Now it's your turn. While you were in Obermeyer's, Mickey told me you were the smartest guy he had ever met. He was really bragging about your science fiction stories. Talking you up. Have you ever entered any contests?"

"Yes, well, sort of … I get some applause for the stories. No medals or ribbons. However, I won a contest in English class last year and got three extra points added to my final grade in the spring semester."

Missy sat up at full attention. "Really? You must tell me all about it."

It was my turn to lie down and stretch out.

"Our English teacher, Miss Hawkins, got the bright idea of having a pop quiz on the Friday before spring break. Me and Squeaky Sullivan had finished trading insults during our weekly fiction tirade, and Miss Hawkins was just killing time until the last bell. She challenged everyone to come up with the best example of alliteration. I won."

Missy cocked her head to the side. "What in the world did you come up with? Something out of one of those campy Japanese science fiction movies? Towering tarantulas topple Tokyo?"

"No. Nothing so mundane and ordinary." I paused for a moment, cleared my throat, and took a deep breath to draw out the drama.

"Bodaciously boobed, bikini bottom, blonde babes baked Big Bill's best black bean burritos before breakfast."

My pretty companion covered her face with her hands and laughed until she lost her breath. It was the happiest I'd seen her. She snorted in a very unladylike manner and wiped tears with the back of her hand.

She said, "Bodaciously boobed? Oh ... my ... god, did you get in trouble for that?"

"Oh yeah. I got sent to the office for causing a riot. Principal Fangman lit my ass up with a paddle made out of a boat oar. Three hard licks. He admitted it was the best example of alliteration he'd ever heard, but told me if it happened again, I would spend the rest of my life in detention. I made an A+ in English. With the bonus points, my final grade average was a smooth 100."

Missy leaned forward, and her hair fell across my face. She kissed me. It was soft and wet and a little salty. A little sticky, and a lot delicious. Every molecule in my body tingled. She lingered over me for a moment, moving her head back and forth, slowly brushing her long raven hair across my face and neck. It was the most exquisite moment of my life. She opened her eyes and looked directly into mine. What does a guy say in a moment like that? Should I tell her I love her? That was stupid. I'd only known her for a couple of days. I told myself to play it cool; *Don't blow it, Theodore. Don't be a dingleberry.*

I whispered, "When my heart stops racing, I'm going to say something really clever."

She rubbed her nose against mine in an Eskimo kiss. "You just did."

Maris called from the second-story window, and Missy sighed. "You better go. Can you come back tomorrow and tie the bandana on top of the gatepost?" I kissed her hand and nodded. Missy smiled broadly as she backed away. "That first day I met you on the railroad tracks, you looked kinda like James Dean. A dirty face, a black eye, and a bloody nose. Shirttail out, and hair disheveled. I knew you were going to be big trouble!"

17

TO SAY I WAS ON CLOUD NINE WAS AN UNDERSTATEMENT. AS I jogged back to town, my hormone-addled mind was flirting with multiple romantic scenarios at once.

A distant siren brought me back to earth. It was nearly 8:00, and I needed to check on Mickey. The cleanup at the Palisades could wait. Tommy and Edna wouldn't mind.

An elderly nurse was locking the front door of the hospital as I arrived.

Through the thick glass doors, she yelled, "Visiting hours are over! Come back tomorrow."

My pleas fell on deaf ears, so I ran around to the ER entrance and caught Brandy and Danni as they were climbing into the Star Chief.

"How's Mickey doing? Has there been any change?"

Brandy sat sideways with the passenger door open, elbows resting on her knees.

"No change. He's sedated. The biggest danger is a blood clot. What am I gonna do, Teddy?"

"You're going to be patient and pray, like everyone else."

Danni startled us both with an explosive exclamation. "That's gross and disgusting! Who would do such a thing?"

Brandy and I gazed at her in confusion. She pointed to a crumpled paper sack on the driver's side floorboard. I reached across Brandy and retrieved the object. There was writing on the outside. "Git reddy Brandee. I'm comming for you." I snuck a peek inside. The sack contained several dirty condoms. Brandy reached for the bag, but I pulled it away. There was no need to add to her distress.

Danni read my mind. "Forget it. Let's just get back to Casa O'Dell and find out the latest news on the manhunt. Do you want to ride with us, Teddy?"

Clutching the sack, I said, "I have to get over to the Palisades and help Tommy with cleanup. I'll be along later."

Brandy held her arms up toward me. I bent over to give her a hug. She nuzzled my neck and grabbed for the sack. Subconsciously, I was expecting the maneuver. Nothing fooled Brandy. She could read a man like a book and spot a lie faster than a polygraph. I jerked the sack behind my back and licked her earlobe. A minor diversion of my own. It worked, and for a fleeting millisecond, there was a look of surprise on her face. She recovered in an instant and pouted her lips as I pulled away. "I'll be waiting for you, Theodore Nutscalder. Hurry home."

The girl could play me like a marionette, but I was learning to tangle the strings a bit.

As they drove off, I took another look at the sack. This shameless sleazeball prank had Galton Grails written all over it. I couldn't outfight him, but I was determined to outsmart him. He would pay.

Most of the townsfolk were preoccupied with the attack, and only eleven movie-goers showed up for the evening feature. Cleanup was quick. Edna decided to close the cinema until the following Saturday, and as we taped a sign to the door, I brought Tommy up to date on Mickey's status and Galton's gruesome gag.

He said, "Grails is getting worse by the day. Sara has been telling me about the rude comments he makes to her and the other girls at school. When we finish with Nollen Embers, we're going to fix that sorry bastard, too."

I didn't elaborate on the evening with Missy, other than the delicious meal. We agreed to meet at the Cusser Club the next day to firm up the plan for harvesting the hornet nest. I told Edna I would sleep at Casa O'Dell, and she said there would be a key under the back-door mat if I changed my mind.

The Knob was unusually quiet, and most of the shops closed early, so I paused by the quarry to gather my thoughts. Even the pot smokers were subdued. Huddled around a small fire, one strummed a guitar as a dozen others sang "Brown Eyed Girl."

The wind gently blew and shadows at the bottom of the quarry undulated in an eerie fashion as the moonlight played peekaboo with slow-moving clouds. I stretched out and rested my head on a cool clump of clover. Humper appeared out of nowhere and plopped down next to me, wallowing on his back, begging for a belly rub. The old mutt was the nearest thing to a genuine pet I had ever had. The warm night, allied with my canine companion, thoughts of Missy, and my favorite Van Morrison camp song soothed my mind. I convinced myself that Mic would be alright. After all, he was the toughest guy I knew. Humper snored, fatigue triumphed, and I was snoozing in an instant.

* * *

Dreams carried me into an Alpine hunting lodge. A blizzard howled outdoors, and a blazing fire crackled in a gigantic stone fireplace. Sara Tyler wrapped herself up in furs on the floor, nibbling pastries and grapes. She smiled seductively and motioned me over. What was I thinking? It should have been Missy, not Sara.

I woke up angry at myself for the imaginary infidelity and pushed the scene out of my mind. Humper was gone. The sun crested over the eastern horizon, dissipating a light fog. One car remained across the way, and all that was left of the fire was a lazy ribbon of smoke snaking skyward in the windless air.

I dozed off and on for a while, enjoying the solitude. Sleepovers at Casa O'Dell were a pleasure, but the inevitable morning clamor was irritating.

Humper's bark echoed up from the quarry floor as an obnoxious mechanical buzzing racket harshed my calm. The familiar, nerve-racking sound of Galton's crotch rocket assaulted my ears. I rolled over on my belly and crawled to the edge of the quarry crater for a look. Mounted on the old army surplus Harley-Davidson, my tormentor weaved a well-worn path between the fractured rocks and abandoned equipment. At various intervals, he would pause and punch a stopwatch, apparently timing his daredevil circumnavigations. Humper foraged around the seep pool, munching on the discarded food scraps thrown over the cliff by the pot heads. A huge clump of trash coalesced on the surface of the slimy green pond.

In a flash of dastardly insight, a plan germinated in my brain. I studied each of Galton's movements until it congealed into a delicious epiphany. A heavy metal cable descended from a twisted crane boom and disappeared underground. It re-emerged on the other side of the bike path and attached to an enormous metal drag bucket. If I could dislodge the cable from the soil and pull it tight across the trail at just the right moment, perhaps I could force a wreck and jump on the bully before he could get up. Pry bars, loose boards, pick handles, and a plethora of other refuse would provide a makeshift weapon.

It was a long shot, but I was determined to take it. My army green shirt blended well with the foliage, so I slithered down the sloping rock face, crouching behind tall stalks of ragweed and scrub brush. By the time I reached the boom, the motorcycle was clattering and smoking badly. Grails stopped and dismounted a hundred yards away. He checked the gas tank, and attempted to kick start the motor, but it sputtered and died. He shouted a string of curses as he pushed the bike up the hill toward the exit.

I missed my chance and bemoaned my lousy luck and indecisiveness.

With Galton's departure, I made my way over to the dragline. Pulling on the cable, it yielded slightly. Determined to work the plan in hopes of a future opportunity, I tugged against the thick metal braid on each side of the bike trail, alternating between the boom and bucket. The roots of weeds and saplings slowed the process, but

I located a discarded shovel blade, and five minutes later, I had most of the cable free. One quick pull would do the trick.

While camouflaging my handiwork with sand and straw, I glanced up to the entrance and saw Grails sitting on the motorcycle at the top of the rim. A bolt of electric terror shot down my spine. I was out in the open. He rolled the bike down the hill and popped the clutch. The engine ignited and he gunned the accelerator, heading straight for me. Searching for cover, I pressed my back against a rusty metal beam protruding from the quarry floor next to the drag bucket.

Dust and exhaust fumes choked my throat as Grails sped past me. My guts turned to water. Was he toying with me? Panic consumed me as I ran for the rock face and started climbing. A glance over my shoulder revealed him maneuvering around curves and jumping dirt mounds, just like before. He was utterly preoccupied and hadn't seen me. So much debris. So many shadows. Rescued by a stroke of dumb luck.

My courage reignited, and determination welled up in my chest. It was now or never. He was at the far end of the quarry, making his last turn back toward my position. He would be on me again in 60 seconds.

Hunkering down, I slid back to the quarry floor, ducked behind the drag bucket, and grabbed the cable. Doubts clouded my mind. This was a stupid scheme. These tricks only worked in the movies. My heart sank as I turned to see Humper carelessly loping in my direction, tail wagging.

Engine clatter reverberated in a deafening crescendo and Galton sped up just as Humper crossed the trail. The collision launched the helpless dog into a thick clump of thorny locust briars.

The heavy motorbike wobbled and weaved, but remained upright. Galton shouted in triumph as Humper thrashed against the vicious spiked briars. Lacerations on his head and neck bled profusely, and he yelped in agony. The impact severed the tip of his left ear off. The malevolent bastard spun around for another attack, and spotting me, he let out a fiendish scream and gunned the throttle. Galton pulled a club out of the side saddlebag and twirled it with diabolic dexterity. The moment of truth had come. As the bully approached, I summoned every ounce of strength I could muster and pulled on the cable. It seemed to snag for a split second before it popped free from the ground.

The drag bucket lurched with a loud metallic *clang* and the frayed strands of the rusty cable ripped the flesh of my hands upon impact. The motorcycle flipped, then the engine backfired before going silent. Time seemed to stand still as I raised my eyes to a surreal vision. Grails tumbled through the air, in slow motion, arms and legs flailing. My soul rejoiced, and for a moment, an orchestra in my head blasted the opening salvo of Richard Wagner's "Ride of the Valkyries." In a moment of paradoxical loveliness, the deranged black demon of mythos sailed through the air, screaming at the top of his lungs. I savored each millisecond of his terror, not wanting it to end. Alas, gravity triumphed, and Galton hit the ground with all the grace and majesty of a gut shot buzzard. A delicate puff of ochre dust highlighted the devastating finale. I raised the shovel blade, screamed like a banshee, and rushed toward my nemesis to thwart any attempt at a counterattack. I needn't have bothered. The Leviathan of my torment twitched and groaned, reduced to a morbid mass of miserable protoplasm.

My palms oozed blood where the cable had snapped and ripped the flesh. It was a satisfying, invigorating pain. A measly fee for a masterpiece of revenge.

I approached my tormentor's carcass with pitiless resolve. He lay face up with the crotch of his pants ripped open, revealing a bald scrotum encrusted with a constellation of inflamed pustules—evidence of a raw razoring at the hands of Otho's dutiful deputies. I ripped off his black shirt and hurried to Humper's side, lifting him out of the tangle of briars. The poor beast was in terrible agony. The sweat-soaked garment was a pathetic poultice for the noble canine, but he calmed a bit with the heartfelt attention. I gathered up the dog and laid him in the shade of a sweet gum sapling. He licked my hands as I dabbed the wounds, silent in his suffering.

"Humper, stay put for a spell and I promise to get you out of here and treat these cuts. I have some long overdue business to conduct with that mean sumbitch on the ground, but rest assured, I'll be back."

Returning to my vanquished adversary, I savored the sight. The boy's chest heaved and his eyes rocked side to side in their sockets like marbles twirling in a washbasin. Bloody spittle drained out of the corner of his mouth and ragged breaths were intermixed with a raspy cough.

Drawing inspiration from Melchior and Dipdottle, I entered a tranquil, transcendental, theatrical state as I squatted down and studied my handiwork. I addressed my antagonist using my favorite Sean Connery impersonation. "Galton, I have never seen you look so well! That was a very impressive feat of acrobatics. You have genuine talent and should have your own television show, just like Evel

Knievel. Of course, you would need a suitable *nom de guerre*. Let's see. You could be Crusty Crotchrot or Shifty Shitstorm. Perhaps something a little more sophisticated like Frothy Flatus or Drippy Dickcheese. Hey, I've got it: Goopy Groovestain! It just rolls off the tongue, doesn't it? You wouldn't even have to change your initials. Hey! You could get some of those tight, crotchless ass chaps to show off your diseased balls. The girls would love that. One look at you, and their panties would just drop down around their ankles. Imagine all the nookie you'd get! Speaking of girls, that prank you pulled on Brandy O'Dell was a classic. Nasty rubbers in a dirty paper sack. I would never have thought of such an ingenious gag. No wonder you are so popular with the ladies. You also impressed Missy Turnbow with your good looks and suave machismo."

Grails gurgled, and his eyelids fluttered. A pack of Parliament cigarettes lay nearby. Ejected from his shirt pocket on impact, no doubt. I rifled through his jeans for some matches and came out with a new Zippo lighter and eleven bucks. I stuffed the money in my shoe, lit up a cig, and blew smoke into his face before continuing my soliloquy.

"I'll give Mickey and Sara your regards. They'll get a chuckle out of our little tête-à-tête. Maybe I'll drag your motorcycle over here and lay that red-hot muffler across your face! I could sizzle your eyelids off. I wouldn't want you to miss a glorious moment of our fortuitous encounter."

Voices yelling from the upper rim of the quarry interrupted my sadistic musings.

The Barge brothers. Cletus was waving a dirty T-shirt and Clydell was screaming; "Hey man. Is your friend hurt? He looks pretty bad. Should we go for help?"

I couldn't help wondering, how much did they see?

I hollered back, "Yeah, I thought he just got the wind knocked out of him, but he might have bumped his head. Y'all go for help, and I'll stay by his side. Please hurry!" I cursed myself for the last remark. I was really thinking, *Take your time. Drink a beer. Smoke another joint. Eat brunch at the damn Country Club.*

* * *

The ambulance was a 1964 long wheelbase Cadillac Eureka. A pontoon boat on wheels. The Detroit monstrosity couldn't navigate the steep serpentine trail from the quarry rim to the bottom, so two pudgy, middle-aged attendants tried wheeling a gurney down the rocky path. Anyone with half a brain could have seen it coming. The contraption got away from them and tumbled down the steep path end over end, ejaculating sheets, pillows, pads, and oxygen bottles all the way down to the bottom. Idiocy is a time-honored art form in Dix Knob, and these hapless creatures were masters of the craft. I laughed. Humper snarled. Galton groaned.

The sheriff and two deputies arrived just as the attendants hoisted Galton onto the lopsided stretcher and began the slow, arduous journey up the hill. I returned to Humper's side and dabbed his wounds while Otho spoke with the attendants.

"The boy doesn't look too good. Get him to the ER, and have the charge nurse call Dr. DeSilva. He probably has a concussion."

He paused by the trail, looked at the bike, kicked the rusty cable, and glared at me.

"What the hell happened here?"

I knew it was futile to tell the sheriff an outright lie, so I concocted a cushioned confession. "It's my fault, Sheriff. Galton hit Humper, and I ran to help and tripped over the cable just as he was speeding by. I guess it caught the front wheel of the motorbike. Next thing I knew, he was on the ground moaning."

He nudged the shovel blade with the toe of his boot, looked at the shirt under Humper's head, and grabbed my wrists. My bloody palms told the true story.

The man shook his head and rubbed his eyes in exasperation. "Teddy, I'm fed up with people lying to me."

"Yeah, I imagine so. He hit Humper, and I snapped. I pulled the metal cable and sent the bastard flying."

"You better pray to God that this worthless sack of shit doesn't die. I'll have to do something then. Something I don't want to do. Something we'll both regret. Get in the car and we'll go to the hospital together. I can't let you out of my sight. C'mon, Humper, let's get you to the vet."

The dog obeyed and slowly limped behind.

The three of us trudged up the hill in silence. As we neared the crest of the quarry, a deputy shouted from below.

"Sheriff, you've got to see this.... we've got us a big ass bloated floater!"

I turned to look, just as the two junior lawmen pulled a naked, swollen body to the edge of the seep pond. There was a jagged gash in the right side of his head.

18

It's amazing how a glorious victory can turn into a steaming pile of shit in the blink of an eye. I prayed for Galton's recovery while imagining myself at the Gatesville Reformatory, wearing a tiara and taffeta tutu. Prom queen. Belle of the ball. The other inmates goosing me, clapping, laughing, and whistling.

Otho ordered the deputies to cover the victim with a canvas tarp until the crime scene could be processed.

"Get some grappling hooks and dredge the bottom. See if there's a weapon, or any clothing or personal effects to help us ID this victim. If there is any evidence, I want it found. Round up the Barge Brothers. Bring them in for questioning. Press 'em hard. Find out if any of the dopers saw anything last night. It's time for some top-notch police work. You got it?"

Both deputies gave a curt salute.

"Ain't this a fine kettle of fish?" Otho muttered as he loaded Humper in the back seat with me. "I told Galton a dozen times to stay out of this old pit. It's going to be a long day. We'll stop by Dr. Terrell's office and drop off this mangy mutt. Get him patched up. Teddy, stick to your original story for now. You tripped over the cable and Galton crashed. Pure and simple. No other details. Got it?" I nodded in grateful agreement.

On the way to midtown, Otho radioed the dispatcher to contact the state police for help with the murder scene. The veterinarian's office was across the street from Kushner County General. When the townsfolk didn't get the answers they wanted from their family physician, they'd walk over to Dr. Terrell's clinic for a second opinion. The veterinarian treated a lot of two-legged animals and had stitched up more late-night brawl injuries than any of the docs in the ER.

Wrapping the dog in an oversized beach towel, he said, "I'll set old Humper up on an IV of saline and antibiotics after I stitch these wounds. Pretty nasty, but I've seen worse." Turning to the sheriff, he asked, "Who's going to pay for all of this?" Both men laughed and simultaneously repeated the standard Dix Knobber response, "We'll take up a collection."

I grabbed the eleven dollars I had stolen from Galton at the quarry and handed it to Doc Terrell. He plucked a one-dollar bill out of the wad and returned the rest.

"Your contribution is duly noted. I'll keep Humper in the kennel for a couple of days. De-worm him and fatten him up a little. When he's strong enough, I'll turn him loose. Y'all get out of here and let me tend to my patient."

* * *

Dr. DeSilva was already in the OR with Galton. Dr. Linquist was scrutinizing a dozen X-rays. Otho stood behind him and cleared his throat politely for attention. The radiologist turned and shook his head solemnly. My heart sank.

"How bad is it?" the sheriff asked.

"Damndest thing I've ever seen. Not a single break anywhere. Not even a stress fracture."

"So he's okay?" I blurted.

"I didn't say that. He has a severe concussion and a subdural hematoma. Bleeding around the brain. DeSilva is doing an emergency craniotomy to relieve the pressure right now."

The spark of hope vanished as Otho glared at me with gritted teeth.

"Beat it, Nutscalder. Get out of my sight. Go sit with Mickey O'Dell. I'll be along after I speak to the surgeon."

Eager to get away from the perturbed lawman, I ran down the hall and peeked in the room where I had seen Mic the day before. The lights were off and the room was empty. Nurse Jurnigan tapped me on the shoulder.

"They transferred Mickey to the indigent ward at the end of the hall. Tommy Crum has been sitting with Brandy. Vera just went home a few minutes ago."

I thanked her and jogged to the other end of the hospital. On the swinging double doors of the ward, someone had scrawled, "Abandon all hope, ye who enter here" in black magic marker. The graffiti had been scrubbed and sanded, but Dante's ominous message remained clearly visible. A plethora of malodorous aromas smacked me in the face when I passed through the doors. Urine, feces, vomit, and sweat, intermixed with alcohol, antiseptic, and pine cleaner. The port-o-potties at the festival smelled like a spring rose garden compared to the beggar's ward. Fluorescent lights hummed and flickered. A maze of gurgling pipes criss-crossed the ceiling. Multi-layered coats of paint cracked and peeled off walls stained with God-knows-what. Beds were separated by track-curtains emblazoned with ridiculous cartoon characters. Rejected remnants bought dirt cheap, no doubt. I peeked in the first cubicle as an elderly gentleman struggled with a plastic pitcher. Trembling hands spilled lukewarm water on the floor as he attempted to fill a paper cup. I stepped in, steadied his hand, and retrieved a straw from a rusted bedside table.

"If I can find an ice machine in this miserable place, I'll get you a proper drink, old timer."

He nodded, took a noisy gulp, laid back, and closed his jaundiced eyes. A thick double curtain concealed the second space with a yellow sign pinned to the drape. "Tertiary Syphilis. Masked and Gloved Personnel Only." I tiptoed past. Mic was in the third stall. Tommy leaned against the wall and Brandy sat on the edge of the bed, dabbing her brother's forehead with a damp cloth. Her hair was disheveled and her mascara was smeared. Both were unaware of the events of the morning. Tommy said, "Mickey wakes up for a minute or two when the sedatives wear off. He is still in a lot of pain, but his fever is down a bit. Nobody checks on him except Dr. DeSilva and Nurse Jurnigan."

Brandy yawned and rubbed her eyes. "I'll stay here as long as it takes. Momma's gone home to check on the young'uns. Bless their little hearts, they're scared them to death. Strangers guarding the house with guns everywhere. I know the men mean well, but the little ones don't understand."

I rubbed her shoulders. Tense ropy knots yielded very little. She leaned back against me and I deliberately willed her exhaustion and sorrow into me. I had grown to care for her deeply and wanted to ease the burden of her guilt.

I said, "Brandy, go home and get some sleep. Tommy and I will take turns keeping watch. Mic won't be alone for a split second."

"Do what he says, girl." A gruff voice startled us from behind the curtain. The Sheriff stuck his head through. "Vera and those little girls need you at home. If he stabilizes, they're going to ship him off to Hermann Hospital in a day or two to let the specialists check him over. You need to be rested to see him off. These two hoodlums will keep an eye on the town hero."

Brandy looked at Otho and then back and forth to me and Tommy. We smiled and nodded.

"God, I *could* use a shower and a pot of hot coffee. Promise me you'll call if anything changes. Good or bad."

We swore oaths to Jesus, Mary, and all the saints we could call to mind. Brandy left, and the sheriff ordered me not to leave the hospital.

"There's a lot of blood on Galton's brain. We don't know how much damage was done. DeSilva is closing him up right now."

Tommy's mouth dropped open, and he started to speak, but I waved him off.

"Sheriff, I haven't told Tommy or Brandy about Galton or the body in the pond."

"You stay put, Teddy. I mean it. No hijinks. No bullshit. I'll be back later. I've got a murder victim to identify."

Sheriff Wheat spun on his heel and left without another word. Tommy's apprehensive eyes appeared enormous behind the magnification of his thick glasses.

"What happened to Galton? I've only been here for a couple of hours and the outside world is going to hell in a handbasket."

We sat on the floor between the wall and Mic's bed. I told Tommy the whole story. Galton, Humper, the Barge brothers, and the body. Nothing held back. I knew he wouldn't gab. He wasn't the type.

"What do you think will happen if Galton dies?"

"Who knows? I'd probably get the same treatment as Pete O'Dell. Or worse."

"Damn Teddy. First Mic. Now you? My circle of friends is evaporating right before my cursed eyes."

"Not so fast, Tommy boy," a voice croaked from the bed above.

We were on our feet in an instant. Mickey had one bloodshot eye open, shooting us the bird at us with his left hand.

"You guys better not write me off just yet. I'm going to be a movie star, like John Wayne, live in a mansion, with an Olympic-sized swimming pool, and a bunch of big-boobed girls everywhere."

Tommy laughed and said, "He's delirious, obnoxious, and cussing. That's definitely a good sign."

"I heard that, you four-eyed pecker. I heard all about Teddy's adventure at the quarry, too. Jeez, I wish I'd been there … arghhhhhhh! … my guts are on fire. I need something to drink. One of you losers go get me a soda."

Nurse Jurnigan jerked the curtain open and said, "If you take a drink and get a belly full of gas, you'll rupture those sutures and bleed to death. Nothing but ice chips for you!" She injected the IV port with a syringe full of a yellow liquid. A moment later, Mic's eyes fluttered and closed.

"You boys know better than to give him anything to eat or drink. Right? He has inflammation in the pancreas, a common complication after a splenectomy. Dr. DeSilva said we may have to delay transferring him to Houston for a day or two until the meds take effect. He's gonna need a lot of specialized care. Visiting hours are nearly over, anyway. Don't worry, I'll look after him. Go home."

I said, "The sheriff told me not to leave, because…"

"You tell Sheriff Otho Wheat I ran you off. If he needs an explanation, he knows where to find me. Now beat it, and don't let the door hit you in the ass on the way out."

An eye peeked out of a gap in the curtain of the syphilis cubicle. I wondered if the occupant had been eavesdropping.

Halfway down the hall, a custodian was gathering meal trays from the private patient rooms and stacking them on a cart. I grabbed a half empty glass of iced tea and topped it off with another.

"That's nasty. You're not gonna drink that, are you?" Tommy asked.

"I promised a fellow a cold drink a while ago. Come with me."

Returning to the ward, I found the old man lying on his left side, listening intently to the soft voice of Syphilis Guy in the adjacent cubicle.

He said, "Keep your chin up, my friend. This high-powered medicine is helping and I'm getting stronger every day. Once I get my legs under me, I'll go get us a six pack of cold beer."

I stuck the straw in his mouth and glazed eyes rolled back in his head as he gulped.

I told the hidden syph guy, "I brought the old timer some iced tea to hold him over until you can score that beer."

"Ahhhh. An angel of mercy condescends to assist a forsaken soul in the indigent ward."

"An angel? Hardly. Just a guilt-ridden mortal, trying to do a good deed and buy back a favor from God. Watered down tea is all I can offer. I suspect the old fellow would prefer a beer."

The mysterious venereal patient mixed a cough with a chuckle and said, "Touche my friend, touche. Benjamin Franklin supposedly said, 'Beer is proof that God loves us and wants us to be happy.' I don't know if the quote is true, but the sentiment certainly is. I confess eavesdropping on your conversation earlier. I'll pray for you. I'm sure your recent escapades had justifiable grounds. Your secret is safe with me and our senile friend. At any rate, I believe The Almighty is amused by the prayers of the guilt-ridden."

"I suspect the Devil is too. Amused, that is."

"I will speak with him on your behalf when I see him."

"God or the Devil?"

"Ha, ha, ha … who the hell do you think?"

19

TOMMY AND I EMERGED FROM THE REAR ENTRANCE OF THE hospital to a twilight thunder shower, so we paused under the ambulance bay to wait it out. Three cars pulled into the adjacent lot in quick succession. Dr. DeSilva's Riviera, Sheriff Otho Wheat's patrol car, and Danni's Star Chief. DeSilva ran up the ramp, not even closing his car door. Otho did it for him and escorted Danni and Brandy O'Dell to the covered bay. The sheriff glared at me.

"I told you to stay put, boy."

Tommy intervened. "Nurse Jurnigan ran us off, Mr. Wheat. She said Mic needed rest. We were just waiting here … oh my god … Dr. DeSilva … what happened?"

Something was terribly wrong. I broke out in a cold sweat. Why was the surgeon in such a hurry? Tommy bolted for the door, but Otho grabbed him by the collar.

"It's not Mickey. It's Galton Grails. The charge nurse called and said he's having seizures." He turned to face me. "It looks bad, Teddy. This could mean real trouble for you. Now you guys come back inside to the ER waiting room and stay put, while Brandy and Danni go with me down to the morgue. We need to know if the body we found at the quarry is our shooter."

"Sheriff Wheat, I want Teddy and Tommy to come with me," Brandy said as the automatic glass doors closed behind us.

"Damn it, I won't allow this to turn into some kind of morbid freak show."

Both girls stopped in their tracks, crossed their arms, and set their jaws.

Otho took off his Stetson, looked up at the ceiling, and silently mouthed something to the Supreme Architect. I couldn't tell if it was a plea or a curse.

"C'mon, let's get this done." He said.

With that minor capitulation, Danni sidled up next to the sheriff and distracted him with her recollections of the suspect. "Ugly bastard. A funny birthmark like a crescent moon on his right cheek. Tattoos of snakes, skulls, and swastikas are all over his arms."

Brandy grabbed my hand and held me back a few steps.

She said, "Arthur Rumkin was at the house and said Galton had a motorcycle accident down at the quarry. He heard a rumor that you bushwhacked him. Galton's momma and daddy are raising a ruckus. Whining and trying to paint him as some kind of poor, retarded angel. Crocodile tears aplenty, trying to get sympathy and begging everybody for money. The Barge brothers had a lot of weed in their car when deputies caught up with them. Some state undercover agents were tailing them too, and threatened to bust 'em on distribution charges. They threw you under the bus, trying to make a deal, saying that you set a death trap for Galton. It doesn't look good, Teddy. They've got you on the ropes. Rick Blaine and Burtis Crum are looking for your daddy. Otho's trying to keep a lid on it, but if the genie gets out of the bottle, and this boils over, it could get nasty, real quick."

As we started down the stairs to the morgue, the realization settled in. I was in deep shit. My knees got wobbly, and I broke out in a cold sweat. Brandy tried to keep me steady, but I stumbled on the last step and fell forward on all fours. The wounds on my hands started bleeding again. Tommy and Danni rushed to my side, and helped me up. Everyone was staring at me.

Otho barked. "Shake it off, Teddy. C'mon, girls, let's get this done."

* * *

Basements are a bad idea in East Texas. Constant humidity, frequent flash floods, and fluctuating groundwater tables cause mold, mildew, and noxious air to flourish in any underground environment. No amount of ventilation helps. The hospital's morgue was small with only six refrigerated slide-in mortuary cabinets. Most of the occupants were floaters. Gas-bloated bodies found bobbing in the mighty Sabine, snagged on a low branch or trot line. Ninety-nine percent went unclaimed. Vagrants and drifters. Unfortunate souls who misjudged the current or their swimming ability. City elders dedicated a special place in Dix Knob Memorial Cemetery to the forsaken, claimed by the merciless waterway. Here lies John Doe #11, claimed by the Sabine River, so and so date, the headstone would read.

The unpleasant, burly attendant sported a black rubberized apron and a sinister smirk. He kept his eyes on Brandy as she timidly stepped forward. He slid the tray out of the wall and pulled back the plastic sheet in one fluid movement. The ghoul had been practicing. Nostrils flared, eyes sparkled, and a perverted grin spread across his face. This was turning him on. Brandy gasped and swallowed hard. The floater's glazed eyes were half open, and the body was purple and bloated. His skull was exposed by the ragged gash on the right side of his scalp. The penis was gnarled and grotesque. The slimy attendant slid on a rubber glove and shook the diseased organ at Brandy and Danni.

"Looks like this Romeo had a serious case of the Ball Head Clap. You ladies want to lean in for a closer look?"

Otho stepped forward, but Danni beat him to the punch. She lunged across the corpse and smacked the snarky bastard in the mouth with a right hook that would have made George Foreman proud. He staggered back wide-eyed, and the sheriff grabbed Danni around the waist as she raced around the table to finish the job.

Otho hollered, "Alright! That's enough of this shit. Is this the shooter or not?"

Brandy shrugged. "I don't know for sure. I don't think so. This guy is too tall, and there's no birthmark on his face."

Danni grabbed the right arm and lifted it up for inspection. Part of the flesh slid away, exposing shiny silver flexor tendons near the wrist. Shaking her head, she dropped the extremity and turned her head to retch.

Between gags she said, "This ain't the guy … no snake and skull tattoos." She looked at Brandy for affirmation.

"Danni's right. We spent a lot of time with the guy at the club. When he showed up at the house, I knew who it was immediately. Even in the dark. He smelled of BO and cheap aftershave, had a heavy Cajun accent, and a short-sleeved yellow shirt with lightning bolts embroidered above the pockets. This isn't the guy."

Trying to save face after his embarrassing misstep with the girls, the attendant pointed to a duffel bag in the corner. "Sheriff Wheat, your deputies brought this in with the body. They said it was all the evidence they dredged out of the quarry pond. I swear to God I didn't mess with any of the stuff inside, but you can see some yellow cloth right there on top. It might be the shirt."

Otho took a pocket knife and cut through the cord, binding the recovered evidence. Sure enough, there was a yellow shirt, just as Brandy described. He shook it out and held it next to the turgid carcass. It was way too small for the dead fellow on the table.

He said, "One more mystery to add to the mix. This body is a red herring. Someone murdered this poor bastard and went to a lot of trouble to make it look like Mickey's attacker. Who the hell is this guy, and where is the perp who shot Mickey?"

20

OTHO QUOTED ALL KINDS OF LAWS, SUB-SECTIONS, AND penal codes if the orderly altered one stray hair on the corpse.

"You sleep on the floor and piss in the sink if you have to. I'm holding you personally responsible for this victim and all the evidence in that bag. Do you understand me?"

Wide-eyed and sweating, the man croaked a meek, "Yes, sir."

As we turned to leave, a petite, auburn-haired nurse met us halfway up the stairs and told Otho a phone call was waiting for him at her station. He jogged to the counter, took the receiver, and listened intently for a few seconds before abruptly slamming down the phone.

"You boys ride with me. Danni and Brandy follow me over to the warehouse on Bolton Street. Things are heating up, and I don't want to let any of you out of my sight until I straighten this mess out."

The nurse tugged on the sheriff's sleeve. "Dr. DeSilva is preparing for another surgery on the Grails boy. He called in a pathologist from Nacogdoches. One of his Cuban friends. He's going to want to speak with you when he gets done."

He replied, "I'll be back as soon as I get some answers about the corpse in the morgue." The sheriff took a card out of his pocket and handed it to the nurse. "Here is the phone number to my office. When the doc finishes, just call the dispatcher and she will relay the message over the car radio."

* * *

Bolton Street was much like Kickapoo. Full of potholes, and lined with overgrown right of ways and abandoned buildings. The warehouse was a dingy, gray, cinder block structure with a high chain-link fence topped with coils of razor wire. There were heavy metal sliding barn style doors, shut tight. Yellow sodium vapor lamps, positioned on high poles at each corner of the property, gave an eerie glow to everything they touched.

Otho looked in the rearview mirror and said, "You guys stay put and listen to the radio. If a call comes in, send one of the girls to get me." He adjusted the volume and squelch before exiting the car.

Nollen Embers and a man holding the leash of a German Shepherd met the sheriff at the gate. The dog's brindle coat, black snout, and dark eyes gave him an eerie, demonic quality in the harsh, artificial light.

Nollen said, "Sheriff, we had a minor incident here at the warehouse last night, and I thought you should know about it." He pointed to the man standing next to him. "Tell him what happened, Butch."

The man shuffled his feet nervously, and the big dog growled. "A guy named Carl Ed Stamper showed up last night, threatening to burn the place down if I didn't release the Chevy Nova I repossessed from him last month. He was real nervous. Kept looking over his shoulder, like someone was following him. He didn't have enough money to catch up on the payments, so I threatened to sic the dog on him and he left."

Otho's eyes narrowed. He wasn't buying any of this tale. He took a little notebook out of his shirt pocket, slid a pencil out of the spiral wire, licked the graphite tip, and took a step toward the man until he was literally nose to nose with him. "So, tell me Butch, why didn't you call the authorities when this happened?"

The man swallowed hard and started to speak, but Embers nudged him aside.

"That is one-hundred percent my fault, Sheriff Wheat. I've told Butch and all of my employees to never call the police unless it's a real, bona fide emergency. I know your resources are stretched thin, and you have better things to do than get bogged down in petty disputes with deadbeats and..."

Otho held up his hand to Nollen's face, never taking his eyes off Butch. The dog stopped panting, squatted behind his handler, and froze.

"I want to have a look at Carl Ed Stamper's automobile." Butch and Nollen exchanged a quick, nervous glance. Otho casually put his hand on his holster and stepped in between the two men. His monumental stature and instinct for bullshit made him a daunting interrogator.

The sheriff said, "I can get a search warrant in about six minutes. All I have to do is get on that radio. Judge Marlin Choate and I are old fishing buddies."

Nolan quickly regained his composure and sported a slimy smile. "No, no, no. You don't need a warrant. I'm just a little embarrassed. Butch isn't exactly a neat freak. The place is a mess, and I'm a lousy record keeper. It might take a while to dig up the paperwork on the car."

The sleaze was stalling, and the sheriff knew it. "Well, Mr. Embers, you start diggin' and I'll get old Butch to give me the nickel tour of your warehouse and the repossessed car."

Butch secured the dog to a post by the gate before sliding back the massive doors of the warehouse. The balanced wheels and well-greased top rails made the maneuver effortless and almost inaudible. Brandy and Danni were huddled on the hood of the Star Chief, straining to see inside. Tommy and I couldn't view much from our position in the back seat of the cruiser. With the doors locked, we would have to climb over the front seat to get out. Neither of us were inclined to do so.

As the men disappeared inside the building, a pebble hit the windshield with a clink. Brandy was trying to get our attention and Danni hunkered down, so no one inside the warehouse could see. Gesticulating wildly, she motioned us to come over. Tommy leaned over the driver's seat, rolled the window down, and slithered out. Ducking his head back in, he said, "Stay put, and keep an ear on the radio. I'll see what's up with the girls." He crawled over to Danni and they both peeked over the trunk toward the building. I didn't see the commotion at first. There was a small window about eight feet off the ground near the rear of the structure. A delicate, feminine arm protruded from the casement, waving a red towel. The hair on the back of my neck stood up. Was someone trying to signal us? Missy? I jumped over the seat and opened the door, activating the dome light. I cursed my stupidity, but apparently no one in the building noticed. All four of us converged behind Danni's car.

Brandy said, "I think that's your girlfriend, Teddy. We need to figure out a way to get you past that dog so you can check it out. Anybody got any ideas?"

Danni laughed. "I believe I can distract the dog using a neat old Indian trick."

She reached into the rear floorboard of her car and came out with an empty quart milk carton. Unzipping her jeans, she said, "You guys turn your heads for a minute." Tommy and I snapped our heads around like soldiers in a parade line. I could hear a stream of liquid reverberating against the bottom of the carton.

Danni zipped up and said, "Okay, Brandy, you're next."

"Sugar, you're mad as a hatter, if you think I'm gonna piss in a milk carton."

"We all gotta do it. It won't work unless we all contribute."

Brandy resisted. "Uh ... Danni ... it's *that* time of the month, and besides that, I've got a shy bladder. I can't work up any pee."

"That's even better, just throw in your dirty..."

Leaping to Brandy's rescue, Tommy interrupted the exchange with a stammer. "Okay, okay ... I might be able ... let me try..."

Danni handed him the carton, and my lanky friend turned away, shuffled his feet, reached into his trousers and heaved mightily as though he was trying to hoist a crocodile into a canoe. Both girls leaned over for a peek. My sight-impaired companion had no peripheral vision, and I didn't have time to warn him. Brandy's jaw dropped, and Danni whistled. Tommy finally finished and handed me the warm cardboard carton.

I said, "No need to turn aside, ladies. Nothing to see here. Nothing of any consequence." Brandy and Danni giggled. Poor Tommy just sat there, befuddled by the whole exchange.

When I finished contributing my meager portion, Danni snatched the container from me and said, "I'll be able to buy you a minute at the most. When I give you the signal, run to the window. Make it quick. Brandy, you follow my lead. Tommy, keep watch."

I learned something that night. Dogs are fascinated by urine. Danni meandered over to the beast, gently sloshing the contents of the carton. She leaned forward and poured a dab next to the gate. The canine stopped barking and his ears perked up. He sniffed the ground and wagged his tail. The ladies slowly sauntered through the gate. Cooing in Koasati, Danni carefully poured the entire contents over the beast's head and back. He shook and licked, snorted and rolled in the dirt. Danni nodded, and I bolted to the window. Not a bark. Not even a growl.

The barren warehouse surroundings and harsh lighting left me conspicuously exposed as I ran toward the window. Missy Turnbow stared down at me in panic. "Teddy, what's going on? How did you get past Satan?"

"Satan?"

"The dog, Teddy, the dog!"

"Oh! Danni poured pee all over him. Some kind of old Indian trick to distract the animal. It worked."

"What's happening? Why is Sheriff Wheat here?"

"I don't know where to start. They found a body in the quarry pond, but it wasn't the guy who shot Mickey. Otho is trying to identify him. Everybody is still on the lookout for the shooter. Are you stuck in a closet or something?"

"I'm locked in the office. Nollen isn't letting me out of his sight. If I make a peep, and the sheriff gets nosey, he and Butch might start shooting. There was an altercation at our house last night. Carl Edwin Stamper knew about the shooter and was trying to blackmail him. Demanding money and his car back from Butch. I saw Nollen hit him with a tire iron. I think he might have killed him. They are making up some story to throw the cops off their trail. I'll bet that's the guy they found floating in the quarry."

"Yeah, it makes sense now. They are killing two birds with one stone. They got rid of Stamper and tried to pass him off as the shooter by planting a shirt that Brandy and Danni could identify, but it didn't work. Otho took the girls down to the morgue for a look. The dead guy didn't have any tattoos on his arms. The body on the slab was too big for the shirt.

"I'm scared, Teddy. Nollen looks calm on the surface, but he's coming unglued. He heard a rumor that some of his own guys are planning to bump him off and take over the business. One thing is for sure. He knows the shooter. They must have taken his shirt and planted it. I don't know if he's dead too, or just lying low. Either way, I've got to get away from Nollen. My mother is in a stupor. She doesn't even know what day it is."

A stone ricocheted off the wall and hit me on the hip. It was Brandy, motioning me to come. She mouthed, "We gotta get out of here."

I glanced back up at the face in the window. That beautiful, terrified face. She blew me a kiss and threw the red grease rag at me. Something was scribbled on it, but I didn't have time to look. I stuffed it in my pocket as I backed toward the gate.

"I'll be back, Missy Turnbow. Somehow. Someway." A sinking sense of hopelessness enveloped me like thick fog. Who was I trying to fool? There was nothing I could do. I didn't have influence or money, and I didn't have a plan.

I paused at the corner of the warehouse and peeked around to the open doors. The dog was barking again as the girls were walking inside.

In a sing-song voice, Brandy shouted, "Otho? Butch? Nollen? There are a couple of ladies out here that are pretty desperate to tinkle. Can we use the restroom?" Danni flashed me a harsh frown and jerked her thumb over her shoulder toward the cars. Tommy was peeking out of the rear window of Otho's Cruiser, glasses glowing like a jack-o'-lantern in the orange light. Satan strained against the leash, snarling. I kicked him in the snout as I ran through the gate and he latched onto a shoe, but the nasty Keds were too much for him and he let go. It's weird what goes through your mind during stressful moments. I thought about my old friend, Humper. A good dog who would never bite anyone. I hadn't checked on him all day. I'd have to stop by Obermeyer's and get a scrap or two for him. My brain was reeling from overload. I had to get somewhere quiet, where I could calm down and think.

I climbed back in the car with Tommy, filled him in on the quick conversation I had with Missy, and showed him the rag. There were some strange letters and numbers written on it.

FOS- 34-46-09 4-5AM

"Missy threw this to me as I was leaving, but I ain't got a clue what it means. Do you have any ideas?"

Tommy held it up to the light, adjusted his glasses, and smiled. "I definitely know what this is!" He scrutinized the markings as he carefully smoothed the cloth out on his lap.

"Don't keep me in suspense. Tell me what it means."

"What's it worth to you?"

"It's worth me not kicking your ass!" I said as I punched him in the arm.

"I'm just kidding, Teddy. Calm down. This is a fallout shelter emergency phone number."

I must have looked completely bewildered, and he chuckled as he handed the cloth back to me.

"It's a special hotline phone number. When you dial FOS, which represents the numbers 3-0-9, it automatically channels the call to a special series of underground cables. The last two digits represent the bunker number. In this case, number 9. This allows you access to all the local fallout shelters. It's like a giant party line. If you ring one, you will ring them all. There might be 10 or 12 on the same circuit. If you dial in from a standard outside residential phone, anyone who picks up on any of the connected phones can talk and listen in. If the Russians start a nuclear war, survivors can still communicate through the protected network. These are exclusive, unlisted numbers, for civil defense. My father told me only big wigs with the local government and utility districts are supposed to have them. There is one in the basement at the Palisades. A couple of times a year it screams like a banshee, and when you pick up the receiver, you get a recorded announcement that it's just a test. Missy must have access to one of these phones. Apparently, some of the rich folks are tied into the network too. Maybe in their wine cellars or storm shelters. I guess she wants you to call between 4 and 5 AM. Hopefully, if she answers on the first ring, nobody else will hear. Most of the nuclear fallout shelters are tucked away under large business buildings. Banks, courthouses, stuff like that. There's probably not a lot of folks around that early in the morning."

"How the hell do you know all this stuff?"

"Like I said, there's one in the theater basement. There is a black booklet attached to the receiver of the telephone. I've read it, and my dad filled me in on some details. Dix Knob is less than 30 miles from the Gulf Coast, where all the refineries and chemical plants are located. This entire area is a prime target for an attack. During the Cuban Missile Crisis in 1962, they assigned everyone in the Knob to a specific shelter, depending on where you lived in town. They did drills and all that stuff. There's something else to consider. When you call, don't use your real names. Keep details as vague as possible, so any eavesdroppers can't put the pieces together."

We both jumped when the two-way radio squawked and a female voice said, "Come in, Sheriff. Are you there?"

Tommy reached over the seat and keyed the mic. "This is Tommy Crum. Sheriff Wheat is questioning Nollen Embers at the warehouse on Bolton Street. He told us to relay any messages."

There was a long pause before the dispatcher continued. "One of the hospital nurses called the station. Dr. DeSilva needs to speak with Otho right away. It's bad news about the Grails boy. Please tell him to get over to the hospital ASAP."

My stomach lurched, and I vomited on the floorboard. "Oh my god. The bastard died. This is it. I'm going to jail for sure!"

Tommy crawled out of the driver's side window, opened the back door, and helped me to my feet. "Don't panic, Teddy. Keep your composure. We don't know he's dead. Stick to your original story. It was all just a spur-of-the-moment decision. An accident." He grabbed Otho's billy-club off of the front seat. "Let's go relay the message."

Tommy steadied me as we headed toward the gate. Satan was barking, slavering, and gnashing his teeth. Tommy swung the club in a graceful sweeping motion and connected with the dog's jaw, stunning him just long enough for us to skip past.

As we approached, everyone inside emerged from the doorway acting all jolly and laughing.

The Sheriff said, "Mr. Embers, I really appreciate your cooperation and the information on the Stamper fellow. I'll look into it sometime tomorrow. If everyone had your keen sense of civic duty, my job would be a lot easier. Come on, ladies, let's leave these gentlemen to their business. Like me; I'm sure they are worn out from a long day at work, and late for supper."

Tommy and I were stunned as he shook hands with Butch and Nollen. Brandy and Danni blew kisses and thanked them for access to the restroom. Butch rushed past us to secure Satan, so we could proceed unhindered. Everything was surreal and unnatural. It felt as though we had descended into a bizarre episode of *The Twilight Zone*.

Brandy put her arm around my waist and quickened her pace. Danni did the same with Tommy as Otho snatched the billy-club from his hand and whacked him playfully in the seat of his pants.

When we got to the street, the lawman whispered, "You girls get in your car, follow me, and don't look back. Nobody looks back."

Not another word was spoken as Tommy and I climbed into the back seat of the cruiser. Otho fired the engine and sped off with Danni right on his tail.

I said, "The dispatcher called and Dr. DeSilva needs to speak with you right away. Galton is real bad."

He nodded and checked his side mirrors to make sure the girls weren't lagging behind. The radio crackled as he keyed the mic three times in rapid succession. "Lois, I want a patrol car to make a pass by the warehouse on Bolton Street every half hour until dawn. Tell the boys on duty to report anything unusual and get me all the information they can muster on Carl Edwin Stamper. S-T-A-M-P-E-R. White male, 25 to 30 years of age. He lives south of town off of the Clayburn Ranch Road. Tell them to meet me at Kushner County General in 20 minutes. No lollygagging."

Zig-zagging through parking lots and alleys, the sheriff reached the hospital in record time. He parked next to the ER, and Danni pulled in a second later. The girls bailed out of the Star Chief before Otho could get our door opened. He huddled us all together on the ambulance ramp.

"Listen and don't talk. Don't tell anyone about the meeting at the warehouse. Keep it under your hat. Not a peep. Y'all go check on Mickey, and stay put until I come and get you. If Nollen Embers, or any of his goons show up, run like hell. I think I was able to put him off, but you can never tell with that bastard. He's dangerous and unpredictable. Go on, while I speak with DeSilva." I had never seen the Sheriff so rattled. The alarm in his voice and the fear in the girls' eyes made my anxiety even worse.

The sheriff stopped at the nurses' station as the four of us hurried to the indigent ward. The lights were off and muffled snores emanated from behind the curtains. Brandy flipped on a lamp at Mickey's bedside table. His color was slightly better, and his breathing was less labored. Both girls felt his forehead and nodded to one another. We all sat down with our backs against the wall.

Tommy whispered, "What happened in the warehouse?"

Danni replied, "Brandy and I went inside pretending we needed to use the restroom. Otho was rummaging through the glove-box of Stamper's car, and as we left the toilet, I bumped against a wall cabinet and the door popped open. It was full of guns. Enough to start a war. Butch shoved me aside and pushed it closed, but not before the sheriff got a glimpse. Otho knew we were sitting on a powder keg, so he started acting all nice and cordial. When Nollen came out of the office with some paperwork, the sheriff thanked him for his cooperation and that's when you guys showed up. If we weren't there, I'm sure there would have been a shootout. On the way back to the hospital, Brandy and I discussed the situation and decided to avoid Muddy Mike's and lie low for a while. Tomorrow I'm heading over to my grandmother's place on the reservation. Nobody can find me there. Brandy can't leave the little ones, but you guys are welcome to come along." Leaning toward me, she said, "What did the little Turnbow princess have to say about all of this?"

Her flippant remark about Missy perturbed me, but I let it slide. "She's convinced Nollen knows the shooter. She thinks the guy in the morgue is Carl Ed Stamper. He was apparently trying to blackmail Embers about his relationship to the shooter. That story Butch told was a bald-faced lie to throw Otho off, in case he realized the body found in the quarry pond wasn't Mic's assailant. The whole thing is all a big ruse. Nollen is terrorizing Missy. Keeping her on a tight leash."

A moan from the bed interrupted me. Mic was awake and listening in. "I'm glad all y'all came back to see me, but keep the noise down. If we make any racket, Nurse Jurnigan will come back in here with that big ass needle of hers and put me back in a coma again. Tuck some pillows under my back so I can sit up for a while. I'm sick of staring at this dirty ceiling."

"There's a linen cabinet by the door with extra pillows and blankets," a voice said from behind the curtain. Mic's venereal suite mate had been listening in on our conversation again.

Brandy wrinkled her brow, shrugged her shoulders, and mouthed, "Who is that?"

I stepped up to the curtain next to the hidden eavesdropper. "I sure hope you are a trustworthy fellow. It seems you know all our sordid little secrets. Can we trust you, or am I going to have to poison your beer?"

The mystery man chortled and said, "Despite my current circumstances, I am a trustworthy fellow, in sympathy with your collective plight. I won't bore you with the details, but I have a vested interest in the demise of Nollen Randle Embers. Your suspicions are well founded. He is a criminal of the most vile and malevolent nature. The bane of my existence. He harmed someone I loved very much."

Danni said, "What shall we call the mysterious man behind the curtain? The mighty and powerful Oz?"

The hidden fellow laughed and said, "My friends just call me Gus."

Tommy returned with an arm full of blankets, and we carefully lifted Mic's shoulders and propped him up in a semi-reclined position.

He adjusted the IV line and rubbed his eyes. "You guys go and get that cute little redheaded nurse. Tell her I need a sponge bath." My heart leapt with joy. Our brave friend was on the mend. Brandy shed tears of relief and wrapped her arms around the pillow, supporting his head.

"Don't smother me to death, sis!" he said. She hugged even tighter, nuzzled his ear, and started whispering thanks for his recovery while admonishing him for stepping between her and the shooter. The rest of us eased outside the curtain to give them a moment of privacy.

I took the interlude to ask Gus about his neighbor in the adjacent cubicle. "How is the old fellow doing this evening? He doesn't say much."

"He's in the final stages of advanced dementia and doesn't even know his own name. No one comes to visit. The good-hearted nurses and doctors are keeping him alive with tapioca and intravenous solutions, but they're not doing him any favors. They should let him go."

Otho Wheat appeared at the door and motioned for me to come. Tommy and Danni took a step toward him, but he waved them off.

"Just Teddy for now. I'll be back for the rest of you directly." I followed him to the hallway.

He said, "Dr. DeSilva is consulting with a pathologist after the surgery he performed on Grails. Something bad is wrong with the boy. I figured you should hear the news firsthand. The situation with Grails, Embers, the shooter, and Stamper is all coming to a head, and I'm afraid it's going to erupt into a shitstorm of epic proportions. You are right in the middle of it all and I'm worried. I don't think I can keep a lid on your involvement in the quarry incident."

He led me to the hospital laboratory where a chubby bald man was peering through a microscope while DeSilva smeared slides with bloody tissue from a glass dish. The surgeon waved us over. "This is Dr. Bolivar from Nacogdoches. I called him in on Galton's case to examine some abnormal brain matter I extracted from the boy during surgery."

I gagged as Dr. Bolivar stood up and presented his diagnosis.

"The boy has a meningioma invading the frontal lobe. The tumor is very large. About the size of a lemon. It's rare in a teenager. Much more common in middle-aged adults. The cancer is not malignant, but can be very destructive. When it invades this area of the brain, there are usually serious behavioral issues. Before the accident, did this patient display any personality disorders? Inappropriate speech or aggression?"

Otho took off his Stetson and ran his fingers along the brim. "Yes, Doctor, the boy is very aggressive, flouting the law and other accepted social norms. Antisocial behavior has been manifesting for a long time."

Dr. Bolivar nodded gravely and continued. "That's not surprising, because these lesions are slow-growing. Symptoms of pain may not show up until the advanced stage. The trauma from the concussion and subsequent bleeding exacerbated the condition, but strangely, it may have prevented further destruction by hastening the diagnosis before it expanded into the optic nerve or temporal region of the brain. This is a very serious disease, but we may be able to salvage some of his mental capacity. Dr. DeSilva and I will attempt to arrange for a consultation with the neurosurgeons at Tulane. They may be able to remove a portion of the mass and relieve the pressure. I'll complete my analysis while Dr. DeSilva speaks to the boy's family."

Dr. Bolivar placed another slide under the scope, and DeSilva escorted us to the surgery waiting room. Galton's mother was a portly woman with a moon face and stringy hair. His father was a big brute with a crew cut and a black patch over his left eye.

When he spied me, Galton's father shouted, "There's the little bastard that hurt my boy! You're gonna pay…"

Otho punched him in the sternum and said, "Before you start throwing accusations around, I advise you to sit down, shut up, and listen to what the doc has to say. The injuries from the wreck aren't the only thing they found wrong with Galton."

Dr. DeSilva said, "The sheriff is right. There was bleeding from the impact of the motorcycle accident, but I discovered a tumor on your son's brain behind his forehead. This kind of cancer can cause aggressive behavior and impaired judgment which undoubtedly contributed to the mishap. My colleague from Nacogdoches may be able to arrange for some specialists in New Orleans to treat him."

Galton's mother covered her face with her hands. Mr. Grails was still fuming and stood up, but Otho shoved him back down into the chair and admonished him.

"Me and my deputies ran Galton out of that damn quarry a hundred times, but he kept coming back. You're just as much to blame as anybody for not keeping him reined in. Galton ran over Humper and Teddy and was just trying to rescue the mutt. It was an accident, pure and simple. Your bellicose behavior is unacceptable and won't win you any friends in this town. Galton is a bully and a troublemaker. Now we know why. The boy has a disease that makes him mean, so stop trying to lay all the blame on Teddy and start thinking about how you're going to get some medical attention to help him recover."

To diffuse the tension, Dr. DeSilva stepped between the men and said, "Galton is still in the recovery room under sedation, but you can see him now. Come with me. I'll introduce you to Dr. Bolivar, the pathologist who made the diagnosis, and we will try to answer any of your questions."

As they left the room, Tommy and the girls entered. Brandy said, "Nurse Jurnigan ran us off again and told us not to come back until tomorrow. She's spoon feeding Mic some chicken broth to see if his gut will move. She's worried about transporting him to Houston, because those injuries will throw a blood clot if they jostle the patient around too much. She said it's going to be a long recovery."

Otho replied, "Burtis Crum told me the same thing this morning. I have to stop by the station and see what the deputies dug up on Stamper. They were supposed to meet me here a half hour ago. Danni, I want you to take Teddy and Tommy home. It's getting late and none of you should be out on the streets."

No sooner were the words out of his mouth when a deputy ran in waving a hand full of documents. "Sheriff, I ran down all the info we had on Carl Edwin Stamper. A couple of drunk and disorderly citations, but not much more. He owes money all over the Delta. Apparently, he's a loner. He fits the description of the floater but I'm having trouble locating a next of kin to identify him. I'll go down to the morgue and try to get some fingerprints off the corpse, and compare them to those we find in his house tomorrow."

Otho said, "Good work. Keep at it. Any news on the shooter's car?"

"The car was definitely stolen, and the VIN number was a dud. Very professional work. It was definitely altered in a first-class chop shop. Not a word from the state boys on the shooter. We've gone door to door, but no one has seen anybody fitting the description."

Arthur Rumkin came strolling up the sidewalk as we were leaving. "Hey Teddy! I've been looking for you. Your dad is home. Rick Blaine spotted him coming out of an AA meeting over at the Baptist Fellowship Hall! That's the last place I would ... oh god, I'm sorry..."

"Think nothing of it, Mr. Rumkin. That's the last place I would have thought to look for him too!"

The sheriff smiled and said, "Arthur, I need your help in a matter of great importance. We need to control the narrative on the situation at the quarry. I believe the floater we found might be the shooter, after all. He probably got involved in a running fight with some other thugs. They shot up his car and threw him in the quarry pond for good measure. Galton has a bad brain tumor affecting his judgment. He ran over Humper, wrecked his motorbike, and Teddy was just in the wrong place at the wrong time." Rumkin was rubbing his hands and licking his lips like a hungry hobo at a Sunday buffet. He would spread this disinformation all over town, with a generous slathering of his own conjecture. The lawman winked at me and shooed us off. "Y'all get on home, keep quiet, and lie low."

As we piled into the Star Chief, Brandy looked at an imaginary watch on her wrist and said, "I estimate it will take about 27 minutes before Arthur Rumkin has the whole town buzzing with Otho's fake revelations. I don't think the actual shooter is stupid enough to come back, and maybe things will settle down until you guys can figure out what we can do to help Missy."

Tommy voiced what I was thinking. "I've been formulating a plan to get Nollen Embers out of the way, at least temporarily. Teddy and I can't do it alone and Missy is going to need some feminine expertise for her part in the scheme. That's where you lovely ladies come in. Teddy will phone her early tomorrow morning and get the inside scoop on the pervert's habits."

I said, "We definitely need your help. Tommy hasn't elaborated on all the details, but I know Missy is going to have to lure Nollen into the greenhouse and get out safely for the plan to work. Embers is a creepy control freak and apparently gets his jollies when he can see the fear in her eyes. She's scared to death."

Brandy said, "I've only got one job skill, but I'm pretty good at it. I think I can teach a little rich girl a thing or two about manipulating men."

21

DANNI DROPPED ME OFF TWO BLOCKS FROM THE HOUSE ON Kickapoo Street. I stayed in the shadows and paused by the Studebaker for a while to assess the situation. I wasn't about to let my guard down and get clobbered again. If anything looked out of sorts, I would hightail it to Casa O'Dell or the Grotto. The ramshackle structure almost looked serene. Nothing seemed amiss, so I took a chance and opened the screen door enough to make the conspicuous squeak, simultaneously plotting a course of retreat if the old man blew a gasket.

"Teddy, is that you? I fried up some pork chops earlier and left 'em covered on the stove. They're edible if you're hungry enough. I stopped by the bakery to get some of those sourdough rolls you like. Mrs. Tyler said she owed you an apology and wouldn't let me pay. What's that all about?"

I took a deep breath and walked in. Nathaniel was sitting at the dinette with a stack of engineering texts and drafting tools. Cigarette butts and coffee cups were scattered all over the place.

Determined to keep things neutral, I said. "The pork chops smell good. I am a bit on the hungry side."

"I tried to make some red-eye gravy with the skillet drippings and coffee like your mom used to do, but I didn't get it exactly right. It's too thick."

"I'm sure it will be fine," I said as I filled a plate and poured a cup of joe. "What's with all the books?"

"A contractor repaired the bridge over Black Cat Creek a couple of years ago, and I told the commissioner at the time it was shoddy work and wouldn't hold up. Well, sure enough, it collapsed today with a couple of cars on it. One driver got out okay, but the other guy busted some ribs. The boss wants to cover his ass and see if we can file a court claim to get the contractor to make it right. I'm reviewing codes and standards, trying to keep busy to stave off the alcohol cravings." He poured a cup of coffee and took a loud gulp before continuing. "Do you want to talk about the events down at the quarry? Rumkin filled me in on the story, but I would rather hear it from you. He has a bad habit of embellishing the facts to the point they're no longer facts. I want you to know that I'll back you up. Hero or villain."

I held up the palms of my hands. "There's really not much to tell. Galton ran over Humper and was bearing down on me, swinging a club and screaming like a madman. In a moment of desperation, I pulled on a metal dragline cable, flipped the motorcycle, and sent him flying. I was over at the hospital an hour ago. Apparently, Galton also has a brain tumor that makes him act like an asshole. DeSilva found it while he was operating on him."

Nathaniel nodded and took a paper sack off the top of the refrigerator, set it on the table, slid it toward me, and said, "It's been an eventful week. You seem to be embroiled in a lot of intrigue. I don't want to butt into your business. God knows I've got no right, but I wouldn't be much of a father if I didn't express some serious concerns."

I ignored the sack and said, "I'll handle whatever comes. I've decided not to roll over anymore. It's as simple as that. Nothing more. Nothing less."

He swigged coffee, stuck two Camels in his mouth, lit both, and handed one to me. "I have one more question. Answer it honestly and I'll leave you alone, and give you all the rope you need to tie up your troubles or hang yourself."

"Deal."

"How does that pretty Turnbow girl fit into all of this?"

"Her stepfather is abusing her in the most awful way. He has some kind of perverted fetish where he gets off on terrorizing her. She's resisted him so far, but his advances are becoming more persistent. She can't hold him off forever. There's no one else she can turn to. Her mother is a basket case, and he's threatening to send her to an asylum if Missy talks. She's between a rock and a hard place. The cops can't do anything, but Tommy and I have a plan."

My father sat for a long moment in silence, slowly nodding his head in thought. He got up from the table, walked to the front door, retrieved his truck keys from the peg, and laid them on the table in front of me.

"I've seen you and Mickey O'Dell driving Pete's old flatbed Dodge down the river roads. The Chevy operates on exactly the same principle. Second gear grinds a bit, so just slide it from first to third. Do what you can to help the girl. I'm bunking with Sudsy Monkhouse and some guys from AA for a few nights while I dry out and get over the DTs. They'll get me back and forth to work." He leaned down and put his cheek on the top of my head. "Son, you're a better man than me." Without another word, he walked out the door.

Mixed emotions welled up in my chest. I didn't know whether to cry or scream. Praise God or curse him. So I just finished up the chops and rolls. My heart skipped a beat as I reached for the sack Nate left on the table. Inside was a shoe box with a brand-new pair of white leatherette Adidas Superstars. The plastic smell was intoxicating. Then the tears came. A torrent of emotional waterworks, complete with sobbing, sniveling, and slobber. Stretching out on the couch, the significance of his final gesture gradually dawned on me. The truck was all he had. The house was rented. The furnishings were rummage sale junk, and past due bills littered the TV tray. I extinguished the spark of hope. I couldn't allow myself to believe he could make a meaningful change in his miserable life. The gentle clatter of the fan lulled me to sleep.

* * *

Tessa sat at Brandy's vanity table, smearing makeup over her face in a vain attempt to hide the cavernous lesions of advanced decay.

"I'm moving on, oh brother of mine! We won't be seeing each other again. Don't feel too bad about letting me choke to death on that frosty February morning seven years ago. It only hurt for a minute. That little rich girl is going to kick you in the nuts and rip your heart out, but it will

be good for you in the long run. It'll help you get all those romantic notions out of your head and toughen you up a little. The next couple of days will determine if you are a real man or just another gutless swine in a long line of gutless swine. That old black witch is trying to help you, but her spells only work if you really believe in them, and you don't really believe. Tommy and Mic do, but you don't. It is time to wake up and face the music, Pussy Boy. The day of reckoning is nigh."

* * *

The stove timer buzzed me out of a fitful slumber at 4:15 a.m. I cursed Tessa, pushing her vexing phantom to the back of my mind, shifting focus to the task at hand. As I reached for the phone, another alarming thought materialized. What if someone could trace the call? A civil defense emergency network might have some kind of system for logging calls. Paranoia was gripping me, but I couldn't let it deflect me from the promise I made to Missy. A solution appeared when I spied the truck keys on the dinette table. There was a phone booth in Rhinelander Park across from Kutz's Cleaners. I could call from there. Suddenly the phone rang, and I nearly jumped out of my skin. Snatching up the receiver, I heard Tommy on the other end.

"Teddy, I couldn't sleep. Have you called Missy yet?"

"I'm on my way to the phone booth at the park. I don't want to take a chance of the call being traced back here."

"Gosh, I hadn't thought about that. Probably a good idea. I filled Danni and Brandy in on the plan while we drove home last night. They have some great ideas. Danni has some kind of psychedelic mushroom concoction brewing. I'm not sure what she has in mind. I'll meet you at the phone booth, fill you in, and then we'll go collect the hive. DeSilva will probably send Mickey to Houston later today. We should be there to see him off."

"See you there, buddy." I scrounged up nickels as I dressed and ran through the idiotic "knight in shining armor" routine in my head. If I could pull this off, I'd be a hero. Dealing with Galton boosted my confidence, and Tommy's plan seemed no more ridiculous than my maneuver at the quarry. How complicated could it be? Cut down a giant hornet nest, stuff it in a bag, wait for nightfall, transport it across town, lure a crafty mobster into a greenhouse, stuff the nest inside, bar the door, and let the brutes sting the bastard into oblivion. What could possibly go wrong?

The truck engine was cold, I forgot how to work the choke, and the carburetor flooded. It sputtered and backfired several times before I finally got it cranked. The clutch was firm, and the gear shift was much smoother than Pete O'Dell's flatbed. The Chevy wasn't much to look at, but Nathaniel kept the mechanical aspect in tiptop shape. My first solo drive was a much needed tonic for the worries about Mic, and misgivings about Tommy's plan. For once I felt confident and even emboldened, letting out a loud "Hell yeah, baby!" as the pickup gained speed down the hill toward town. The rubber soles of my Adidas squeaked against the clutch as I shifted from first to third. I thought about Sara driving her dad's delivery truck. I wondered if she had ever had this much fun. Why was I thinking about Sara? Missy needed me.

Traffic was light, and I reached the park in no time. The square looked completely different in the predawn hour. It was peaceful. Clouds of gnats silently swarmed the antique street lamps, whip-poorwills cooed in the fragrant magnolias, while crickets chirped and tree frogs croaked. I relished the chill as my lungs drank in the cool morning air. I didn't have time to dawdle. Missy was waiting.

The booth was a replica of the red British style phone box, erected during more prosperous times of yore. Paint peeled and the delicate panes of glass were pockmarked with pings and fish eyes from random slingshot pebbles and BBs. Such is the fate of any exposed glass in an East Texas town. Even the bulletproof glass at the First National Bank had pecks and pings aplenty.

I pulled the rag out of my pocket, studied the number for the hundredth time, put two nickels in the slot, and dialed.

After one ring, Missy picked up. "Teddy?" she whispered.

"Yeah, it's me. Where are you?"

"In the storm shelter. My father put the fallout phone in years ago, but the dialer is broken, so I can't call out." There was a long pause before she continued. "Nollen cornered me last night in Mom's room. He's giving me an ultimatum. Either I give in, or he will send my mom … oh god, he killed that Stamper fellow, I'm sure of it." Her voice faltered and trailed off, replaced by muffled sobs. I filled in the blanks for myself.

"Missy, I am so sorry. I should have told the sheriff how Nollen locked you in the warehouse office. He would have called reinforcements and come back for you. He saw all of the guns Nollen and Butch had hidden in a cabinet. Don't think for a minute that Otho was fooled by anything he said. I spoke with Tommy a few minutes ago. He explained his plan to Brandy and Danni yesterday. They are eager to help. We'll do it tonight. If we fail, I'll figure something else out. Don't give up. How can I get in touch with you later?"

"Tie something to the gatepost…" *Click.*

I slid down to the floor of the phone booth in an avalanche of shame and anger, furious with myself. I should have told the sheriff. He could have called in the cavalry and rescued her. My imagination ran wild, and atrocious images of Nollen's lecherous advances stoked a rising rage. I'd failed Missy once. It wouldn't happen again. Guilt, shame, and cowardice gradually gave way to a seething resolve. A destructive thought seeped into my brain. I could go back to the house and grab Nate's gun and fill the bastard full of holes. I'd never fired the revolver, but how difficult could it be?

Tommy tapped on the glass, interrupting my interlude of self-loathing.

He said, "I figure we've got an hour before sunrise. The hornets won't be docile for much longer. There is no time to waste."

I replied, "As luck would have it, I've got Nate's truck today, while he dries out and gets over the shakes. Let's get it done."

* * *

Tommy gripped the dash as I negotiated potholes, corners, and curves. I recounted the brief conversation with Missy. "It's now or never, Tommy. Missy is desperate and we can't let her down. That bastard is making his move. Remember the first day we met her on the trestle? She's stuck in a tree, the forest is on fire, and it's up to us to get her down."

"Maybe we should just tell the sheriff and let the authorities handle it. Embers has all those weapons, and he has already proven he's capable of murder. We're likely to end up like Mickey O'Dell, or worse."

"I've already considered telling Otho, but I just keep thinking about the girl over in Kirkcaldy last year. She was even younger than

Missy and got trapped in the same situation. Her stepfather was diddling her nonstop for years, but the press and the courts ended up dragging *her* through the mud. The authorities already knew the guy was a molester. He got caught trying to sodomize the retarded kennel boy at the animal shelter. In the end, they said it was just her word against his. Victim shaming at its worst. He got off with a slap on the pee-pee and moved away. Now she's stuck in that piss-dribble town with all the embarrassment and humiliation."

"You're right. Any official investigation would expose her crazy mother and that would end up hurting Missy even more. She is so protective of Maris. The daughter is the caretaker of the mother, instead of the other way around. Arthur Rumkin says there aren't any relatives nearby. All they have is each other and Nollen knows it, and uses that as leverage against them both. You are absolutely right. We have to handle this and go through with the plan."

There was a glimmer of light on the eastern horizon as I turned onto the Riverfront Levee Road. I pulled up to the wisteria and said, "I don't think there is any reason to be clandestine at this point. Do you?"

Tommy shook his head. "After what we saw at the warehouse and what Missy just told you on the phone; I don't give a damn about anything but the matter at hand. Let's grab that nest and give Nollen Embers a dose of his own medicine."

We crawled through the opening and made our way through the brush to the awning. It wasn't as cool as I had hoped and some of the creatures were already crawling around on the outside of the giant hive. I was struck by the sudden realization of being completely unprepared.

"I was so preoccupied with the phone call to Missy that I didn't bring a ladder or anything. What do you have in the sack, Tommy?"

He produced a roll of twine, a single pair of leather gloves, and tin snips. "Hoist me up on your shoulders, Teddy, and I'll slip the bag over the hive and secure the top with twine. Then I'll cut the stalk away from the awning with the snips. Easy peasy."

You always jinx yourself when you say stupid stuff like "nothing to it," "easy peasy," or "piece of cake." You might as well kiss a chainsaw or stick your dick in a sausage grinder.

I braced my back against the wall, and hoisted Tommy up on my shoulders. His shoes dug into my muscles and I couldn't help but squirm. Immediately, he started swatting as the angry insects emerged from the single opening at the bottom of the nest.

"The bastards are stinging me!" he screamed as he dropped the bag on my head and stumbled backward. Flailing, he reflexively grabbed at the awning. Rotten boards gave way, and the nest seemed to hang in the air like a paper balloon for a split second before it fell and hit the ground right at my feet. Tommy's glasses flew off into the grass as he landed hard on his back. The nest trembled as he scrambled to retrieve them.

"Forget the glasses. Cover up the damn nest before any more of 'em get out!"

I pinched the opening shut just as two of the vicious brutes hit my left arm in rapid succession. Tommy jerked the waxed offal sack over the vibrating hive and secured it using a rapid lark's head knot. Two more stings penetrated my right shoulder.

"I'll grab your glasses. Head for the fence before these suckers kill us."

Tommy took off like a gazelle, the bag bouncing on fragile twine behind him. Yellow puffs of pollen exploded as tall stalks of thistle, ragweed, and toadflax parted in his wake. I grabbed the glasses and stumbled after him, swatting wildly at the demonic tormentors.

Bald-faced hornets are unique among the insect order hymenoptera. When the nest is threatened, they swarm in a dark, undulating cloud formation much like a flock of blackbirds at dusk. Flying toward an invader, they flex their abdomen forward right before contact to drive the stinger in deep. You can actually hear the impact. Unlike honey bees, they don't die after a sting, so the ruthless critters have no reluctance to strike again and again and again. A cotton shirt won't stop them.

Thwack, thwack, thwack, three more in the back.

I caught up with Tommy just as he reached the perimeter, but the bag wouldn't fit through the hole under the fence, so we heaved it over the top. It snagged on a loop of rusty barbed wire and twirled for a moment before coming loose and hitting the ground on the opposite side.

My head swam. Arms and legs tingled, went numb, and rebelled against mental commands. Emerging from the wisteria, I saw Aunt Tilde waving her arms and yelling at an elderly gentleman in a jon boat near the opposite shore. That's the last thing I remember. The world turned a weird shade of green. Ears roared, muscles convulsed, and the world went dark.

* * *

My head was filled with loud static as I awoke. After a moment, I realized the buzzing was actually inside my head. My face was covered, but I couldn't remove the obstruction because my arms refused to respond to any command with anything other than a spastic jerk. Voices in the room sounded like they were coming from the bottom of a cave.

Tommy said, "I'm so glad you spotted us and got Aunt Tilde's help. Your medicine is soothing the stings."

A girl's voice with a musical Cajun accent replied, "You have the prettiest tan I've ever seen. You're a shade darker than me. The swelling on your neck is already going down, but I couldn't help noticing there is a swelling in your pants that seems considerably larger than it was a minute ago. What's going on down *there*?"

"Well, Monique … that there is … er, uh … it's a long story."

"Yeah, I can see. It's definitely a very long story. Perhaps I should have a look at it. You may have an injury that needs some special attention."

Someone had me laid out on a pile of quilts in Aunt Tilde's living room. My left arm finally reconnected to the motor cortex of my poison-addled brain and I pulled a wet cloth off my face while struggling to focus my eyes. Tommy was sitting on the floor, propped against the opposite wall, and a pretty Creole girl with hazel eyes and caramel skin was kneeling between his legs, dabbing a white paste on the whelps covering his bare chest. His glasses were off and for the first time, I realized how handsome Tommy was. Slender. Chiseled features. Slightly disheveled sandy blond hair contrasted perfectly with a rugged bronze complexion. The girl named Monique certainly thought so. She was being salaciously attentive.

Monique leaned in until she was literally nose to nose with him. "Your story is getting longer every minute. Would you like me to examine it for you?"

Tommy swallowed hard and let out a deep groan. "Pro … prob … probably not a good idea. We might get something started that I can't stop."

Monique ran her fingers through his hair. She said, "Perhaps this is the best time to get that first awkward kiss out of the way."

She licked her lips and puckered, but before she could follow through, Aunt Tilde emerged from the kitchen with a pitcher of tea and said, "Monique, quit aggravating the boy. You better watch her, Tommy. She delights in stirring up trouble and torturing young men. Her momma was the same way when she was young. Redbone girls are just too pretty for their own good. Men can't resist 'em."

Monique arched her back, leaned forward, and forced her cleavage against my friend's face. "Aw. Auntie, we were just having a little fun playing doctor. Tommy says he can get me free movie tickets anytime I want."

Tilde shot her a stern look as Tommy self-consciously buttoned up his shirt.

The old woman turned to me and smiled. "I'm relieved to see you back in the land of the living, Theodore Nutscalder. Drink some tea and rest while my herb and goat's milk plasters pull the poison out of your body. Monique, make yourself useful and go find out what Titus did with that big bag of bees."

Monique winked at me and blew Tommy a kiss as she headed out the door. The tea was ice cold and syrupy sweet. Just the tonic to jolt my body back into action and clear the cobwebs out of my foggy noggin.

I said, "It looks like you rescued me again, Aunt Tilde. You always come through at the crucial moment. I believe the time has come to help the girl you saw in the vision. Tommy has a plan for those vile hornets. Please don't kill 'em."

At that moment, Monique returned with the elderly man who was guiding the jon boat across the river as I blacked out.

He tipped his hat to Tilde and said, "I put the critters in the abandoned smokehouse and covered the bag with lavender and rosemary stems, just like you said. It's nice and cool in there. I won't say they are comfortable, but they won't die."

Tilde nodded at Titus and motioned toward the kitchen. "There's a biscuit and gravy on the stove. Hot coffee in the pot. Go make yourself a plate, but don't run off. These boys are going to need a boat ride to the Knob side as soon as they are strong enough. Shouldn't be too long."

Tilde put the pitcher on the table and followed Titus to the kitchen. Monique poured Tommy a glass of tea, straightened his collar, and kissed him right on the mouth. "You come back and see me real soon. I'll be here all summer, studying with Aunt Tilde. She's teaching me the finer points of the craft, if you know what I mean. I would like to visit the projection booth you were telling me about. It sounds like a nice private place to fill me in on the rest of your long story." She made a playful grab at the crotch of his pants, but pulled back before contact.

Tommy made a little choke-gasping noise. "Urg … humph … did I mention a well-stocked concession stand is included in the deal?"

Monique ran the tip of her tongue along her upper lip. "You really know how to tempt a poor country girl, Mr. Crum. Are you trying to seduce me?"

"Well … uh … yeah, I guess so. How am I doing?"

A hearty laugh came from the kitchen door as Titus walked through, wiping gravy off his chin with a handkerchief. "I think you're in way over your head, young man. We better get you fellas back to the Texas side before Missus Kellum puts a hex on all of us. She will have us all squawking like ducks or rooting around for bugs with old Rufus."

Monique and Tommy peeled the plasters off my back. She wrinkled her nose, but I actually enjoyed the pungent medicinal smell. Something akin to pine tar mixed with pipe tobacco. Titus stepped over and handed me a silver quarter.

"I don't have any idea what you boys are planning to do with those bees, but it must be pretty important to take such a risk collecting the nest with no protective clothing. Take this quarter and buy a block of ice down at the farmer's co-op to help keep 'em calm and cool until you need their … services."

"I'll do exactly that, Mr. Titus. We appreciate you ferrying us to safety. Tommy and I will let you know how the adventure goes. We don't have 100% of the plan worked out yet."

"Let's get you boys back to the Knob before it gets any later. It's already after seven o'clock and the streets are getting busier by the minute. Prying eyes could throw a wrench into your project. Better get those varmints hidden away quickly."

The old smokehouse smelled of sowbelly and hickory. Discarded meat hooks littered the floor around the offal bag. Tommy grabbed two of the tools and gathered up the rosemary and lavender stalks. I carried the bag to the river's edge. The clawing and buzzing racket was unnerving. Monique steadied the jon boat while Titus pulled the starter cord on a small motor.

Monique approached Tommy and said, "Aunt Tilde told me to give you these." She handed him a paper sack, and he pulled out two elaborately carved ebony wood voodoo masks, adorned with sharp silver teeth and white crosses painted on the forehead. She said, "These will protect you. Auntie blessed them with special powers, but I don't know how you are going to get it over your glasses."

"I've got an old pair. I'll pop the lenses out of the frames and mount them on the mask with glue."

The Creole beauty giggled and kissed him on the cheek. "You be careful. I expect you back real soon, Tommy Crum. Don't disappoint me or my first hex is gonna be on you." She playfully slapped him on the rump as he climbed into the boat. Titus twisted the accelerator and expertly angled the tiny craft against the current. Ninety seconds later, the old fellow skillfully slid the skiff to rest on the sandy bank in front of Casablanca. As we disembarked, he made the sign of the cross and shook our hands. "My prayers are with you. I have a couple of secret hideouts back in no-man's-land, if the plan goes bad and y'all have to make a run for it. I'm in the white house behind Tilde's place. The back door is always unlocked."

We thanked our new friend, grabbed the masks and the offal sack, and headed for the truck.

Tommy said, "We can hide the hornets in the Grotto. It's cool in there."

"I already thought about that. Rick's place will be teeming with locals this evening, and they'll certainly see us recovering the bag. Let's keep it close at hand, where we can keep an eye on it. I was thinking about hiding it in Pete O'Dell's tool shed. We'll do what Mr. Titus said. Get a block of ice to keep it cool. Besides, we are going to need Brandy and Danni's help anyway."

"Yeah, you're right. Danni's got some secret native concoction mixed up for Missy to spike Nollen's scotch decanter with. She says it'll make him loopy, and throw him off balance."

I kept the old pickup in low gear and puttered down Riverfront Levee Road and turned onto Pearl Street when the sheriff passed by, beeped his siren, whipped around, and pulled me over.

My heart skipped a beat when the lawman stuck his head out of the window and yelled, "What the hell are you doing behind the wheel of a motor vehicle without a license? Just because we give Sara Tyler some slack doesn't mean you two delinquents can flout the rules."

I had to think quickly. If he spied the hornets, the gig would be up, so I put the pickup in neutral, pulled the emergency brake, and jumped out with a silly grin on my face. "Hey sheriff, I was heading over to the O'Dell's, to see if there was anything I could do to help. Nathaniel is drying out at Sudsy Monkhouse's place with some other guys from AA, and I promised to clean up the truck and mow the lawn on Kickapoo Street if I can get Pete's old mower working. That's why I brought Tommy along. He's pretty handy at mechanical stuff. I appreciate your visit with Nate. He's been a lot nicer since you had an … er … talk with him."

Otho looked at me suspiciously. Suddenly, a loud, bone-rattling explosion reverberated through the air, and all three of us looked up simultaneously. At first, I thought it was a sonic boom. Occasionally, the jet pilots from Barksdale Air Force Base would hit the afterburners and break Mach One, but there were no shrieking jet engines or vapor trails anywhere to be seen. Our unspoken speculations ended abruptly as an ominous black plume of smoke arose from the direction of the town square.

"Good God Almighty, what the hell is happening now?" Otho bellowed as he slammed the door and sped toward the square, sirens blaring. I breathed a sigh of relief and realized I'd even peed a little.

Tommy said, "Let's get these critters stowed away and go find out what's happening uptown. Gosh Teddy, these little hellions are a lot more trouble than I ever imagined."

22

As we pulled into the gravel driveway of Casa O'Dell, Vera was standing on the porch with all of Mic's sisters staring at the smoke billowing up from midtown. Brandy said, "Uncle Murl called and said Kutz's Cleaners caught on fire. The whole town is gathering on the square to fight the blaze." Tommy jumped out of the truck, pulled her aside, and whispered in her ear. She glanced in the back of the pickup, nodded at me, and pointed toward the backyard.

Using the meat hooks and a wire coat hanger, we suspended the offal bag from the rafters of Pete O'Dell's tool shed. Brandy hooked an extension cord up to an old squirrel cage fan, salvaged from an evaporative cooler, and propped it on a workbench so it blew directly on the suspended sack, causing it to rock gently back and forth. The cool air and hypnotic motion seemed to calm the hive.

Mic's shapely sister wore a colorful tie-dye T-shirt and a pair of faded bell-bottom jeans. She had her hair pulled back in a French braid and wore no makeup. I told her about the conversation with Missy, and Tommy related the comedy of errors with the hive and Tilde's timely rescue. My friend mercifully left out my fainting spell and purposefully omitted details of his arousing encounter with Monique. He showed her the masks and explained his plan to affix the old lenses to the disguise. Her demeanor was uncharacteristically subdued and businesslike. She studied the masks and said, "I've got a better idea. Come with me."

We followed her to her bedroom, where she retrieved a pair of sheer pantyhose from a pile of laundry at the foot of her bed. Taking a pair of scissors, she cut the leg out of one. "Come here, Tommy boy, take your glasses off and hold the mask over your face." He did as he was told and Brandy carefully pulled the hosiery over his head, securing the mask in place. The vixen took his glasses and held them over the eye openings. "Can you see through the material? I can tie a rubber band around the ear pieces and secure it to your hair with a bobby pin, or..."

"I can see just fine. The hose are sheer enough that they hardly obscure my vision at all. Let's try it this way." Tommy pulled the hose and mask off and replaced his glasses. He then held the mask over his spectacles and directed Brandy to replace the stocking.

He said, "This works even better. It's uncomfortable, but I can stand it for a few minutes." He attempted to dislodge the get-up by shaking his head in all kinds of comical gyrations, but the disguise stayed in place perfectly.

Tommy asked, "What do you think, Theodore? Do I look like a deranged sorcerer? Will anyone be able to recognize me?"

"Man, you look utterly evil! If we put one of those velvet Cusser Club robes over your shoulders, you would scare the Devil himself."

He crouched down in front of Brandy's vanity mirror. "Perfect. Absolutely perfect." Brandy used the other stocking to affix my disguise. Her ingenuity was remarkably effective.

Distant sirens sounded in the south. Tommy ran to the open window and cocked his head to listen. "It sounds like the volunteers from Vidor are coming in to help put out the blaze. Let's go see what's happening."

* * *

Tommy sat in the pickup bed with the three youngest sisters, while Vera and Brandy rode in the front with me. Fire engines blocked Division Street, so I parked in the alley behind Tyler's Bakery. Everyone piled out of the truck and ran toward the town square except Brandy. She put her hand on my knee and watched the others retreat until they were out of earshot. "Dr. DeSilva is shipping Mickey off to Houston this afternoon, and I want you to be there with me to see him off."

"Of course, I'll be there."

"I'm getting a terrible foreboding. I've been having bad dreams that something terrible is going to happen. I'm afraid Nollen Embers is going to send that crazy shooter to finish him off." She locked her hands behind her head, closed her eyes, and rested her chin on her chest.

"You're worrying needlessly. That would be a stupid move on Nollen's part. He doesn't want to attract any more attention. He's trying to appear respectable, and this incident with Mic is threatening to derail his campaign plans. The shooter is probably long gone. Embers undoubtedly has him hidden away somewhere or buried in a shallow grave.

"Sweet Jeezus, my whole life is a big mess. I'm disgusted with myself, acting like a cheap floozy."

I said, "You can't blame yourself. You didn't ask for that guy to follow you home. You didn't ask for Papa O'Dell to be sent to prison on a bullshit manslaughter charge. And you damn sure didn't pull the trigger on the gun that shot Mickey. You stepped up to earn money for your family, doing … well … doing what was necessary with the lousy hand life has dealt you."

Brandy kissed me on the cheek before stepping out of the truck. She peered in the passenger door side mirror, inspecting her face and hair. "I look awful. No one should appear in public looking like this. No makeup. No hair spray."

I bent over and laughed until I was breathless. Brandy gazed at me with a sad, hurtful look on her face. I finally composed myself, walked over, and straightened a tiny wisp of hair on her forehead, exactly like she had done to me a few days earlier. "Well, if you are trying to look less attractive in this hippie outfit with no makeup, you're failing miserably."

It took her a moment to process my back-handed compliment. When it finally dawned on her, she smiled and hugged me so hard, it squeezed the air out of my lungs. Nothing sexual. Nothing flirtatious or taunting. Just a genuine, affectionate embrace.

"Teddy, you always know the right thing to say."

"We will get through this together. Don't worry, everything will work out. Trust me. C'mon, let's catch up with the others and see what's going on with the fire, and then we'll go see Mic at the hospital."

We emerged from the alley to a hellish sight. They cordoned off the town square, and firefighters were hosing down what was left of Kutz's Cleaners from every angle. Otho Wheat was questioning bystanders, trying to determine if anyone was in the building. Suddenly, the roof caved in and the brick walls collapsed. Ash and cinders erupted and came raining down in a black blizzard. Townsfolk doused, swatted, and stomped in a chaotic dance to keep the fire from spreading. Arthur Rumkin, Sudsy Monkhouse, and my old man were straightening hoses and working the fire hydrants. Nollen Embers' campaign billboard smoldered around the edges, and his picture distorted into a dastardly image, as scorch marks deformed his creepy smile into a monstrous sneer. All that remained readable of his name was "Embers." A fitting demise to his gaudy effort at respectability. Brandy hustled her sisters and Vera to the far end of Rhinelander Park, away from the smoke. Tommy yelled at me from the sidewalk in front of Tyler's Bakery.

"Teddy, come give us a hand with this broken window."

The blast shattered the storefront plate glass. Sara and her mom struggled to tape cardboard over the opening while Tommy swept shards with a big push broom. Sara's father cowered behind the counter with a wet towel over his mouth and nose to filter out the smoke.

Buford Tyler enjoyed poor health. The pale, pudgy hypochondriac had a variety of vague disorders which baffled local physicians. Dropsy and rheumatism with water on the knees. Kidney trouble, gas, bloating, and flatulence compounded by elusive parasites in the bowel. The pharmacist loaded him up with harmless homeopathic remedies to soothe his obsessive desire for medicine. The neurotic milquetoast used illusory illness to get sympathy and shirk work. He languished in his sickbed while Sara and her mom worked their fingers to the bone.

Tommy and Sara stood outside, frantically applying strips of duct tape, while Mrs. Tyler and I supported the corrugated patch from the inside. Mr. Tyler muttered some vague suggestions, but his wife wasn't in the mood. "Take your ass back upstairs, Buford, and get under the covers. Stay out of the way and I'll let you know when it's all over." It was an awkward conversation, so I changed the subject.

"Thanks for the sourdough rolls you gave to Nathaniel. He said you wouldn't let him pay."

She shook her head without looking at me. "Sara got mad at me for the comments I made when you gave her the necklace. I don't know what she sees in you. She's like a lovesick puppy, and I wish you wouldn't lead her on."

"I don't have much to offer Sara. All I have is a couple of bucks in my pocket, and the clothes on my back. That's about it. I'm not making excuses, but..."

The woman surprised me with a sudden swift slap across my face. Not a vicious blow, but it stung.

"Theodore Nutscalder, I'm not talking about material things. I'm talking about integrity. I'm talking about kindness. I'm talking about consideration for a sweet girl's romantic fantasies. God knows there are enough dipshit Casanovas in this town. Don't be one of them. Now get the hell out of here before I say something I regret."

The firemen finally had the blaze under control, and as I walked outside, Tommy was playfully thumping bits of ash out of Sara's hair while she giggled. They both jumped when I came into view and donned a guilty look, as if I had caught them doing something naughty. I pretended not to notice. A tender moment passed between them. I felt a pang of jealousy, and then shame at feeling jealous. Had I stumbled upon a budding romance?

"Look at you guys, playing patty cakes and grooming each other like a couple of baboons. Cut it out."

Sara slapped me across the face. Hard. I've been punched, pummeled, kicked, stomped, and gouged, but never slapped. Now twice in a two-minute period, by a mother and daughter, no less.

With uncharacteristic anger, Sara said, "You're just as bad as Galton Grails. Y'all both think I'm some kind of dumb, big-boobed gorilla."

I replied, "What are you talking about, Sara? The baboon comment was nothing personal. It's just a figure of speech. I was thinking about the documentaries we watched in science class and the *Wild Kingdom* TV show."

"Liar! You and Galton both make spiteful remarks right to my face and think I'm too stupid to realize you're insulting me."

I stood speechless, mouth agape, literally gathering dust and ash. Tommy stepped forward and gently put his hand on Sara's shoulder. "Sara, I really don't think Teddy meant anything malicious. His sarcasm cuts to the quick sometimes, but he does it to everybody. Even me and Mic. What did Galton say to you?"

The girl folded her arms and scowled at us both. "He sits behind me in Social Studies and whispers things like, 'I'd like to rub your monkey, or let's go lather up our chimps, or meet me behind the gym and I'll play monkey slide with you.'"

Tommy and I both clapped hands over our mouths to keep from laughing straight in the poor girl's face. Her innocent naivete was absolutely adorable. Tommy pulled Sara aside and whispered in her ear. Her eyes widened and as she slowly gleaned the true meaning of Galton's repulsive remarks.

"Oh god, I'm so sorry, Teddy. I … I didn't realize he meant … that's disgusting!"

I laughed and waved her off. "I had it coming, Sara. Don't worry about it. Galton brings out the worst in all of us. Let's get over to the hospital and say goodbye to Mickey."

23

As TOMMY, SARA, AND I ENTERED THE INDIGENT WARD, A nurse was stripping the sheets off the bed in the first cubicle. I paused for a moment and opened my mouth to inquire about the senile fellow, but she sensed my presence, glanced up, and shook her head in silence. Gus' cubicle was empty, too. Tommy pulled my sleeve. "Looks like the old timer's suffering is over. Let's put on a cheerful face. Mic needs us."

Brandy, Vera, and the girls were hovering over Mic's bed, lamenting his imminent departure, promising hearty meals, and round-the-clock attention upon his return. He spied us, put on a terrified expression, and said, "Boy, am I glad to see y'all. Come rescue me from all this feminine affection before I start blubbering like a pregnant bride, abandoned at the altar!"

Mic's color was better, and his warped sense of humor helped ease my anxieties. Vera was inconsolable and Brandy uttered soft words of encouragement between sniffles of her own. Dr. DeSilva and Nurse Jurnigan pulled back the curtain, hustled us out of the ward, and told us to wait outside the ER entrance while they performed one final examination before loading him on the gurney.

A joyous sight awaited on the ambulance dock. The whole town turned out. Folks still smudged with soot and ash cheered as we emerged from the ER waiting room. Vera held up her arms and announced Mic was close behind and the merry mob had a hearty laugh at their premature hooray. Nathaniel was the only one with a frown on his face.

"Son, get back inside, now," he said, shoving me toward the door. I tensed, preparing for an assault. Tommy, Sara, and the O'Dell's were already mingling with the crowd and didn't notice the exchange. Entering the room, I crossed my arms in front of my face in a defensive posture, but Nate took a step back and held out his hands.

"Teddy, I just came to warn you. Arthur Rumkin told me the blood in the shooter's car was from an animal. It wasn't human. The whole thing is some kind of elaborate trick to throw the cops off. He's probably still out there somewhere. We don't want to alarm Vera and the girls, but Burtis and I are going to take turns watching the O'Dell place tonight, just in case he returns. The fire chief from Vidor found evidence of arson at the cleaners. Marlon Kutz got some late-night threats a few weeks ago when some citizens floated the idea of running him for mayor. All of this skullduggery points right to Nollen

Embers. If you know anything about that guy, you need to tell me right now. He's dangerous and shouldn't be trifled with."

Nate trembled as he leaned back against the wall. Withdrawal from the alcohol was taking its toll. For a moment, I considered spilling the plan, but thought better of it.

"No need to worry about me. I'll see Missy later this afternoon. If I learn anything about the shooter or the fire, I'll go straight to the sheriff. I promise." Crossing my heart, I stepped toward the door. Nate grabbed my arm.

"Teddy, don't get caught up in a situation you can't control. I know you're concerned about the girl, but Nollen is a crafty criminal. He always seems to be one step ahead. He wouldn't hesitate to..."

The swinging wooden doors at the far end of the hallway clattered and boomed as the petite redheaded nurse pushed Mickey's gurney toward us. She struggled to maintain control of the stretcher, and Mic reached out on either side of the safety rails with muscular arms to keep it from banging against the walls. He raised his head off the pillow, grinned, and shot the bird at me. I shot it back, and Nate gently whacked me on the back of the head. "Don't be disrespectful. You guys shouldn't act so crude in front of a lady." The redhead winked, stuck her tongue out, and playfully tousled Mickey's hair.

"I've waxed his woody, and emptied his bedpans. At this point, I'm inoculated against his crudity. Completely immune!"

Cheers arose from the assembled townsfolk as we pushed Mic's gurney down the ramp to the back of the waiting ambulance. Rick Blaine handed the nurse a wad of cash. "Knobbers took up a collection, and we're depending on you to keep the town hero in line, and make sure those big city doctors do their job." She stuffed the bills in her bra and playfully pinched Mic's chubby cheek. "I'll make sure Dr. DeSilva gets a report every evening."

O'Dell crossed his eyes and grinned ear to ear. Vera and the girls gave him one last hug before the attendants loaded him and the cute caretaker into the transport. Tommy, Sara, and I pressed our cheeks against the window and made kissy faces. Mic held a pillow tight against his wound as he laughed and gave us a thumbs up. We all got misty eyed as the ambulance pulled away. Brandy hugged Sara, Tommy, and me in turn and said, "There are a lot of good people in this town. I have to stop and remind myself that the sleazeballs don't outweigh the Samaritans. Speaking of sleazeballs, are we doing the dreadful deed tonight?"

My mind flashed back to the warning from Nate. "Tommy and I work better alone. He's polishing the plan, and after Missy lures Nollen into the greenhouse, I'll barricade the door from the outside while Tommy helps her escape through the mulch butler. Piece of cake."

Brandy frowned and punched me in the chest. "Listen here, guttersnipe, you ain't gonna leave me on the sidelines. I've been thinking about some stuff to help Missy lure Nollen into the trap. Danni's magic mushroom recipe is fermenting in the drawer of my vanity table as we speak. It should soften him up a little. Missy will need to spike his scotch decanter, so I'm not leaving this plan up to you two amateur hooligans."

There was no talking her out of it. Tommy was explaining the plan to Sara, who was listening with great interest.

Tommy said, "Teddy, we're going to need all the help we can get, and besides that, how will we get away if something happens to you? I can't operate the pickup. Brandy would have to drive."

Tommy unknowingly gave me the excuse I was looking for to keep Brandy on the sidelines. "Well, that's the problem, Tommy boy. Brandy can't drive worth a shit. Mic tried to teach her how to use the clutch and shift gears in Pete's old flatbed pickup and she almost ran over Widow Woolerton as she was walking to her mailbox. Now, the poor old woman soils her granny panties every time she hears a backfire."

Brandy kicked me in the shins. Sara stepped between us and said, "No problem. I can do it! I'm an excellent driver. I'll keep your dad's pickup idling in the alley. Besides that, you'll need a lookout. If anybody comes around, I'll beep the horn."

Tommy piped up. "Not a bad idea, Teddy. The ladies could be the key to making our ambush work. The option of a quick getaway sounds pretty appealing to me, especially if Nollen gets wise and the plan goes south."

I squirmed as all eyes turned to me. "You may be right, but I still don't like it."

Tommy pulled the watch out of his pocket. "It's ten minutes until 11:00. The window of opportunity is closing in on us. Let's use our time wisely. Sara and I will stop by the bakery and make sure everything is secure there. Teddy, you take Vera and the girls home, meet with Missy, and get an update on the situation with Nollen. We'll meet you back at Casa O'Dell by three o'clock. That will leave us two and a half hours to get in position before sunset. We can fine tune the details then. Don't forget to stop off and get that block of ice that Mr. Titus mentioned. We don't want our little nasties getting heat stroke before the big game."

24

I WAS OVERRULED AND DIDN'T OBJECT. TOMMY WAS TAKING THE lead, and the ladies were in full agreement. I breathed a little sigh of relief. Truth be told, I was grateful the yoke of leadership was off my shoulders for a while. Tommy and Sara took off as Brandy climbed into the passenger seat of the truck.

She crossed her arms and glared at me. "You didn't have to embarrass me like that. I would have admitted I can't drive."

"I just don't want to take a chance on anything happening to you. Your family needs you more than ever, now that Mic is gone. In case you haven't noticed, I have a genuine affection for you and all I wanted..."

She reached over and whacked me on the back of the head. A kittenish smile spread over her face. "Just shut up and drive, lover boy. Momma and the girls are across the street in Dr. Terrell's parking lot, petting Humper."

A rickety card table was set up on the sidewalk of the veterinary clinic, piled high with casseroles, pies, and grocery bags for the O'Dells. Humper was minus one ear, but wagged his tail and barked excitedly as we approached.

As Vera and the girls loaded vittles in the truck's bed, Dr Terrell said, "Humper bounced back pretty well for an old mutt. Everybody in town pitched in their pocket change and dropped off table scraps for him. Those catgut stitches in his neck will dissolve and fall out on their own in a few days. Keep an eye on him. If he needs anything else, bring him back."

A shrill scream followed by peals of laughter interrupted our conversation. Millicent McLeod was walking Damsa to the clinic, and Humper promptly mounted her, ignoring the owner's protests. Damsa crouched down on her forelegs, leaving her rump high in the air. Humper let out a throaty growl as his forepaws tightened grip on Damsa's hindquarters. His rear toenails scratched desperately on the concrete sidewalk as he struggled to maintain position. Vera covered her face, and I couldn't decide if she was shielding herself from the embarrassing scene or trying to hide her laughter. The three youngest O'Dells admonished Humper in unison, saying, "Naughty dog! Naughty dog!" I shushed them and Dr. Terrell separated the copulating canines while reassuring Millicent no harm was done. Brandy lifted Humper into the bed of the truck and instructed her sisters to keep him away from the food. Vera sat in the middle next to me on the way back to Casa O'Dell. Brandy closed her eyes and lolled her head out of the passenger side window, enjoying the sunshine and cool breeze against her face.

Vera absentmindedly patted my knee and said, "I really appreciate all you've done during this ordeal. I know Nate is trying to dry out, so I hope you will come stay with us until Mickey gets home. Having a man around the house would be a great comfort."

Brandy jerked her head inside, winked at me, and said, "Momma, that's a wonderful idea. Theodore is such a wholesome lad. I can make a pallet on the floor in my bedroom and he could sleep in there with me."

"Brandy Jolene O'Dell, shame on you! This is no time for joking. I am at my wit's end. Stop teasing Teddy."

The girl pouted and shyly sniffed, "I'm not being nasty or anything like that, Momma. I've been crying myself to sleep every night. Teddy could rub my back and sing me a lullaby like Daddy used to do when I was little." I thought how Melchior and Dipdottle would have been hysterical at this comment.

During the rest of the short drive, I filled my mind with dog snot, gopher guts, and dysentery, to avoid arousal at the thought of sleeping in Brandy's bedroom.

It didn't work.

* * *

After unloading the pickup, I checked on the hive in the tool shed. The offal bag swayed quietly to the rhythm of the fan. Reassured, I slipped through the back door of the house to the hallway. The phone rang as Brandy snuck in behind me. "We've only got a minute while Momma is on the phone." She pulled me into her room, opened the drawer to her vanity, and retrieved a small amber medicine vial and a half pint of cheap gin. She switched on a table lamp and held the vial up to the light. "It's been steeping since last night, and should be ready. Hand me those tweezers next to the ashtray." I did as I was told and, using the pincers, she fished a wad of slimy matter out of the bottle, careful to let the residual liquid drip back into the vial. Spreading the gunk on a tissue, I realized it was a clump of tiny mushrooms. She pulled the largest fungi aside and meticulously separated the cap from the stalk, teasing apart the gill-like structures underneath. "Look here, Teddy. Do you see how these slits underneath have turned a dull orange color? That means the spores have dissolved and released the psychoactive chemicals into the liquid." She topped off the vial with gin, replaced the cap, and shook it vigorously. "To maintain maximum potency, Danni says to keep it cool and out of the sun. When you see Missy, tell her to pour this in his scotch decanter as soon as possible. It should be stable for eight to ten hours. Come with me to the kitchen and I'll put it on ice."

As we entered the kitchen, I could hear one side of the phone conversation as Vera said, "Oh Burtis, do you really think it's necessary? Well, okay, we will see you between 6:30 and 7 o'clock. I'll bake a pie and make a big pot of coffee." Vera hung up and waddled to the pantry door, mumbling about pie crust and apple filling. Brandy placed ice cubes on a sheet of tinfoil and wrapped the vial up in a neat ball. "This should last long enough for you to get it into Missy's hands. Danni left us a bag of stuff out of her car trunk, before she took off to the reservation. It's on the porch. Take it with you on the way out. It sounds like Burtis and your dad are back on the night watch again. We'll need to get the hornets out of here before they show up. I'll see you at three o'clock. Go, go, go!"

25

After saying goodbye to Vera and the little ones, I gathered up Danni's bag and headed to the North Side. As I cruised by the hospital, Mr. and Mrs. Grails were walking in with a young girl of 10 or 11 trailing behind. Dejected, they all hung their heads, trudging along. Bile bubbled up in my throat as a pang of guilt gripped my gut. Nobody in town seemed to care about their plight. I reminded myself that Galton was someone's son and brother, despicable though he was. I resolved to put in an appearance after the meeting with Missy if time allowed. As I drove around the square, Butch was putting out campaign placards in the park. The signs read: "Elect Nollen Embers for Mayor. A New Opportunity for Growth and Expansion." Shopkeepers swept ashes off the sidewalks. Tommy and Sara flirted while securing plastic sheeting over our makeshift window repairs. A lone fireman doused the remaining cinders of Kutz's Cleaners. No one noticed me.

The ebullience of the previous hour waned, and an oppressive sense of gloom invaded my thoughts. Doubts were creeping in. Doubts about Mic's recovery. Doubts about my fate if Galton didn't recover. Doubts about the plan to stop Nollen's incestuous assault on Missy. Anxiety turned to panic. What the hell was I doing? I had no experience in these matters, and complex plans always go awry. Nollen was a career criminal, and would never let himself get caught in an amateur trap. I should just grab Nathan's 38 Special out of the nightstand and shoot the bastard. I thought better of it and kicked those destructive musings to the curb. I would never get away with it, anyway. Texas courts would certainly try me as an adult, and I would end up frying in the electric chair.

As I turned into the alley behind the Turnbow residence, a complication arose. Mr. England was walking Brutus and waved me down. I cursed my bad luck, but forced a smile and rolled down the window.

The old man said, "You're pissing against the wind if you are coming over to court Missy. Her folks keep an eagle eye on her, and they aren't going to let a South Side boy anywhere near their precious darling."

"I know that, Mr. England. She's way out of my league. I just promised to give her an update on Mickey O'Dell. He's making a slow but steady recovery. DeSilva shipped him off to Houston this morning. He's apparently going to need some long-term care."

"Yeah, I heard about that." The old codger squinted his eyes and pointed toward the gate. "There was a lot of activity at the

Turnbow place last night. A bunch of guys in a big panel truck loading and unloading stuff. Nollen was shouting orders from the second-story window. I'd be careful if I were you. That guy is shifty."

"Sounds like good advice, Mr. England. I won't linger long. You and Brutus have a nice day."

He got a faraway look in his eyes and whispered, "They left ruts."

"What did you say? I don't understand."

"They left ruts. With the panel truck. They must have been hauling something very heavy, and there was a strong smell of petroleum."

I followed his gaze. There were deep tire impressions in the soil next to the gate.

"You are giving me the jitters, Mr. England. Do you think something's wrong?"

The man never changed expression or diverted his eyes from the gate.

"I'm just a suspicious old man with too much time on my hands. You should be careful nonetheless."

With that, he turned and walked away. I put the Chevy in first gear and eased forward. With all the distractions, I forgot the bandana to tie around the top of the gatepost. Infuriated by my stupidity, I stopped by the fence and searched for an alternative. Nate hadn't left a rag, rope, strap, or string anywhere in the vehicle, so I reached in the sack Brandy sent along. It contained two wigs. One black and one blonde. A fancy masquerade ball mask adorned with feathers and sequins. There was lipstick, rouge, mascara, and several other cosmetics I couldn't identify. At the bottom lay a white satin robe and sheer negligee. The robe had a thin belt attached. That would have to do. As I climbed on the fender to reach the top of the finial, the gate flew open and Missy rushed out.

"Get in the truck and drive before someone sees me!"

I jumped behind the wheel and sped down the alley. "Where do I go from here?"

She said, "Turn left at the end of the alley and head north. Gypsy Camp Road is about a mile up the way. Turn right and we'll hide down by the dirt pits."

Missy clutched her chest and gasped for air. The girl was in full panic mode. Her hair was mussed, and she had on two different shoes. I shifted into third gear and gunned the engine. A minute later, I turned onto the oil top path and dropped back down into first. Cottonwood and black gum trees lined the narrow lane, blocking out the sunlight. Abandoned shanties, overgrown with weeds and Virginia creeper, marked the remains of a seasonal village where carnies and circus folk wintered during the '40s and '50s. After two miles, the path opened up into a four-acre field, pock-marked with dirt pits and mounds of gravel and asphalt crumbs. The property served as a repository for sand, clay, and mud used in municipal road repair and levee projects. More secluded than the quarry, it was a popular spot for teen couples to park and smooch on evenings and weekends. I came to a stop behind a backhoe and killed the engine. Missy was hyperventilating, so I emptied the contents of the bag on the floorboard and shoved it in her hands.

"Hold this over your mouth and breathe slowly." She shook her head and pushed my hand away. "Nollen ... he..."

"Did Nollen rape you?" She held her head down and clasped her hands tightly in her lap. I said, "Maybe Tommy was right all along. It's time to tell the sheriff."

She replied, "He drugged Mom. I was in her room, but that didn't stop him. He held a pillow over my mouth and used his fingers to … penetrate… He was laughing the whole time. Taunting me. Grabbed me by the hair and held my face next to hers. 'Go ahead and tell her,' he said. 'She can't hear you, and if you say a word to anyone else, I'll give her some more dope and turn her into a turnip.' Even if I went to the sheriff, it would just be my word against his. That's always the way it goes, isn't it? No one believes the victim."

She rocked back and forth just like she did when we found her at the Grotto. Desperation was eating away at her insides.

I've always been baffled by the term "quiet rage." I always thought it was an oxymoron bandied about by not-so-clever writers when they had nothing else to say. In a profound epiphany, I finally grasped the concept. Clarity of thought. Tranquil courage. Steel resolve. I reached down and picked up Danni's paraphernalia from the floorboard, meticulously placing each item back in the sack, neatly folding the top. Reaching under the seat, I retrieved the tinfoil ball containing the mushroom concoction, shaking the condensation off on the hot dashboard, watching it evaporate in the heat of the sun. Unnerved by my deliberate movements, Missy cocked her head to the side, gazing at me, bewildered.

I unpeeled the tinfoil and held the vial up between my thumb and forefinger. "It's time to give Nollen Embers a dose of his own medicine."

Missy shook her head vigorously. "I can't do it, Teddy."

"Yes, you can, and you will. Just pour this in the scotch decanter. Tommy and I will do the rest."

"He ... he's dangerous."

"Oh yeah? Well, I have some news for you. I'm dangerous too. Do you know why? I'm invisible. I'm nobody. He'll never see me coming. Just take it one step at a time. It will only take a minute to spike his liquor. Then find a place to hide and stay out of sight until tonight. Tommy and I thought about hiding you in the Cusser Club building, but he will get suspicious if you disappear for too long. Stay out of your mom's room. I know it sounds cruel, but the more attention you give to her, the more likely he'll harm her. Think about it. Am I right?"

Missy put her hands over her face and stomped her feet on the floorboard in frustration.

"Of course, you're right. God, I'm a mess. I need someone to think for me. Maybe I could hide in the attic or the garden shed at Mr. England's."

I flicked a few more drops on the dash. "The attic will be too hot. Better plan on the garden shed. Take a treat for old Brutus. He'll keep you company."

She reluctantly nodded. "Could we just sit here for a little while? I'm dead dog tired and I need a few minutes to get myself together. You must think I'm a lunatic. Hell, I just realized I have on two different shoes."

A sudden gust of wind stirred up a dust devil a few yards in front of the truck. Eager for a diversion, I said, "That's good luck. Danni Redhawk says that whirlwinds and sand twisters are the spirits of our ancestors coming back to help us."

Missy laid on her side, curled up on the seat, with her head resting in my lap. I pulled her hair away from her face, tucked it behind her ear, and rubbed her back. Looking out over the dirt pit and piles of iron ore gravel, I studied the shanties in the distance and said, "I wonder what it was like for the carnies and circus folks. On the road nine months out of the year and never putting down permanent roots. I suppose it's a tough life, but I can't help being envious in a weird sort of way. Moving from town to town is preferable to being stuck in the Knob and rotting from the inside out."

She closed her eyes and rested in silence, basking in the quiet patch of peace.

After a while I said, "I have to get back to Casa O'Dell before 3:00. Do you have any idea what time it is?"

Missy reached into her jeans pocket and pulled out a dainty gold wristwatch with a broken clasp. "It's ten after two. Don't you have a watch?" I shook my head. "Here, take this one. Daddy gave it to Momma for Christmas a long time ago. I took it out of her jewelry box. I didn't want Nollen getting a hold of it."

"Aw Missy, I can't take it. I'd feel awful if something happened to it."

She straightened the twisted band and rubbed her thumb over the scratched crystal. "It's just a stupid watch. It's not really worth anything. You can give it back later. After this is all over." She stuffed the timepiece in my shirt pocket and threw her arms around my neck. "I'll try to do my part. You guys are the only true friends I've ever had. I'd better get back to the house. Maybe Nollen won't try anything while the housekeeper and gardeners are around. I'll do like you said and hide in Mr. England's shed until you come and get me."

I cranked the Chevy and drove down the narrow, tree-lined road. Dark clouds gathered and overhanging limbs scraped against the top of the truck, as if they were trying to relay an ominous warning.

Missy started huffing and gasping the closer we got to Fairhaven. I eased off the gas and pulled over toward the curb, but she reached for the steering wheel and said, "Keep driving. I've gotta do this while I still have some nerve."

Mercifully, there was no one in the alley. I raised her hand to my lips for a quick noisy smack, and said, "I'll hang out here for a minute with the engine idling. If anything is amiss, come on back and we'll make a run for it."

She peeked through the gate for a moment and then flashed the okay sign. I forced myself to ponder on any other problems that might arise and derail the plan. I opted for a quick drive around the neighborhood, to familiarize myself with the street layout in case a quick get-away became necessary. Mr. England lived on a cul-de-sac, so the block north of Fairhaven was useless. Lamar Street was one block south and at the end of the street, a gravel trail ran next to the greenbelt and up the hill to the town's water tower. I eased the pickup over the curb and made my way up to the base of the steel reservoir and parked. The entire neighborhood was visible from the high vantage point. The path descended into a wooded area on the other side, so I walked down the steep, overgrown trail rather than risk getting the vehicle stuck. Two hundred yards down the way, it opened up next to the parking lot of the Piggly Wiggly on Division Street. The Chevy might make it down the hill with a little luck. It was a hazardous path, but no other options were available. Walking back up the hill, I made a mental note of stumps and boulders that might get in the way. After reaching the truck, I climbed the ladder of the water tower 20 feet up for a better view of the neighborhood. Everything appeared peaceful. The Kuykendalls were still gone, and Mr. Hildebrand was waxing his Mercedes in the driveway.

Just as I started down, a large white van with a red cross emblazoned on the side pulled up to the Turnbow place. Missy's worst fears were coming true. The Nut Wagon was coming for her mom. I had to do something. I cranked the truck and raced around the block to Fairhaven Street just as two attendants emerged from the house with Maris in a wheelchair. The wild-eyed woman's head flopped side to side like a toy bobblehead dog. Nollen and the maid restrained Missy on the front porch.

That same voice I heard on the train trestle started repeating like a broken record in my head: *Do something, dummy. Do something.*

I pulled up to the curb, partially blocking the drive, and beeped the horn. Nollen jerked his head around, allowing Missy to wrench loose and run back into the house. He paused in a moment of indecision, looking alternately at me and the front door. He couldn't decide which way to go. Chase Missy, or confront me. I decided for him. Jumping out, I donned a goofy grin, stuck my hands in my pockets, and sauntered up to the porch. "Hey, Mr. Embers, I hope I haven't interrupted anything. I can come back later if..."

"Get to the point," he said tersely. Out of the corner of my eye, I could see Missy frantically waving her arms behind a nearby window.

"Well, I ... I ... came by ... really for two reasons. You promised a reward for finding your sweet Meroticia. I'm not asking for myself, but for the O'Dell's. They're at a real low point with Pete in prison and Mic just now shipped off to Houston. Remember Mic? He was on the front page of *The Tattler*. You bought us breakfast..."

Crimson veins on his forehead pulsated as he took a step forward and stared me straight in the eyes in a malignant challenge. For a split second, I considered throwing down the gauntlet. Tell the vicious bastard I knew everything and give him all the details to prove the point. Tell him I knew all about the bite marks and the taunting. Tell him what I thought about a vile coward that forcefully finger fucked a fifteen-year-old girl, while her mother lay in a stupor on the bed. Quiet rage tamped down my runaway emotions. The calm voice in my head whispered, *"Don't tip your hand. Just show him the watch."*

Fumbling around in my shirt pocket, I said, "I found this in the old Studebaker where Missy spent the night. It must be hers. Would you give it to her?"

Taking a step back, Nollen knitted his eyebrows, studying the object. Recognizing the timepiece, his countenance softened. "Yeah, that's her mother's watch ... I'll give it to her. And here is a little something for the O'Dell family." He produced a wallet and shoved a $50 bill in my face.

I grabbed the cash and shook his hand vigorously. "God bless you, Mr. Embers. This will go a long way to help the O'Dells. I don't care what everybody says. You're a swell fella. I appreciate your generosity."

An ambulance attendant held out a clipboard and pen. "Mr. Embers, I need your signature on some documents."

I took advantage of the momentary distraction, bolted back to the truck, gunned the engine, and made a U-turn. Missy was already waiting at the end of the street. I slowed down, and she jumped on the running board and leapt through the open window like a circus acrobat. Shifting into third, I stomped the accelerator and turned south.

She screamed, "That son-of-a-bitch finally did it! Shipped Mom off to the nut house. What am I going to do?"

Reaching into Danni's bag, I said, "The first thing you're going to do is put on this blonde wig. We don't want anyone recognizing you. The situation may not be as bad as you think. Nollen won't hurt her. At least not right away. If he allowed those doctors to perform any harmful treatment, he would lose his leverage over you. They might put her in a straitjacket or a padded cell, but he knows he will lose his advantage if they do anything drastic. Think about it. She's probably safer now than if she stayed at home. He plans to dangle that threat in front of you as long as possible, to keep you compliant. We can focus on getting her back home after we deal with him. We've got an ace in the hole. If need be, I can tell Arthur Rumkin what's going on and everyone in town will know about it in less than an hour. That will stir up a nice ruckus. All the right people will start asking questions. Let's concentrate on the task at hand. Did you spike the decanter?"

"Yeah. While you had him occupied."

"Good. The ball is in motion now. Hold tight for a minute while I make a quick detour by the farm co-op."

26

THE ICE HOUSE WAS BUSY AS FARMERS LOADED LUGS OF tomatoes and squash onto tractor trailers heading north to the wholesalers in Dallas. Fifty cents got me two thirty-pound blocks. I tossed them in the bed and we were back on the road in less than five minutes. Missy tucked her raven locks under the blonde wig and fluffed the fake hair, covering her forehead and cheeks. A casual observer would be hard-pressed to recognize her.

Cars lined Pearl Street up to the driveway of Casa O'Dell. Good-hearted townsfolk milled on the porch, visiting with Vera and the girls. Tommy and Sara sat on the railing, holding hands and playing footsie. Brandy motioned me to the back yard, so I pulled up under the shade next to the shed.

I said, "Come with me, Miss Turnbow, and I will introduce you to our unwilling co-conspirators." I led her into the tool shed and thumped the suspended offal sack. A sudden symphony of vibrant humming attested to the wellbeing of our ill-tempered friends. Tommy, Sara, and Brandy entered and closed the door behind them.

Tommy made introductions. "This is Sara Tyler and Brandy O'Dell. Ladies, this is Meroticia ... er ... uh ... Missy Turnbow."

Brandy cut her eyes over to me in a coy look, acknowledging the girl's beauty and my silly smitten-ness. She said, "That's quite a disguise you've got there, Missy. I assume you're incognito for a reason?"

Missy blushed, and I brought them up to speed on the events leading to our arrival, leaving out the gory details of Nollen's assault. I could tell by her expression that Brandy filled in the blanks for herself.

Tommy praised my actions during the confrontation with Nollen. "Good thing you stayed cool, Teddy. It'll keep him guessing for a while. Let's continue this conversation at the Cusser Club, and put the finishing touches on the plan. Brandy, do you have a flash-light handy?"

"I've got something better than that." She reached on the shelf and pulled down a large kerosene hurricane lantern. Handing it to Missy, she said, "It's full. You guys grab the bee bag. Sara and I will get the masks and a few other items and meet you out front."

Tommy and I wedged the hornets in the truck's bed between the ice blocks. He said, "As long as we keep them out of direct sun-light, they should stay cool enough. Missy, were you able to spike the scotch decanter?"

"I poured it while Teddy had Nollen distracted. I'm still not sure what that is supposed to do to him. Poison him? Make him sick?"

"The psilocybin will cause hallucinations if taken in large doses of two to three grams. He won't get very much, since it's diluted in the liquor, but maybe it will make him woozy enough to throw him off balance and give us a few extra seconds to get you in and out of the mulch butler. I hope it doesn't backfire on us."

"Oh god. I'm already terrified. What if I can't do it? What if he grabs me before I can get out of the greenhouse?"

I reached inside the door of the shed and grabbed Mic's old baseball bat that hadn't been used since we were in Pee Wee league. Blowing off the dust, I struck a 'batter up' pose. "I've got contingency plans. Let's get over to the Cusser Club, where we can practice unobserved."

Tommy and Sara rode in the back, and Brandy jumped in the cab with Missy and me. She pulled the masks and hose out of the sack, did a quick inspection, and told Missy the details. "Tommy and Teddy will use these for a disguise and hide behind the greenhouse. I'll find a place in the shadows to stay out of sight. After you lure Nollen inside, they'll get you out. Sara will keep the pickup idling in the alley in case we need a quick getaway."

Missy said, "I don't know if I can do it. What if I panic and freeze up?"

"Don't worry about it. Look, I'm a pro at dealing with horny guys. You'll be able to throw him off his game when I get finished with you. We'll do the rest. Ain't that right, Theodore?"

"I have the utmost confidence in your abilities. I have absolutely no doubt that Missy will be prepared for her part in the scheme!" It was a lie. I had doubts aplenty, but I wasn't about to voice them.

Tommy and Sara giggled as they tumbled around in the back, trying to avoid getting wet in the melt-off from the ice blocks. For a fleeting moment, I hoped Monique might see the couple and cause a scene, but immediately chastised myself for the petty thought.

"Looks like they are having a good time," Brandy said as she reached behind Missy's neck and thumped me on the ear. "I guess Sara figures she needs to move on now that there's another love in your life."

I felt the blood rise in my face. A combination of irritation and embarrassment. Instead of responding to Brandy directly, I addressed my response to Missy, knowing I could never win a verbal sparring contest with an O'Dell. "Brandy delights at stirring up the manure pile and embarrassing me in particular. Sara and I have been friends forever, but there's never been anything between us." I leaned forward and looked directly at Brandy. "She is free to pursue whatever romantic path makes her happy. With my blessing." It was not an outright lie. Just a little obfuscation. Brandy snorted in derision. She knew better, but let it slide.

Missy grinned at me and said, "So, who's this new love interest she's referring to?"

27

TURNING ONTO THE RIVERFRONT LEVEE ROAD, WE WERE ALL surprised to see Casablanca overflowing with cars. Groups of men filled the porch and clustered in the parking lot in intense conversation. I recognized several of the town's elders.

I said, "There's Preacher Perkins talking to Mayor Grissom and Marlon Kutz."

Brandy leaned forward, studying the crowd. "Look, there's the Baptist preacher talking to Father Donahue from Immaculate Conception. What are *those* guys doing at a saloon?"

I pulled over and backed the truck off the road under the shade of the mimosa tree next to the wisteria. Tommy and Sara stood up in the bed and broke branches off to make a canopy over the offal bag. Brandy and Missy made their way under the fence while Tommy and I helped Sara out of the back.

He said, "I wonder what's going on at Casablanca? It's unusually busy for this time of day."

Sara replied, "There's my dad's truck! He never leaves the apartment unless it's something really important."

I slid under the fence first. Sara was next, with Tommy pulling up the rear. Poor Sara had to roll over on her back and stick her arms through, with me and Brandy pulling, while Tommy gently maneuvered her bosom under the chain links. His dexterity was impressive. Compress a little here, shift a little there. Pull, push, squeeze. Walla!

Missy bent down face to face with Sara. "I'll bet the mean girls at school make fun of you all the time, don't they?" Sara meekly smiled as Tommy brushed dirt off her back. It was a bonding moment. The girls nodded knowingly to one another as an unspoken understanding passed between them.

Brandy chortled. "Yeah, that's the difference between you girls and me. Before I dropped out of school, I loved it when those snotty bitches snickered and huddled in the hallway, whispering behind my back. I'd just saunter up to the nearest handsome jock and 'accidentally' rub my tits on him." Pulling a strand of hair over her face and transforming into a bashful babe with a thick Southern accent, she exclaimed, "Oh Roger, I'm so sorry. I didn't mean to brush my breasts against you. I swear, these unruly girls have a mind of their own. Please forgive me." Adopting a deep, gravelly, masculine voice of the mythical "Roger," she answered herself, "Oh, don't worry, Miss Brandy! You can rub yo' tig ole biddies against me any day!" Everyone laughed at Brandy's legendary irreverence.

As we made our way through the tall weeds, Tommy instructed the girls in a comical serpentine maneuver to avoid detection. This added to the lighthearted atmosphere, and I was relieved to see Missy allow herself another smile. Brandy and Tommy were well aware of the beneficial effects of their shenanigans, and hammed it up. Sara sidled up to Missy and whispered something in her ear. They both glanced back at me and giggled. I'm sure it was an unflattering remark, but at that point, I didn't care. Anything to get her mind off her troubles. Even a jab at my expense. Humper greeted us at the door and licked our faces as we shimmied through the opening. Enthralled by our trespass into the abandoned building, the girls curiously examined the Custer mural and secret panels as Tommy provided a nickel tour.

"The Knights of the Mystic Chalice smuggled booze during Prohibition and kept this private speakeasy running all during the 1920s. They undoubtedly made a fortune. After the federal government repealed the anti-liquor law in 1933, the Custer Club Taproom operated until Hurricane Audrey wrecked the building in '57. Ever since it was condemned, old Humper has been the sole occupant. Ain't that right, boy?!" Tommy said as he rubbed the mongrel's head.

Missy turned to me and said, "So, this is your private club now?"

"Yes, we've taken over the secret society. Tommy is the Subterranean Horluth. I'm the Serpentine Wyvern, and Mic is the Imperial Cyclops. I know it sounds ridiculous, but this old building kinda grows on you after a while. I like it, and no one will bother us here. Let's venture upstairs to the hallowed halls of the KOMC lodge and I will introduce you to the founder of the order."

Tommy lit the lantern, and we ascended the treacherous stairs single file, cautioning the ladies each step of the way.

Entering the second-floor chamber, Sara yelped as several crows screamed and fluttered out of the shattered skylight. "Wow. This place is creepy. You guys are crazy for hanging out here. It smells like a crypt."

Missy pulled off her blonde wig and swirled it around in a vigorous effort to disperse the dust and musty odor.

Brandy hip bumped her and said, "Not exactly the Sabine Valley Country Club, eh, North Sider?"

"Definitely ... uh ... an interesting place," Missy replied as she ran her fingers over the carvings of a decorative wall panel. "This is first class architecture. It's a shame the building has fallen into disrepair."

Tommy stood below the portrait on the wall, took a deep bow, and announced with a booming Shakespearean flare, "This is the most honorable Faustus Muffberger, founder of our noble order. This sad portrait is the last vestige of his existence. He now lies molding in the grave, dismissed by history and by the world, forgot!"

The ladies gawked at us as though we had dung beetles crawling out of our ears.

Shrugging off the less than enthusiastic response, he nodded to Brandy and said, "Perhaps we should get to the matter at hand. I figure we have two hours until sunset. The floor is yours, Madam."

She rolled her eyes and gave a brief curtsy. "You guys sit down and keep your mouths shut. I'm fixin' to show y'all how a professional performer woos a crowd. Sara, you might as well join the lesson too. Every girl should have some seduction instruction. You never know when it might come in handy."

Tommy and I followed orders and sat cross-legged on the floor while Missy and Sara leaned back against the altar. Humper laid down between, resting his head on my foot.

Brandy closed her eyes and shook her arms from side to side, getting into character. "Come here, ladies, and copy my movements. Don't worry, it will come naturally. I'll make pussycats out of you in no time."

Missy and Sara timidly tried to mirror her movements. Brandy pulled her T-shirt over her head and dropped it on the floor, revealing an impossibly tight white bikini top. She licked her lips and stuck out her tongue, touching the tip of her nose. Dropping her gaze to her chest, she squeezed her arms together, accentuating her cleavage, simultaneously exposing a delicious tan line. The beach bra struggled valiantly to contain the sultry spheres. Straining the fabric almost to the point of failure, she quickly released the tension, resulting in a delightful bounce.

"Wow!" I blurted before I could stop myself.

Tommy whacked me on the back of the head. "Don't interrupt the show. I'm trying to concentrate."

Sara kicked his shin. Light from the lantern cast provocative shadows on the wall, and I couldn't help but wonder if the old Cusser Club building had ever witnessed such a risqué performance. A breeze whistled through fractured walls in ethereal approval, and curious crows lined the edge of the skylight, peering down in silent fascination. Missy and Sara's initial movements were awkward and rigid, but quickly smoothed out under expert tutelage.

Brandy nodded in approval. "Move like a wave. Smooth and fluid. You girls are catching on quick. Here, let me show you a few more moves. We must recruit as many of the male senses as possible. Sight, sound, and smell are the Holy Trinity of seduction. Touch and taste only as a last resort. Just remember, ladies, once they get a little glimpse of heaven, all of their intelligence drains from the big head on their shoulders to the little head in their pants."

I should have been offended, but my mental focus was already migrating south—a scathing indictment of the male mindset.

Brandy demonstrated lip and tongue movements combined with impeccably timed moans and coos. Titillating choreography, born of countless hours at Muddy Mike's Gentleman's Club. "Give this move a try," she said, undulating her pelvis with intermittent quivers while letting out erotic, barely audible gasps. The younger girls repeated the procedure and Sara even laced her fingers on top of head and swirled her hair. She was a natural.

Tommy shifted uncomfortably and gulped, "Oh my goodness."

Missy was having some difficulty getting into the groove, so Sara sat down next to Tommy while Brandy patiently tutored her on the finer points of breast heaving and tushy jiggling. "It's easier if you close your eyes and pretend you're in the shower. Imagine the warm water flowing over your body as you rinse off the suds. Arch your back like a cat."

Missy put her hands over her face. "Brandy, I feel silly. I don't have ... uh ... the equipment. I'm not as well-endowed as you and Sara."

"Oh really? You don't believe you have what it takes? Let's get Theodore to assist us in proving my point." Brandy turned and motioned for me to stand up. Missy stared down at the floor in embarrassment.

It's amazing how women can manipulate men so easily. I followed her instructions without the slightest hesitation or trepidation. I should have known better. She casually unfastened the top two buttons of my shirt. I protested, but she pinched my lips together and said, "Just bear with me for a minute, Mr. Nutscalder. This is a very important part of my demonstration." She slipped behind me, patted me on the back, and said, "Relax, big boy."

That should have raised an alarm, but my hormone-addled brain swallowed the innocent gesture hook, line, and sinker. The vixen suddenly grabbed my collar with both hands and jerked the shirt down to my elbows in a straitjacket posture, leaving me completely helpless. She wrapped her arms around me to secure the hostage position, reaching around to the front of my pants with her right hand, grabbing at my measly manhood.

Pressing Little Willie against my jeans, she said, "See Missy? I told you so. Just as I suspected. Not the biggest one I've ever seen, but hard enough to cut diamonds!"

Missy and Sara collapsed in peals of laughter. Tommy's eyes widened to the size of silver dollars behind his spectacles. Brandy released me and rushed toward him as he desperately back peddled on elbows and heels. She tackled him, spun around, straddled his chest, and grabbed the crotch of his jeans, energetically tracing his mannish endowment halfway down to the knee.

"It's a universal law, ladies! A guy may lie to you with his mouth, but the pecker in his pants speaks the truth every time!"

Perturbed by the embarrassing display, I grabbed Brady by the belt loops and hoisted her off Tommy. "You've proven your point! Everyone is in complete agreement. You are the undisputed expert in male emasculation." I turned to Missy and Sara, who were whispering conspiratorially. "Do you ladies have any more questions for the Marquesa de Blue Balls, or are you content with your current level of instruction?"

I must have had an irritable edge in my voice because both girls snapped to attention. Sara nodded and Missy shook her head. "Well, which is it?" I yelled, louder than I should have.

"I ... I think we've got the general idea," Missy murmured.

Tommy stumbled between us, tucking his shirttail and rearranging his pants. "Okay, okay, mission accomplished. Let's re-focus, review the plan, and get everyone on the same page." All three girls leaned against the altar and focused attention on our lanky strategist. "Teddy and I will position ourselves behind the greenhouse and place the hive in one of the mulch butler drawers. Brandy will dress Missy in the outfit Danni Redhawk provided, and see to it that she makes an alluring target to coax her stepfather into the ambush position. Once he is inside, Missy will jump into the mulch butler and Teddy will pull her outside to safety. At that point, I'll untie the bag and release the hornets. Who's going to block the door once Nollen is inside?"

Missy said, "There's a two-inch gap where the flagstone walkway abuts the threshold. We can wedge any sturdy stick or stone into the crevice and block the door so he can't escape."

"No problem," Brandy answered. "I'll hide in the shrubs, and once he's inside, I'll slip something into the crack. If Missy has trouble getting out, I'll bang on the glass and make a ruckus to distract him."

Tommy nodded. "How does that sound, Theodore? Do you see any flaws in the strategy?"

I was secretly thinking of a thousand things that could go wrong, but I didn't want to cast doubt on the plan. I said, "Sara will keep the pickup idling in the alley. Let's pray Mr. England doesn't get too nosey. I've scoped out a quick getaway route along the water tower access trail at the end of Lamar Street. Other than that, I've got nothing to add. Let's grab the robes and see how our disguise looks with the voodoo masks. Sara, you and Missy climb up the spiral staircase to the porthole window and see what's happening at Casablanca. We don't want any witnesses delaying our departure."

Tommy gathered the robes and inspected the ceremonial swords as the two younger girls ascended the stairs to the station of the Serpentine Wyvern. Brandy pulled me aside.

"Teddy, I'm real sorry about embarrassing you guys, but I'm trying to throw a little starch into Missy's collar. She's scared to death. I've got to ask you, if the wheels come off the bus and this plan goes south, what are we going to do? Nollen isn't going to be amused by our antics, and we'll have a real fight on our hands."

"I've been thinking about Plan 'B'. If Embers don't take the bait, we'll hightail it out and regroup. If he escapes the greenhouse and comes after us, we'll just beat the shit of him, pure and simple. I've got Mickey's baseball bat and Tommy is gathering swords as we speak. They weren't designed for fighting, but we can damn sure poke a hole in him. There are four of us, five counting Sara, so the son-of-a-bitch is gonna have a hard time whooping us all at once. The real key is our disguise, and keeping you out of sight so he can't identify any of us."

"Hopefully it won't come to that, but an O'Dell never runs from a fight. I'll wrap up in one of these old cloaks and stay in the shadows. I'll be your ace in the hole."

"You can count on me as well, Teddy boy!" Tommy said as he twirled a sword, lunging and parrying with dexterity bordering on elegance.

The girls applauded from the alcove above, and Sara said, "It looks like the party's over at the bar. The parking lot is clearing out."

Tommy and I donned the robes and held the masks over our faces. "How do we look?" I asked.

"It's a great disguise and looks much more formidable than I imagined." Brandy replied. Sara and Missy nodded in agreement. The girls brushed the dust and cobwebs off the garments as Tommy and I struck a menacing pose with the ornamental swords.

I said, "We are as ready as possible at this point. No need to clutter our minds with endless speculation. Tommy, how much time do we have before sunset?"

"A little over an hour," he replied as he removed the mask and spread his robe out on the floor. "Let's rest for a few minutes and say a prayer for Mickey. He's gonna be sorry he missed this party!"

Sara retrieved two more capes while Brandy swabbed makeup on Missy's face by lantern light.

Sara positioned herself directly under the narrow shaft of sunlight filtering through the hole in the ceiling, laid on her back, and instructed Tommy to do the same. "Let's make a Magic Wheel, so all our dreams will come true."

Tommy asked, "What's a Magic Wheel?"

"It's supernatural. Like a Ouija board. Everyone just lies face up, with our heads together in the center and our feet pointing out like spokes on a wagon wheel."

Brandy said, "Yeah, I remember Granny O'Dell telling stories about the Magic Wheel a long time ago. It's some kind of Irish folklore. I think you're supposed to lie down in an enchanted forest or some other magical place, so I guess the Cusser Club is probably as close as we're gonna get to that, here in the Knob. Sounds like a lot of fun. I'm just about finished with this little minx. What do y'all think?"

The makeup job was flawless. The eyeliner and mascara gave Missy an oriental flare. Lipstick accentuated already voluptuous lips, and a touch of rouge under the cheeks made her look even more provocative. No matter what facial expression she assumed, it translated into a 'come hither' look. Satisfied with the war paint, both girls followed Sara's advice and reclined on the floor. Brandy shot me a wink as she patted the space between her and Missy. I feigned exasperation, but plopped down between them. In reality, there was no place in the world I would have rather been.

"So, how does this game work?" Tommy asked.

All three girls answered simultaneously.

"Not a game—"

"Old Celtic magic—"

"Mystic spell craft—"

I said, "Has everybody in the world heard about this stuff but me and Tommy?"

Missy playfully pinched me on the arm. "Just concentrate on your goals and dreams, and then verbalize them to your friends, and the universe opens a path to fulfillment. Take deep breaths and clear your mind. Sara, you go first, since it was your idea."

"Okay, I dream of a day when everyone quits making fun of me. I dream of a day when people see the real me. Not an airhead with frizzy hair and a big set of boobs."

We all laughed and Sara exclaimed, "See, that's what I'm talking about! Even my so-called friends think I'm a ditzy twit."

Brandy gently scolded her. "Girl, quit letting other people define you. Look at me. The whole town calls me a tramp and whispers behind my back, but I don't give a damn what they think. I'll do whatever is necessary to survive. Not caring is actually kinda liberating. You ought to try it."

Missy chimed in. "We aren't taunting you, Sara. I know exactly what you're talking about. Just like all those girls at your school that we talked about earlier. They're just jealous. Hell, I'm jealous! If I had a bust like yours, I'd buy a Jane Russell bra and point those puppies up at the sky for everyone to see. I wouldn't wear anything but T-shirts and tube tops."

Brandy replied, "Amen, sister!"

I was delighted by the friendship forming between the girls. Their background couldn't have been more diverse, but their common plight struck a chord of human sympathy that drew them closer together with each passing moment.

An interval of sweet silence passed as we lay on our backs with our heads together, staring at the wispy clouds passing over the ruptured skylight. The crows lost interest and abandoned us as soon as we ceased our antics, bored by our calm repose.

"Everybody in town knows what I want," Tommy said as he took off his glasses and held them at arm's length toward the opening in the ceiling. "My vision is getting worse and, at this rate, I'll be blind in a year."

Sara replied, "There has to be a doctor somewhere that can help."

"My mother wrote a letter to a specialist in New York. We're waiting to hear back from him. I'm afraid the cost is going to be staggering. I have a recurring nightmare. Standing on the street corner with a tin cup begging for change." An awkward moment followed. None of us knew what to say. Tommy finally broke the uneasy silence. "Enough of my troubles. What about you, Brandy? What do you want, other than to get Pete and Mic back home, safe and sound?"

"I want to meet a nice guy. No knight in shining armor. No handsome hunk. No rich playboy. Just a plain, regular, hardworking chap, with eyes only for me. Every time I dance at the club, I search the room for a quiet guy with a kind smile, sitting in the shadows, away from the stage. Maybe a little shy. But he's never there. I've come to the cruel realization that no one is coming to my rescue. Nothing but a bunch of horny whoremongers, leering and groping. Isn't it ironic? The last thing you're going to find at a gentlemen's club, is a gentleman." Brandy sniffed and wiped her eyes, exposing a tiny chink in her otherwise impenetrable armor.

"I get where you're coming from," Missy whispered. "I just want to be normal. Y'all are going to laugh, but I envy the girl that runs the cash register at Piggly Wiggly. She's as plain as a potato and limps when she walks, but I'd trade places with her in a minute. She's always happy and laughing. Everybody loves her. Folks wait in line to see her, even if the other cashiers are open. You can't help but smile when she speaks to you. When people look at me, they just sneer and turn away."

Sara said, "I intended for The Magic Wheel to be fun. This is downright depressing!" Everyone burst out laughing and the crows reappeared at the rim of the skylight, cawing at the ruckus.

Brandy said, "What about you, Teddy? What's your secret desire?"

"Nothing special. I just want to be an author. Get away from the Knob, and write. Not a *New York Times* bestselling novelist or anything so lofty as that. I would be happy to write pulp fiction, like those *Flash Gordon* and *Buck Rogers* paperbacks you buy at Perry's Five and Dime Store."

Tommy said, "He gets stellar reviews in Miss Hawkins' English class. Isn't that right, Sara?"

She replied, "Teddy is a talented storyteller. He'll be famous someday. I'm sure of it."

At that moment, a blast of wind shook the building and Faustus Muffberger's portrait fell off the wall with a thunderous crash. Sara and Humper leapt to their feet and bolted for the door. Brandy and Missy screamed and ran.

Tommy snatched up the swords, threw the robes at me, and yelled, "Let's get outta here! I think the spirits of the Cusser Club are fed up with our sacrilege!"

28

THE GIRLS WERE ALREADY HUDDLED IN THE FRONT SEAT OF the Chevy when Tommy and I emerged from the wisteria. Sara was behind the wheel, engine running, windows rolled up tight, with the doors locked.

Tommy tapped on the window, but Sara shook her head. "That place is haunted and I ain't opening this damn door. Y'all get in the back. I'll drive."

She drove slowly and kept to the back streets on the way to Fairhaven. A couple of the hornets squeezed out of the opening of the offal bag, so Tommy stomped them and tightened the string. Clouds gathered and a low rumble of thunder heralded our arrival to the alley gate.

Everyone bailed out of the pickup, and Missy peeked through the fence slats and said, "Damn! Butch's GTO is in the driveway. What are we going to do now?"

I said, "That throws a wrench in the works, but we can't postpone the plan until tomorrow. The little beasties in the bag won't last until then. We can't stay here and wait. Mr. England or one of the other neighbors might see us and get suspicious. Maybe we could hide out at the dirt pits on Gypsy Camp Road for a while."

Brandy shook her head. "That won't work. If kids aren't parked out there already, they will be soon, smooching and getting busy. We can't go back to Casa O'Dell either. Burtis and Nate are watching the place in case the shooter returns. Missy, is there any way we can see what's going on inside the house?"

"Nollen and Butch are probably in the library at the front of the house. There's a side window next to the driveway. If I hide in the hedges, I might be able to sneak a peek without being seen by anyone inside the house or on the street."

Brandy replied, "I'll go with you. Everyone else stay in the truck. If anyone comes by, stall 'em. Just tell them you're helping look for Missy."

The girls crept through the gate, and Tommy arranged the cloaks and masks on the tailgate. Sara stood in the bed, peeking over the fence. "I don't know about you guys, but I'm getting nervous. What if something goes wrong? What if we get caught? What if...?"

Tommy interrupted her. "Don't worry, Sara. If anything goes south, Teddy will think of something."

I was about to reply when the other girls returned.

Brandy was grinning ear to ear. "The scotch decanter is empty. Both of those sumbitches are as drunk as Cooter Brown. They're smoking pot too!"

Missy was shaking with trepidation. "The scotch decanter was over halfway full when I spiked it this afternoon. I imagine he's pretty high. Sometimes he gets violent when he's high. I'm sick to my stomach. I don't know if I can go through with it."

Brandy grabbed the fancy masquerade mask out of Danni's sack, took off her T-shirt, adjusted the straps on the bikini top, and said, "I'll put on this disguise and sneak in with you, just in case we need to distract old Butchey Boy. We'll catch 'em off guard. I know Nollen is a control freak and likes to call the shots, but I guarantee he'll follow you into the greenhouse. Just remember all the stuff I taught you. Assume your positions, boys. The show is about to start. Turn your backs while Missy puts on the negligee."

Tommy and I donned our robes while Sara and Brandy helped Missy change. My heart was thumping against my bruised ribs and Tommy's hands shook as he positioned the hosiery over his voodoo mask and glasses. He looked like the Angel of Death. I gasped as Missy emerged from the cab of the truck. She couldn't look me in the eye. I briefly reimagined the Alpine Lodge dream, with *her* wrapped up on the bed of furs instead of Sara.

Tommy punched me in the arm. "No time for distractions, buddy. I'll carry the bag while you grab the baseball bat and swords."

Sara hugged Tommy for five Mississippis and me for two. "You guys be careful. I'll keep a lookout."

"Let's do this before I lose my nerve," Missy said as she locked arms with Brandy and slipped through the gate. Tommy and I followed as Sara slid behind the steering wheel. The full moon cast an eerie glow through the clouds and a gentle breeze billowed Tommy's cloak, transforming him into a malevolent floating phantom.

A single Agro light positioned over a tray of seedlings was the only illumination inside the greenhouse. Tommy placed the offal bag in a drawer and positioned the string so a single pull would open the top. Brandy motioned me to join her on the patio steps and handed me a little plaster garden gnome.

"I'm going in with Missy. Use this to block the door once Nollen and Butch are inside."

I said, "Are you crazy? That'll foul up the whole plan. We can't get *both* of you out through the mulch butler!"

"Settle down! I'll have to take Butch out of the equation. I'll try to lead him away from the greenhouse, but just in case it doesn't work, put the baseball bat inside the door and tell Tommy to take the offal bag out so both drawers are open. Once we're out, you can shove it back inside. There is no other way. Missy's petrified and can't do it on her own. Grow some balls, Boudreaux!"

The insult stung, but I knew she was right. I propped the bat inside the door against a shelf of African violets and readjusted my mask in the glass reflection. The girls peeked into the house through the sliding patio door and whispered to one another. A long hallway ran past the kitchen to the front foyer next to the library. Missy tugged at the bottom of the satin robe, trying to obscure her thighs. There was a little birthmark shaped like a cat's paw just under her left heinie cheek. I couldn't help wondering if I was the only guy in the world who had ever seen it. There was a soft swoosh as Missy eased the door open. They tiptoed down the hallway to the library, pausing for a moment to listen. Missy turned back toward me with a terrified look. Suddenly, Brandy took her hand and pulled her into the light emanating from the room. Following Brandy's lead, Missy did a little tushy shake and then leaned forward, blowing kisses to the occupants. I suddenly realized I hadn't told Tommy to remove the bag. As I rushed to his position, an ear-splitting scream pierced the air. We were past the point of no return. "Take out the bag! Brandy's inside with Missy and we are going to need both drawers. It's do-or-die!"

I crawled on all fours toward a topiary plant shaped like a lamb. Another blood-curdling scream. Missy burst forth from the patio door with Nollen Embers hot on her heels. Brandy was nowhere in sight. Missy leapt over the steps and scampered into the greenhouse, pausing for a split second to topple a Ficus tree in her stepfather's path. I slammed the door, shoved the gnome into the gap, and rushed to the rear of the structure just as Missy jumped in the mulch butler. She crouched down and Tommy pulled on the drawer, but couldn't get her out before Nollen caught up and grabbed her by the hair. It was a Mexican stand-off. Halfway in and halfway out. Missy screamed in pain as we struggled to hold on to the box. Tommy grabbed a sword and tried to saw through her hair, but the dull blade wasn't up to the task.

"Stab him in the hand!" I yelled, yanking the drawer with all my might. Missy reached overhead and grabbed her assailant's arm and pulled. It was just enough. Tommy drove the tip of the blade into his wrist. The bastard bellowed in pain and let go. I hoisted Missy to safety, and in one fluid movement, Tommy threw the bag into the container, pulled the string, and shoved it inside.

Missy screamed, "Butch has Brandy trapped inside the house. You've got to help her!"

Nollen flung terra cotta pots against the door and pounded the glass with his fists. I grabbed both swords and turned to Tommy. "Take Missy back to the truck. I'm going after Brandy. Tell Sara to drive around and meet us out front."

The hornets didn't swarm and Nollen lunged against the greenhouse door, splintering the frame. A bewildered look crossed his face as I came into view, and he growled. "Who are you? You dare to fuck with me? I'll slit your throat and send you straight to hell!"

Tunnel vision focused on the deviant. The voice in my head whispered, "*You have him right where you want him. Stay the course. See it through to the end.*"

I pressed my mask against the glass as he hammered with his fists, and quoted Shakespeare. "Send me to hell? Hell is empty and all the devils are here!"

Uttering the line from *The Tempest* was the magic spell. A black cloud emerged from the back of the structure and coalesced into an undulating vortex of demonic rage. I crossed the swords over my head and backed away as the onslaught began. Like a giant blunderbuss, the rabid insects pummeled Nollen's body and smashed themselves against the clear glass panes. There was nowhere for him to hide. Screaming in agony, the man stumbled and swatted, knocking over tables and shelves. He uprooted a pygmy palm, swinging it wildly in a futile effort to deflect the airborne assault. Each movement just enraged the creatures even more.

Another scream from the house jolted me back to reality. Bolting up the patio stairs and into the hallway, I reached the door of the study just as Brandy and Butch tumbled into the foyer, locked in a desperate struggle. Nollen's lieutenant had her in a choke hold, squeezing the air out of her lungs. I stabbed her assailant in the ass with both swords, driving the tips deep into his right butt cheek. Butch reflexively arched his back, allowing her to twist free of his grasp. I crouched with weapons at the ready as he spun around and jumped to his feet. He snatched a Tiffany lamp off of a Bombay chest and hurled it at my head. I reflexively ducked, and the mask deflected some of the blow, but left the right side of my face momentarily exposed. As he searched for another weapon, I yelled, "Leave her alone, dickhead!"

His eyes narrowed, and he chortled with a derisive sneer, "Shit, you're just a piss ant kid, hiding behind a Halloween mask!" He shattered a thick porcelain vase at my feet, forcing me to backpedal into the kitchen. The bastard grabbed a toaster off the countertop, and bashed my face. The mask recoiled against my nose as the bone split away from the cartilage with an audible crack. An explosion of blood splattered against the inside of the mask and into my eyes. Blinded by the hemorrhage, I swung the swords in wild desperation, but he hit me with a dining chair and pinned me to the floor. I braced for another blow, but it never came. Instead, the chair tumbled to my side and a heavy weight fell onto me with a squishy thud. I froze, addled by the injury, unsure of what to do next.

"It's okay, Teddy," Brandy grunted as she rolled Butch's body off me. I felt her hands gently pulling the sticky disguise off my face.

"Oh my god. Lie still, your nose is broken. Let me get you a towel."

I sat up and managed to wipe some of the blood out of my eyes. Butch was lying prone on the floor, head to one side, drooling. A broken glass scotch decanter lay beside him. Brandy returned with a wet cup towel and a baggy full of ice. Her voice was hoarse from the strangulation, but she appeared okay, other than that. My guardian angel gritted her teeth and winced as she wiped clots of blood off of my upper lip and placed the cold pack over the bridge of my nose. "Hold this in place and let me help you stand up. Your nose is real crooked, and we're going to have to take you to the hospital and get it set. Did Missy get away?"

Before I could answer, an explosion of shattering glass erupted behind us. Brandy screamed and pointed toward the patio. Nollen, baseball bat in hand, stumbled up the steps, clad only in boxer shorts, his eyes swollen and arms bloody. He raised the bat, roaring like a wounded bear as he stormed into the kitchen. Swinging wildly, he yelled, "I'll kill all of you bastards!"

Leaving the cloak and swords behind, Brandy pulled me down the hall and out the front door. Still dazed from the blow to my face, I got dizzy and fell down the last step onto the lawn. Brandy lifted me up and wrapped my arm over her shoulder to steady me.

She screamed, "He's got a gun, Teddy! We have to get out of here."

A shot discharged and Brandy collapsed beneath me. "My leg!" she screamed. A surge of adrenaline shot through my veins and I grabbed her arm and dragged her into the neighbor's hedgerow as Nollen staggered into the street and fired two more rounds in the air.

"Brandy, where are you hit?"

"My left leg!"

Another shot rang out as Embers squinted and jerked his head around, searching for a target. "I'll kill all of you! Nobody gets the drop on me … Meroticia? Where are you?

As he turned toward us, headlights flashed in the street, bathing our attacker in a beam of brilliant white. Nollen's face was swollen to the point his eyes were mere slits. Hundreds of red blisters covered his exposed skin, evidence of the hornet attack. A split second later, Nate's old Chevy sped past, careening headlong into the madman. Tires screeched, followed by a heavy thud. I turned to see the bastard tumbling through the air, hitting the pavement 20 feet away. Missy, pulling up her jeans, jumped out of the truck, and ran toward her stepfather. He rolled over and crawled on all fours, patting the asphalt, searching for his gun. The revolver lay in the gutter a few inches away and I screamed at Missy to retrieve it. She had other plans. Her sprint morphed into an agile skip, and with a graceful arc of her right leg, she planted her foot squarely in Nollen's ballsack. The sound was glorious. Kind of like dropping a cinder block on a toad. He rolled over, clutching his genitals as a fountain of projectile vomit erupted from his gullet. The man gagged and screamed as Missy repeatedly stomped his groin. All the shame, rage, and abasement from years of abuse poured forth from the girl in a torrent of sweet revenge.

I turned my attention back to Brandy. She had her pant leg rolled up, revealing a nasty gash in her calf. "I think the bullet ricocheted off the concrete and grazed me. Take my belt and let's make a tourniquet." Just as I unbuckled her belt, Tommy appeared with Danni's paper sack and poured the contents on the ground next to us. "I figured there might be something in here you could use," he said, looking alternately from my nose to Brandy's leg.

Brandy rolled up the satin robe and Tommy helped me secure the makeshift bandage with the belt.

Sirens sounded in the distance as Sara jumped out of the truck, picked up the pistol, and tossed it into a nearby storm drain. "C'mon, guys, we've gotta get out of here before the cops see us!"

Tommy grabbed Missy around the waist and pulled her away from her stepfather. I gave Sara directions to the water tower as I lifted Brandy into the passenger seat. Just as Tommy and I climbed in the back, the GTO fired up in the driveway. The engine revved, and we braced ourselves as Butch backed out at breakneck speed. In a wild-eyed panic, he struck the rear bumper of the Chevy, launching me over the side onto the pavement. Tires spun and smoked as he stomped the gas, speeding down the street just as two patrol cars pulled onto Fairhaven. One vehicle missed him. The other one didn't. The clash of metal was deafening. Missy and Tommy helped me up. Otho Wheat stumbled out of the crashed vehicle while two deputies piled out of the other. Converging on the GTO, they dragged Butchey Boy out kicking and screaming like a sissy bitch. Jack boots stomped, billy clubs flew, and 10 seconds later, he lay motionless on the pavement just like his boss.

Too late to flee, Sara pulled the pickup over to the curb and killed the engine. Nollen sprawled in the street, moaning. We quietly gathered on the lawn and Missy said, "What are we going to tell the cops? This whole thing is about to blow up in our faces!"

A resonant voice answered from the shadows, "Four guys in a black Cadillac with Louisiana plates. Big bastards, and heavily armed. You kids got caught in the crossfire. Wrong place. Wrong time."

We all turned toward the mysterious commentator. Mr. England stepped out of the shadows, Brutus in tow.

"Yeah, that's right," Brandy said. "Four guys. Black Caddy. Everybody got it?" She looked at each of us in turn as we nodded in agreement.

Mr. England said, "The sheriff is heading this way. I advise you all to sit quietly on the grass. Coppers like to tower over people. Less threatening. Speak only when spoken to."

Otho approached Nollen, who was still clutching his balls, and nudged him with the tip of his boot. Taking a deep breath, he shook his head and walked toward us, holding up the index finger of his left hand. His right hand on his holster.

"One person. I want to hear the story from one person."

I opened my mouth to speak, but he shot me an angry glare. "Not from you, Nutscalder. I don't want to hear a damn word from you."

After scanning the faces, he settled on Missy. "Meroticia, would you condescend to enlighten me on this shit show?"

"Nollen sent my mom away this morning, and I was inconsolable. My new friends came over to visit and comfort me. They told me about a play they were planning to raise money for Tommy's eye operation."

"*Macbeth,*" Tommy said, holding out his arms to display the Cusser Club robe.

"That's right," Missy answered. "I invited them to practice here in our back yard. Then some men arrived in a black car, and a fight broke out. They started shooting. We all panicked, and my sweet Teddy got hurt. Nollen was screaming. I … I …" She covered her face and sobbed. Brandy patted her on the back. "There, there, Missy. It will be okay. The sheriff will sort things out." Melchior and Dipdottle would have been absolutely euphoric.

Mr. England stepped to Otho's side. "Sheriff, may I have a word?" The elderly gentleman spoke in muted tones while pointing alternately at Nollen and the gate next to the alley. The deputies pulled up in the undamaged patrol car with Butch face down on the floorboard, hands cuffed behind his back.

The junior lawman in the passenger seat rolled down the window and said, "Boss, your car is still drivable, but just barely. We radioed for a wrecker to pick up the GTO. An ambulance is on the way for that pile of shit whimpering in the street."

Otho said, "Put out an APB on any late model black Caddy in the area with Louisiana plates. Four perps. Ask their business. Get names. They're probably armed. This would be a good time to answer that call about suspicious activity at the warehouse on Bolton Street."

The deputy looked puzzled. "I haven't heard of any calls about the warehouse. What are you talking about?"

Gritting his teeth, Otho bent forward while pointing to Embers and Butch. "Remember, Deputy? We *just* got a call about someone snooping around that big warehouse, and it's our duty to investigate!"

"Oh … oh, yeah … that call. I remember now. I'll round up some guys. We'll have a real thorough look."

The sheriff turned to our ragtag group as the deputies drove away. "Sara, I want you to take Tommy and Brandy home. Park the truck at the bakery. I'll have Nathaniel pick it up later. Miss Turnbow and Mr. Nutscalder will come with me." He grabbed my chin and turned my face to the streetlight. "Dr. DeSilva needs to set that snout. It's gonna hurt like hell, but don't worry, Nurse Jurnigan and I will hold you down, where he can work it back in place real nice and straight. You ain't going to be very pretty for a while."

29

AS SARA, TOMMY AND BRANDY DROVE OFF, WE FOLLOWED Otho to his car. He shoved me in the back and opened the front door for Missy. The engine clattered and shook for a minute when he cranked up, but smoothed out a bit as he drove toward midtown. He pulled into Kushner County General but parked at the furthest point from the hospital entrance. He knew we were lying. I could imagine the questions rattling around in his head.

Why was Mr. England covering for these kids?

How did they get the drop on two hardened criminals?

Why are these South Side kids sticking their necks out for a rich girl they hardly know?

Finally, he spoke to my companion. "So, they shipped your mother off to the psych clinic?"

"Yessir."

"Is that why y'all did .... whatever it was ... y'all did?"

"There's other stuff," Missy whispered.

He positioned his rearview mirror to see my reaction. He was baiting me, so I kept my eyes down and my mouth shut.

He let Missy recover her composure.

"Do you want to tell me about the other stuff?"

Missy wiped her eyes and leaned against the passenger side door, facing the sheriff. She unbuttoned her blouse and pulled it down, not bothering to stop at the crucial point. Otho gasped and punched the dashboard so hard it left a dent.

I said, "That's Nollen Embers' handiwork. And *that* is the crux of the matter."

Missy placed her hands between her legs. "There's more down here."

The sheriff shook his head. She buttoned up.

Otho keyed the mic on his radio. "Dispatch? Lois? This is Otho."

"Yessir?"

"Call Patti and tell her I'm bringing a guest home tonight. Missy Turnbow. She may stay a couple of days while I sort out a few things. Also, see if you can locate Nathaniel Nutscalder. Theodore got himself a broken nose, horsing around trying to impress some girls. I'm taking him to see Dr. DeSilva. Nothing serious."

"10-4. Anything else?"

"Yeah, call Judge Marlin Choate. I need a search warrant for the Turnbow place. Over and out."

He cranked the car and pulled into the ER entrance. "Missy, just stay in the car while I take Theodore to the doc. C'mon, you delinquent turd, let's get that schnoz straightened out." Missy leaned over the seat and gave me a kiss on the forehead as Otho opened the back door for me. He put his hand on the nape of my neck and squeezed as we ascended the ramp. The waiting area was empty, but a group of hospital workers gathered at the far end of the hallway, taking turns peeking into a brightly lit exam room. They chortled and parted to let us pass. Nollen Embers sprawled out, spread eagle, naked on a gurney while nurses hooked IV bags into both arms. DeSilva was palpating his enormous purple scrotum, muttering to himself about testicles on the verge of rupture. The physician glanced at me and arched his eyebrows.

He said, "Sheriff, take him into treatment room number five. I'll be there as soon as I … drain some fluid off this … uh … patient."

A nurse followed us into room T-5 and stuck wet swabs up my nostrils. It stung like hell and my eyes watered to the point I couldn't see.

She said, "This astringent will stop the bleeding. Hold still while I get some more ice."

Otho crossed his arms and leaned against the wall. "Why didn't you come to me with this problem?"

"You know damn well why we couldn't come to you. Everybody remembers the girl in Kirkcaldy. Nollen would have weaseled out, and you know it. There's no justice for a girl in Missy's situation. Her word against his … so we handled the situation."

He said, "Just for the record. Four big guys? Black Caddy? Louisiana plates?"

"Yessir."

"Trouble follows you everywhere you go and I'm weary of it. Stay out of my sight for a few days. I don't want to see hide nor hair of you. Not a peep. Understood?"

"Yessir."

"I'm going to take Missy home to Patti. They'll talk. It will be good for the girl. Maybe they can pay Maris a visit and assess the situation. No telling what Nollen had planned for her, but Marlin Choate and I will see that no harm comes to the poor woman."

Otho left as Dr. DeSilva entered the room with a nasty-looking syringe.

The surgeon said, "I'll have to numb your nose so I can set it." He pulled the swabs out of my nostrils and I closed my eyes as the needle went in. The hornet stings were worse. "Hold still. This will only take a second." A bolt of lightning behind my eyes followed a nauseating snap.

"The worst is over. I'll give you a shot of morphine for the pain. Nurse Jurnigan will pack your nose and tape the splint. You can sleep in the recovery room tonight." A prick on the shoulder was the last thing I remembered.

30

I DON'T KNOW HOW I GOT TO THE RECOVERY ROOM. WHEN I awoke, daylight was filtering through the louvered blinds. Desperate to pee, I grabbed a bedpan off the side table and unleashed Little Willie just in time. My cursed bladder wouldn't have held another minute. Residual swelling blurred my vision, and I teetered with every step. Stumbling down the hall, I found myself at the entry of the indigent ward. I hadn't seen Grails since the attack and a mixture of curiosity and guilt got the best of me, so I eased inside.

All the curtains were open and Galton was lying in Mic's old bed. A young, freckle-faced girl with dishwater blonde hair lay curled up, asleep on a cot beside his bed. My arch nemesis lay face up, eyes open, but unaware. Thick bandages wrapped the top of his head, secured by pink diaper pins. His toes tapped the footboard, as if keeping time to some jolly tune reverberating in his damaged brain.

He worked his lips in a puckering motion while blowing spit bubbles like an infant.

"Who beat the shit out of you?" the girl said as she sat up, rubbing her eyes.

"It's a long story. And very boring."

"If you came here to finish him off, go ahead. I won't tell."

"No … oh god, no … I just came to check on him and see if there was anything I could do to help. I feel awful. It really was an accident."

The cute little ragamuffin shrugged her shoulders, yawned, and stretched. A perfect picture of indifference.

She said, "I'm stuck here till lunch. Someone has to stay with him all the time. He gets choked a lot. The doctor said he might suffocate, so I'm supposed to run and get help if he stops breathing."

"Are you his sister?"

She nodded. "Ginny with a 'G,' not a 'J.'"

"Pleased to meet you, Ginny. I'm Teddy. You must love your brother very much, to spend all night in this dreary place, looking after him."

My statement clearly surprised her.

"Love him? Are you kidding me? I hate the cruel bastard. I'm only here because my dad made me stay. If Galton starts choking, I'm going to hold his nose, and make damn sure he's good and dead before I call for help."

I burst out laughing before I could stop myself. Ginny with a 'G' laughed, too.

She straightened the blanket on her cot. "Come over here and sit beside me. I could use some company."

As I sat, Ginny pulled up her dress, exposing a nasty burn scar on her thigh.

"When I was seven, Galton pushed me into the fireplace when I refused to fetch him a biscuit. Daddy wouldn't take me to the doctor, so Momma treated me with turpentine and bacon grease. She's a little retarded. It festered, and I ran a fever for days. Do you think that pile of shit ever stuck his head in the door to say he was sorry?"

"I thought I had it bad. You have to live with him. I had a twin sister once. She died when we were seven. I'd give anything to have her back."

The girl leaned forward and rested her elbows on her knees. In a barely audible whisper, she replied, "I'd give anything to have him gone."

Ginny's stomach growled, and I asked if she was hungry. She had no money, so I fished two dollars from my pocket and told her I would watch Galton while she went to the cafeteria.

"It's the least I can do for a kindred spirit."

"For a dollar-fifty I can get the Lumberjack breakfast. Bacon, eggs, grits and a pancake. I'll bring you the change."

"I had a windfall yesterday, so keep the change for a snack later on."

Without another word, she vanished. Leaning over the bed, I studied my vanquished foe, memorizing every aspect of his face. My stunt at the quarry had reduced the town bully to a drooling, ball-scratching idiot. For a fleeting moment, I entertained the thought of finishing him, like Ginny suggested. I imagined Satan crouching in the corner, whispering; "You're going to hell, anyway. Just hold a pillow over his face. It will only take a minute."

The swinging doors burst open, and Nurse Jurnigan barged in with a cart of bandages, balms, and sponges.

"Where is Ginny?" she said as she adjusted her glasses and inspected the splint on my nose.

"I gave her some money for breakfast and told her I'd watch Galton while she went to the cafeteria."

"Good for you. She's a sweet girl, trapped in an unfortunate family situation. How's your nose?"

"Throbbing, but not unbearable. I don't even remember you coming in to fix the splint."

A sly smile spread over her weathered face. "You were semiconscious, blabbering on and on about a girl named Missy."

"Oh, my god! Jeez, what did I say?"

"Plenty! But don't worry, I'll never tell. Sedatives and painkillers act like a truth serum. You wouldn't believe the stuff I've heard over the years. The evening shift said Nollen Embers prattled on for hours about all the crimes he's committed, going all the way back to his childhood. The entire staff got an earful. None of it is admissible in court, but it will certainly put Otho Wheat's investigations on a fast track. You should rest up and let that fracture heal. Go home while I tend to this boy."

31

I SET OUT FOR TYLER'S BAKERY, CURIOUS TO FIND OUT WHAT happened after we split up the previous evening. Fresh air and the three-block walk to the town square helped steady my feet and clear my head. My eyesight was still blurry and a bizarre spectacle emerged as I arrived at Rhinelander Park. At first, I thought I was hallucinating. Colorful crepe streamers swung between the trees. Dozens of helium-filled balloons bounced in the breeze, attached to lamp-posts, benches, and the Dix Statue. Nollen Embers' campaign signs covered the lawn, but there was something odd about the placards.

Upon closer inspection, I realized pranksters had expertly altered each one to read:

"Elect SWollen MEmbers for Mayor—A New Opportunity for Growth and Expansion." Attached to the bottom of each sign was a photograph of the bleary-eyed candidate, spread eagle on a gurney, his scrotum swollen to the size of a casaba melon. Townsfolk milled about the grounds, laughing and joking with one another. A large group held up the insulting posters while a photographer from *The Tattler* snapped pictures. Arthur Rumkin was in his element, slathering commentary on curious onlookers as he squatted like a troll on the base of the Rhinelander statue. He glanced my way and motioned me over.

"Ooowee, young Nutscalder! I heard you made a pass at the Turnbow princess and she decked you with a left hook."

I wondered if this misinformation was part of my co-conspirators' attempt at a coverup. It wasn't the most flattering lie, but it would certainly avert a lot of awkward questions, so I ran with it.

"It was actually a right hook, Mr. Rumkin. Walked right into it. Rich girls are a peculiar breed. I really should have listened to you last week when you warned me about her."

"Like Romeo and Juliet, some relationships are destined to end in tragedy. Keep your chin up, Theodore! That ugly honker will heal eventually, and some other little filly will come along and catch your eye, now that you've screwed the pooch with Missy *and* Sara."

"I haven't completely given up on Missy, but Sara has moved on. I think she and Tommy have a special friendship. He's a bigger man than me, anyway."

I meant the statement figuratively, but Arthur took it literally. He bent over and dangled his arm between his legs, guffawing at his cleverness.

"I really didn't mean it like that, Mr. Rumkin. I wouldn't want to start another rumor that might hurt Sara. She's already endured enough teasing for a lifetime."

"I was merely amused by your choice of words. What do they call it? A double entendre? There isn't much to laugh about in this sad little town, but gonad humor never gets old!" He leapt off the pedestal and patted me on the back. "I've got a roof leak to patch at Doc Terrell's place, so I gotta run. Stop by Casablanca this afternoon. There's going to be some interesting stuff going down."

Sara was busy tending to a full house at the bakery, so I headed to Casa O'Dell, hoping to get the scoop from Brandy. When I arrived, it surprised me to find Murl O'Dell sitting on the porch varnishing a barstool, while the three younger sisters took turns playing with a hula hoop in the yard. The girls came running when I walked into view. The sight of my battered face didn't faze them at all.

The oldest said. "Brandy came home with blood all over her clothes and Momma got real upset. She thought someone had shot her. Brandy told her the blood was yours after you fell and broke your nose."

"That is exactly what happened, and I just got out of the hospital a few minutes ago. Where is Brandy? I would like to thank her for helping me."

"Her and Momma have gone off to Huntsville to see Papa. They left on a Greyhound, and won't be back until the day after tomorrow. Uncle Murl is taking care of us until our Aunt Coleen can get here from Lufkin."

Murl said, "Teddy, you look like you've been in the ring with Smokin' Joe Frazier. You should go inside and grab a clean shirt out of Mickey's closet, and clean up a little."

The girls dragged me into the house, and thirty minutes later I emerged with hair perfectly coiffed (and heavily sprayed), a blue dress shirt (that matched my eyes) and some cold cream (generously applied by the youngest) to soothe the bruises. I said goodbye and headed back toward town. Reaching the end of Pearl Street, I peered across the river into The Grove. Aunt Tilde's rocker was empty and Monique was engaged in an agitated conversation with Titus and several other folks on the porch. Something was wrong. I hightailed it across the trestle and found Monique taping sacred heart talismans around the door while whispering incantations.

She said, "Thank God you're here, Teddy. Aunt Tilde has been in a transfixion all night. Deeper than I've ever seen. Come inside. Maybe you can help her snap out of it."

Candles filled the living room and a black cloth covered the soapstone skull and crystal ball. Tilde's bedroom swam in a cloud of incense. She was propped up in bed with Titus gently fanning her. Everyone jumped when she suddenly bolted straight up and pointed to me.

"A storm is coming! Danger and death! Prepare. Pray!" Her eyes rolled up in her head and she fell back and shuddered with a brief convulsion. A peaceful countenance spread over her face and her breathing eased.

Titus felt her forehead and checked her pulse. "The paroxysm has passed. Let's pray for her."

Titus and Monique knelt by the bed, and I followed suit. They took turns invoking the intercession of the Virgin Mary and a lot of saints I'd never heard of. A strange sense of purpose descended upon me. I felt my heart strangely warmed, and before I knew it, I was praying aloud as well. Something I had never done.

I said, "God, I know I ain't got no business asking for a favor, but if you can do anything for Aunt Tilde right now, you can just take it off my account in the end. I owe her more than I can ever repay, and the world desperately needs more kind folks like her."

Monique squeezed my hand and Titus said, "Amen, and amen."

I lingered on the porch with Titus for a while, exchanging stories about Tilde's influence on the community, and me in particular. I told him about the attack on Nollen and lamented the fact I dragged my friends into the fray.

He said, "Sometimes you have to do some bad things in order to accomplish a greater good."

Monique reappeared and announced that Aunt Tilde was resting easy. Titus offered to ferry me across the water, but I told him I'd walk over the trestle back to the Knob. It would give me time to reflect. Tilde's warning rattled around in my brain while I made my way back to the Grotto. The cool, quiet cave was a welcome comfort, and I laid on my back, focusing on the iron ore ringlets staining the ceiling. Humper wandered in, gave me a lick on the cheek, and plopped down across my legs. A strange sense of tranquility spread over me and I dozed off into a dreamless sleep.

32

When I awoke a couple of hours later, Otis Redding's "Sitting on the Dock of the Bay" echoed up the hill from the Wurlitzer, mixed with laughter and the smell of fried food.

My throat was parched from breathing through my mouth, and I was desperate for a drink. I crept down the hill to the service steps at the rear of Casablanca and eased around the porch to the nearest window. Mayor Grissom, Arthur Rumkin, and Coach Mason were standing next to the jukebox. Dr. DeSilva joined Nurse Jurnigan and Burtis Crum at the bar. Miguel worked the beer tap and barked orders to the cooks.

"Well, well, well! If it isn't the Vigilante of the Knob," a gravelly voice said behind me. I turned to face Rick Blaine, sporting a sly smile.

"What do you mean, Mr. Blaine?"

"You know exactly what I mean. Don't think for one minute you fooled anyone with that little stunt you pulled on the North Side last night. The word is out. You're a celebrity! Come on in and I'll treat you to brunch."

"Since when did you start serving brunch?"

"Since they talked me into running for mayor."

"Aha! So that was the reason all the bigwigs were gathered here yesterday?"

"Yes, indeed. I never dreamed the townsfolk would consider a barkeep for the position, but I guess they decided I was the lesser of two evils."

A hush fell over the crowd as we entered. Coach Mason gave me a thumbs up. Miss Hawkins held her hand over her mouth to hide a broad smile. Burtis Crum gave me a subtle salute. Rick pulled out a chair at the bar and popped open an RC. All eyes were on me. The awkward situation was unnerving.

Arthur Rumkin said, "The floor is yours, Master Nutscalder. Please regale us with your account of the Turnbow-Embers affair!"

Coach Mason knitted his eyebrows together and shook his head.

I took a long swig of an RC and said, "Well, these four goons in a black Caddy showed up and…"

Everyone erupted in laughter, pounded the tables, and exchanged knowing looks. I had no idea what version of the story was out, but apparently my part in the ordeal was quite comical. Following Coach Mason's advice, I kept my mouth shut. Whenever someone new walked in, Arthur converged on them and surreptitiously filled them in on "The Scoop." Winks and nods were exchanged, and the secret that was not a secret was discreetly divulged. The whole situation made me uneasy, and I was relieved when everyone turned their attention to Murl O'Dell, who strolled through the door with the barstool I had seen him polishing earlier on the porch at Casa O'Dell. He walked to the center of the room, placed the chair on the floor, and slid a dainty, velvet-covered tray from underneath the seat and latched it into place.

Placing a satin pillow on the tray, he said, "I've been trying to find a suitable home for this masterpiece, and inspiration struck this morning. Out of consideration for our unfortunate mayoral candidate, Nollen Embers, I respectfully request that this chair be reserved only for him. Ladies and gentlemen, this is a very special barstool. Not only does it provide excellent postural support, it also has a comfortable tray … to prop up his gigantic balls!"

The patrons erupted in applause and Rick bought a round of drinks in honor of his humiliated mayoral opponent.

Murl's arrival was just the distraction I needed to make my escape. As I eased out the door, I came face to face with my father ascending the stairs. Otho Wheat walked behind him with a solemn look on his face.

A hush fell over the crowd as the lawman announced, "Nathaniel Nutscalder, are you the legal guardian of this minor child?" Nate kept his eyes on the floor and nodded. Otho approached me, wrenched my arms behind my back, locked me in handcuffs and said, "Theodore Roosevelt Nutscalder, by order of the District Attorney of Kushner County, I am placing you under arrest for the attempted murder of Galton Gideon Grails. You have the right to remain silent. Anything you say can and will be used against you in a court of law. You have the right to speak with an attorney. If you cannot afford an attorney, the court will appoint one for you. Do you understand these rights?"

"Yessir."

33

NO ONE SPOKE AS THE DEPUTIES STRIPPED MY CLOTHES AND changed me into drab orange jailhouse coveralls. They silently escorted me to an interview room where Nate sat alone.

He said, "The preliminary hearing is tomorrow morning. Judge Choate will set bail. The DA wants to charge you as an adult. Teddy, I don't know what we're going to do. We don't have the money for bail and a lawyer. Even if I sold the truck, it wouldn't be enough to…"

"Don't do it. Don't even think about it. That truck won't bring more than a couple of hundred bucks. I got myself in this situation and I'll take the consequences. None of this is your fault, or anyone else's, for that matter."

"You don't understand, Teddy. This isn't a petty theft charge, where they will let you off with a few days in juvie and six months of probation. Attempted murder is a serious felony."

"Regardless, I got myself into this, and I'll take the hit."

Otho stepped in and addressed my father. "Nate, we don't have facilities to hold a juvenile for the long term. I know the Jacksonville police chief up in Cherokee County. He's pulling some strings for me. They have a new transition center for youth offenders and he's agreed to hold Theodore there until the trial. I'll arrange for transportation as soon as the hearing is over tomorrow. Teddy, keep your mouth shut until then. Do you understand?" I nodded. The sheriff hollered out the door, "Deputies, take him to solitary."

I yelped as the jailer slammed the door of the tiny cell. Peeking through the slot, he said, "You better get used to that sound. You're going to be hearing it a lot."

It was the longest night of my life. I went over the quarry scene a hundred times, and it always ended the same. The Barge brothers on the witness stand recounting how they watched in horror as I carefully positioned the steel cable, and pulled it, flipping the motorcycle and launching Galton into the air. How I rifled through his pockets and taunted him with no compassion for his injuries. A jury would find no justification in my pathetic excuses.

Jailhouse breakfast consisted of a stale biscuit and a mealy piece of fried fatback. The coffee smelled like roofing tar. They let me take a two-minute shower after the adult inmates finished and provided a fresh pair of coveralls. Deputies shackled my hands and feet for the trip to the courthouse. No one spoke. People milled around me, but I felt totally alone. After an hour in the holding cell, they took me up the prisoners' elevator to the second-floor courtroom. It was empty except for a janitor and a court reporter. The bailiff sat me down at a table, and using a padlock, he attached the foot shackles to an eyebolt on the floor. Voices were shouting outside the door, but I couldn't understand what was being said. The DA arrived and sat down at the table to my right. Immediately behind him was a grotesquely obese fellow fumbling with a briefcase and an arm full of law books. He sat down beside me and extended a sweaty hand.

"I'm Percival Gaunt. I came up on rotation for public defender, so that makes me your lawyer. Bail is probably going to be about ten grand. Anybody in your family got that kind of cabbage?"

"No way."

"I didn't think so. Sit tight while I review the charges and come up with a strategy."

My heart sank as Pudgy Percival sank down next to the DA and started talking about a guilty plea.

The bailiff cracked the door and shouted to the people in the hallway. "Quiet down, folks! There will be no talking while you are in this courtroom. Families of the victim and defendant are allowed first. Then those with a press pass. Other interested citizens as seating allows. Anyone causing a ruckus will get slapped with a hefty fine and thrown out."

Galton's parents sat behind the DA. Ginny smiled and waved, but Mrs. Grails swatted her hand. Rick, Burtis, Tilde, and Titus sat directly behind me. Nate was nowhere to be seen. I heard Brandy O'Dell arguing with a deputy, but he wouldn't let her in. I wondered about Tommy, Sara, and Missy. The bailiff closed the doors and took a position in the front.

"All rise! This court is now in session. The honorable Judge Marlin Choate presiding."

Everyone stood at attention as the judge entered. He had a ruddy complexion with white hair and a white beard, neatly trimmed. Judge Choate had been on the bench for 20 years and was respected by all. He had the reputation of being harsh with career criminals, but showed mercy when it was warranted. Choate recused himself from Pete O'Dell's case, much to everyone's dismay, because they were both members of the Knights of Pythias fraternal order.

Judge Choate said, "You may be seated. The district attorney will present the charges against the defendant, Theodore Roosevelt Nutscalder, who, I am told, is a 15-year-old minor. Is that correct?"

The smug prosecutor rose to his feet, cleared his throat, and announced, "That is correct, Your Honor. I represent the State of Texas vs. Theodore Roosevelt Nutscalder on the felony charge of attempted murder. Facts will show that on or about May 29, 1969, the defendant, with premeditation and malice aforethought, set a trap for Galton Gideon Grails in the abandoned sandstone quarry, causing the victim to wreck his motorcycle, resulting in great bodily harm from which he is unlikely to recover. Furthermore, the defendant not only failed to render aid, but attempted to delay aid, by downplaying the injury when two witnesses offered to seek help. I will move to certify the defendant as an adult, and request that bail be set at ten thousand dollars."

The judge turned to my lawyer, who was still fumbling with items in his briefcase. "I see that Percival Gaunt is the public defender. Mr. Gaunt, is your client prepared to enter a plea at this time?"

"Your Honor, we are not prepared at this time. I only got appointed to this case late yesterday and I have not spoken to the boy's parents. The evidence is very compelling and I will consider a plea of guilty if the DA will…"

A booming voice from the back of the courtroom shouted, "There will be no guilty plea!"

I turned to see a tall, distinguished gentleman in an impeccable black three-piece Italian suit stroll up to the center of the room, with my father following behind, hat in hands. The judge squinted his eyes and leaned forward. "You look familiar. Are you an officer of the court?"

"Augustus D'Armond for the defense."

An audible gasp arose from the room, followed by three rapid raps of the judge's gavel.

As soon as the ruckus subsided, the judge leaned back, smiled, and laced his hands behind his head. "The infamous Dark Horse D'Armond? I thought you were dead."

"To paraphrase Mark Twain, the rumors of my demise have been greatly exaggerated. I have been on a spiritual sabbatical for quite some time, but rest assured, I'm still in good standing with the State Bar. I have been retained by the Nutscalder family to represent the defendant in the false charge of attempted murder. I apologize for the theatrics, but I must speak with my client before we proceed."

Before the DA could object, Judge Choate struck his gavel and announced the hearing would reconvene the following morning.

Nate walked up to me and whispered, "Otho Wheat showed up at the house with this guy and shoved a bunch of legal papers in my face. I was desperate and took a chance and signed them."

D'Armond snatched a folder of documents from Gaunt, shoved him aside and sat down beside me.

"Who are you?" I asked.

"My friends call me Gus."

34

WHEN I ARRIVED BACK AT THE JAIL, THE DEPUTIES escorted me into an interview room, where a big greasy burger and a basket of fries were waiting. I gobbled the last bite as Gus appeared and sat across from me.

"Did you get enough to eat?"

"Yessir."

"Were you surprised to see me?"

"I didn't know who you were, and I certainly didn't know you were a lawyer."

"I know you don't have any reason to trust me, so I'm going to tell you a secret. Actually, a couple of secrets. This way, you'll know I'm being straightforward and honorable. I have a vested interest in your case."

"I don't know where you're going with this."

"Teddy, the truth is I'm dying. I have cancer, not syphilis. Dr. DeSilva checked me into the indigent ward under an assumed name so he could treat me with an experimental drug we smuggled in from Brazil. Hanging a venereal disease sign on the partition ensured that none of the staff or visitors got too inquisitive. The only people who spoke to me were a senile old man and a 15-year-old boy. If news of this got out, it would harm Dr. DeSilva's reputation. He might even lose his license. I'll trust you with the secret, so maybe you'll trust me with your case."

"I don't have any choice. Pudgy Percival was going to surrender before the fight even started."

"I like you, Teddy. You're a good guy who got caught up in a situation that spiraled out of control. Otho Wheat says things are looking bad. The Barge brothers got swept up in a dragnet with some major dealers. A state task force took over the case and is throwing the book at them. They will do anything to get a lighter sentence, and you are their sacrificial lamb. They are telling everyone you set a trap for Galton at the bottom of the quarry. Galton's father is clamoring for justice. Attempted murder is a major felony, and the DA is going to petition the court to certify you as an adult. He has lofty political ambitions and, in his opinion, felony convictions are gold. The Pete O'Dell manslaughter case actually emboldened him. No one outside the Knob blinked an eye. If he succeeds and takes you to trial, he's going to drag all your friends in to testify. Mic, Tommy, Sara, Missy, and Brandy. As well as all of your other classmates at school. Everything you have ever said about Galton will come out. If they tell the truth, it will play right into the prosecutor's hands. If they lie to protect you, he will pick apart the inconsistencies and, likewise, it will play right into his hands. It's a no-win situation. The average juror can't read between the lines and sort out the subtle truths. Furthermore, the press loves this kind of story. Missy and Brandy will come under scrutiny and all of their tawdry secrets will be laid bare. All the people you love will end up getting hurt. And there is another big problem. Once certified as an adult, you are *always* an adult in the eyes of the Texas judicial system. If something happens to Galton, and he dies six months or a year from now, they could prosecute you for murder as an adult. Even if he just falls out of bed and bumps his head, any medical examiner would have to admit that the underlying injury contributed to his death. Do you see where I'm going with all of this?"

It was all so completely hopeless. My mind flashed back to the first time I met Missy. A beautiful girl standing on a train trestle, contemplating suicide. I never understood the deep sense of despair that made a person consider self-harm, until that moment.

"So, I will just spare everyone the humiliation, plead guilty, and spend the rest of my miserable life in prison?"

"Not necessarily. The odds are stacked against us, but I believe we have one ace to play in this high-stakes poker game. First and foremost, I will fight vehemently against certifying you as an adult. I will also attempt to discredit the Barge brothers, as they are unreliable witnesses. Arthur Rumkin is collecting every scrap of dirt on those two cretins as we speak. I'll throw every bit of that in the DA's face, and perhaps persuade the judge to disallow some of their testimony. It may not work, but I'll try. Do you remember when we were talking at the hospital and I told you I had an interest in the demise of Nollen Randle Embers?"

"I remember. I thought it was strange that you knew his full name."

"Well, this is my second secret. I had a sister who was married to one of Nollen's business rivals. Embers ordered a hit, and she got killed in the crossfire. I don't have much time left, but I'm determined to see the monster brought to justice before I die."

"I know the pain of losing a sister, and I sympathize, but how is that going to help me? I planned the attack at the Turnbow house, but Embers had nothing to do with the incident at the quarry. I doubt he even knows Galton or any of his family."

"We may be able to use Embers as a bargaining chip with the DA. Over the years, I have collected an extensive dossier on the man. Not enough to convict him, but my information, combined with other recent revelations, might be enough to tip the scales of justice and get him sent to prison."

"Nurse Jurnigan said he confessed to all sorts of stuff while they drugged him up at the ER, but it's not admissible in court. I guess I'm just stupid, Mr. D'Armond. I still don't understand how all this stuff fits into my case."

"I believe God has given me one last opportunity to redeem myself by doing two good deeds at once. I will offer the DA an olive branch. If he will sign off on a good plea deal for you, I will give him everything I have on Nollen Embers. This would be a high-profile case for him. Any kind of conviction would provide more political clout than sending you up the river for life. It's a big fish versus a little fish situation. I can't make any promises, but I'll throw my heart and soul into it. Teddy, you are going to have to do some jail time. It's inevitable, but maybe we can keep your incarceration local. Anything is better than Huntsville or Palestine."

My heart leapt. "Thanks, Gus. I thought it was completely hopeless."

"There is one more thing, and you won't like it. You can't have any visitors. Anyone who comes to see you may be forced to testify and we can't take any chances. It's best to cut all ties with the outside world. At least for now. From this point forward, there are only twelve words in your vocabulary. 'I-need-to-take-a-shit' *and* 'I-want-to-see-my-lawyer.' Do you understand?"

"Yessir."

35

THE NEXT MORNING, GUS THREW EVERYTHING HE HAD AT the DA. After Judge Choate had him repeat the charges, Dark Horse D'Armond stood up in a packed courtroom and launched my defense.

"Your Honor, Theodore Roosevelt Nutscalder enters a plea of not guilty. The evidence will clearly show this was an unfortunate accident. Theodore was trying to rescue a stray dog viciously injured by the plaintiff, Galton Gideon Grails. In a moment of panic, my client pulled a rusty cable across Galton's path in an attempt to divert his motorcycle and prevent further injury to the animal. The sheriff will testify that he, and many other law enforcement officers, had warned the Grails boy on numerous occasions to stay out of the quarry because of the inherent dangers therein. Now to the matter of the so-called witnesses to the incident. While under the influence of illicit drugs, Clydell and Cletus Barge made the outlandish assertion that my client set a trap for Grails. Cletus and Clydell Barge are well-known drug dealers and are currently facing indictment by a state task force. Furthermore, details from their eyewitness statement would have been difficult, if not impossible, to view from their vantage point on the west rim of the quarry."

Judge Choate said, "Due to the youth of the defendant and severity of the charges, I will have counsel for the prosecution and defense meet me in chambers to set some parameters for the trial. Looking out over the crowd in this courtroom, I can see there is intense public interest in this case. I will not allow this to turn into a circus. Bailiff, clear the courtroom."

* * *

Escorting me back to solitary, Sheriff Wheat said, "If the judge agrees, I will have Deputy Boyles transport you to the Cherokee County Juvenile facility tomorrow. With any luck, you will only be there for a week or two. Perhaps Gus D'Armond can pull a rabbit out of his ass."

I said, "How's Missy doing?"

"She's pretty bummed out. Patti has been counseling her. She wants to see you, but I told her no. It isn't in anyone's best interest right now. We're trying to get Maris transferred to the Rusk State Hospital, where she can get a professional evaluation and first-rate care. The mental institution is in Cherokee County too. Maybe if things cool down, Missy can swing by and see you when she visits her mom. Butch made bail, and Nollen Embers vanished from the hospital and skipped town early this morning. No one knows where he is. Just keep your head down and ride this out."

* * *

A heavy thunderstorm blew through Dix Knob overnight, and the jailhouse flooded. I awoke to find six inches of water on the floor, along with a three-foot water moccasin. The nimble snake struck at my leg but didn't penetrate the heavy cotton coveralls. Climbing on the toilet, I swatted the creature with my pillow to keep him at bay, while yelling for help. I couldn't figure out how he got in my cell and decided the jailers probably placed him there as a sick prank. That theory fell apart when the guard opened the door and the reptile swam between his legs. He screamed like a six-year-old girl and ran off without closing my cell. Jesus wasn't the only guy who could walk on water.

Within an hour, they brought in sump-pumps and issued brooms and mops to all the inmates. Cleanup was a welcome diversion. When other prisoners tried to speak to me, the deputies would yell at them to shut up. They got the message that a conversation with me was *verboten*. Breakfast consisted of shit on a shingle. A mixture of lukewarm meat by-product smeared over cold toast.

Otho came in just before noon and took me to the second floor to shower and change clothes. Nurse Jurnigan showed up, unpacked my nostrils, and reset the splint. She gave me a big hug before she left and we both got misty-eyed. When the sheriff returned, he produced a bottle of green Aqua Velva aftershave, stood back, and doused me in a manner that reminded me of a lily-livered priest slinging holy water on a leper.

He said, "Have you brushed your teeth?"

"No sir, they never provided a toothbrush."

The sheriff ducked his head out the door and yelled, "Hey, any of you guys got any gum or peppermints?"

Several officers appeared at the door with a variety of confections—bubble gum, lollipops, peppermints, and butterscotch.

He gathered them up and shoved them in my hands. "Start chomping."

"What's going on, Sherrif?"

"I'm in deep shit with my wife, and you're fixin' to make it right."

Thoroughly befuddled, I followed his order and crammed in the sweets. He led me down the hall to his office, sat me down in a chair against the wall, and looked at his watch.

"Five minutes, Nutscalder ... five minutes. Not a second more."

He slammed the door so hard the pictures on the walls rattled, leaving me alone in the dark room and thoroughly confused. I dared not move.

Moments later, the door eased open and Patti Wheat peeked inside. She turned and whispered to someone in the hallway. Missy Turnbow stepped through and closed the door behind her.

I started to speak, but she shushed me, put her hand over my mouth and said, "I don't want to talk right now."

I had re-lived our first kiss a thousand times. This one was different. There was soul in this one. There was sorrow and desperation in this one. There was a farewell in this one. Five minutes passed in an instant, and a knock on the door triggered a torrent of tears. Missy swore to visit. She would be waiting when I got out, and we would start a life together. She tried to convince me of something she didn't believe herself. Fairytale promises, whispered between kisses. She pretended to love me, so I let her pretend.

I knew I would never see her again.

Patti whispered through the door. "Missy, it's time."

36

STORM CLOUDS BILLOWED IN FROM THE GULF AS A LONE deputy loaded me into the van for the trip to the juvenile detention center in Jacksonville. I would be held there until the trial. A wide-eyed Stinky Rucker pounded on the window of the vehicle and told me that God was coming. Otho gently pulled him away and told him to go home. I sat at the rear, alone with my thoughts.

At the city limit sign, the deluge began. Three miles down the road, rain came down in sheets, forcing the driver to pull over.

Then came the hail. Dime-sized at first, then golf ball, then baseball. A deafening cannonade battered the roof, and windshields shattered. The deputy attempted a desperate U-turn, but the van slid off the shoulder on the opposite side and got mired in the mud. Tires spun as he helplessly jerked his body back and forth in the seat in a futile effort to dislodge the vehicle. In any other situation, it would have been quite comical.

Then the hail suddenly stopped. A heavy ozone smell permeated the air, and it was deathly quiet for a moment, then the rumble started building. Stinky's prediction came to pass. The gargantuan black finger of God descended from the heavens, forming a mile-wide funnel that bore down on us as a constant barrage of lightning laced the swirling clouds. A cacophony of ear-splitting cracks resounded as trees and utility poles snapped. The deputy yelled something at me, but the fury of a hundred locomotives drowned him out.

I don't know how many times the vehicle flipped. I curled up in a fetal position and bounced around like a pinball in an arcade. The van finally came to rest upside down in the bar ditch with the unconscious driver halfway out of the door. I crawled through a smashed side window, pulled the dazed deputy to the tree line, and propped him against a splintered pine stump. I rubbed his face with hail fragments and slapped his cheeks. His eyes fluttered, and he finally spoke.

"What happened?"

"A tornado flipped the van over. You were thrown out. Can you walk?"

He screamed in pain as he tried to stand. "I think my hip is broken."

"Is there a radio in the van?"

"Yeah, but it ain't gonna work because the antenna is buried in the mud, so you'll have to go for help. Head back to the Knob. A couple of miles down the road, just before you get back to the city limit sign, there's a beer joint on the right. The owner lives in a cabin directly behind. His name is Lansing. Tell him Deputy Vic Boyles sent you. Hold your hands high over your head as you approach, so the sumbitch don't shoot you in that orange jumpsuit. It will be dark in a couple of hours. Take the flashlight under the seat and bring me the first aid kit, and emergency road flares out of the glove box."

* * *

Lansing's beer joint was leveled. Not a brick or board left standing. I called out, but no one answered. Just as I turned to leave, a county dump truck pulled into the parking lot. Sudsy Monkhouse rolled down his window as I approached, nonplussed by my prison garb.

He said, "Are you making a run for it? If you are, I won't tell."

"No sir. There was a terrible accident. A tornado wrecked the van and Deputy Boyles has a broken hip and can't walk. Can you help?"

"We've got a road crew a couple of miles north on County Road 2208. Maybe we can use the dozer to get to him. It might take a while. The straw boss has a radio in his car, but all he's getting is static right now. Most of the guys are going door to door trying to find a phone that works so they can contact their families."

I told Sudsy I'd head back to the Knob, turn myself in, and let them know about Boyles. So much debris clogged the road it became downright impassable as I approached town. The Missouri-Pacific railroad track provided a more direct approach and the wide right-of-way appeared less obstructed. Settling into a jog, I finally emerged behind the demolished junior high. There was no electricity, and everything was eerily quiet. No chirping birds or croaking frogs. A lone siren in the distance was the only sound. Random thoughts bounced around in my brain. Should I try to escape or return to the jail like the deputy said? Maybe the house on Kickapoo Street was still intact. I wanted to see my friends, but the thought of further entangling them in my crimes made me toss the idea. I finally settled on the privacy of the Grotto.

The thick kudzu vines deflected most of the rain, leaving my cave mercifully dry. I poured water out of the Adidas and wrung out my socks. Grabbing my Captain Kidd spyglass, I peered into The Grove. Other than some broken limbs and Titus' overturned jon boat, damage across the river was minimal. The storm blew a bunch of debris under the pilings of Rick's place, but otherwise, the bar was mostly intact. Half of the Cusser Club roof had collapsed.

An odd clatter echoed up the hill from Casablanca. A peculiar wood on wood scraping sound, like someone moving furniture. As I eased down the embankment for a look-see, the wind shifted and an overpowering odor of gasoline burned my swollen nostrils. Something was terribly wrong. Taking a stealthy approach, I crawled under the pilings to listen. Gasoline dripped between the floorboards, creating a noxious vapor, and I struggled to stifle a cough. There was an intruder in the building, with arson on his mind.

I waited for the scoundrel to enter the kitchen, rolled out from under the building, and crawled up the front steps on all fours. Dusk was falling and visibility was fading fast. Edging along the wall to the jukebox, I crouched in a position where I could see through the serving hatch between the grill and mahogany bar.

The hair on the back of my neck stood up when I spotted the interloper. Skull, snake, and swastika tattoos covered his arms. My mind reeled. I had never actually seen the shooter, but Brandy and Danni's description was unmistakable.

He backed through the swinging kitchen doors, shaking the last remnants of gas from a jerry can. He produced a lighter from his pocket and thumbed the striker.

I screamed, "You're gonna blow the place sky high, you stupid bastard!"

Eyes wide, he spun around to face me. "Who's there, mutha fukka?" A metallic click sounded and a glint of steel flashed in his hand. He twirled a switchblade and lunged.

I swung a chair to deflect the thrust, but the intruder was too quick for me. In an instant, he had the knife pressed against my throat. His lip curled up in a sinister sneer as he twisted the tip of the blade against my gullet and forced me back against the jukebox. "Hands above your head!"

I said, "You ain't exactly a genius, are you?"

"Smarter than you! Who's got a knife to his throat?"

"Yeah, I guess that's true, but those gasoline vapors will ignite in a flash fire if you strike that lighter. It'll blow us both up. You should have used diesel fuel or kerosene, like you did at Mr. Kutz's Cleaners."

A surprised look came over his face as he dug the knife tip deeper into my Adam's apple. "How did you know 'bout that? Nobody seen me. I wuz in and out of there in a minute."

"I know a lot of shit. I know all about those two girls from Muddy Mike's. I know you shot…"

"I don't give a fuck what you know! All you need to know is, I'm gonna carve you up and make you squeal like a pig before I burn this place down on top of you. Now, get your hands up like I told you!"

Reaching for the sky, my knuckles bumped the shelf above the Wurlitzer, knocking over the Maltese Falcon. There must have been a wayward angel looking over me. In a stroke of divine providence, the ceramic figurine rolled right into my hands. I brought the statue down with all my might, and the big black bird smashed into his face with a delightful, squishy thud. He stumbled backward, and I swung again, cracking his left temple. The falcon's head broke off, leaving a sharp, jagged edge to prod my opponent to the floor.

I pummeled the maggot, jabbing the collarbones, thereby stunning the nerves to his arms. Galton Grails had taught me that during the fight at the railroad tracks.

Screaming for mercy, he slithered over to the brass foot rail beneath the bar and tried to squeeze under to deflect the blows.

With a mighty heave, I turned over the Wurlitzer and slid it against his body, wedging him firmly underneath the metal tube.

He whimpered, "Sweet Jesus, I give up. I won't give you no more trouble."

Quiet rage chuckled in my head. *Leave him for the sheriff.* Leaning hard across the jukebox, squeezing the air out of his lungs, I said, "I'm Theodore Roosevelt Nutscalder. That guy you shot was my best friend, Mickey O'Dell, and *I'm* going to burn this place to the ground with *you* in it."

The shooter bawled like a calf at the slaughter as I buried him. Everything I could find—tables, chairs, kegs of beer, sacks of potatoes, and boxes of booze. On top of the pile, I perched the Maltese

Falcon, re-attaching the broken head using a big wad of chewing gum scraped off the bottom of a barstool.

We visited for a while. Between sobs he admitted shooting Mic. Butch kept him hidden in a camp shack down the river so Embers wouldn't kill him, and he decided to burn down Kutz's Cleaners and Casablanca, in an attempt to get back in Nollen's good graces. He figured it would dissuade others from running for mayor, giving his boss a smooth path to victory. He didn't know Rick very well. I told him to stay put and I wouldn't drop the match, but if I heard so much as a bottle clink, I'd burn the place down and cook him alive. Of course, I had no intention of doing so. He was wedged tight and wasn't going anywhere.

I walked back to the kitchen and unscrewed all the fuses in the electric service box, to prevent a spark from setting off the fumes if the utility company restored power.

37

SATISFIED MY HANDIWORK WOULD THWART ANY EFFORT AT escape, I retrieved my flashlight, tossed the intruder's lighter out the window, and headed down Riverfront Levee Road toward town. If I reported to the jail voluntarily, perhaps Judge Choate would take it into consideration at my trial and sentencing.

Residents of The Grove had a bonfire going on the opposite riverbank. Those poor folks were always the last to get back on the grid when the power failed, but they always made the best of it by cooking up all the food in their freezers before it could thaw out and spoil. I was seriously considering a visit across the water when my ear detected a faint howl coming from the storm-damaged Cusser Club building. Ducking behind the wisteria, I shimmied under the fence and ran to the pub door. A pile of rubble blocked the entrance. Shining the flashlight upward, I realized a portion of the brick facade above the awning collapsed during the storm. The entire length of the eave sagged to the level of the awning where the hornet's nest had been. Humper's mournful howling seemed desperate. Was he trapped? Hurt? I tried to pull away the obstruction, but the eave came crashing down, followed by a cascade of moldy shingles. Scrambling to the top of the pile, I pushed against the boards covering the window. One gave way and then another. Shining the flashlight into the pub, I spied Humper on his hind legs, desperately pawing at the walls of the dumbwaiter shaft.

"Hey Humper, are you okay? Be a good dog and come to me. This old building is fixin' to fall down around our ears, and we need to get you out now!"

He didn't budge or even look at me. He just kept whimpering and clawing at the opening. I dislodged another board and managed to scooch inside.

When I reached for Humper, he bit my hand. He didn't have enough teeth to bring blood, but the uncharacteristic betrayal shocked me. Something had him in a tizzy, and whatever it was, it was in that shaft. I spoke calmly, and he would lick his chops, whine, and wag his tail occasionally, but never took his eyes off the opening.

"What is it, boy? What's got you all stirred up?" He calmed a bit and allowed me to stroke his back. I slowly squatted down, nudged him aside, and pointed the flashlight up into the duct leading to the second floor. The force of the storm shifted the building and there appeared to be a big bundle of cloth wedged in the tunnel about eight feet up. I squeezed in and stretched, but the obstruction was just out of reach.

"C'mon, buddy. The storm dislodged a bunch of old costumes those guys used to wear to scare folks like you and me. That's all."

A huge chunk of plaster fell from the ceiling, and the wall behind the mural split and buckled inward, causing General Custer's mouth to gape in a silent scream.

"C'mon, Humper, we've gotta get out of here now!"

As I grabbed for the mutt, the bundle came loose and fell to the bottom of the shaft with an odd hollow clatter. Humper threw his head back and let out a pitiful, warbling yowl.

As the plume of dust settled, I rubbed my eyes and lurched back in horror. Humper crouched by a twisted, mummified body, or what was left of it. Bile bubbled up in my stomach with the realization that we had been just a few feet from the corpse each time we entered the building. The leathery skin and sinew crumbled as the dog pawed at the remains. For a moment, morbid curiosity overcame my fear. Who was it? A vagrant? A murder victim? Whoever it was, they had been there for years. I broke out in a cold sweat at the thought. What a horrible way to die, trapped in a narrow space with no way out, and no one to hear your screams.

I figured the corpse had been lodged in the shaft for 12 years, since the building was condemned and the fence went up. Humper rested his head in what remained of a lap. He had a connection with this person. Was this his long-lost master? He tried to nudge me away as I knelt by the body. The skeleton had delicate features. Long blondish hair clung to the gruesome skull, and delicate teeth were frozen in an eerie frown. A female.

Then I saw it. A leather bag wedged under her pelvic bones. The dry-rotted pouch tore open as I pulled, and a cascade of gold spilled out.

This was the bandit that 'got away.' Wounded, and running from the posse, she tried to hide and got trapped when the gale force winds of Hurricane Audrey caused the building to shift. Helplessly caught between floors in the dumbwaiter, with no way out and no hope of rescue. I couldn't imagine the sheer terror of slowly dying, alone, in the narrow, lightless tomb.

Adrenaline shot through my veins as the entire building shuddered. Jolted back to reality, I scooped up the crumbling leather bag and threw it out of the window. Humper wouldn't budge. He growled and gnashed his teeth as I tried to pull him away from the corpse. I had no choice but to leave him. Debris from the ceiling battered my head, and I dove through the window just as the roof collapsed. The walls buckled inward, and a gargoyle landed on the pile of rubble, rolled off, and bashed into my right ankle. Gritting my teeth against the pain, I stuffed my pockets with as many of the coins as I could scoop up from the ground, including a small clutch purse and locket.

Humper's howl went suddenly silent.

Choking and blinded by a cloud of century old dust, I crawled to the fence and wriggled under to safety. Hobbling on my wounded foot, I made my way to Casablanca, and retrieved a bar towel to swab the blood out of my shoe and bind my ankle.

The shooter sobbed and pleaded for mercy, but I wasn't in the mood for pity.

Limping up the hill to the Grotto, I lay down, closed my eyes, and listened to the Cusser Club's death rattle for hours. A rumble, a crash, a plume of dust. A repeating rhapsody of ruination, until the forces of nature reduced the grand old edifice to a sad pile of stone. Everyone in The Grove witnessed its demise. No one from the Knob did.

I lit a fire in the pit and studied the treasure. Thirty-one coins in all. A small fraction of what rested beneath the ruins, but a fortune nonetheless. There was a driver's license at the bottom of the clutch, along with a locket containing the picture of a handsome Black man, with a broad smile and shoulders like a linebacker.

The name on the license was Elsa Blaine, born November 7, 1940. She was just seventeen when Hurricane Audrey hit in 1957. This was the same couple I saw pictured on the wall at Tilde's place. Rick Blaine's sister? Perhaps her companion was Aunt Tilde's nephew?

The revelation created as many questions as it answered. My theory, for what it was worth, filled in some blanks that bedeviled the folks of Dix Knob for years. Humper had been around for at least 11 or 12 years. I had heard stories of loyal dogs standing guard over their masters' graves until they got sick and died themselves. Rick Blaine came to town immediately after the Hurricane Audrey and set up a business in a declining quarry town. Folks often wondered why. Did he know about the robbers? Was he searching for his sister?

I remember my parents taking me and Tessa to the Palisades to see *Old Yeller* when we were five. I was the only one who cried at the end of the movie. Everyone made fun of me. Tessa most of all. Humper was the closest thing to a pet I'd ever had. I bit my lip and squeezed the wound on my ankle, determined not to shed a tear.

Damn stubborn dog.

38

THROBBING IN MY RIGHT ANKLE WOKE ME UP BEFORE DAWN. I wrapped the coins in the bloody bar towel and buried them in the embankment beneath a thick clump of kudzu, marking the spot with my Captain Kidd spyglass. I reminisced about the times I had peered across the river at Tilde rocking on her porch, staring back at me with those old opera glasses.

My mother bought the toy at Montgomery Ward, and I remembered feeling cheated when Tessa got a cowgirl costume, complete with a hat, boots, and cap gun. To hell with 'em. I'd take the last laugh on this one.

The extent of the tornado damage was heartbreaking. Tommy's house had a tree through the roof and Murl's cabinet shop was demolished. Upturned roots from the big cottonwood tree behind Casa O'Dell knocked over the tool shed, but most of the house was spared, thank God. Arriving at Rhinelander Park, I was relieved to see Tyler's Bakery still intact. Preacher Perkins was leading a prayer service next to the base of the toppled Dix statue. Arthur Rumkin, Otho Wheat, and a photographer from *The Tattler* had their heads bowed, so I waited until the final "Amen" before interrupting. Rick Blaine pulled up in his big blue Mercury sedan as I approached.

Rick jumped out of the car and noticed me first. "Jeezus, Teddy, you look like hell, and you're leaving a trail of blood behind you! What happened?"

"I injured my foot trying to get Humper out of the Cusser Club. He didn't make it. Have you been to Casablanca yet?"

He looked at me in alarm and said, "No, I drove up to Marshall to meet with a distributor yesterday after they shipped you off. The roads were closed after the tornado, and I couldn't get back to the Knob until just now."

"The bar is still standing," I said as the photographer snapped pictures while Otho pulled up my pant leg.

The lawman growled, "That don't look good. You're going to need to see the doc before we throw you back in the hoosegow. I'm gonna keep you here in the Kushner County jail until the trial. Deputy Boyles told me how you pulled him out of the wreckage. Where the hell have you been for the last 12 hours?"

"It's a long story. I ran into Mickey's shooter trying to torch Casablanca, but there's no cause for alarm. He's wedged under the brass footrail of the mahogany bar with the Wurlitzer and all the furniture on top of him. Sorry about breaking your jukebox, Mr. Blaine."

Rick grinned, lit a cigarette, and took a long drag. "I'll buy another jukebox."

The photographer got right up to my face and snapped another picture. Otho shoved him aside and said, "Do you mean to tell me you got the drop on that slippery sumbitch and he's just waiting for me to pick him up?"

"Yessir, and he confessed to the fire at Kutz's Cleaners too."

"Was he armed?"

"With a switchblade."

"How did you subdue him?"

"I broke the Maltese Falcon over his head. I'm sorry for busting your antique statue, Mr. Blaine."

Rick grinned and winked. "I'll get some glue."

39

THE SHERIFF TOOK BRANDY AND DANNI WITH HIM TO identify the shooter at Casablanca. They found him sniveling like a sissy bitch, crying for his mommy. The district attorney loaded him up with every charge imaginable. Nollen wasn't around to bail him out, so the putz sang like a canary. When all was said and done, Otho had the name of every car thief in East Texas and South Louisiana, along with a lot of other juicy leads on Nollen Embers. In appreciation for helping Deputy Boyles after the tornado, the jailer made sure I got plenty to eat in the days leading up to the trial. Gus mounted a powerful defense and the Barge Brothers withered on cross-examination. The DA regretted not taking advantage of Gus' offer for a pre-trial plea deal.

When the final gavel fell, the jury took pity and downgraded me to second degree felony assault, and sentenced me to three years in the Gatesville Reformatory. With good behavior, I might get out in two.

Three days before the transfer, a deputy slipped me a note from Brandy. I shudder to think about the price she paid to bribe him. Mic was progressing well, but was throwing a walleyed fit because the doctors wouldn't release him in time to come home and see me off. Grails made a rapid physical recovery, but emerged from the ordeal with the mind of a six-year-old. Stinky Rucker relinquished his crown as the village idiot to my old tormentor. Galton developed a keen interest in roadkill. Walking the streets at night, he gathered dead animals, placed them in cardboard boxes wrapped with colorful scraps of paper, and gave them an illustrious Viking burial on the turbid waters of the Sabine. Lighting the makeshift coffins on fire, he would release them into the current to be devoured by catfish and alligator gar. Sort of a submersible barbecue for the bottom feeders. Residents of the Knob left nickels and dimes next to the mangled remains of coons, squirrels, and armadillos as a tip for the fledgling undertaker. Arthur Rumkin convinced Galton the money was a gift from the Carcass Fairy. Sort of like the Tooth Fairy, only different. News of the macabre ritual spread to surrounding towns and the nightly event was gaining a cult-like following. Folks would gather on the opposite shore and railroad trestle with binoculars to view the solemn ritual. The muddy river waters would churn and roil as giant gar and catfish fought over the tenderized delicacies. Galton's new obsession was threatening to become a genuine tourist attraction.

Other than my father, Otho allowed me one visitor before shipping me off to Gatesville. I chose Tommy Crum. It was a sunny Sunday, and the sheriff let us talk through the fence in the exercise yard. He, Sara, and Monique were getting along splendidly. The girls developed a special friendship and neither seemed to be jealous of the other. I found myself envious of Tommy.

He listened in disbelief as I relayed the story about Humper, the mummified corpse, and the treasure. I told him where to find the coins and made him swear to use the money for his eye surgery and to take care of Sara and the O'Dells. I told him about Elsa Blaine and my theory about the bandit couple, and left it up to him to relay the news to Rick and Tilde, knowing he would do the right thing at the right time.

Tommy said the Turnbow mansion was up for sale. Judge Choate ordered the psychiatric clinic to release Maris, and she immediately skipped town with Missy in tow, to destinations unknown. For a few days, I kept up hope for a phone call or a letter. Nothing came.

Apparently, I gained an unexpected ally in Ginny Grails. She teamed up with Arthur Rumkin to spread the word about her brother's personality improvement after the "accident." Tommy promised to make sure she had some new clothes when school started in September.

Brandy O'Dell and Danni Redhawk went to work waiting tables and serving drinks at Kelli's Kitten Klub in Pasadena. The money wasn't as good but the clientele was more refined.

40

Everyone in town was waiting when Otho Wheat led me out of the jail. Officers had the area barricaded and roped off to form a path through the parking lot to the prisoner transport at the curb. Clamoring for a statement, a mob of reporters pushed through, camera bulbs flashing.

"Hey man, the wire services are picking up your story! They want to know how you caught Mickey O'Dell's assailant."

"Rumors are flying that you led the attack on Nollen Embers, and forced the mobster into hiding. Are you afraid of retribution?"

"Did you have a secret affair with the Turnbow girl?"

"Who else was in on the assault?"

"Are you just going to just take the rap and leave us all in suspense?"

The sheriff barked orders and deputies rushed in and shoved the journalists back behind the barricade.

Otho unlocked my handcuffs while Tommy and Brandy slipped through the crowd and approached with a large cardboard box. Inside was a brand-new Smith Corona typewriter, several spare ribbons, and a ream of fancy linen paper. Otho directed a deputy to stash it in the van.

Tommy said, "A companion of Alexander the Great made a contribution to get you some snazzy new tools to launch your writing career."

Brandy reached up and touched a curl on my forehead. "I would tell you to stay out of trouble, Theodore Nutscalder, but I know it wouldn't do any good. Come and see me when you get out." Her voice cracked and tears welled up in her eyes. Tommy turned away. The shapely reporter from Channel 3 stuck a microphone in my face, shook her head sadly and said, "So, this tragic tale comes to an end. Our river bottom Romeo has lost his Juliet. What is to become of our heartbroken hero?"

"In matters of the heart, the hero's ultimate fate is always that of a monster or a fool."

"Hemingway?"

"Nutscalder."

Epilogue

THIS IS A MESSAGE TO THE BEAUTIFUL GIRL I MET AT THE Eastern Star banquet hall in Jacksonville, Texas during the winter of 1971. I'm sorry I couldn't help you. I hope you escaped your abuser.